Foiglman

Aharon Megged

FOIGLMAN

TRANSLATED BY

Marganit Weinberger-Rotman

The Toby Press

First English language Edition 2003

The Toby Press LLC

POB 8531, New Milford, CT. 06676-8531, USA

& POB 2455, London W1A 5WY, England

www.tobypress.com

Translation by Marganit Weinberger-Rotman

Cover: *Dove in Flight*, 1994 (tempera on panel) by James Lynch (Contemporary Artist) The Maas Gallery, London, UK/Bridgeman Art Library

ISBN 1 59264 032 X, *hardcover*

A CIP catalogue record for this title is available from the British Library

Typeset in Garamond by Jerusalem Typesetting

Printed and bound in the United States by Thomson-Shore, Inc., Michigan

Chapter one

I am not a young man. I shall be sixty-one in August. Nine months have passed since the death of my wife Nora, and five since the death of the poet Shmuel Foiglman. It's as if I'm being corroded by sorrow. It is a kind of slow, incessant burning. I'm neglecting my work: three weekly lectures on Thursdays, and my research on the Petliura pogroms, which I carry out without any enthusiasm. I am not sure I will complete this research. I even have doubts if any good will come of it. Foiglman's funeral haunts me like a bad dream.

When I was notified about his death, I told myself: I'm not going to his funeral. No way. I can't.

Yet half an hour before the appointed time, I left home and went there.

About thirty or forty people had gathered in front of the funeral home.

His son, his daughter, his brother and his family, a large group of Yiddish writers, several men and women apparently from his hometown. Many of them came to shake my hand, as if I were related to him or was his closest friend. As if it were my personal bereavement.

Meanwhile, all the time, I felt a kind of heartburn, an inner burning, and could not utter a word.

Nora's suicide is crying out inside of me, and time cannot silence that cry.

I turned aside and leaned against the wall of the yard fearing that I might collapse. A kind of hushed commotion stirred up the little crowd of Yiddish writers, as if they were engaged in some clandestine affair, as if there were some last-minute arrangements to be made before a trip in some pre-war railway station in Poland. Then a certain poet, whose name escapes me, mounted the podium before the coffin. He had sunken cheeks, a pointed thin-skinned nose, and protruding blue veins on his temples. He delivered a eulogy in Yiddish about the departing member of this united yet quarrelsome family whose ranks are gradually shrinking. He spoke heatedly, with an enthusiasm that sounded like anger. Then a loud cry suddenly burst out of his heart, half in Yiddish, half in Hebrew, *"Geshtorben? Neyn! Geharget!** Yea, for Thy sake are we killed all the day long!"*—a sort of protest, an accusation, which he hurled to the four winds of the town, the whole country; it hovered above like a wounded bird in the hot afternoon air. And it seemed to me that this man, who only a few minutes earlier, silently, with a bowed head, had shaken my hand as a brother-mourner, was now aiming his outcry at me! At me!

Then the son, Irving, who had come from England for the funeral, said *Kaddish*, the mourner's prayer. He read from the prayer book slowly, stumbling over the words, bringing the pocket-sized book closer to his glasses, then away from them to decipher the small print; he pronounced the verses in an estranged tone while his sister, who had come from France, stood at his side with a handkerchief clutched to her nose. They stood next to each other—he, tall, skinny, in impeccable suit and tie, and she, chubby, broad-faced, with unkempt yellowish hair that made her look frightened. In her stature and blue eyes, she resembled her father.

When the mourners got on the bus to go to the cemetery, I could have slipped away unnoticed in the street. Many did just that.

---

* *Geshtorben? Neyn! Geharget!*—Yiddish: "Died? No. Killed!"

But my legs would not obey my impulse. When I stood on the step, most seats on the bus had already been taken, and again I felt the urge to turn back and leave. It was like finding myself in some East European Jewish quarter whose breaths, smells and whispers would be repulsive to me. Yes, I know, it's a despicable feeling. And the embarrassment: standing like that on the doorstep with your eyes roaming around trying to decide where to sit, next to whom, who will be your neighbor for the next half hour; while all you want, if indeed you are destined to be cooped up in this fold, is to be by yourself, away from the others, not to be bothered.

I shouldn't have gone to that funeral. It was like a desecration of Nora's memory. Morris Goldman, who was sitting in one of the back seats, motioned to me to come and sit with him. He patted the seat next to him, and when the bus started on its way, he said to me softly, "How do you explain this, Professor?"—he always addressed me as 'Professor' the few times we had met, and I seemed to discern a note of irony there, as if he were saying: You, who study the history of our people, who are so versed in our heritage, who can fathom the mysteries of various phenomena—"How do you explain this, Professor, that not even one representative of the Hebrew Writers' Union, or the Journalists' Association, or the Municipality's Department of Culture, or even the publishing house that put out his book, has showed up at his funeral?"

I said nothing. I looked around at the passengers trying to find Zelniker, the translator, but he, too, was not there. To avoid an argument, I said dryly, "I have no explanation." Morris Goldman—in a light suit, powdery face and thin white hair meticulously brushed back, that made him look like a respectable businessman, had been the owner of a Jewish publishing house in Uruguay before coming to Israel in the sixties. Here he had a travel agency, but out of a smoldering love for Yiddish literature, he financed various publications of its writers' union and, it was rumored, he also secretly supported some impecunious individuals.

"You have no explanation," he looked at me with a bitter smile on his thin, pale lips. For a moment I was seized with indignation; was I responsible for the whole 'Hebrew' state, for all its institutions

3

and organizations?! Am I to be held accountable for all the accusations brought against it! I restrained myself and said, "People don't come to other funerals, either."

Goldman continued to look at me. "Yes, you're right. The dead increase and the mourners decrease."

A fog clouded my eyes, and again I felt a pressure on my heart. I was reminded of Nora's funeral. Many, many people attended her funeral. More than a hundred. Perhaps two hundred. The old settlers of Rehovot, who knew our families, employees of the Biological Institute, my colleagues from the University, who came from Tel Aviv, her girlfriends who had studied with her in Jerusalem. They dispersed like a flock of sheep around the tombstones of the Old Cemetery. Many cried bitterly when the grave was sealed over her, and Yoav—in his officer's uniform—who has been to so many funerals of his friends and subordinates, and whose harsh combat experience should have hardened and steeled him, covered his face with his hands as the sobs gushed out of him, like coughing. It infected the others who wiped the tears from their faces, as if the sorrow of seeing such a robust man break down and weep like a child was greater than the sorrow of death itself.

"To be buried next to my father and mother." Those were the only words she wrote on a note before taking her life. For months afterward, days and nights, these words haunted me and lacerated my heart; again and again I turned them over in my mind, puzzling over what she wanted to convey to me: was it a message telling me that she wished to be separated from me in the next world, too, to be gathered only to her fathers, as it were? I was tormented by the question. Why only these few words, and not one word addressed to me, or to our son? Why shroud everything in mystery?

We got off the bus and mingled in the big Jewish crowd gathered in the forecourt in front of the gate. Family by family, group by group, they made their way to the mortuary, from which they emerged and parted along seven paths. Something weird hung in the air. Perhaps it was the desperate wails of a woman in a red shawl that trailed from her head to her arms, who was supported on both sides by two strong young men, apparently her sons. Perhaps it was shreds of howling that the wind wafted from afar, from the vast desert of tombstones stretching as far as the eye could see. A busy, nervous, traffic of coming and going, gathering and dispersing, filled the square, as if it were a marketplace of the dead. And in that motley crowd—a medley of faces, clothes, and headgears probably unseen at funerals anywhere in the world, where a respectful, somber, somewhat ceremonial silence invests the mourners with a uniform aspect. Our outlandish group was moving to and fro, trying not to lose sight of each other, waiting, not sure for what. Like a railway terminal in a big city, where a loudspeaker announces the arrival and departure of trains, the announcer now called out the names of the departed being carried on their last journey.

Then something embarrassing, disgraceful, grotesque happened: a name ending in 'man' reverberated in the air, and someone from our group pulled my sleeve and said, "Now! Let's go!" We whispered to each other and hastened to gather behind the coffin, which was being carried from the mortuary by the people from the burial society. We had barely made a few steps toward the cemetery when we found ourselves surrounded by people we didn't know, dressed in overalls, in rustic clothes, two or three in army uniform, some of whom were hastily approaching the coffin; and among us, right in front of me, some dressed in black, including one woman who keened loudly in a language that sounded like Rumanian to me. Even before reaching the first tombstones, we realized our mistake and, ashamed and embarrassed, we returned to our starting point.

When Shmuel Foiglman's name was called out loud and clear, my heart leaped. I saw him, alive, before me, as I had seen him the last time at his apartment door when he told me, his face all flushed with confidential optimism, "There is an alternative, indeed there is! We'll talk about it some other time. But there is!"

It was a long trek to the plot, along rows of barren tombstones. The six men who took turns carrying the coffin looked as if they were seizing the horns of the altar. Behind them walked the daughter, Rachel, her arms joined with her aunts' and cousins', followed by Shmuel's brother, Katriel, and his two daughters, then Irving, walking with measured steps, his head held high, and behind him and around him, the rest of the mourners. About half way, when I realized the distance between myself and the others had widened, I quickened my steps and caught up with him, to walk along with him. When he noticed me, his face lit up in surprise, and he whispered in English, "Thank you for coming."

"What about your mother?" I asked.

"She's in Australia. Couldn't make it in time." His faint smile seemed to say: just as well. Then he added that she had been giving performances there for two months. After many attempts to reach her by phone, his sister finally tracked her down in Melbourne, but then it turned out that the earliest flight would get her here in three days. The funeral could not be delayed. "She has been distant from him for years," he said with half a smile. I felt a sense of affinity, of brotherhood toward him, welling up inside me, as if the two of us, marching side by side, were the only outsiders in this group of mourners. The plot was at the edge of the cemetery, and beyond it stretched the yellow sands.

It was hot. People wiped the sweat from their faces and necks with large handkerchiefs. Irving stood still, his head bowed, his hands clasped, watching the skillful work of the lowering of the body into the grave and the removal of the boards. The other mourners tossed earth in, passing the spades to each other, eager to perform the sacred duty; they shoveled the earth diligently, like expert sextons, with sweat dripping from their faces. The cantor chanted the prayer for the dead, and then, just as one of the mourners—Foiglman's neighbor—was about to deliver a eulogy on behalf of the tenants in his house, someone grabbed my arm—a short, thin man with a long nose—and took me aside, among the tombstones. From a tattered leather briefcase, he took out a thin volume and handed it to me.

"I was going to mail this to you, but seeing that you're here…." he said, one leg poised on a tombstone. On the cover of the book, which had a dark human shadow cutting across it diagonally, was written: *"Lang is di Veg—Lider—*I.I. Segalovich."

I thanked him faintly, stifling a sigh, and he—with an embittered look in his narrow eyes, whose pupils seemed to pierce his interlocutor—stretched his hand toward the book and said, "If you have any comments after reading, I shall be delighted to hear them."

But this is exactly how the whole affair with Foiglman started, I said to myself, standing among the tombstones, five paces from Shmuel Foiglman's freshly dug grave, the affair that brought calamity on my life! It all started with a book, with one book of poetry! And as soon as the ceremony was over, when the wooden marker had been posted on the grave, I fled from there. I hastened my steps toward the main gate, leaving the group far behind me. When I reached the road, I hailed a cab and returned to the city.

But in spite of all this, *in spite of all this*, I say. As if there is some kind of determinism that governs the behavior of man—that 'biological creature,' as Nora used to say with a dash of irony—so that he cannot break away from predetermined patterns dictated by his DNA. Because, for all my determination to stay away, not to get sucked in, to flee—the next evening I went to pay my condolences.

There were about a dozen people seated on the sofa and chairs around the room, which was quite familiar to me. Rachel and Foiglman's sister-in-law were serving tea and cakes. While still on the threshold, I asked Rachel about Irving, and she said, "He's in the next room, keeping to himself. I'll tell him you're here."

"No, leave him alone, he must be tired of seeing people," I stopped her. "We'll have a chance to talk before he leaves." I entered the room and sat down on an empty chair next to Katriel, Shmuel's twin brother. "He asked about you. Quite often," he put his hand on my shoulder. "I didn't want to bother you. I knew you were very busy, and besides…you have troubles of your own…"

I apologized and said that I did not know that his brother was sick until he, Katriel, called me, and I had no idea it was so serious. Since I had such a heavy workload at the end of the semester, I'd kept putting off visiting him at the hospital. "Yes, it all happened very fast. The end came very fast," he said, and added that at first the doctors thought it was a common intestinal problem, and he himself made light of it. Then, when he started losing weight, and within one month lost twenty-six pounds, they discovered the malignant tumor in his intestines. It was operated on, and he felt better and seemed to regain his health. He wrote, made several trips to Jerusalem, had great plans which he "kept under his hat," was full of optimism, as was his nature. Only three weeks before the end did the doctors discover that the cancer had spread to the liver and the gall bladder, and that it was hopeless.

"I didn't know about it, I had no idea..." I said, "In the last few months we somehow lost contact..."

"Yes, I know," he said ruefully, and added in Yiddish, *"Er hot aykh shtark lib gehat!"**

I shuddered from head to toe. I seemed to hear Shmuel's own voice, his turn of phrase. *"Lib gehat."*† Yes, this is how he used to express himself, with such embarrassing frankness, and to use the verb 'love'—always in Yiddish—when talking to me.

The twins were not alike in all things. Although both had stocky, peasant-like bodies, wide faces and bluish eyes, Shmuel's hair was all white while his brother's had only begun to turn gray. The expression in their eyes was different, too: Shmuel's was a bright, open, almost childlike expression, while this one's was humble, submissive, reserved. But now there was the voice! It was the same voice: thick, warm, a little moist, coming from deep down in the chest. The kind of voice that seemed to achieve its full spiritual quality only when speaking Yiddish.

"You know..." Katriel started saying in Hebrew, but at that moment Rachel sat on his other side and he put his hand on her shoulder and continued in Yiddish, "It reminds me of that well-known story about Death coming upon a man in the marketplace and telling him: I'll see you in Samarkand. This is how it was with my brother. He lurked and stayed in wait for him, for both of us, all the time we were there, sickle in hand, but he didn't raise it, he only whispered, 'I'll see you in Samarkand. It's been almost forty years—and it's here, in Israel of all places...'"

We were silent. The other people in the room chatted with one

---

* *Er hot aykh shtark lib gehat*—Yiddish: "He loved you very much."
† *Lib gehat*—Yiddish: "loved you."

8

other, walked around, helped themselves to fruit and pastries from the bowls on the table. Snatches of conversation reached my ears, something about a recently published book, a television interview. Rachel said, her face flushed, "When I sat by his bed at the hospital, and he could barely talk, he said to me, 'I'm telling you, it all started there! It's them!' And he told me that when the Americans were approaching Kungskirchen and the German guards fled, all the survivors broke into the camp kitchen and grabbed everything they could find there. They gorged themselves on raw potatoes, beets and canned meat. Dozens died on the spot as a result of this overindulgence. He was seized by terrible cramps and was taken to hospital. It was dysentery, and he recovered. But all those years he knew the disease had not left him; the snake was lodged in his belly and would one day rear its head. And then he said: 'I mustn't complain. I received a gift of forty years. I don't deserve it.'" And she dabbed her eyes with a handkerchief.

Rachel, the faithful daughter. She had been born in Paris, but had no trace of Parisian chic in her. She neglected her appearance, her clothes; she used no make-up, made no attempt to refine the peach-like face and the puffed lips, or to pluck the thick, blond eyebrows. Whenever Foiglman spoke about her, tears would come to his eyes. "A disaster!" he would say, "A disaster!" and he would relate her tale of woe, she married a Jewish boy from Algeria, a shiftless good-for-nothing, who deceived and bamboozled her, extracted money from them, her parents, under false pretences, and finally deserted her and disappeared. She was left alone, with a little daughter and a small boutique in Orleans.

Rachel got up, and I followed her. When I reached the door, I said I'd pop into the next room to say hello to Irving.

Irving was seated deeply in an armchair, his limbs crumpled, an open book in his hand. When I came in he raised his eyes to me, as if he did not recognize me, or as if he were still wrapped in his reading reverie. "I see I'm disturbing you," I said, and he got up, displaying his customary civility—even here, inside the house, he wore a tie, and a white striped shirt over his narrow chest—and apologized: "I…I saw no point in sitting there…I can speak only a broken Yiddish, and they don't speak any English, or French…" and he asked me to sit down. I turned the cover of the book he was holding toward me to see its title, and he grinned: "I didn't know my dad was interested in electronics...interesting..."

I myself was surprised. It was a French book by one Bourjon about the invention and development of laser beams. I glanced at the books Foiglman had brought with him from Paris. Most of them were in Yiddish, a few were in Hebrew; in French he had Verlaine, Baudelaire, Apollinaire, St. John Perse, as well as Proust's *A la recherche du temps perdu* and Sartre's *Les mots*. I had been in that room several times—in Foiglman's study—but that book had escaped my notice.

"I suppose there were a lot of things you didn't know about your father," I said, "you lived apart...for how long?"

"Eight years, maybe more. Yes, that's true. I was sure he was absorbed in Jewish affairs... Look here, he even made notes to himself," and he opened the book to show me. In the margins, next to the French text inlaid with diagrams and scientific formulas, some Yiddish words were scribbled in pencil. A wave of warmth, affection, and pity came over me when I saw the tiny Hebrew letters—like a miniature reflection of their author—next to the Greek and Latin characters of the formulas. "Perhaps he was thinking of the medical use of those beams," I speculated aloud. "Don't you think? But he had brought the book with him from France, before he took ill...that's strange..."

Facing me, on the wall, behind the armchair to which he now returned, hung a picture of his mother—Hinda, as she was called by her husband, Henrietta Fogel, which sounded "less Jewish" for her stage name, in the role of Berenice in Racine's play; she was clad in a Roman toga, with long black hair cascading to her shoulders. I was struck by the resemblance between her and her son: the same oval face, the thin nose, the delicate sensuality in the nostrils, in the lips, a sort of 'spiritual' sensuality. From whom did he inherit his talents, this young man who at the age of twenty-four had already received a doctorate in the philosophy of science at Oxford?

"A prodigy!" his father used to brag about him. And yet, whenever he spoke about him he would sigh: "He will never get married, not this one."

"What was he looking for in this country father, that is? What made him come here in the first place?" A sad smile flickered in his eyes.

"He was looking for family," I said.

"And did he find it?"

"No, he didn't." He looked at me silently, then bent down, his head bowed to his knees, and when he straightened up again, he said: "What's going to happen here, in your land? Wars, wars... And your generals, when they crossed the Litani River, probably saw themselves as Caesar crossing the Rubicon. The die is cast!"

I told him that in my opinion the invasion into Lebanon was indeed a sin, but since the army was already crossing the Litani on its way back, it was a kind of repentance. The look he darted at me showed he expected another response. "Your original sin...is perhaps the State itself...whatever followed from there..." He paused for a moment and smiled, "It seems to me that you are living by nineteenth-century concepts...all this business of incursions beyond your borders...interfering in the affairs of your neighboring states...it's anachronistic, don't you think?"

Like many Oxford graduates, he, too, had the habit of stammering and truncating his speech in a manner that indicates not hesitancy but overconfidence. His views on Israel were familiar to me from our first meeting, two years earlier, and I had no desire to engage in an argument with him. His long fingers, twitching nervously, were interlaced over his stomach. A slight tic traversed his face from time to time. "Hubris..." he said, "don't you think you are guilty of hubris?"

Suddenly I felt a sharp stab in my heart as I thought of my son, Yoav, who had left with his family two months earlier to live on the other side of the globe.

As if he were fleeing from me. And not yet written a word. Only 'Regards' on the margins of Shula's letters. And again, as every time I'm reminded of it, I was devastated by the things he had said to me on the eighth day after the tragedy, when we were left alone in the house...

"There is one thing I don't understand, Dad...why, when you

found her in the morning...you didn't right away call...it sometimes happens that..."

It was outrageous! As if he were accusing me of murder!

Irving continued talking. He mentioned Sparta. Beads of perspiration glistened on his forehead, and he whipped out an immaculate and neatly folded handkerchief from his pocket and wiped his face and neck. Sparta conquered the whole Peloponnesus, Laconia and Messina, reached all the way to Persia...they fostered ideals of frugality and abnegation, subservience of private will to public benefit, courage, heroism, sacrifice... What was left of Sparta at the end of the fourth century? A small, unimportant village...

His words smacked of cold 'scientific objectivity.' As if these were not matters of life and death for people to whom he, too, perhaps against his will, was related by blood. There was something feeble, slightly unwholesome in his appearance: the thin body, the round face with the large glasses, his soft hands and arms. "You...are building a fortress here. Closed and confined."

Suddenly a smile lit his face, he bent forward, his arms hanging between his knees, grinned and said, "But you haven't got public toilets. I was walking around the town...couldn't find even one... A fortress without a toilet..." A thin, effeminate laughter trickled from his mouth.

I wondered about him. I wondered how such a shoot came forth out of his father's stock.

"Your father," I said after a short silence, "in one of our last meetings, told me that he had started compiling a *Lexicon of the Holocaust*, from A to Z, from Auschwitz to Zyklon B, as he phrased it. I have no idea which letter he managed to reach."

He straightened up, and a glimmer of memory or of surprise lit his eye. "Yes?" he said, and then immediately—as if curbing his excitement—commented derisively, "That's his nostalgia."

I was flabbergasted. "Nostalgia? For the Holocaust?"

❧

"It...sounds paradoxical, I know..." he stammered, "but there is such a thing... No, not longing for those days, of course...but rather for the sense of uniqueness, for having been chosen...for being singled out in the world, in human history, for being the select..."

I was overcome by sadness. A curtain of despondency suddenly enveloped everything: the room, full of his orphaned books, the figure of this dainty young man, so restive, so inwardly perturbed, the nocturnal world that stretched beyond the window. I took off my glasses and wiped them with my handkerchief. "Absurd," I muttered.

"Otherwise...otherwise I can't explain this...constant and continuous digging and poking." His face became flushed with excitement, "Thirty, forty years...such pleasure in burrowing and rummaging in a pile of ashes...and what for? At any event, it's nothing but 'a tale told by an idiot, full of sound and fury, signifying nothing.'"

I got up, and he saw me to the door, but when I put my hand on the doorknob, he said, "One more minute...I wanted to ask you something..." He went to the table, picked up the book about laser beams, leafed through quickly and brought it to me open, pointing to four words in his father's handwriting, at the edge of one of the formulas. "Could you tell me what this means? You know I don't understand Hebrew..."

The four words, so heavily underlined they almost tore the paper, were: "So perish all thine enemies!!"

I translated it into English for him.

His eyes opened wide with amazement.

I looked back at the four words, my heart sinking, and I closed the book.

Standing on the threshold, he said, with a thin, contrite smile, like an excellent student who has erred, and now stands repentant before his master, "I'm sorry. I'm afraid I said a lot of rubbish..."

Rachel, with an imploring look, said, "I'll see you again, won't I? I have something to give you."

I came once more, at the end of the *shiva*—the seven-day period of mourning—in the afternoon. Irving had already left for England. Tranquility pervaded the room. The square table that stood in the middle was covered with the yellow lace tablecloth with the tassels, and on it an empty, crystal vase. On the wall hung a three-tier bookcase: on its top shelf his own books, about five or six, on the middle shelf some of his colleagues' books, and on the bottom shelf—just like the days when I used to visit him, nothing had changed—three bottles of drinks: one Napoleon cognac, one Israeli red wine, and one cherry liqueur. As soon as I had walked in, he would take down the bottle of cognac from the shelf, put it on the table with a thud, produce two glasses, pour, and importune me—actually force me!—to drink a *glezele*, a small glass. To decline would have been perceived as an unforgivable, major insult. Against the walls stood a couple of two-seater sofas with orange upholstery. The furniture was spare, as in a temporary lodging.

Rachel brought two glasses of tea, and cakes she had baked herself. "The world has emptied," she said, and laid her corpulent, albino arms on the table. I asked if she had spoken with her mother, and she said, yes, her mother had been calling every day. She was broken hearted, but she was not going to return just yet. "The show must go on," she had said. Her father would often say those words too, in times of trouble. 'The show must go on.' When she was a child, she said, they had often been hungry. They subsisted on the pittance her father received for articles he published here and there, and from what her mother earned in the occasional roles she performed with an itinerant theatrical company in the provinces. "But father was an optimist. The show must go on, he used to say."

"Yes," I agreed, "I always found him in high spirits."

She lowered her eyes to her glass, which she rolled back and forth with both hands—she hadn't touched her tea—and when she raised them again to me, she said, "He was not happy here. No. From his letters I sensed that something had snapped in him." She spoke a beautiful, natural Yiddish, which she had learned from her parents. Yes, that was true. He had not been happy here, and I was well aware that the "high spirits" he displayed were a mere pretense, or a desperate attempt to cheer himself up.

"Recently we didn't see too much of each other," I said. "We haven't met for several weeks."

"Yes, I know." And after a moment's pause, she gave me a look full of 'Jewish sorrow' and said, "He wrote me about your tragedy."

The tragedy. A small tongue of fire leapt from the ashes in

my chest. The ashes that have not cooled, that will never cool. But how could she have known about the connection between the two tragedies?

I swallowed hard, and to distract us both from that unfortunate affair, I told her what her father had once told me—something that demonstrated his optimistic humor: he said that Hebrew had a severe and stern face, while Yiddish had a smiling, happy face. And he cited an example. It says in the Passover Haggadah, "With a mighty hand did God bring us forth from Egypt," a sentence which bespeaks seriousness and gravity. However, Yiddish took this Hebrew expression '*Hozek*,' meaning, 'might,' and changed it into '*Khoyzek*,' meaning to mock, to deride, to travesty. What is harsh in Hebrew becomes soft in Yiddish. Troubles that Hebrew tackles with pathos, Yiddish treats with humor. And there was something else he had said to me. "You speakers of Hebrew are as hard as cypress trees, whereas we are as pliable as a reed. Strong gales will break the cypress, but they only bend us. Don't marvel then when you see Yiddish speakers walking around bent and bowed down—bent they may be, but they endure better than you!"

Tears of laughter sparkled in her eyes. She told me that when she was a child, her father—even though he was a *Bundist**—insisted that she learn Hebrew, and sent her to a Hebrew day school in the afternoons. After two weeks she ran away and never returned. "I had such internal resistance!" She put her hand on her chest. "I felt like a traitor! As if I were really committing an act of treason!"

I asked her how long she intended to stay in the country, and she replied that she had to go back to France right away. She had left her five-year-old with friends, and she had already been here for three weeks. But she did not know what to do with the apartment. Should she sell it? Should she rent it out? And what about all the things in it, the books? Her mother was not going to come here from Australia. She was going straight back to their apartment in Paris. "An empty house is like a heart that has stopped beating."

---

* The *Bund*—'General Federation of Jewish Workers in Lithuania, Poland and Russia,' a Jewish Socialist party founded at a conference in Vilna in 1897

And saying that, she got up, went to the other room, and returned with a parcel. It was wrapped in crumpled brown paper and tied several times over with a frayed string. "Father asked me to give this to you." She put the parcel on the table. "I think there are notebooks inside."

When I came home, I opened the parcel. Yes, it contained five notebooks, gray, Israeli school-type notebooks; next to "Student's name" he had written his name, and next to "Grade" he had written his address in Tel Aviv. I peeked inside. A journal? Philosophical ruminations? There were little asterisks between the passages. I rewrapped the notebooks in the same crumpled paper, tied the string around them, fetched a ladder, and put the parcel on the top shelf of my library, on a pile of other brown envelopes which also contained old notebooks.

On the last day of Nora's life, in the morning, I saw her watering the geraniums in the flowerpots that hang from our front porch. She was wearing a light, bright suit, and she went from plant to plant with a little sprayer in her hand. I called to her from a distance: "Why are you watering them? Everything's still wet from the rain?"

She did not answer and went on watering. Then, when she was done, she came closer and asked me softly, almost imploringly: "Shall I give you a lift?"

I said it was not necessary; I could take the bus to the university. "Good bye, then," she said, and there was tremendous sorrow in her eyes. I left the house and did not return until eleven that night. In the afternoon we had a staff meeting, and in the evening I had dinner at the Sheraton hotel with a Jewish-American donor from whom I solicited a donation for a research grant for one of our brightest students. When I came home, I saw that there was light in her room, but the door was closed. For several months now we had been sleeping apart—she in the bedroom and I in my study. One night, at the end of a short argument, I picked up my bedding and told her, "I need my rest, Nora." I had hoped she would stop me, but she said nothing. I moved my bedding to the couch in the study; I felt a heaviness in my legs, my arms, and my chest. We spoke very little. The "soul-searching talks" I tried to initiate, mostly during

meals, would sink very fast, like water in sand. "How will it all end?"
I finally asked, when all words failed me.

"There will be an end," she said with a rueful smile on her lips,
and her eyes radiated a kind of affection, perhaps even love, toward
me. I wondered where she got the strength to maintain such long
silences, not to succumb to the temptation to "thrash things out." In
the mornings she would go to the institute, return in the afternoon,
do her chores around the house—obligations she fulfilled meticulously—and in the evenings, when I worked at my desk, she would
watch a little television; but in the middle of a program, she would
get out of the armchair, turn it off and retire to her room. I seemed
to hear her sighing behind the wall. So strong!—I would say to myself
when I heard her vigorous steps going to her room—So strong!

Once in a while she would go out in the evening. I did not
ask her where she was going.

When I woke up the following morning—earlier than usual, it
was five thirty—the light was still on in her room. I walked in and found
her dead. Her face serene, pure, as if she had finally found peace.

૨૯

Last night, at one AM, I called Bogota. Shula answered the phone,
warmly, cheerily. How are you? How are things in Israel, how is the
weather? They are fine, terrific. Sarit is okay. She misses me. Why isn't
Grandpa coming, she keeps asking. "You probably want to speak to
Yoav. Just a minute." I waited for a long moment. As if a negotiation
is being conducted behind the scene. "How are you"—he sounds
very restrained. And then with forced jocularity:

"How is Petliura?" And then—with Shula whispering in the
background—suggesting that I come visit them over my winter
vacation—which is summer there—for two or three weeks. "What
for?"

"To rest. If you want, you can work here." They would allocate
me a whole floor in their villa. It's quiet there, you only hear the birds.
"I'll send you a ticket. Don't worry about the money."

"I'm not worried about money," I said, and he did not insist.
"What's new apart from this?"

Apart from what?!—I wanted to shout—apart from what? What do you want me to do, Yoav? You want me to disappear, to vanish from the face of the earth?

Why do you bear me a grudge? What could I have done that I did not do?

The news of their departure had hit me like a blow. It was Shula who broke the news to me, barely two weeks before their trip, two and a half months after Nora's death. She came with the child. They already had the tickets. They had already rented out the house in Ramat Efal. She tried to soften the blow; they were going for only two years. In any event, if Yoav had accepted the job offer he had been given here—after thirteen years' service in the army—they would anyhow have moved to Beer Sheba and I wouldn't have seen them that often. Sarit sat on my lap, hugging me, demonstrating her reluctance to be separated from me. To Colombia?—I said stunned—What is he going to do in Colombia?

The letters I received—once every few weeks—were all written by Shula. Long letters full of descriptions of the Colombian land-scapes they see on the long car-trips they take. Detailed descriptions of the local customs and beliefs. They have three servants in the house—a villa situated away from the center of town, surrounded by a large garden. And Shula, who from early childhood was accus-tomed to doing the household chores by herself, finds it hard to adjust to this luxury. Six-year-old Sarit is driven every morning by a chauffeur to the Jewish school in town. Luckily, her teacher is an Israeli. "Warm regards from Yoav." Not a word in his own handwriting.

I have no idea what he is doing there. It's confidential.

He knew from the start about my falling out with his mother. It was in the air. And perhaps he overheard a few exchanges during his short visits. In the beginning, he tried to dispel the tension by cracking a joke every once in a while. Then, when the crisis intensified, he made a point of never coming by himself, but always accompanied by Shula and Sarit. We would busy ourselves with our granddaughter, chasing her around the house, playing with her. He would shun me, ostracize me. Once, before leaving, he stood at the door with Sarit in his arms and said to me, with suppressed hostility in his eyes: "I don't understand you, Dad, I just don't understand!"—and left.

What did you want me to do, Yoav?

The love between him and his mother! From his childhood! Gently she used to guide him with his studies, never raising her voice to him, never losing her patience when he encountered a difficulty in solving problems. She treated him like a little gentleman. On holidays she used to take him with her to the Institute, show him the marvels of biological experiments, and he came back exhilarated.

When he was twelve or thirteen, she used to put her arm around his shoulder and the two of them would walk in the street like pals, proud to be seen together. When he grew taller than she—first in a soldier's uniform, then in an officer's—he would put his arm around her shoulder protectively. He was proud of her good looks, of her youthful appearance, of her vitality. He would introduce her to his friends saying, "Meet my beautiful mother."

And the 'telepathy' that existed between them when he was in the army! A radar on which she traced his moves. On the night of October 16, when he was injured during the crossing of the Suez Canal—he was then squadron commander in the Armored Corps—she had a nightmare. In the morning she told me, quietly but with complete certainty, "Yoav was hit." And she stretched her spread fingers as though releasing their tension. She kept spreading and clenching them. I grabbed her forcefully by the hand and said, "We don't know anything, calm down!" But that same evening she was by his bed at Tel Ha'shomer Hospital. His injury was slight: some shrapnel in the shoulder and chest. She did not try to detain him when, ten days later, he returned to his unit.

What a perversion of nature that it is Shula who is now acting as mediator between us, that only through her can I now talk to him! Shula, whom Nora—unlike me—intensely disliked before they got married.

When the two of them left our house after the first introduction, Nora put her hands on her head in a desperate gesture and said with a bitter grin, "I don't understand anything!" Shula looked so pitiable to her: a face like a bird, huge glasses with a dangling chain, swarthy complexion, skinny, tongue-tied. She sat on the couch, huddled as if cold, her answers to our questions barely audible, looking at us with suspicious eyes. She was born in Be'er Tuvia, she told us, graduated from a seminary for kindergarten teachers. No, she did not think she would teach kindergarten. Her answers were laconic, dry. Yoav put his hand on her shoulder, to protect her. "What does he see in her?" Nora wondered. She thought he deserved someone prettier, better educated. She said she always marveled at this strange yet common phenomenon that handsome boys, beloved and desired by the prettiest of girls—a wink and they would tumble in their arms—end up marrying the dullest, most unglamorous girls.

Only after they were married did Nora start to see some merit in her: 'practical wisdom,' common sense, manual skill, love of nature—Shula surprised her with her familiarity with the Latin names not only of wild flowers but also of the common garden varieties—and her greatest virtue: whole-hearted love for and devotion to Yoav. After Sarit was born, she acted like an older sister toward her. Quite often, when I arrived home, I found the two of them having an animated conversation, like two contemporary friends. Once I caught snatches of their conversation about polygamous tendencies in humans and in animals...

Then, after the tragedy... There were maddening things he said to me the first day after the *shiva*.

The doubt! As if it were I...

Since then he almost never came by himself. The two of them would sit down, he would let Shula do the talking. He himself kept still, was impatient. Soon he would get up, rattle the car keys in his hand, "Well, we have to go."

Or he would pop in for a few minutes—as if impelled by a sense of duty to his widowed father or, perhaps, his conscience bothered him a little—between one errand and the next, to ask if he "could do something." He would wander from room to room, check here and there, as if the house needed supervision. He would go out into the stairway, open the electricity box to make sure the fuses were okay, turn on the television for a few seconds to see if there was 'snow' on the screen, walk into the bathroom and declare that the faucet was leaking and that he would replace it the next time he came. "Well, I'm in a hurry now. Take care."

Then, without any notice he left the country. To Colombia! Yoav, how could I have anticipated this fatal entanglement?

Chapter two

Aand it all started one day, about four years ago, when I received a parcel from Paris in which I found a book of Yiddish poetry, *Oisgeboygene Tsvayg*—"The Crooked Bough"—by a poet whose name was unfamiliar to me, Shmuel Foiglman. On the title page, underneath the title, was a long dedication which stretched across the width of the page in large Yiddish script: "To the very important author of *The Great Betrayal* who, with sharp vision and a warm and loving heart, penetrated to the crux of the awesome tragedy of the murdered Jewish people, the ashes of whose six million are scattered over the earth of Europe—with heartfelt esteem and admiration. Shmuel Foiglman." Over the 'G' of 'Foiglman' was drawn a little bird, and underneath the name, the poet's full address, in Paris' tenth arrondissement.

My book, *The Great Betrayal*—the study of Chmielnicki's uprising and the massacres of 1648–49 which describes and analyzes how the Polish landed aristocracy betrayed their Jewish lessees—had, indeed, appeared in French translation a few months earlier, published by the University of Mainz. It enjoyed a circulation that quite surprised me as well as the publisher, due to a rave review in *Le Monde* by a noted historian, a gentile, in which he draws an analogy between what I describe in my book and the situation of the Jews in the French "free zone" and the Vichy regime's betrayal of its "protected Jews" during the Second World War. But it was strange—and also exceedingly embarrassing, because of the hyperbolic dedication—to receive, as a token of gratitude and appreciation for a scholarly study such as this, a book of poems, and in Yiddish to boot. A scholar is flattered by commendations from his colleagues, not from an unknown poet.

I had learned Yiddish when I was about thirty-five. My father, who was an archeologist, was a fanatic Hebraist, and my mother, who was a native Israeli, spoke no other language. When my maternal grandmother immigrated to the country—I was nine years old then—and came to live with us in Rehovot, I picked up a few words and phrases of her tongue, until I was able to conduct a halting conversation with her on domestic affairs. The great affection I felt for her—a quiet, refined woman, who walked on tiptoe around the house and went out of her way not to upset our daily lives—was extended to her language, too. But it was only when I started my intensive investigation of the history of Eastern European Jewry, and realized that a large part of the material I needed, in books and documents, existed only in Yiddish, that I mastered the language thoroughly. To this day, however, my speech in Yiddish is not fluent.

I have to admit to a deficiency: I am not interested in poetry. When I read the literary sections in the weekend papers and my glance wanders—from the corner of my eye, as it were—toward a poem printed in the outside column, I usually scan its five or six opening lines before I despair of comprehension and return to the articles. It is very seldom that I find a poem that really excites or enthralls me. One of my colleagues at the university, who is also a poet, is in the habit of presenting me with a gift of every poetry book he publishes. I leaf through the books, out of obligation to a colleague, but when I linger over this or that poem and try to fathom them, I suffer. Yes, it is suffering, quite literally; I stumble over the words, crushing them like gravel in my teeth; I cannot see the connection between the lines. I find no musicality in them that would entice me to keep on reading, to overcome the hurdles in my way. After all, musicality in a poem is in itself a source of enjoyment! And the metaphors—the metaphors in those poems seem to me like contrivances the author has laboriously sweated out of his brain in order to put the greatest distance possible between the image and the correlative. So I shake my colleague's hand whenever I meet him, pay him some empty compliment, and we never mention the subject again. He nods smil ingly as if to say: I know you're not enthusiastic about the poems, perhaps you never even read them, but I forgive you. You're really under no obligation.

Yes, it is a flaw in me, a deficiency. Since I dedicated myself to research, my work has taken up almost all my time, day and night, it has consumed all my thought and energy, and consequently, I have deprived myself of many pleasures that enhance and enrich the spirit. I have almost totally given up reading *belles lettres*; I rarely go to the theater or the movies. If it were not for Nora, who kept renewing our subscription to the Philharmonic Orchestra, I would probably have given that up, too, even though I derive enormous pleasure from music. I could listen to César Franck's sonata for violin and piano a hundred times, and there would still be tears in my eyes. I have erected a kind of barrier between my own realm and several other realms in which exciting, exhilarating, magical and mysterious things are happening. Yes, it is a serious flaw.

It isn't that research 'dries you up' as many would say who have no contact with scientific endeavor. Research carried out without enthusiasm and passion for the subject, without the joy of curiosity and discovery, is a barren undertaking. But a scientist—even one dealing with a precise science, let alone with history, which is a humanistic discipline and not a 'precise' one—can endow his research with wings, so to speak, if he suckles the 'divine nectar of the Arts.' Whenever I read the historical monographs of Plutarch, my eyes light up at the interpolated passages of poetry; interspersed in the text like cornflowers and buttercups in a cornfield are the verses from Euripides when describing Alexander the Great; from Sophocles when discussing Numa; from Homer when depicting the exploits of Coriolanus. There is so much grace, nobility, and high-mindedness in such practice. The verse helps soften and lighten the 'great tragedy of

25

science,' which according to Erich Heller, is inherent in the fact that "ugly facts often do away with the most wonderful hypotheses."

Unfortunately, I have distanced myself from those springs of life, from the arts, of which poetry—more sublime than even History, as Aristotle maintained—is one. One day, a long time before I received Foiglman's book, I was invited, together with some other colleagues of mine, to an evening of poetry reading at the university auditorium. The hall was full to overflowing, with people sitting on the stairs and standing by the walls. One by one, several of our bright young poets appeared on the stage and read from their poetry. The audience listened with bated breath, then applauded enthusiastically. As for me, as if touched by a magic wand, my heart opened up and I understood. Understood the very same lines which, when my gaze wanders over them in the newspaper, make me recoil and discard them. It was a kind of revelation for me. I suddenly realized that all those images, metaphors, verbal constructions that I had always considered contrived and remote from any actual experience, are the epitome of capturing moments in time, of imprinting their essence on the soul, in a way no other mode of expression can capture. Radiating sparks, not unlike the 'holy sparks' in Hasidism. Was it the human voice, the sound of the poets as they uttered the words and phrases—flying out of their mouths like pigeons from a magician's mouth—which wrought in me this miracle of understanding? Or was I, too, influenced by the atmosphere of admiration and empathy that permeated the audience? When I came home, I told Nora about it. I told her how much we were missing by not reading poetry. She replied: "When I look through a microscope and see a virus floating in a solution of flounder cell, meandering through mounds, bubbles, stars and comets, in some sort of magnificent, multicolored paradise—this is a perfect universe of poetry! The poets who compose odes to nature know only the macrocosm; it's a pity they don't know this microcosm." And I said: "On the contrary, they write about the micro inside the macro!" And we both laughed. But she knew by heart many poems she had learned at school. Once, when we stood facing the sea, she recited Tchernichovsky's poem, *The Full Extent of the Azure Sea*, from start to finish.

During our period of quarrels, some of which were so fierce that I would rush to close the windows lest the sounds be heard outside, I once cried: "Let's separate, then!" She fell silent, blanched, her lips grew livid; she dropped into an armchair, gave me a long, distant look, as if from the world beyond and quietly, resolutely said: "No, we will not separate."

But the real separation between us had occurred long before we withdrew from each other for the night; it happened when she stopped telling me her dream: I showed Nora the book I had received from Paris, and when I translated the dedication for her, she said: "A funny man." When I pointed to the bird drawn over his name, she said, "Not very clever,"

I said, "A poet's whim."

I leafed through the book, scanned a few poems, and found them not to my liking. Most of them were lamentations—written by a man who obviously lived through the Holocaust—about the destruction, the killing, the annihilation. Or there were poems harking back to the world that existed once and was no more. Since I am not in the habit of reading poetry, I was not qualified to analyze it. However, those poems elicited in me, as a layman, a certain sympathy for the author, compassion, though not much appreciation. The poems were 'melodious': one could glide along the verses, cruise, sometimes hop, from rhyme to rhyme, and finally reach the safe haven of the concluding couplet. Yet it was precisely this 'melodious' quality—absent in so many contemporary Hebrew poems—which alienated me from them. The gentle flow, so light, so mellifluous at times—for all the sighs, the jeremiads, the gushing forth of obviously authentic anguish—that unfaltering flow, never stopping for even one moment of dismay, of silence, or of furor which might upset the rhyme and reason of the verse—seemed to me in jarring contrast to the reality of atrocities and anxieties of which the poems themselves spoke. And the images, the metaphors—they seemed to me too familiar, as if I had encountered them countless times before: weeping trees, drops of blood on the snow, extinguished memorial candles, fading stars, the heart as a smoldering firebrand, life as a dark night.

I put the book on a shelf in my bookcase. I said to myself: when I find the time, I'll write him a thank-you note.

It often happens that when you put off an unpleasant obligation from one day to the next, before long the matter is relegated to the back of your mind, and then it becomes altogether 'obsolete.'

I was appointed head of the Jewish History Department, and the administrative work—the bothersome, harrowing job that distracts you from the important business, from study and research—consumed most of my time. The book of poems completely slipped my mind. Two months had passed since its arrival when Professor M.S. saw me in the corridor and said, "I have regards for you from Shmuel Foiglman." The name sounded familiar but I could not place it. Only when he went on to say that the man had lavished the highest praise on me and on my book, *The Great Betrayal*, did it ring a bell. I felt terribly ashamed. The book. The dedication. The outstanding debt. "Yes, he sent me a volume of his poems," I said, "but I don't know him personally." And M.S. told me he had met "that Jew" at the Sorbonne, at an international conference on the study of the Holocaust. He came to every lecture, sat in the small audience, which was comprised of some two or three dozen, and after my colleague's lecture, approached him and told him about me and my book. He asked him to convey his regards to me. I asked what kind of "a Jew" was that Foiglman, and he said, "A warm kind of Jew, a bit ridiculous… During recesses, between lectures, at the cafeteria, he tried to buttonhole various participants…a professor from New York, a lecturer from Geneva…he talks in an exuberant manner, gets into arguments…"

"Does he speak Hebrew?"

"Fairly well. His Hebrew is a little old fashioned, but he does speak it. A poet, you say? He didn't tell me that."

That same night I sat down to write the thank you letter that was two months overdue. The letter that was the 'original sin,' so to speak, the primal cause of everything that ensued.

❧

An explanation is in order. But I doubt I can supply a satisfactory one. For I am the exact opposite of the poetess Rachel who wrote, "Only about myself can I write." For the last twenty-five years I have been committing words and phrases to paper. Scores of publications, two thick books. I deal in events that happened in distant times, in far-off places, in which I had no personal involvement. I have never written a diary. In letters—including those intended for friends and family—so far as they concern myself, I put down only facts, and frugally at that. Dealing in history all one's life makes one humble in its presence, reduced to a miniscule grain of sand. "Poor in worthy deeds," as it's said in the Yom Kippur prayer. My study resembled a chamber at the top of a watchtower from which I looked out, into the expanse of time, through transparent glass which does not reflect one's own image. Suddenly you are hit on the head; death has penetrated your well-protected chamber, and you hear a voice commanding you: Look inside, man; examine your ways!

I must explain how a strange man entered my life and destroyed it. Completely destroyed it! For had it not been for him and for this whole relationship between us—this unexpected, uncalled for, one might say compulsive relationship—Nora would have been alive today. We had a happy life. Yes, Yoav, we had a happy life. Do you doubt it? Don't you know that I did everything in my power to bring your mother out of the depression she sank into in the last few months?

Despite everything I knew? Things you did not know, and could not know? I wrote to Foiglman because I felt guilty. Doubly guilty.

First, for my ingratitude. For having put off for so long expressing my thanks to a man who took the trouble to send me—by air mail—his book, with an affectionate, heartfelt dedication. Had I thanked him immediately, I could have acquitted myself with a few polite words, and thus put an end to the matter. There would have been no follow-up.

And secondly—secondly, the man is a Holocaust survivor. When I reread the book, prior to writing my letter to him, so as to know what to write—this time I read it poem by poem, dwelling on each one—I slapped my forehead and said: How could I so ignore and slight a man who had poured into those poems his entire soul, his anguish and mourning for the loss of his family, his home, everything he owned in the world! Only a cynical, insensitive brute could behave like this!

So, I wrote him a long letter, two and half pages long, full of praise and compliments. No, I was not being untruthful and I did not write lies. Upon rereading the poems—actually reading them for the first time—I discovered in them many 'sparks,' surprising and original metaphors.

Such as the line where he compares a cry to an "arrow of lightning that froze in tempestuous skies." Or, "The white lake of my mother's silences." Or the description of the clock whose ticking continues to sound in a house that had burnt down, in his haunting poem entitled: *On the Death of Dreams.*

Moreover, the book contained a whole section that completely escaped my notice the first time I leafed through it; it was called *In the Backyard* and had no bearing on the Holocaust or on the world of childhood that had perished. Those were mostly short poems, comprising eight to ten lines—all love poems, to a wife, a daughter, friends—and poems about nature, animate and inanimate. Those poems, so concise and original in their perceptions, were to my mind, the best in the volume.

But the poem that impressed me most profoundly was the last one, which I had not even reached when first scanning the book. It was a twenty-four-stanza poem called: *The Ballad of the Old Child Who Was Never Born.*

"A lonely old child stands in front of a locked gate and knocks"—thus opens the poem. The locked gate is the gate of Heaven, "a gate of light blue splendor," and through the gate the child talks to three righteous men: Noah, Daniel and Job. He asks them to open the gate for him, so he can stay with them in that Temple of Splendor, and they ask him, each in turn, what entitles him to join them there. His suffering entitles him, he says. To Noah he explains that he has been through a more horrendous flood than in his days; to Daniel—that he was thrown into a den full not only of lions but of every beast of prey, and they tore his flesh; to Job—that his house burnt down, his family perished and none survived. "But you are still only a child," the three men say. "A child cannot have lived through so much. Even if you lived as long as Methuselah you could not have been through so many misfortunes." The child says he is like a thousand-year-old, and seventy generations have not seen what his eyes have seen. If he is so old, the three say, what are the good deeds that entitle him to a place in Heaven? The child is silent. He has no good deeds to his credit, since he is only a child. "My good child, my innocent child," Job says to him, "Naked you came out of your mother's womb, and naked must you return there. When the angel Gabriel has taught you the secrets of the world, he will also show you the way to us."

"Righteous Job, wise Job," the child says, "how can I return to my mother's womb when it was ripped in front of my eyes..." And the ballad concludes with the words: "And the three righteous men of the world stand silent, watching the wondrous transformation of the child into a bright star."

It was mainly about this poem that I wrote to him. I may have exaggerated a little in the praise I heaped on him, but I did not lie.

Three weeks later I got a letter from Foiglman. Seventeen pages long. I had written to him in Hebrew and he responded in Yiddish.

I was so overwhelmed by the length of the letter that I laid it at the corner of my desk and did not pick it up until three days later, on Saturday.

I am not used to great intimacy in my dealings with people, especially with strangers. The letter—although the author treated me with the utmost respect—was written in a very intimate, emotional tone, as one might write to a brother. He started by saying that he had read my letter with tears in his eyes. The day he received my letter was "one of the happiest days of his life." And he explained why: It was not the first time that his ballad had garnered high praise; it had already been included in many anthologies and translated into several languages, though not into Hebrew, and much had been written about it. His wife, who is an actress, includes it in her recital tours in various countries around the world, and everywhere it is received with great enthusiasm. "People come backstage to kiss her hands." But all this is nothing compared to the 'soul warming' that my letter generated. What made him most happy was the fact that his poems have elicited such praise from an 'admired' scholar whose language is Hebrew, who not only lives in Israel, but is a native of Israel, as he had found out from the back cover of my book, *The Great Betrayal*.

Over five pages the author then laments the great tragedy of Yiddish, the thousand-year-old tongue that has lost its people, "roaming around the world like a ghost," like "the shadow of Peter Schlemiel, separated from its owner"; a language whose speakers, readers and writers are constantly dwindling. They are the last generation. "And I—sometimes at night, I wake up from a terrible nightmare in which I'm shouting: *gevald!* and nobody understands my language."

All that was not new to me; I had often read such comments, delivered in the same mournful, elegiac tone, but this time it was coupled with a note of disappointment and harsh accusation: the sole hope of Yiddish 'after the great destruction,' he wrote, was that it might rise, like a phoenix, from its ashes, in that same land where the remnants of the destroyed house are now gathering to build their new home. Yes, he is well aware that in a country where the twelve dispersed tribes are gathered from East and West, Hebrew must be the 'official language of the state.' He also knows that the 'family feud' between the two languages, which had such ugly manifestations during the twenties and the thirties, has long subsided. But the 'reconciliation' that has since prevailed offers only small consolation. "We are like the wretched maid in the mistress's house."

And into these matters of public interest creeps a bitter note of personal peeve: he has visited Israel three times—his brother lives in Ramlah—and walked about it "like a beggar at a wedding." Except for a handful of Yiddish writers, nobody had heard his name; nobody had read his poems. Once, out of curiosity, he went to a big conference of Hebrew writers, and nobody greeted him. When he introduced himself to the secretary, the man did not even offer him a cup of tea; he walked away and left him alone. Would he have accorded the same treatment to an English or a French author, or even to a German author, the son of a murderous nation, if he had come there as his guest? If a nation's culture is compared to a family, with father, mother, sons and daughters—what, then, happens when you drive the mother out of the house? If Hebrew is the 'father' of Jewish culture, then surely Yiddish is its 'mother'! It is Yiddish that inherited and fostered, treasured and safeguarded the wealth of folk wisdom, proverbs, legends, jokes, lullabies; it was she who infused the house with warmth! Why, for that very reason Yiddish is dubbed *mame loshen* and not *tate loshen*! And now, present-day Israel is a sovereign state with glorious deeds to its credit and pomp and circumstance too—but mother is not there!

In the second part of his letter Foiglman explains why he was so enthusiastic about my book and why he saw fit to send me his own book, something he rarely does with people he does not know: first, he found my book, although a work of research, written "from the heart, with great love, and full of soul, and from this respect it seems affiliated to poetry"; second, he himself was born in Zamosc—a town mentioned many times in my book—which in the last three hundred years has been victim to three massacres: first Chmielnicki, then Petliura, and finally the Nazi murderers. When he was eight years old his family moved to Warsaw where his father, who was a journalist and a *Bundist*, got a permanent position on the newspaper *Haynt*. But as soon as the Germans entered the city—he was thirteen years old—he and his twin brother were smuggled back to Zamosc, which had been captured by the Russians at the outbreak of war; there, it was hoped, they would be safe from the murderers. When the German-Russian pact was signed, the town fell into German hands again, and in April, 1942, on the eve of the great deportation—when all the Jews of the town and its surroundings, about ten thousand people, were executed—the two brothers managed to flee the ghetto and hide, for a high ransom, in the barn of a Polish peasant who had been almost a member of the household before the war and who had been helped out of prison by their uncle. This very peasant turned them over to the Germans two weeks after he had given them shelter—and thus Shmuel Foiglman witnessed first hand 'The Great Betrayal.' He had heard, in his childhood, about the other 'Betrayal' at the time of the Petliura pogroms. It was frequently mentioned in

33

their house, and the "horror stories of women howling in the streets were interwoven with the lullabies sung to us."

What he endured in the ghetto, and later, when handed over to the Germans and sent to Majdanek, and from there to labor camps in Poland and Germany, and how he survived all that—"this is a matter for a book of a thousand pages of blood and tears which I will not write," he wrote; but when he read *The Great Betrayal*, he realized that more than any other researcher of Jewish history in modern times, I had grasped the core of that 'grotesque absurd play' of the unfortunate and fallacious relationship between Jews and gentiles in Europe in recent generations, and that was why he was so taken with my book.

At the conclusion of his letter—written in rounded, pictur-esque, lucid handwriting—he expressed a wish to meet with me "speedily and in our time," so he can have the honor of meeting me personally and talking to me face to face; and if I chance to be in Paris—I am always welcome in his house. His apartment was far from being a palace, but "a friendly talk and a smile make a house roomier," as the saying goes, especially in view of the fact that his wife is often on tour, so I could have a room all to myself. "My house is your house, my table your table, my bread your bread," he concluded in Hebrew.

And above his signature—again the drawing of a little bird.

It was with mixed feelings that I read that letter. It was not only out of a sense of duty and gratitude for his generosity that I hastened to respond to him. By that time I had already started col-lecting material for a comprehensive study of the Petliura pogroms and the relationship between the Jews and the Soviet authorities on the one hand, and the Ukrainian rebels on the other. The mention in his letter of 'family stories' that circulated in his house about those pogroms, were like a gift from heaven for me. I consider myself a rational person, not given, normally, to superstitions. Nora, whose preoccupation with biology brought her closer to 'the secrets of life'—used to tell me, however amicably, that I had an understand-ing of the 'overt' but not the 'covert,' and hence I should beware of its unexpected assaults. And yet, whenever I am engrossed in a certain study, and accidentally come across a document, a piece of information, an unexpected clue, I see it as a sign that I am on the right track and that I should pursue that course. Thus, I immediately wrote back to Foiglman, asking him if he knew of any first-hand written testimonies of those pogroms.

In less than two weeks I received a large envelope containing, in addition to a letter, (a short one this time) a ten-page photocopy of an article written by his late father and published in the *Ykuf Almanach* in 1935, entitled: "Memories from the Burning Cellar." It contained detailed descriptions of the Ukrainians' raids on Jewish homes in 1919: the devastation, the plunder, the massacres, the brutality and atrocity, the few attempts at self-defense, the abandonment by the Bolsheviks, and so on.

In January of the same year, in return for my letter of thanks, I received a page from the Parisian Yiddish journal, *Unzer Velt* containing a long poem of his, *A letter to Yehuda Halevi Across Seas of Fire*, and underneath the title—to my utter astonishment!—a personal dedication to me, to wit: "For my dear friend, Professor Zvi Arbel, with love." *Mit Libshaft.* And across the top margin, was written in Hebrew: "Warm regards—S.F."

Chapter three

This morning, when I walked into the office of our department, before my lecture, the secretary offered me a cup of coffee and asked: "Aren't you well, professor?"

"Why?"

"You look a little pale..."

There is something annoying, malicious even, in these remarks of hers about my health and looks, which purport to express concern for me. But the truth is that in the last few weeks I have been plagued by migraines, which must show on my face. I have to take pills, which for the most part help alleviate the pain, but if I take them too late, when the headache is in full swing, pounding like hammers on my left temple, threatening to smash my skull, then the pills are of no use.

And this is what happened today. When I walked into the lecture hall, a dark fog clouded my eyes. I spoke about the 'Council of the Four Lands' and the words emerged from my mouth as if the jaws and lips were numb from a narcotic drug. I counted the students present: eleven. In the beginning of the previous year, before Nora's death, there would have been some forty to fifty people. A big commotion before my entrance, then an expectant hush as soon as I ascended the podium. Sorrow wears me down, and I lack the courage to declare surrender. When Gibbon finished writing *The Decline and Fall of the Roman Empire*—he was fifty-one at the time—his own decline and fall set in. And after the death of his close friend Deyverdun, he knew no joy. In the last six years of his life he wrote only his memoirs. I will be sixty-one in August.

When I remember those moments, when I stood by my desk with the page from the Yiddish newspaper in my hand, stunned at the sight of my name in the dedication, barely cognizant of the verse itself—I am amazed to recall the agitation that seized me. I slumped into my chair. My ears flushed. A mixture of rage, indignation, shame—but not a shred of gratitude. He shackles me with bonds of 'affection'!—I said to myself—*mit Libshaft!*—what grants him such presumption, considering that he does not know me at all! Is this the price I have to pay for asking a small favor?

By nature I am not a very sociable, amiable person; my relations with my colleagues are matter-of-fact. Seldom did we invite any of them to our house or accept their invitations. And even that was only in order to enhance good working relations. In the academic world, where there is so much competition and behind-the-scenes intrigues to usurp one another's place, some fraternization of this kind cannot be avoided. Even when your position is secure and you have tenure, you need two or three allies just to further your own causes. At those parties with my colleagues, when the conversation was always about the same topics, I would sit impatient, raging inwardly over the waste of time, thinking about the book left open on my desk. Sometimes I would find an excuse, apologize to my hosts and depart, leaving Nora to find herself a ride home with someone else. When you are absorbed in a study of a given subject, there are subtle, tense relations between you and the material you are working on, not unlike the relations between a man and a woman. First you woo your subject—sometimes it requites your love and sometimes it simply turns its back on you. It happened to me more than once that I 'wooed' a certain research idea, but had soon to relinquish it because it 'turned its back on me.' But even when the match takes and an

intimacy weaves itself between the two of you—day after day, night
after night, you keep each other's company for long hours—the tension never disappears; sometime you think it is eluding you, evading
you, 'cheating' on you; you are jealous when you find out someone
else is casting glances in its direction, or puts a hand on it. You want
it to be yours alone, and even when it yields to you, the gratification
is not always complete. Perhaps this is why I instinctively shy away
from people who try to get too close to me; I erect a barrier between
me and them, as if fearing they might come between me and the
object of my true love. I am not surprised, therefore, that many people
who tried to make friends with me, while I—though gently—kept
them at arm's length, interpreted it as arrogance and haughtiness on
my part.

It was only after long moments—when my agitation abated
there was certainly something unseemly about it—that I opened my
eyes to read the poem. In the style of Itzik Manger's dialogues with
historical figures, Foiglman talks here with Yehuda Halevi, argues,
expostulates, reasons. You, he tells him, wrote that your heart was in
the East while you yourself were at the distant end of the West, but
with me it is my very heart that is split, rent, between my brothers
who are reviving the land in the East, and my brothers who were
murdered in the land of the West. You found it easy to leave behind
all the riches of Spain in order to see the ground where the ruined
temple stands; you—you yearned to hurl yourself to the ground and
kiss the stones of our fathers' land, and to prostrate yourself at their
tomb in Hebron, while I—I have no grave and no tombstone here
to throw myself on, because my fathers' ashes were blown in the
wind and I cannot bid their souls goodbye. You—only saw with your
mind's eye how the dogs drag your nation's lions and the crows pick
at its eagles' carrions, while I—saw with my own eyes how the dogs
tore off babies' limbs and the crows scoop down on heaps of cadavers.
Like you, I am a violin making melodies, but my strings, all but one,
are torn, and that lone string emits shrill sounds of bleak desolation
that drive all listeners away. But as long as there is breath in me, I
shall wander from East to West, with my violin in my hand, and play
it wherever there is a Jewish soul fluttering and yearning.

I sat for a long time facing the newspaper page on my desk, unable to rise from my seat. A cloud of sadness enveloped me.

The next morning, at breakfast, I showed Nora the poem and the dedication above it. "What?" she cried alarmed, but the next moment she raised a smiling face to me: "He's immortalized you!"

I laughed: "This isn't the first time, you know, that my name appears in print!"

"Yes, but poetry is immortal!" And then she asked: "How is the poem?"

"Strong," I said and told her what it was about. "Yes, yes," she said gloomily, but I detected a note of skepticism in her voice. When she got up from the table, she said, as an afterthought: "Still, you'd best be cautious of him."

I did not write to him. I did not thank him for the poem and the dedication.

Five weeks later, toward evening, when I picked up the phone and heard the words: "Am I speaking to Professor Zvi Arbel?" I knew instantly—was it a premonition or just the heavy Hebrew accent that gave him away? Or was it the fear I had harbored all these weeks, knowing the moment would arrive—that it was he. The blood rushed to my face. Confusion raged in my heart. But I restrained myself and calmly replied: "Yes, that's me. Who is speaking, please?" When he told me his name I cried with exaggerated glee: "Welcome, welcome!" and asked when he had arrived, where he was staying and so forth, and then I hastened to add, terribly embarrassed, that yes, I am in his debt, a long overdue debt—I thanked him for the poem, for the dedication, I apologized, stuttering, for not writing to him, I had been so preoccupied...serious troubles, so unexpected, at the university... He was calling from Ramlah, from his brother's house. I hastened to invite him over. At last we'll have the chance to meet face to face, I said.

Chapter four

When I opened the door for him, Foiglman stepped back a little and gave me an astonished look, as if he had come to the wrong address; in his left hand he was holding a leather briefcase, and his right hand was outstretched as if asking a question; only after a moment did a smile light up his eyes, and with a great swing, as if he intended to strike me, he planted his right hand in mine, "*Shalom Aleichem!*"*

Then he extended his hand to Nora, bowed deeply, and asked if she understood Yiddish; when she said she did not, he said, "Then we'll speak Hebrew. I'm breaking my teeth speaking Hebrew, but as it says in the Bible, 'Thou hast broken the teeth of the ungodly.' As you can see, I still remember what I learned in childhood..." Again, he examined me with his eyes, "I didn't expect you to be so tall...and you're much younger than I thought..." I said I had long passed my fiftieth birthday, and when he asked how long ago and I told him, he said, "Then I'm much younger than you! Two full years!"

I, too, was surprised at his appearance. Because of the dark

* *Shalom Aleichem!*—Hebrew: "Greetings to you!"

nature of his poetry and those letters suffused with bitterness, I had imagined him as a somber, hunched, embittered-looking man. Instead, I saw a broad shouldered man before me, with the arms and hands of a peasant, a firm chin and light blue eyes with a cunning, whimsical glint in them. His long, scraggly hair, yellowish-white in color, came down to the nape of his neck and on both sides of his wide forehead. His black bowtie, slightly tattered, gave him the appearance of an old-fashioned bohemian.

We sat in the living room; he bent down, opened his briefcase, and said in Yiddish that first of all he had to unburden himself. He took out a bottle of French cognac and put it on the table. When Nora protested and said, "What for? You needn't have! We never drink at all," he said, "Then it will be for your guests! *Shoyn!*" And trying to put us at our ease, he said he had bought it cheaply at the airport, so we needn't worry about the expense. Then he whipped out a heavy tome from his briefcase and laid it in front of me. "A little present for you," he said, and patted the cover with the palm of his hand. I opened the book. *From Nearby and from Afar* was the title, and Foiglman, while turning the pages with me, explained that it was a collection of articles about writers and artists he had met during the last thirty years in France, America, England, Poland and Israel.

"When you have a little time, between the *Minha* and *Ma'ariv* prayers, you can take a look at it," he said, and bending his head toward us, he whispered, "Do you have a policewoman in the building?" He must be jesting, we thought. "When I came into the building," he continued whispering, "a woman walked in with me. About thirty, slim, straight body, as if manufactured in a carpenter's shop. She was wearing a tight brown dress with two rows of buttons, and she had green eyes. On a leash she was leading a big black dog that came up to her waist. I stood aside to let her go first, but she stood there, staring at me hard, saying nothing, waiting for me to go up the stairs first. Being the gentleman, I said, 'Ladies first,' and motioned to her with my hand to go by, but she said nothing, just stared at me with those green eyes as if I were a thief. Perhaps she thought I was a beggar looking for a place to sleep. When I saw that she wasn't budging, I walked in front of her. The dog behind me was panting like a bellows and I was afraid he might attack me any moment. Finally, they entered an apartment on the second floor and I felt relieved. So tell me, is she a policewoman?"

We laughed. We told him she owned a boutique, that she lived alone, and was always scared, hence the big dog that never left her side. "Why did you assume that she was a policewoman?" Nora asked, amused. "She had such eyes!" and he glared at us menacingly, "but if she's just scared, that's all right...it's all right..." And he, too, laughed.

Nora got up and went to the kitchen to bring some refreshments. He looked me straight in the face, with an inquisitive yet radiant look and said, "Finally!"

"Yes, it's good to meet each other finally," I said pleasantly. He continued to look at me, with glowing eyes, as if confirming to himself that I was indeed the man he had been corresponding with all along and said, "*The Great Betrayal*, eh?" And a moment later he repeated aloud, as if announcing to the whole world, "The Gr-eat Bet-ra-yal!" then fell silent, gazed around at the walls, examined them and pronounced, "Nice place you have."

I explained that we had inherited most of the paintings from Nora's parents.

"Daumier, eh?" he said, pointing to a drawing of Don Quixote on his horse, and then turned back to me, "And now—Petliura?"

"Yes," I assured, "I'm already knee deep in the material." A distant smile gleamed in his eyes. "You know that Itzik Manger wrote a poem about Petliura, don't you?"

No, I actually didn't. *Di Ballade fun Petliura*, he said and quoted a few verses in Yiddish:

Black bird of the night,
Why have you brought Petliura hither
With the bloody hands, with the dark eyes?

At that moment Nora came in and put tea and cakes on the table. He turned to her and translated the verses into Hebrew, and related the content of the ballad. Underneath Yankele's crib lies a slaughtered young goat. It is a sinister midnight hour and Petliura the Haidamack is standing outside the window. The child asks what

43

the man wants, with a sword in one hand and an ax in the other, and the mother says he has come looking for a spade to bury the dead father. When he asks the black birds why they have brought him hither, they say he has come looking for a rope to hang himself. The poem ends with a curse: May the wind blow him away every midnight; may he roll in the dust with leprous dogs; may our tears burn him to death.

"Let's talk about happier things now," said Foiglman, and peering at Nora's face added, "If I'm not mistaken I would guess, the lady is a *sabra*, a native-born Israeli."

"As a matter of fact, no," Nora laughed, and told him that she was born in Munich and had been brought to Israel with her parents at the age of three, on the very eve of Hitler's rise to power. "Munich, yes..." Foiglman nodded, "Frauenkirche, eh?"

We wondered what he meant, and he explained. Frauenkirche is an old, fifteenth-century cathedral in Munich. "I'll tell you something funny," he said. "My brother, the one living in Ramlah, is my twin. We were together in the ghetto; we were together in Majdanek... Two months after the war we found ourselves in Munich. Destitute refugees, we didn't know what was going to happen to us. The town lay in ruins, but the old cathedrals stood in their place. We went to see the Frauenkirche, which is famous for its twin towers. We stood on the ground in front of the cathedral and looked up. Suddenly we both burst out laughing. Here we are, two twin boys, and up there, two twin towers... We laughed and laughed and couldn't stop laughing until we left the place."

When he realized that his anecdote had saddened us, he clapped his hands and said in a cheerful voice: "But then we were already fine! Oh, yes, then we were fine indeed!"

"And what about you?" Foiglman was now asking about my origins. I told him that on my mother's side I'm a third-generation Israeli, and that my father emigrated from Riga, Latvia. "Riga!" he called out, and proceeded to tell us that in Riga, before the war, an important Yiddish newspaper was published, *Frimorgn* was its name, whose editor, Stopnicki, later committed suicide in the Warsaw ghetto by drinking poison. That was during the first deportation, in 1942.

One of the frequent contributors to that paper was Mark Razumni. He was surprised that I had never heard of Razumni, since, he said, apart from being a noted journalist and a humorist, Razumni also wrote poetry, stories and fascinating travel accounts.

While he was talking the telephone rang; someone asked if Shmuel Foiglman was there and could he please talk to him. "This is for you," I said and handed the receiver to our guest. "Must be my brother," he said, and while he was talking to his brother in Yiddish, his eyes beamed at us, as if he were aiming his words at us. "Yes, everything is fine," he said, "I arrived safely, I found the house, a nice home, beautifully appointed… I am being treated very well… I'm even served tea and cake… The lady of the house is pretty as a picture…" he winked at us, "Yes, Thursday night… Tell them I'll be there… I'll read, of course, how can I come and not read?… What should they put in the ad? Tell them to write that the eminent author, the great luminary, the towering genius… Listen, Katriel, let them write their own ad, why should I tell them how to phrase it?"

When he sat back in his chair he told us that on Thursday next week there was going to be a memorial service for the Martyrs of Zamosc. He had been asked to read some of his poems. He could not very well refuse. So many great men of letters came from Zamosc! Y.L. Peretz, Eichenbaum, Zederbaum, Schiffman, Reifman…all destroyed, not a trace remained. Could we, too, come to the service? "No, don't come! There's no point!"

I asked him why his wife had not joined him, and he said she was on a tour in Argentina, enjoying considerable success. Many people don't even know that she was his wife, because she goes by the name of Fogel. "When I came to France after the war," he said, "People tried to talk me into eliminating the '*yod*'—the letter 'i'—from my name, so it would sound more respectable, less *Ostjude*.* But I told them there's no way I'd give up on the *yod*, the 'i' in my name; there's no way I'd change it from Foiglman to Fogelman! That's the essence of my Jewish identity. My sanctification of the Holy Name! My wife, however, is another matter. Actors are wandering stars, as

---

* Ostjude—a derogatory term for Jews from Eastern Europe

Goldfaden used to say, they follow their fortunes—a change in name
may bring a change in fortune.

In response to Nora's questions he told us that his wife was
born in Paris, the daughter of the Yiddish writer Richard Boimel, and
that she was equally fluent in French and Yiddish. When he first met
her, she was an actress in the French theater and had appeared in a
movie with Simone Signoret, with whom she was still friends. But
the theater is a cruel environment of ruthless competition, and Hinda,
his wife, was not one to tread on corpses. Thus, five years ago, she
decided to embark on a one-woman show of reading and acting in
Yiddish. Since then she has been very successful, but the trouble is
that most of the year she flies around the world like a bee gathering
nectar, while he, the male, is bound to the hive.

I asked him when he started writing poetry, and he said that
he wrote his first poem in the work camp in Kungskirchen when he
was seventeen. He wrote it on a piece of paper he had torn from a
cement bag and hid in his shoe. "It is included in the book I sent
you." He motioned with his hand. "It's called 'Once There Was' and,
at the bottom, it's signed Kungskirchen, 1944!"

"I didn't remember," I said.

"Let's take a look at the book," he said.

And then something rather unpleasant happened. I walked
into my study—he followed me—and started looking through the
bookshelves, one by one, section by section, scanning them, shifting
them around—while he, in the meantime, took stock of my library,
admired its scope, examined some rare titles he found among them
that he recognized—but I could not find his own book. The longer
it took, the more frenzied I got. I felt hot, in my chest, in my face. I
was getting hysterical, rummaging, yanking books from the shelf and
then replacing them with trembling hands. "It can't have disappeared!
It's got to be here!" I cried.

Nora came in and joined me in my search. A blue cover with
a picture of a bough and bird, I reminded her. We kept on looking
for a few more minutes, and then we gave up. Foiglman, all the while,
did his best to alleviate my embarrassment. He suggested I had lent
the book to someone and had forgotten about it. He said that sort

of thing often happened to him. And besides, it didn't really matter. As soon as he would leave the house, the book would come out of hiding. It must have felt ashamed in his presence and that was why it went into hiding. Just as you lose things inadvertently, so you find them inadvertently. He even quoted an adage to the effect that a person ought to regret days lost but not lost books.

When we returned to the front room he stopped by the drawing of Daumier's Don Quixote and said, "Ah, Rosinante, Rosinante…" and turning to us added, "Even Cervantes himself did not understand the soul of that horse as Daumier did… A crying horse! Have you ever seen a horse cry?" He pointed to the picture, "So much suffering in this long face, in this skin and bones…" Nora said the picture had been given to her by her father. He had brought this big reproduction from the Pinacotheque in Munich, where the original hangs. Foiglman, his hands behind his back, looked at her with a pursed smile, murmuring, "Yes… Munich… Yes," and then, as if emerging from a reverie, said, "Do you remember the episode with the death train in *Don Quixote?*"

Since neither of us remembered, he proceeded to tell it to us in a mixture of Hebrew and Yiddish. "After the affair with the three village maids from Toboso…don't you remember? Sancho, this shrewd rogue, had arranged an entire production for the benefit of the poor knight. He conned him into believing that one of the girls was Dulcinea, and fell to his knees in front of her jackass. And Don Quixote wondered: How is this possible? Her face resembles a potato, and what's worse, she reeks of garlic. Is it possible that his divine lady would smell of garlic? Well, they ride on and meet a cart carrying a troupe of actors. And who are these actors? One is Death, another the Devil, yet another Caesar… What man is not afraid of Death? But our Knight of the Mournful Countenance here shows himself defiant of Death…"

With great animation, gesticulating with his hands, raising and lowering his voice, his face expanding in a smile, then contracting in a menacing expression, he told how Don Quixote ordered the Devil, who was the coachman, to stop the cart; how the clown of the troupe waved his belled scepter over his head until Rosinante got so frightened it bolted, made its way to a field, collapsed on the ground, and toppled its rider.

"I must have read *Don Quixote* at least twenty times." A whimsical glint showed in his eyes. "And every time I said to myself: If I were a novelist instead of a poet, I would write a great novel about Rosinante; how this wretched horse, carrying its mad rider from town to town, from village to village, receives nothing but blows and curses, gets injured in battles with windmills and by all manner of wayfarers, both innocent and villainous, and has no idea why all this is happening to him... How would he regard all those crazy adventures? And at the end of the novel...no, not at the end but toward the end, I would let him grow wings and he would rise from the ground, flying, flying in the air..." And he flapped his arms like a huge bird trying to take off from the ground.

He was standing in the middle of the room, his arms rising and falling, striking against his ribs, and his eyes narrowed in a smile. But it was an anguished, injured smile, devoid of any mirth.

Nora felt awkward and muttered, "You...you would turn it into Pegasus..."

"Pegasus!" Foiglman made a long face. "No, Pegasus is Greek while Rosinante is a sort of Jewish beast, not unlike Mendele's nag." His eyes lingered on our faces as if he were waiting for our approval, and then he turned to me and said, "Sancho put it very aptly when he said to Our Hero, 'Sir, sorrow was not created for beasts, but for humans, but a man who has no feeling in his heart for the beasts, has himself become a beast!' Nice, isn't it? But didn't King Solomon say, 'A righteous man regardeth the life of his beast'... Well now, I have taken enough of your time, and I have to get to Ramlah tonight."

I offered to see him to the bus stop, but he would not hear of it. He thanked us warmly for our hospitality, showering praise on the 'gracious hostess,' and standing on the threshold said, "Light! There's so much light in your country. At noon I am almost blinded by the light."

A couple of minutes later, when we were clearing the table, he rang the bell. He apologized profusely and asked to use the bathroom.

"In Hebrew you say: 'For a man's life is as a tree,' whereas in Yiddish we say, 'A man's not made of wood.'"

We heard the water flushing in the toilet. He came out, apologized again, thanked us again and once more took his leave.

We sank into the armchairs in the living room and exchanged smiles. "Well?" I asked. The smile gradually faded from Nora's face. "When he was flailing his arms like that...it was a little crazy, wouldn't you say?"

"Yes, a little bit..." I half agreed.

Then Nora said, bemusement on her face, "When he was telling us about the maid from Toboso who reeked of garlic, I wanted to say, 'And what about you?' He, too, had bad breath. Some kind of garlicky Polish sausage... It wasn't very pleasant."

A few minutes later the doorbell sent us scurrying again. Foiglman was standing in the doorway like a penitent child. "You can kill me!" he muttered. "Instead of repaying my hosts' kindness, I'm making their lives miserable. Devil's own luck! I get on the bus, open my wallet to buy a ticket and realize that I have no Israeli money, only francs. I pleaded with the driver to accept it, but no, he won't take foreign currency. I had no choice but to come back here and ask that you convert my..." And he handed me a couple of French notes with a trembling hand.

I quickly took out my wallet and put all the shekels I could find in his hand. However, I refused to accept the francs. "You'll pay me some other time," I said.

"Somebody must have cast a spell on me," he said apologetically to Nora. "How could I come without so much as bus fare... What a head I've got!" and he thumped his fist on his forehead.

"This is some bird!" Nora laughed when she had closed the door.

It was only at the end of that week, when I opened the bottom drawer of my desk—where I keep Xerox copies of documents needed for my work—that I found Foiglman's book, on top of the papers.

Chapter five

A few days later he phoned me again. I informed him happily that the prodigal son had returned. "Did he tell you why he was hiding?"

"He was hiding from me, not from you," I said. "Yes, I'm used to his turning his back on me." And then he asked if and when we could meet again. I could not avoid him, so I set a time for a week later.

"I have a delicate question for you," he said, "I don't want to impose, of course, but would it be terribly rude of me if I brought my brother along? He has heard so much about you, from me and from others, and he is longing to meet you and, of course, your noble wife. She made a great impression on me. Great impression."

"Gladly," I said. "Of course! We'll be happy to meet him."

When I told Nora about the scheduled visit, she recoiled, crying, "What!?" Then she added, "You'll excuse me, I'm busy that evening." Yet she did stay long enough to welcome them when they arrived, to save me the trouble of serving refreshments.

Shmuel's twin resembled him in build, height and facial features, yet his hair was black and combed back in strands to cover a

bald spot; a black skullcap was pinned to his head. A modest, def-
erential, self-effacing smile, hovered on his lips. He carried a leather
briefcase.

Nora sat next to him; she seemed to have taken more of a liking
to him than to his brother, since she was lending an attentive ear to
his answers to her questions. He told her that he had immigrated to
Israel in 1947. He 'was just in time,' as he put it, to be incarcerated in
Cyprus, 'just in time' to fight in the War of Independence, with the
Moriah Battalion, in the battle over the Old City of Jerusalem, and
then in two subsequent wars… He told all this in an unassuming tone,
in fragmentary sentences, as if discounting his own experiences. He
had spent two years in the Hiriya immigrants' camp, then tried his
luck at Moshav Mishmar-Hashiva, unsuccessfully… He now owned
a little electric shop in Ramlah…had three daughters, two of them
married, and a son doing his military service…

He opened the briefcase and took out a big package, wrapped
in coarse brown paper, and put it on the table. A small gift he himself had made, he said, opening the package; it was a three-branched
candelabrum, resembling boughs on a tree, with candle-like bulbs.
We thanked him heartily, and Nora—although the gift was probably
not to her taste—expressed great admiration for his handiwork, and
put the candelabrum on the sideboard for all to see. Katriel got up
and tried to plug it into a socket in the wall, but it turned out to be
two-pronged while the plug was three-pronged. He looked around
the room for another socket, and when he realized that all the sockets
were similar, he shook his head at us and said, concerned, "This isn't
good. You mustn't have these…it's dangerous…you should change
the sockets. You have metal fixtures, and every time you touch
them…"

Nora promised to follow his advice, saying we had been meaning to change them, but somehow never got around to it. Then she
apologized to our guests, saying that she had a prior engagement she
could not call off, and left.

When they resumed their seats, I asked Katriel how he became
an electrician. "Oh, it's a long story," he smiled, "and not a very
happy one either." His brother urged him to tell the story, but he

tried to evade it. "What for...let bygones be bygones...why let the demons out?"

But after many entreaties he consented. For over an hour he unfolded the story of the brothers' experiences during the war.

The next day, when I returned from the university, Nora told me that a few minutes after she arrived home, at four-thirty, the doorbell rang; when she opened the door she saw Katriel Foiglman, in his overalls, with his tool-kit in his hand. He apologized profusely for not letting her know in advance about coming, but he had not been able to sleep that night out of fear for our lives. He asked her permission to change all four sockets in the living room. "One could live for a hundred and twenty years, but death, God forbid, can come in a second." Though she was stunned and embarrassed by this unexpected intrusion, she could not stop him. He worked for two hours, threading grounding wires into the walls here and there, inserting new electric points. He refused to accept any money, and when she offered him at least some refreshment, he hastened to leave, bidding her farewell and proffering best wishes.

"I know how to take precautions against troubles," Nora said, "but I still have to learn how to protect myself against favors."

"The queen has been conquered in her own palace," I teased.

ҿ

What the twin brothers endured during the war is not in my power to 'document,' nevertheless I feel compelled to do so—it is the historian in me that has the urge to commit their story to paper, now that one of them is dead and the other is not a man of letters.

Just as there is no 'banality of evil' in the world, as Hannah Arendt defined it (quite fallaciously, in my opinion), there is also no 'banality of suffering.' Thus, any attempt on my part to chronicle, in the language I use for my studies, the brothers' lives from the day they were betrayed to the Germans, to describe the atrocities they underwent at Majdanek and in the work-camps, would deprive the events of their uniqueness, since suffering is always a unique experience, and render them banal. In this case, to 'document' would mean to describe what they underwent during each of the millions of minutes they lived under the shadow of the crematoria and the gallows, where every minute in itself was 'an entire world.' This is something that even those who themselves experienced the barbarities find beyond their power to depict. Hence, I shall content myself with mentioning only a few 'bare facts'—a brief account of what I heard from Katriel Foiglman, a soulless summary, just enough to explain how the brothers survived the devastation.

After the Polish peasant, in whose yard they had been hiding, turned them over to the Germans, they were taken to the Lublin Citadel and from there, together with several hundred detainees, both Jews and gentiles, were transported to the nearby camp of Majdanek.

On the fifth day after their arrival the first 'selection' took place; those found unfit for work—children, the sick, the old, most of the women—were sent to the crematorium at the end of the camp. The rest were divided into work groups.

The two brothers, who were fifteen years old at the time, claimed that they were seventeen, and they were assigned to the camp works commando. Their task was to transport rocks in wheelbarrows from one end of the camp to the other, a kilometer each way, from six in the morning to six in the evening continuously except for a one-hour break at lunchtime, their lunch consisting of a bowl of watery soup and a slice of stale bread. The camp commandant, Anton Thumann, supervised the workers with the help of two German shepherds whom he used to set on the laggards, lashing them with his whip. Those who fell down were bludgeoned to death by the guards.

Shmuel—the weaker of the two—is already exhausted by the third day: the skin on his palms is peeling off, he has sores in his armpits, his arms cannot carry the load of the wheelbarrow. It is his brother's 'device' that saves him from being beaten to death or from the gas chamber. He found a rope, tied it to the handles of the wheelbarrow, and hung it on his brother's neck, thus lightening the burden on the arms.

A week later, at the role call on the camp square at three in the morning, the prisoners are asked if there is an electrician among them. Five people step forward, Katriel among them. His experience consists of having once assisted an electrician in some repair job at their home in Warsaw: he handed him the tools and observed him at work. Now a miracle happens: Thumann chooses him out of the five.

He is sent outside the camp, to a manor house confiscated from a wealthy Polish farmer to accommodate an SS officer and his family. He is commanded to install electricity in three rooms. He had 'good hands and a good head on his shoulders' as his brother described him. Putting on a knowledgeable expression, he sets to work: drills holes in the walls, puts pipes in, pulls wires out, etc.

In the camp, dozens are dying every day from disease, from the cold, from hunger. Katriel manages to save some of the food he gets at the officer's house, hides it under his clothes—bread, sausage, vegetables—and at night smuggles it back to his brother. The officer's wife takes a liking to him and when the electricity job is finished, she asks the camp commandant to let him stay there to do the gardening. There is a large vegetable garden around the house and he cultivates, waters and fertilizes it. The fertilizer comes from the camp. It is ashes from the crematorium; it comes in sacks and is rich in all the minerals that human bones contain.

One evening, on his return to the barrack, he cannot find his brother. They tell him that he has collapsed at work. The *vorarbeiter* hit him hard on the head and he was dragged to 'Gamel Block'—the barrack where the hopeless cases were put. Those were either shot and later dumped in a pit, or else sent off to the furnace.

In the evening, when coffee is doled out from kettles, Katriel steals away from the line and rushes to 'Gamel Block.' This is the sight that greets him: on the barrack floor, people are rolling in blood, filth, and excrement, writhing in pain, groaning, shrieking. Many lie dead. He finds his brother among the bodies, lying motionless on the floor. He shakes him, calls out his name, and when his brother comes to, he stands him on his feet and, in the darkness, carries him back to their barrack.

Once more Katriel's resourcefulness saves his brother from death. Since the twins look very much alike and are hard to tell apart, he decides that every few days they will switch the numbered patches they wear on their clothes that serve as identification tags. This they do. Then, one of them goes to work at the officer's house, then the other, and they alternate. In this way they take turns at renewing their strength. Winter comes. Snow covers the ground and work in the officer's garden is suspended.

Together with several hundred inmates, the brothers are transferred by train to Auschwitz. After a 'selection' there, they are sent to work camps in Germany. One to Ravensbruck, the other to Kungskirchen. For a year and a half, neither of them knows anything of the other's fate. When the camps are liberated by the Americans, both are near death. Only after several weeks' stay at hospitals are they able to stand on their feet. And then both of them—from their separate places—make their way back to their hometown of Zamosc, to see if any of their relatives has survived. There the two meet in the street and fall on each other's shoulders. And then they continue their wandering through Europe.

Chapter six

Yesterday afternoon, for the second time since Nora's death, Elyakim Sasson showed up.

And just like the previous time: no advance notice, no letter, and no phone call. He walked in, tall and robust, looking the same as when he was eighteen (except for the sprinkling of white in his thick, black moustache), a tight-fitting blue army jacket, a haversack slung on his shoulder, and without any introduction, but with a waggish smile in his black eyes, asked if I could put him up for the night. "If I may find favor in your eyes," he says in his usual jocular, high-flown manner, "would his worship grant a lodging for the night to a very weary wayfarer?" And in the same whimsical vein, a token of our long-standing friendship, I reply despite myself, "It would surely be a great honor…"

Since I live alone now, he regards my home in town as a hostel where he can spend the night. It does not occur to him that this might be an inconvenience. The bus to his kibbutz in the Arava leaves only twice a day. I cannot say no to him. So, I invite him into the living room, but he goes into the kitchen first. He takes a couple of big persimmons out of his sack and puts them on the table. "A cure for anything that ails you, in body and in soul," he pats me on my back. Later, in the living room, five minutes after we had sat down, he gets up, walks to the cupboard. "Will his worship allow me?" He opens the compartment where the drinks are, and takes out a bottle. He darts one of his irresistible smiles at me. "May I offer his worship a glass of vodka?" and he pours for both of us.

A brief friendship was struck up between us in the days when he was a scout in the Etzioni Battalion and led the troops to battle. The kind of friendship that, by all accounts, and because of the differences in character, occupation and lifestyle, should have ceased the moment we went our separate ways. But for reasons that elude me, he has hung on to it, and for many years would not let go. "I'm watching you from afar," he used to admonish me. And when an article of mine, on whatever historical problem, would come into his hands—somewhere in the blazing Arava—he hastened to send me his reactions: reservations, counter-arguments, praise. His epistles were strewn with quotations from Scripture, from the poetry of Bialik and Alterman, and always in a humorous tone. He would open thus: "Esteemed and revered sir, shining light of the world, the paragon of our generation!" or, "My friend, crown of my head!" And he would sign: "Your humble servant," "I'm the dust beneath the soles of your feet," "Your ignorant friend, the horseman of the Arava," and so forth. And the letter itself would sometimes be written entirely in the third person. "Would his worship deign to elucidate why he has written…?"

Elyakim Sasson was born in Jerusalem to a family of Persian origin. As a member of the No'ar Oved youth movement, he joined a kibbutz in the Beit Sh'ean valley. But years later, "in order to renew my youth," as he put it, he joined a new kibbutz in the Arava. He was at least fifteen years older than the other members there. He had one *idée fixe*: growing roses.

After Nora's death he sent me a heartfelt letter, this time devoid of flourishes. He wrote how, every time he visited us, he had always been impressed by "her mental equilibrium and sense of humor," and that's why he was so stunned when he learned that she had taken her own life. Once, he told me, he had visited her at the

Biological Institute to find out about the mildew that infested his rose conservatory. His spent half a day there, and she showed him all the departments and the new equipment and, with great humor, explained to him "the crazy, adventurous, tricky and capricious life of the fungi and viruses" they saw under the microscope, and they never stopped laughing. Further on in the letter he reminded me that he was witness to the kindling of love between us. It was at an Independence Day party at the home of the artist Amira, where he watched us dance and then go out into the garden. When we came back, he already knew...

Two years after he had been married—that was in the first kibbutz—his young wife left him and moved to the city. He has never remarried. After the second drink he starts pleading with me—just like the previous time—to come and stay with him on the kibbutz, for two, three weeks, for a month. He would get me a room, a palm-thatched hut, a bungalow, a pavilion, anything I want. Birds would chant to me morning and evening, and deer dance before my eyes. He claims that I'm a 'pessimistic historian' the reason being that I spend my life cooped up with books, cut off from nature. "I have let my heart"—and he quotes a verse from Alterman—"grow dark in a room, without the stars that were left outside." I should come to his place, see the Arava bloom, appreciate the new variety of roses he has bred. All his varieties of roses have been given 'optimistic' names: 'Happiness,' 'Paragon of Beauty,' 'Majestic Glory.' "Not all is vanity, Zvi, not everything is vanity of vanities, as our friend Nathan the Wise claimed."

He knows whole poems of Nathan Alterman by heart, from the collections *Stars Outside* and *Joy of the Poor*. I promise him I will come one day when I find the time. "You spin a web of lies around me, Zvi! What a dishonest man you are! Last time, too, you promised to come, but in your wayward heart you've thought: He will forget and I won't come. With all due respect for your professorship, the scholar, too, can be taken to task!"

After the fourth drink he urges me to sing. He starts singing a liturgical hymn that he used to sing in the old days. He sings it in an oriental melody, his fingers tapping on the table: "My heart yearns for

Zvi/ No shepherd has he..." And he reminds me of a certain night, at Tanus House in Jerusalem, after we had failed to break our way through to the Old City during the War of Independence, and he heaves a big sigh in remembrance of the many casualties in that war, four or five of whom he mentions by name, but he quickly shakes himself and starts singing another song, his voice hurling into the distance like the wailing of a jackal: "To the de-se-rt..."

He stole out of the house early in the morning before I was up.

Chapter seven

Amira's party in Abu Tor took place on Independence Day Eve during my last year at the university. There were some hundred people there, most of whom I did not know. Some came from Tel Aviv. They sprawled around the spacious rooms of that old Arab house—the war scars in the stone walls had not yet been repaired—and roamed around the walled garden. At times the music coming out of the loudspeakers sounded wild as if blaring out of the jungle, and at others soft and surreptitious.

I was standing by the wall watching the dancers. The lights dimmed as the music grew softer. A tall girl with fine blonde hair tumbling around her neck, stretched out her arm, and with a smile of ironic affection in her eyes, as if there were some secret about me she had discovered, drew me into the circle of dancing couples. While we were slowly dancing I asked her name.

"Does the name Abramson mean anything to you?"

"Abramson from where?"

"From Rehovot."

"The architect?"

"I'm his daughter, Nora."

I stopped and stared at her, her face so close to mine, her breath brushing my mouth. Their house was not far from ours, just around the corner. "You won't remember. I was still in kindergarten when you were in third or fourth grade. I attended your mother's nursery. She insisted upon calling me Nurit."

I laughed. There was a sort of past kinship between us. We continued to spin slowly to the music. Nora whispered in my ear; she used to see me almost every day, playing ball in the street, or returning from the club in my scout's uniform 'looking so proud,' or with my father, in his dusty jeep which would take me to the four corners of the land. Then, she said, I disappeared from her life for years, until one day she discovered me in a corridor of the university. She hesitated for a moment, wondering if she should approach me, then decided it would be ridiculous. "After all, I was only a little girl then." Since then, every time she saw me or passed me by, she would smile to herself. She was a biology student. Third year.

The music in the loudspeakers now changed from soft to frenzied, raging. Nora—virtuoso of all dance rhythms—took charge of our movements: drawing, parrying, spinning, turning, clinging, breaking away. She seemed inexhaustible. I got all sweaty while she, a smile hovering on her face, enjoyed spinning me around in a dance.

We went out to the garden for a breath of air. We sat on a wicker bench facing each other, and we laughed. There was a kind of clandestine pact between us, a secret understanding, something we both had harbored in our hearts for years. The pine trees emitted a cool fragrance and the night air dried our perspiration. In the distance, across the city sky, fireworks sputtered upward, exploding into iridescent stars, trailing sheaves of light and expiring. When I put my arm on her shoulders, she leaned her head on mine.

I was intoxicated by the scent of her hair, the smell from the sweat of her armpits where thick clumps of reddish hair sprouted, from the softness of her rounded shoulder and plump arm, from the summer-like heat that shone from her brown eyes. We were silent. A few minutes later she tore herself away, raised her head and asked if I would like to join a group that was going on a hike the next day to the woods near Mevo Beitar. I need to bring only some food and a blanket, she added, and mentioned the meeting point.

We left town in the afternoon. We were about twelve people, including three female students, two teachers and two fellows I knew from the time when we escorted convoys to Jerusalem. A Palmach veteran, a scout who knew every rock and bush on the way, walked in the vanguard. We walked in single file, through narrow paths. Nora walked in front, I in the rear. When we got to the grove at the top of the mountain, the sun was already setting.

With a stick in his hand, the veteran scout pointed out sites, in every direction, describing events that had taken place in each of them. He was as knowledgeable about the battles of the War of Independence as about ancient history. He pointed to the village of Battir and told us about the battles that had raged there in October 1948; then he described the siege the Romans had lain to the ancient fortress of Beitar during the Bar-Kochba Revolt. A ruined wall and some fortifications remained from that period. Nora, who was standing near me, whispered in my ear: "How is your father?"

I turned my head to her and laughed, "Still digging. And yours?"

"Still building," she smiled. "Were you there?" She pointed with her head to the hill facing us. I smiled and replied that I had not been there, but I was quite familiar with the area since I had been with the Etzioni battalion when we took Wallaja, and I pointed to the village facing Battir. She looked in my eyes and laughed, as if indicating that that was not at all what she meant.

We gathered wood, made a tripod, lighted a fire. The women prepared the food and laid it on a blanket. When we sat down and started to sing, two armed guards emerged from the dark. They came from a nearby settlement. We asked them to join us, but they declined and stood on the side watching the sparks and listening to our muted singing. Before departing they asked where we intended to spend the night. The scout said we would sleep in the grove, as we were planning to watch the sunrise from the top of the mountain. The guards hesitated for a moment, then left.

When the fire had died and the group started getting ready for sleep, the two of us walked down the hillside, spread a blanket on a couch of pine needles under a cliff and lay down.

Everything happened naturally, as if by a tacit agreement. It was as if for years we had both been anticipating this moment of passionate embrace.

"There's no fortuity in mating," Nora would say to me years later, when we reflected on our first night. "Genes. It's all in the genes."

When I opened my eyes, at early dawn—a heavy, gray stillness enveloped everything, not a bird was twittering—Nora was already up. She was sitting wrapped in a blanket, her arms hugging her knees close to her chest, her chin resting on her knees. She was gazing at the valley and the slopes stretching before her as they shed the night's darkness, pine needles dotting her loose hair. I rose from my couch and put my arm around her shoulder. She turned to me, her eyes smiling like a child caught in a mischievous or forbidden act and whispered, "I'm happy. Are you?" Then she said, "You won't believe me, but when I was nine or ten and used to watch you walking down the street, book bag in hand, so erect, so confident—you had such a dandyish forelock tumbling on your forehead—I said to myself: one day this boy will be mine."

I laughed. We kissed. Then we rose to watch the sunrise.

❧

Everything happened naturally. Two months later we went to Rehovot to inform our parents that we had decided to get married. My mother was delighted, as if a prodigal daughter had returned to the fold. "Nurit!" she hugged her shoulders and beamed at her. She said to me, "Her mother adamantly refused to Hebraize her name. But I insisted on calling her Nurit!" And she told us anecdotes about Nora's exploits at the day care center. My father joked: biology and history—what a perfect match. Human life in a nutshell: body and spirit. Then he complained about me to Nora: he had hoped that I would follow in his footsteps and study archeology. But I abandoned things that are real, concrete, rooted in the ground, in order to pursue 'flying-off letters.' Doesn't it say explicitly in the Bible, "Truth shall spring out of the earth?" Anything that is not buried in the earth itself, in con-

64

crete soil, is suspect, unsubstantiated. I had to confess there and then that when he used to take me on tours to the ancient sites—Gush Halav, Bir'am, Belt She'arim, Tel Sheva—I found it boring. Stones, dust, shards. Hypotheses and conjectures about dates and provenance that I found hard to credit. On school holidays, he would 'volunteer' me to help in the digs, plant a spade and a basket or a sieve in my hand—tedious work in the scorching sun—it was real suffering for me. "Suffering!?" my father burst out, his black eyes pretending to strike terror in us, his Charlie Chaplinesque moustache twitching, "When we were digging at Gezer, weren't you happy when we unearthed those shards with inscriptions from the Israelite period? And in Jericho, didn't you run around like a drunken donkey among the ruins of the palace, looking for the pool where Miriam the Hasmonean bathed, as if you expected to see her appearing naked in front of you?"

"And you were looking for Aristobulos' body." I teased him. "Well, well," my father nodded and again complained to Nora that he wanted to turn me into an Israeli, whereas I—he had no idea where that came from—had reverted to the archetypical Jewish scholar, steeped in books, expounding texts. "But Nurit, on the other hand," my mother pointed to her blonde, short-nosed future daughter-in-law, "is neither Israeli nor Jewish. We always called her *'shiksele'*."

Nora had told me about the state of affairs at their home even before our trip to Rehovot. The threat of divorce had been hanging over their heads since her childhood; her two younger sisters had been sent to a kibbutz in the Valley of Jezreel, whose veteran members were German Jews, where they attended boarding school. Her father, whom Nora both adored and feared, was a proud, pedantic, irascible man. He would spend most of his time in his office or traveling to Jerusalem and Tel Aviv, and when he came home he exchanged a few pleasant words with her at supper, then shut himself in his room. With his wife he discussed only practical matters which were unavoidable, but quite often, early in the morning, before leaving for work, or late at night, the house would resound with his outbursts—always in German, he always spoke German to her—and the girls would hide in their room fearing that he might hit their mother, whose voice was not heard at all, or worse, leave the house for good. Those outbursts were always brief, lasting only a few minutes, like a hurricane striking the walls, and then passing away—afterward the house fell silent, or a door was heard slamming followed by the sound of receding steps. Nora never knew the reason for the profound hostility her father felt for her mother, a hostility captured in his silence, in her banishment from his life. His bursts of fury were triggered by trivial matters: a shirt that hadn't been ironed, an overdue bill, a book lent without his consent, an undelivered telephone message. When she heard him scream at a neighbor to turn off the radio, she knew he was venting his wrath at her mother, and when he got into his car, he was seeking shelter from her there. Was it an 'old, outstanding account' from way back in Germany, as she had overheard relatives say?

Her mother, Susie, opened the door for us, and a black and white St. Bernard leaped on my chest with its paws. Nora hugged the dog and, stroking it, brought it with us into the living room where she made it crouch on the rug. The western wall was all glass and opened onto an expansive lawn bordered with trees and hedges.

"I wouldn't have recognized you," her mother said, examining my face. I said it was not surprising as I had been away from the village for the past eight years, and only came to my parents' house for short visits. Would I drink something? Brandy? Cherry liqueur? She walked over to the bar in the wall, made of inlaid mahogany squares, and with slow, languid motions brought a decanter and goblets to the marble coffee table. She was dressed in a long, form-fitting gown that reached to her ankles, and the lime colored leaves printed on it complemented the flaming copper color of her hair. She had too much eye shadow on, which made her dark eyes look narrower. A polite smile never left her eyes, but the strain to maintain it had left tiny wrinkles at the edges and gave her face a bittersweet expression. She did not ask us about our impending wedding or about how we had met, but she did ask many questions about Jerusalem: Did I know this or that professor from the old guard, those who had come from Germany; did I go to the concerts at the YMCA? She deplored the fact that the Old City was no longer open to us. She said that "in the good old days when the city was not yet divided" she once stayed at the American Colony Hotel for two weeks, and she described the hospitality she had enjoyed there, the civility, peace and quiet, the meals served in the inner courtyard with the water trickling in the fountain…

In the middle of her speech, Nora got up from her armchair, bent down by the dog crouching on the rug, embraced its neck and stroked it.

"It's a pity things have turned out like this," Susie Abramson said wearily, and her fingers started playing with a golden clock that had a crystal ball rotating between four little columns. "The days when we could all live together peacefully, Jews and Arabs—and English, too—those days will never come back, apparently."

"Peacefully?" Nora smiled at her, still hugging the dog's neck.

Susie turned her gaze to her, her hands still toying with the clock, and studied her face as if trying to figure out how to respond. Then she said, "You need a haircut, Nora, your hair is beginning to look unruly."

At that moment her father entered the living room from a side room, his steps almost inaudible, like a tiger; a tall man, in white trousers, T-shirt and cloth slippers. He walked over to his daughter, who got up from the floor, kissed her cheek, then turned to me, gave me his hand and said, "I understand that you are our future son-in-law. I'm pleased to meet you." And he sat with us at the table.

Otto Abramson was an 'impressive man': handsome, athletic physique, shiny silvery hair, cropped short in the 'Roman' fashion, he looked younger than his wife. He poured liqueur into the three goblets that were standing empty, hesitated for a moment, then went to the bar to get a fourth goblet, filled it, too, and made a toast. Then he said, "I would have thought it more logical to wait until Nora's graduation, but if you've made up your mind, you must have your reasons, I suppose." He had a niggardly smile, which made his face pucker a little, and the look in his deep sunken eyes was misty, vague and distant.

Susie went out to bring coffee. Otto—his voice sounding deep and ponderous—discussed the practical aspects of our married life: where we would live, my prospects at the university, what we would live on until I obtain a position. He was very generous with us; he was prepared to pay the rent for an apartment in Jerusalem until we settled down, and later, when we decide to buy a house, he would contribute half. If Nora chose to continue her studies abroad, he would pay for the fare and tuition.

"I'll impoverish you, Father," Nora leaned her head on his shoulder. "This will be your dowry," Otto said, stroking her hair, "instead of a chestful of silk dresses and jewelry, or two pigs and potatoes."

He emitted a hearty laugh that turned into a cough. When he had cleared his throat, he explained that the peasants in southern Bavaria used to give two pigs and ten sacks of potatoes as dowry.

Susie brought a tray of tiny china cups, silver decanters and silver spoons, and placed it on the table. She asked where we going to spend our honeymoon. When we said we had not yet thought about it, she said, "As long as you don't go to Cyprus, with all the vulgar hoi polloi." She sat down to pour the coffee and added, "Perhaps Switzerland after all: there man hasn't yet succeeded in destroying nature." Then she told us that when she was a young girl, her father, who was an art collector and a great devotee of the Bauhaus school, took her to Lucerne to see the community center designed by Walter Gropius.

All the while she was talking, Otto sat with bowed head, rotating the china cup between his fingers. When she had finished extolling the works of Gropius, Klee and Kandinsky, he turned back to us and resumed the discussion of our marriage plans: the wedding date, its place, and the guest list.

Susie got up and went to get cigarettes and lighter. She sat down to smoke, then got up again and brought an ashtray. She smoked half a cigarette, stubbed the butt in the ashtray, got up a third time and gathered the coffee cups on the tray. Before we left, as we were standing at the door, she turned to me and said, "How come you picked Jewish history as your subject? It's so boring, isn't it?"

"Boring? Shocking!" I smiled.

"Yes, shocking, that's true," she looked at me sadly.

"Poor father," Nora said as we came out of the yard.

※

The wedding was a modest one; we did not have it in a hall but at the Abramsons,' on their spacious lawn. The dignitaries of the village were there as well as friends and relatives on both sides. My parents and Nora's parents spoke very little to each other. My father's vibrant temperament—he mingled with the guests, fast-moving, fast-talking, exchanging pleasantries—had no affinity with Otto's stern, reserved, refined aloofness. Nora's mother—very impressive in her long brocade gown adorned with an oriental necklace of silver bells, and her crown of red hair surrounding her face like a wheel—deigned to stand and talk with my mother for a while, but she had the manner of a noblewoman condescending toward a woman of the people. Nora greeted everyone brightly, cordially, unselfconsciously, receiving the guests at the door, mixing in the crowd, engaging them in pleasant conversation. Nora's voice, her warm, full-throated, sensual voice.

We rented a small apartment in Talbiah in Jerusalem. Nora continued her studies; I became an instructor in the Jewish History department. Even though Nora was five years my junior, she possessed an amazing maturity and self-confidence. She was endowed with that 'talent for happiness' which I lack, a talent to enjoy, without inhibition, the little gifts that fate puts in our way, and to be amply, wholeheartedly grateful for them. In the morning she would open her eyes with a smile, as if waking from a sweet dream, stretch her arms, and greet each day like a holiday.

I, on the other hand—as Nora would tell me several times during our life together—could see only what's 'revealed,' never what's concealed underneath in the dark.

Chapter eight

A few days after the brothers' visit, Foiglman called again, saying he had to return to Paris the day after tomorrow, and would it be too much of an imposition if I were to meet with him one more time. In order to spare Nora the aggravation—or dismay—I suggested he meet me at the university; this way he could visit the institute where I work, and where even Yiddish studies are taught. "Gladly, gladly," he said.

He arrived about half an hour late, his face flushed from the sun, wiping the sweat from his brow and from his neck, holding a tattered briefcase in his hand, like the Wandering Jew. He said he had been given wrong directions, told to take the wrong bus, and here on campus, it took him fifteen minutes to find the building and the office. "America!" he stretched his arm to the view from the window, marveling at the open spaces, at the greenery, at the beautiful buildings. I ordered soft drinks and asked about the memorial service for the martyrs of Zamosc that he had attended. "What could you expect?" he nodded. "The same old lamentations, the same wailings. Tears never brought anyone back to life."

When he had refreshed himself with a cold drink—even now,

in the heat of the day, he was wearing his customary bow-tie—he told me that at the memorial service there was an American guest who told the crowd about the terrible experiences he had undergone; he was among the last Jews deported from the Zamosc ghetto to Izbica, about twelve miles away. He described their death march and how the "black guards"—Ukrainians and Gestapo officers, shot anyone who staggered on the way, and trod on the corpses and on the dying writhing in their agony with their blood and bone-marrow oozing out. When they reached Izbica all of them, several hundred people, were herded into a movie theater and locked inside. For eight days they were imprisoned in that hall, with neither food nor water, horribly crushed together. Children and old people died of suffocation, hunger and thirst, but they would not let them clear the bodies. Later, the survivors were taken out, in groups of thirty and forty, led to the Jewish cemetery, and shot. He was the only one to survive. He was taken for dead, but in fact he was only injured in the thigh and lay under the corpses. Later that night, when the murderers had left, he got up and fled to the forest.

"Enough!" Foiglman thumped with his hand on the table. "No more of that for now!" Again he raised his eyes to the window, admiring the view. The Sorbonne, he said, with its somber walls, was medieval. This here is the Modern Age. There—the past, here—the future! "What light! What light!" he called, laughing, "Not light to the gentiles, but light to the Jews!"

He scooted his chair closer to the table, rested his arms on it, leaned toward me and said, "My dear friend—allow me to call you friend because I feel that there's a closeness between our hearts, even though you don't say this to me since you are, I've already noticed, a taciturn, reserved person, unlike me, who gushes out like an overflowing barrel of fat… Well, you may ask, my dear friend, what a Jew like me, a Yiddish poet, is doing in Paris? I'll tell you. I don't know myself! What is there for me? Three or four newspapers, whose readers decrease in number from day to day, a writers' club that is more like an old folk's home… Have you ever been to an old folk's home? The air is dense with hatred, petty jealousy, suspicion, meanness of spirit, the kind of bitterness bred of ulcers…and the smell…

Although—and this I must stress—we are an exceptionally united family. What a family! Always hugging and kissing. Paying each other lavish compliments—in alphabetical order, like the acrostic in the Haggadah. Every six months it's somebody's jubilee, and when we celebrate a jubilee, the praises just pour out from the podium... We adore you and worship you! The guest of honor almost melts from the warmth that the speakers generate... So what am I doing there, in Paris? Well, yes, there are Jews there, many Jews, more than in any other capital in Europe. But for me, these are just statistics. I have nothing in common with most of them. Although I'm an atheist, as you know, I sing the prayer, *Adon Olam* in a different tune...what can I tell you?" He broke off and then, choking with emotion, cried, "My dear friend! When I'm in Israel, I feel that my true place...my true place..." Tears welled in his eyes.

Sitting with my back against the wall, only the table between us, I felt constrained, fenced in, I wanted to extricate myself from this cloying, excessive sentimentality that was pouring forth from him toward me; I felt like getting up and taking him outside, to the fresh air, where we could engage in idle talk, just chat about this and that. His slightly jocular speech, spiced with broken verses from the prayer book, clearly concealed some great distress, which, against my will, he was going to make me share. All the time he was talking I could not help see in his face, the face of a man nearing sixty—like superimposed photographs—the face of the boy pushing wheelbarrows full of rocks, under the cracking whip, ready to collapse at any minute. His brother Katriel, too, had the same manner of speaking: lightly, almost jokingly, he had told me about the horrors of Majdanek, shifting his wide palm on the table, from place to place, as if he were marking lines and dots on a map; here was the gate, here the barracks, here the crematorium, here the German officer's house, and all the while a smile glinted in his eyes.

I told Foiglman that our door was always open for him. If that was how he felt there, in Paris, all he had to do was pack his belongings and come over here.

His face clouded. "Yeah, but how... Who knows me here... an anonymous, nameless person..."

I said there was a large community of Yiddish readers, Yiddish writers, Yiddish scholars…

He dismissed my remark, as if pitying my naiveté. Of all the Yiddish writers, he said, there were two, perhaps three, whose names were familiar to the general, educated public, and who garnered great honor mainly thanks to the fact that they had been translated into Hebrew.

"Then translate your poems into Hebrew!"

"Who?" he countered with a cry, "who will translate them?"

The blue in his eyes dimmed and his face assumed an expression of pain and humiliation. He said that a few years earlier, a poem of his had been translated into Hebrew and published in an Israeli literary magazine. A month later one of his friends—"May God protect me from such friends"—sent him a newspaper clipping of a review of that literary magazine. The reviewer had called his poem "utter kitsch."

"I want to show you something." He bent to his briefcase and pulled out a big album that he laid on the desk and opened. It was a collection of newspaper clippings pasted onto brown cardboard, pages from Yiddish papers published in France, the United States, Canada, Argentina, Brazil—reviews of his poetry books or individual poems that appeared in various publications. The complimentary comments were underlined in red.

I turned the pages, my eyes flitting over the underlined phrases, and told him that very few Hebrew poets received such praise. "You have certainly ensured your place in the Pantheon!"

"Sure, next to Victor Hugo." He thrust his chest forward mockingly. "We Jews used to say, by the eastern wall."

And he told me that in Zamosc, before the war, there was a wealthy merchant who, every year before the High Holidays, would ensure himself a seat by the synagogue's eastern wall in return for a large contribution to the synagogue. Sometime later he came down in the world and had no money to give, but he did not want to relinquish his seat. So instead he offered to sing the central prayer—he had a fine singing voice—*El Malei Rahamim* ("God, Full of Mercy") at funerals. It was accepted; he served as *hazan* at funerals without payment, and kept his seat at the eastern wall. He used to joke about it and say, "Mercifully, I have retained my seat."

૨૬

He turned a few more pages in the album, showing me photographs of himself delivering speeches at literary banquets, seated at the podium, or in the company of such celebrities as Leivick, Marc Chagall, Zadkin, Sutzkever, raising a glass with Chaim Grade, both smiling at each other...

Suddenly he seemed to have shrunk in my eyes. A little Jew, I said to myself, just a little Jew. He leaned forward to put the album back in his case, and when he straightened up he said, "There's something else I'd like to say to you, Zvi. May I address you by your given name? Or perhaps I should call you Hirsch?* Zvi is an exalted attribute! An apotheosis! "Zvi Israel"—the beauty of Israel! You know, in the *Hymn of Praise* 'Zvi' is mentioned four times, as 'Glory,' as 'Crown of beauty'... Hirsch on the other hand—is how people talk to each other..."

I laughed. I said he could call me any name he was comfortable with.

"Well, what that windbag wrote about me, about my poem being kitsch, well, as a matter of fact, he was right! He himself did not realize how right he was! If you ask me, our entire Jewish history, is one big kitsch story, from the Exodus to this day. If you were to watch it on the stage—the theater of world history—you'd say it was utter kitsch and melodrama! Outrageous hyperbole that no person of intelligence or taste would credit! Such cloying, mawkish sentimentality! Both the laughter and the tears. For what is the Holocaust if not a cheap melodrama? Can a sane, cultivated person really believe that such a thing happened, that thousands of naked men, women and children were crammed into a bathhouse and gassed like insects? A cheap play by a third-rate playwright, aimed only at shocking a foolish audience! A tearjerker for maudlin women! Or take the reverse case, not of horror but of happiness! My brother and I, after a year

* In Yiddish *hirsh* means "a deer," which in Hebrew is *zvi*

and a half of hovering between life and death in two different camps, certain that we would never see each other again, suddenly meet in front of the ruined house where we were born, in a town empty of its Jews, falling on each other's necks, hugging and crying… Isn't this a melodrama? And there were hundreds of cases like this after the war. Son and mother, husband and wife, brother and sister—suddenly meeting each other in the street of a ruined town, at a railway station, in a restaurant, in a DP camp… And what happens here? If anyone in Hollywood were to write a fictional script showing the Israelis, sons of the Maccabees, demolishing the entire Egyptian air force in one hour, and in six days conquering an area five times bigger than their country, charging forward to the Red Sea, to Mount Hermon, blowing the *shofar* at the Western Wall—wouldn't people say: this script is for idiots, any intelligent person would find it ludicrous. And what about Entebbe? Isn't that kitsch? Believe me, Hirsch, all of us, in our entire history—including the pathetic scenes of martyrdom—are all ham actors in a cheap melodrama!"

I was fascinated, by his words, by his face. A metamorphosis was taking place right in front of me. No more the 'little Jew' trying to impress me with paper clippings and photos. A soft light now shone from his blue eyes, his brow cleared, its wrinkles smoothed. A glory seemed to have descended on his face, the kind of 'divine splendor' surrounding a *Tzaddik* when he delivers a sermon with an ecstasy that transcends material existence. The tips of his fingers touched the edge of the desk, softly, feelingly, like a pianist resting his fingers on the keys before starting to play. At that moment his whole bitter life experience seemed to have been purified and purged of the 'foul material' that had clung to it, and he was able to transcend it and to look down upon it and upon the vast expanses of history. So much courage is required—I thought to myself—for a man like him, to put a distance between himself and his biography, to be able to view it as part of some metaphysical entity, with both sadness and irony.

I said, "Foiglman, your poems must be translated into Hebrew and published here, in Israel. This way you won't be anonymous when you come to live here!"

His eyes narrowed in an expression of either suspicion or mockery, "Do you really think so?"

We went outside to tour the campus. Again he was full of admiration for what he saw, the spaciousness, the greenness, and the bright light everywhere. He stopped by one of the sculptures that dotted the lawn and critiqued it as if he were a great expert of modern art. He recounted something that Melech Ravitch once said to him when they were looking at a Brancusi. "Fine," the poet had said, "this is the framework, now it has to be filled with content!"

We went from building to building. He said he had already been to Beth Hatefutsoth* on one of his earlier visits in Israel ("a cold house" he now commented as we walked past—"they've got everything there except two things: Life and Death"). Then I suggested introducing him to a professor of the Yiddish language.

When I said to Professor L., "May I introduce Shmuel Foiglman," he gave him his hand and nodded, but it was obvious he did not recognize the name. "A Yiddish poet from Paris," I added. "Yes, yes," he scrutinized him as if trying to remember, and asked him to sit down. Foiglman bore the insult bravely. He asked how many students there were in the program, what the syllabus was, and got into an argument with the professor when the latter mentioned the *Khalyastre*†. Foiglman claimed that those poets were "divorced from their people and its literary tradition and were merely trying to imitate German expressionism." He asked which of Y.L. Peretz's works they were teaching and, by the way, mentioned that he, too, like Peretz, was a native of Zamosc…whereupon the conversation between the two became livelier since, even though L. himself was born in Radom and came to Israel just before the war, he knew a great deal about Zamosc; he mentioned many rabbis and authors familiar to both of them, as well as Frischmann's *The Vision of Zamosc*, Peretz's *At Night in the Old Market* and *Four Generations, Four Deaths*… Suddenly he stopped short, his glasses glimmered, and like a man

---

* *Beth Hatefutsoth*—The Museum of the Diaspora, in north Tel Aviv
† *Khalyastre* ("the gang")—nickname for a literary Yiddish group in Poland before the Second World War

finding a lost coin in a haystack, he cried, "*Oysgeboygene Zwayg,* right?"

"Among other things, yes…among other things," Foiglman smiled.

"Of course! How could I forget?!" L. slapped his forehead, and immediately stirred to action, got up and said we must go to the library to check if the book is there. He was quite positive it was.

Thus the three of us marched purposefully along the hallways, like a delegation sent on a sacred mission, and made our way into the library. While Foiglman and I browsed among the shelves, L. conferred with the librarian, checked the catalog, and a few minutes later, returned to us, a gleam of triumph in his eyes, and handed the poet his book. Foiglman was elated. He opened the book, leafed through, his eyes caressing the lines affectionately, then looked up at L. and said, "What about readers? Are there any readers?"

"The truth is," said L. "that we don't have many readers, but those that are interested, read."

We stood there a little longer, while the two of them deplored the fate of Yiddish in Israel, and before we took our leave of L., Foiglman said to him, "I will return here, I definitely will."

I saw him to the bus stop. We were both moved. We kissed. I felt a tremendous closeness to this man and tears stood in my eyes. In a trembling voice he said, "Through you I found *Eretz Yisrael* anew." Then he reminded me to give his regards to my wife, "who is a true aristocrat," and added, as the bus was pulling up, that his house was always open for me, and if I find myself in Paris, not to go to a hotel, God forbid…

When I came home I told Nora about our meeting and our leave taking. "You have become so sentimental," she smiled at me.

"It must be my age," I said.

"He's Yiddishizing you!" she laughed.

At that moment the phone rang. Nora got it. "It's your friend." She handed me the receiver and left the room.

Foiglman, in a wailing voice said, "What should I do, Zvi? When I came home I realized that the album with the pictures and the reviews was gone. I must have left it on your desk. Did you by any chance take it?" I said I hadn't noticed it, but it may still be lying on my desk. "What should I do? Tomorrow at six I'm flying to Paris, and I need that album as a cock needs its comb. This week I'm meeting with an important editor and I have to present it. Maybe I ought to take a cab to the university, and you'll let them know…" I said my office was locked and the key was with me…

"Woe is me, I'm such an impossible person, Zvi…"

I had no desire to meet with him again, after we had said our goodbyes, but I'm not good at evasive tactics. I said I'd go over there and bring the album home, and he should come at seven to get it. "I feel like Tartuffe, Zvi. It's awful! It's as if some demon is foiling all my good intentions."

When I told Nora what it was all about, her eyes opened in amazement. "You're not really going to the university now to find it for him?!"

I said I had no choice; my office was locked, I could not send him there by himself, and it would have taken him two hours to get there from Ramlah.

"Is there no limit to what you're prepared to do for this bore?"

Later, when she realized that it meant another visit of Foigl-man in our house, she protested, "Why here? Why didn't you at least arrange to meet in some café?"

It hadn't occurred to me, I said.

"There's no respite from him…"

I drove to the university. I found the album on a pile of books on my desk. At seven o'clock promptly the doorbell rang. When I opened the door I was greeted by a huge bouquet of red and purple gladioli, about twenty in all, adorned with green twigs, but with no wrapping, and Foiglman's face hiding behind them. He walked through the hallway and into the living room without saying a word, still hiding behind the blaze of colors, turning this way and that, as if playing hide-and-seek with us. Even Nora had to laugh, despite herself.

Finally with a deep bow he handed her the bouquet saying, "I'm ashamed to show my face, Madam, I'm simply ashamed!"

And immediately turned to me, "Did you find it?"

I brought the album from my study and handed it to him.

"I'm off!" He took the album from my hand. "I'm speechless!" and he stole to the door and left.

"Are you sure he's flying to Paris tomorrow?" Nora said.

Chapter nine

Nora loved the sea. On Saturdays, on holidays, she used to take Yoav—she had taught him to swim when he was five—to beaches far and near, spend long hours there, coming back refreshed, sun-drenched, a languid gleam in her eyes. I myself was rather pleased. They enjoyed themselves and I was none the worse for it. This way I could work uninterrupted and accomplish a great deal. I never cared for these forays into the bosom of nature, let alone to the beach; the sea emits chill and strangeness, sometimes fear. I barely know how to swim.

I remember one Saturday—Yoav was nine or ten then—when I acceded to Nora's importuning and went with them to the beach at Tantrum.

The sea was raging, small froth-crested waves fluttered and capered to and fro, slapping my face from all directions. Nora and our son pounced on them joyfully, and in a few minutes they were out of the cove and swimming away in the open sea. After a short dip I returned to the beach, stretched in a deck chair and started reading the book I had brought with me. From time to time I would raise my eyes and see the two heads, one fair, one dark, sticking out of the water, tiny as two nuts, bobbing up and down among the strips of waves.

About half an hour later I saw Nora rise from the water: erect, proud, her blond locks dripping, her arms, her thighs, her long legs glistening with beads of water, a blissful expression on her face; a nymph who had beaten the Medusa! She reached me, deeply breathing the sea air. "Wonderful!" She grabbed my book, "Enough! You hop right in and swim!" Yoav came running, kicking the sand with his feet, and Nora, provoking me, inciting him, "Let's throw Daddy into the water!"

"Yes! Yes!"

He knocked over my deck chair, and the two of them dragged me, each by an arm. My glasses fell to the sand, but before I could get them, Yoav grabbed them and refused to hand them back to me. "First you swim!" We laughed, we tussled, the three of us, rolling in the sand. Then I went into the water to wash the sand off. When I came out, Nora was standing there, a towel wrapped around her shoulders, and in her eyes a smile both affectionate and mocking. She looked like a Nordic figure from a distant race. At that moment a thought flashed through my mind; she had made a mistake marrying me. She should have chosen someone else, different from me, for a husband. Me, I only put shackles on her feet.

On the way back to town, we stopped at an excellent restaurant. Nora ordered a plate of shrimp. She pounced on them with the same zest with which she had earlier pounced on the waves. She had a passion for shrimp, something I could not understand. She used to go to a special store in Jaffa where she bought kilos of shrimp. She would then fry them in butter, sprinkle minced garlic, parsley, spices—and on the side a huge bowl of fresh lettuce in oil and vinegar.

After the beach, at home—we made love. All the sun's warmth she had absorbed, the frolicking in the waves, now radiated, flowed out of her ardent body. Afterward, she fell into a deep sleep.

Once, on Purim* Eve...

It was not such a long time ago, perhaps eight or nine years,

---

* Purim, (Hebrew: "lots")—the festival commemorating the rescue of Persian Jewry during the time of King Ahasuerus, through the mediation of Esther, from the threat of annihilation engineered by Haman. According to the *Book of Esther*, the extermination was fixed by lot for *Adar* 13.

we were invited to a costume party at some friends' house. Many of my colleagues were going to be there. I told Nora I was not going. I hate such parties. I'd much rather sit at home and work. I told her to go by herself. I encouraged her to go. "I won't go by myself!" she declared. And then, as if trying hard to contain some suppressed fury seething inside, "All these years you've been trying to drag me, pull me with a rope, into that black hole where you're stuck, stuck…"

"Nora!" I tried to calm her down.

In the following days she tried to persuade me…"Then don't put on a costume, if you think it's beneath you… Just be my escort, that's all. Are you incapable of a simple gesture of chivalry?" I told her again I wasn't going.

Confident that eventually I would submit to her will, she busied herself preparing a costume for herself.

Just before the party, at about ten o'clock, as I was sitting in my study, with books and notebooks on my desk, Nora was at the door, like a huge, black Bird of Paradise. A fitted black dress wrapped around the length of her body, a black fan-tail spread proudly like an arch behind her, a black feather tassel sprouted from the top of her head. Only the white face was exposed, with the rosy blush of painted lips blooming out of the whiteness. I held my breath in astonishment.

With a frozen face, whose whiteness underscored its chilliness, she said, "Are you going with me?"

"You're beautiful. Minerva who has turned into a peacock!"

"Make up your mind: choose either me or…" she stretched her hands toward the books on my desk.

I laughed. "I'll drive you there and come back here."

"I don't need you to drive me. You either stay with me there or I'm going by myself."

"What will you do with the tail?" I said jokingly. "You can't sit on it."

"I'll stick it in the aerial mast. Have you decided?"

A moment later her steps were heard going down the stairs.

She came back at three or four in the morning. "How was it?" I asked waking up. She did not answer. Quickly she took off her costume, wiped off the make up, got into bed and covered her head with the blanket.

At eight o'clock she woke up, called me and muttered, "Call the Institute and tell them I'm sick," and wrapped herself in the blanket again.

She got out of bed in the late afternoon, walked into the kitchen to have a bite. Her face looked squashed, yellow, its luster all gone. I asked her again about the party.

"I danced," was all she said.

"Did you enjoy yourself?"

"I danced all the time. I didn't even notice who was there," she said listlessly. After two cups of coffee she rallied a little and said, "For a whole hour I danced with the same young man…studies theater at the university, he said…wouldn't let go of me for a moment, his compliments made me sick."

I looked at her, as if her face were a reflection of the tempestuous events of the previous night. "You were very impressive in your fantastic costume…"

"They chopped off my tail…" she smiled. Then she added, "Everybody asked about you."

"What did you say?"

"That you're working." We both laughed.

"Now tell me, should I have gone there?" Nora kept quiet. She got up, took the cup to the sink and said, "No."

Quite often I would send her to parties at friends' houses by herself. The following day—almost invariably—she would be troubled, as if possessed by an evil spirit. She hardly spoke, acted hastily and nervously, blew her top at the most trivial things—why I didn't take down the laundry from the line as she had told me to do; why were the books scattered all over the house; was I too dumb to realize that when I leave the windows open all day, dust covers the furniture? There'd be tears of anger in her eyes. Once when I forgot to turn off the gas she screamed, "You wanted to kill me! To suffocate me!"

Or she would stay in bed until very late the next morning, and then, suddenly, at ten or eleven, jump out of bed quickly, put on some clothes, and while still combing her hair, go out to the Institute.

She would come back unusually late, without taking any food, would rush to her bed, cover herself up in the blanket and sink into a deep sleep, for twelve, thirteen hours.

One day, after one of those parties, when I was certain she was asleep, she suddenly opened her eyes and asked if I was still seeing that librarian who… The old suspicion, from years back.

Once, when I mentioned those 'lapses' of hers into depression and anger, she replied, "You had better get used to the idea that you're living with a woman who doesn't feel like springtime every day and who can't greet you with sunshine all the time." And a moment later, "Why do you keep sending me there anyway?"

In two or three days she would calm down, regain her composure, her self-control, apologize on behalf of the demons raging inside of her, breaking all restraint; again she would become the lady of the house, in full command of her will and actions.

About a year prior to Foiglman's arrival at our house, she attended a biologists' conference in Salzburg that lasted five days. I went to the airport to pick her up. After a long wait outside I saw her coming out of Customs, pushing the luggage cart in front of her. She looked so European in her dark blue suit, the fin-de-siècle rounded velvet hat. At her side— with only a large carry-on in hand—walked a tall, elegant, middle-aged man. Fair skin, auburn hair covering half his forehead. After we kissed, Nora said, "Meet Dr. M. from the Faculty of Agriculture at the Hebrew University. He, too, attended the Congress." A polite, rather mysterious smile on his smooth face, a curious look in his eyes. With a broad motion of his arm he gathered his smooth crest of hair in his hand and pulled it back from his forehead.

On the way home, in the car, Nora told me about the famous people she had met at the Congress: one from Harvard, another from Stanford, an epidemiologist from East Berlin, a fascinating woman from India, a bacteriologist, a whole delegation from the Soviet Union…

At home she took out of her suitcase a woolen Tyrolean sweater and necktie that she had bought for me. They were green, brown and yellow. She told me that on Sunday a group of participants went on a trip to the Taunus Mountains, to a ski resort.

They climbed on foot, in the snow, watched the skiers, ate at an inn, drank wine and sang to their hearts' content... On their way back to the funicular her toes froze and two men had to carry her in their arms... In the middle of her story, she looked around the room and said, "We have to change the upholstery on those armchairs. They are completely worn out."

At night, in my arms, she sobbed. I asked what was wrong. She said her whole childhood had come back to her there. Rose from the depth and surfaced. I said, "You were only three when you left Germany, what can you possibly remember?"

"I don't remember and yet I do." In Salzburg she had spoke German, listened to German spoken. The castles, the snowy mountains, the pine and fir woods, her childhood there and her childhood here, with the miserable life her parents had, the fights, the constant threat of divorce, her own fears.

Two days later she was her cheerful self one again. She went to the balcony to water the flowers and when she came back, watering can in her hand, she said, "Home! There's no place like home!"

Once, in England, we went to the Tate Gallery in London. We stopped in front of Henry Moore's huge bronze 'Family Group': the primordial man and woman sitting on a bench embracing their child on both sides. Nora said, "This is my ideal: domestic happiness."

After Foiglman's return to Paris, we did not mention him for several months. Except for a short, impassioned letter he sent us immediately after his arrival there—which I thought required no answer—he did not write.

On occasion, when I came across the name Zamosc in a book or a document, I was reminded of him, but I tried not to think about him. I was absorbed in my study of the Petliura pogroms.

Chapter ten

Santayana's famous maxim: "Those who cannot remember the past are condemned to repeat it," cannot be predicated on Jewish history, because in this case, even those who remember the past are doomed to relive it. Take a small town like Zamosc. In the past three hundred years alone, it has undergone three horrible carnages (apart from 'little' pogroms that took place in between) Chmielnicki's massacres, Petliura's pogroms, and the annihilation by the Nazis. Even though each wave of destruction was different—the first followed a popular uprising of peasants against the aristocracy and landowners; the second followed a nationalistic revolt of Ukrainians against Russians (and against the spread of Russian Bolshevism); and the third as part of the 'Final Solution' to exterminate the Jewish people—from the victim's point of view there was not much difference between the events: dependence on a segment of the local Christian population—or on the authorities—to provide shelter against the attackers, in exchange for sizable bribes or 'ransom' money—and the crushing disappointment that came with the realization that all those means were in vain; shelter was not provided, all promises were blatantly, shamelessly broken. The ransom was indeed taken, but so were the lives. The memory of each catastrophe was etched deeply in the heart of the Jewish inhabitants of the town, and passed on from generation to generation—but no lesson was learned from past events, and when the next catastrophe occurred, it always came as a surprise, always evoking tremendous astonishment, as if it were the first time in the town's history; and in its wake—always the belated disillusionment.

Through this prism, Jewish history in the last few hundred years, with its replication of events—unlike the history of other peoples—appears to be lacking in 'progression.' In other words, it does not flow in any direction, but rather seems to be stagnant, like a fetid bog, or a 'miry pit' to use Nathan Neta Hannover's phrase in his chronicles of the 1648–49 massacres.

An historian dealing with a given period typically is faced, at every stage of his research, with questions of alternatives for which he is seeking answers, and which are the trigger and the challenge for his investigation. What would have happened if? Which direction would events have taken if a certain personality or group of people had acted differently? What would have become of the Roman Empire if Cleopatra's nose had been longer, to use the facetious classic example. And by the same token: What course should have been taken—according to the researcher's light and bias—for the 'whirligig of history' to take the turn that most suits his views?

If the historian does not subscribe to a deterministic viewpoint, if he does not hold that everything that happens on earth is decreed by Providence and is a manifestation of 'divine will'—as von Ranke maintained, who regarded the historian's task as describing "actual facts at the time they were taking place," without passing judgment, then he is bound to pose the cardinal question of the alternative.

What the student of Jewish history in the Diaspora finds most exasperating is, in fact, the meager, almost total lack of alternatives. In other words, questions like "What would have happened if…?" can find no other answers but what the facts suggest.

No other people has sanctified the memory of destructions and disasters as the Jewish people has, by commemorating them in fast days, memorial services, public assemblies, by composing lamentations, prayers, liturgical hymns, by designating days of mourning and grieving. Even our holidays and feasts are stamped with the memory of past destructions. But these memories that are so indelibly etched in our consciousness have never spared us a repetition of the same tragic events, which are visited upon us again and again—with almost no variation in the patterns of our behavior or that of our attackers, except, perhaps, for the differences in magnitude.

Would the pogroms, massacres, pillages, destruction and annihilation have been prevented had the Jews converted? Assimilated? Had they faithfully observed the letter of Halachic law? Switched camps? Organized self-defense? Faced their oppressors proudly and ignored their promises? Emigrated en masse? And where to?

What so clearly distinguishes Jewish history from the history of any other nation is that the forces that "in every generation have risen against us to annihilate us," as it is said in the Passover Haggadah, were ahistorical forces: an irrational, timeless hatred going all the way back from the Pharaohs, Apion, Thucydides, to the present, essentially unchanged, merely assuming new guises—religious, social, national, racial, ideological, etc.—defying all causal explanations. The chronicler and researcher of this history—if he is not content to merely describe the events, but attempts to interpret them—finds himself deprived of his status, in a sense, when he is up against this dominant ahistorical element which perforce turns him into a 'nature researcher,' a biologist—as history becomes biology…

Yes, I am a 'pessimistic historian,' as Elyakim Sasson said about me. It is often claimed that every historian is a 'frustrated novelist.' But not I. I have never had the desire to be a novelist, since I don't have the talent to create imaginary characters or situations. But if there is one attribute I do share with the novelists it is the strong tendency to identify with my historical protagonists in the same way that an author identifies with his imaginary protagonists. While researching the Chmielnicki massacres, and later the Petliura pogroms, as I was poring over countless authentic documents, in Hebrew, in Yiddish, in translations from Polish and Russian, all describing what happened in Nemirov, Tulchin, Czernikov, Zhitomir, Bratslav, Proskurov, Dubovoy, Baranov—in hundreds of communities all over Ukraine,

Russia and Poland, where waves upon waves of marauders swept across like Scythian hordes, butchering, burning, tearing to pieces anything that stood in their way—then I feel as if I myself were there, in the 'towns of slaughter,' among those fleeing to the fort, trying, unarmed, to defend themselves; among those huddling together in the synagogue, terrified of the moment—that no prayer or supplication could stave off—when the gates would be thrown open and the barbarians' swords would slaughter every soul; among those hiding in cellars, finding refuge in "outhouses, pigsties and other excremental places,"* watching from their holes how the women were defiled, "each woman under seven uncircumcised brutes."

Even now, while writing these lines, I can hear the wailing carried from one end of the town to the other. The wailing in Zamosc. I found two pages, written in Yiddish by a woman named Rachel Tannenbaum: memoirs from the Petliura pogroms. On Saturday night a rumor spreads across town that Ukrainian soldiers are preparing a massacre. The Jews hurry to their homes as if fleeing from an impending thunderstorm. In a few minutes the streets are empty. A deathly silence descends. The shutters are closed, the doors bolted. Nobody goes in or out. Rachel, who is twelve years old at the time, and her family of seven are hiding in the cellar. Her four-year-old sister starts to cry. They stop her mouth, almost strangling her. Suddenly they hear horrifying shrieks from the butcher's house across the street, and his wife's blood curdling cries: Jews, help! They are slaughtering us! And soon afterward from another house, at the end of the street and from the neighboring street. Wails, wails. The wailing of children and of women. The air is full of wailing. Through the chinks in the shutters twelve-year-old Rachel sees two Cossacks dragging the butcher, blood gushing from his head, into the street, and under the street lamp one of them yanks his gold teeth with pliers. The butcher's wife, her mind deranged, flees from the house, her fingers chopped, her hands dripping blood. A moment later they hear banging on their door. They cower in the corner, hiding behind sacks of coal, but when

---

* The paragraph is taken from a poem of H.N. Bialik's about the Kishinev pogrom in 1903, entitled *In the Town of Slaughter*.

the shouts increase—Damn Yids, open the door or we'll murder all of you!—the eldest brother, sixteen years old, decides to go up and open the door. He'll tell them he's alone in the house, and they are free to take whatever they like. The face of the four-year-old is turning blue from asphyxiation. Upstairs the rioters are heard storming in, threatening, smashing furniture and dishes, trampling with their nailed boots, flailing and thrashing…

And the piercing cry of the boy. Then silence. And the wails, the wails that rend the air of the town from end to end. What, then, is left for the historian, who delves into such material and is unable to fit it into any system of 'historical logic'—except empathy?

✿

It's been two weeks since I touched this manuscript. A dull headache, like a cloud, hangs inside my skull, on the left.

But this is not the reason. At night I wake up, and scenes from our thirty-three years together rise in my memory and haunt me. Suddenly, I am shaken—as if it happened only yesterday—by the death of our little girl, Aviva, in the fourth month of her life. It was three years after Yoav was born. As soon as she was brought to Nora's bed at the hospital, we knew. The slanted eyes, the creases in the eyelids, the tongue sticking out of her lips. Two weeks later we discovered the yellow stain on her back. But she was a beautiful baby. An angelic smile hovering on her face, her hair light and soft as down. When she looked at us, a kind of other-worldly wisdom seemed to radiate from her eyes. And she never cried. I used to stand at her crib when she was asleep, watching her rounded face, her short nose, the clenched fists with the short, thick fingers, and think of her as a precious loan from God—a rare manifestation of the divine 'Potencies'—which we should guard with our lives. Nora used to hold her in her lap for a long time after she finished nursing her, face to face, eye to eye, they seemed to conduct a long and secret dialogue.

We knew what was in store for her and for us when she grew up, and that knowledge turned our love into a mysterious pact. One night her temperature suddenly shot up. Her face burned, as if an internal combustion was quickly consuming her. 'A holy fire.'

91

For weeks afterward Nora was tormented by guilt. She said it was she who was responsible for the baby's defect. Between silences she explained that the congenital deformity was caused by a 'chromosomal deviation' in her blood or in an ovum. One redundant chromosome, in addition to the standard 46. Her own genetic make-up was irregular, she said, and she herself had inherited it from either her father or her mother. Our lives were invaded by such mysterious natural processes.

We never spoke about it all those years. We erased the tragedy from our memory. But Nora resolved not to bear any more children. It was the fear of propagating defects, 'unclean spirits.' She brought home an enormous philodendron and put it in the living room. Then she added the flowerpots on the balcony, with dozens of different plants that she tended with great devotion. And they flourished.

When our granddaughter Sarit was born, she lavished on her all the love she was unable to grant her own daughter. Every evening she would go to their house to help Shula take care of the baby. When the child was three, four years old, she spent hours with her, reading stories and poems. She knew by heart poems by Fanya Bergstein, Miriam Yalan-Stekelis, and Kadya Molodovska, which she had remembered from my mother's nursery. And the fairy tales of Andersen and Grimm.

Another night—I wake up remembering a fight she had with her mother. It was about twelve years ago. I walked home and found the two of them in the midst of a tense conversation. I left them by themselves. Very seldom did Susie or Otto visit us, and never together. Through the door I heard Susie say, "You always provoked me...and in front of father, on purpose...for every mistake I made... When a plate slipped from my hand, you'd burst out laughing, such mean laughter..." And a few minutes later, in response to whispers I could not catch, "The soul? You think the soul is a pretty doll? A beauty in a crystal cage? The soul is a whore, yes, a whore...even you know that, though you won't admit it..."

Nora did not see her to the door when she left.

I walked into the room and asked what had happened. She was sitting in an armchair, pale, her eyes red, furious. She did not answer my question. I could tell her nerves were almost bursting with tension. Suddenly she grabbed her head in her hands and shouted, "She's driving me crazy!" Then she looked at me and calmly said, "You don't see anything. You don't want to see."

And I am reminded of one day, when we talked about her refusal to have any more children, and I said her argument was 'unreasonable.' She was seized by a great fury and, as always when she was angry, she held her palms against her temples, as if she was struck by a headache and cried, "I'm exasperated, exasperated, when I think that for you everything is controlled by reason! And you don't realize, you're incapable of realizing, that in life things don't work like this! Not at all! There are much stronger forces than reason and logic that make people tick! Can't you grasp it?"

When she calmed down she added quietly, "This is also true in nature."

Chapter eleven

One summer night, about four months after Foiglman's departure, I received a phone call from someone speaking English. His voice sounded opaque, as if coming over a long distance. He said his name was Irving Foigl, and when I asked him to repeat the name, he said he was Shmuel Foiglman's son. His father sent me regards and also asked him to deliver a little package. I said I would be glad to see him. He was calling from Jerusalem, he said. He was here only for a few days, giving three 'unimportant' guest lectures at the Philosophical Society conference. He was going to be in Tel Aviv for a day, maybe two, before returning to England. I invited him to come over in the evening. He sounded uncertain, disinterested, as if the task he had undertaken was bothersome to him, interfered with his plans. It was even stranger to hear him ask—in a phone call from Jerusalem!—if there was a bus going from there to Ramlah, as he had promised his father—and that, too, was said with a note of reluctance—to visit his uncle who lived there.

We arranged to meet at four, but he did not show up until six. Nora, who had been waiting with me, lost her patience after an hour, and resenting his rudeness in not letting us know he would be late, went off to Yoav's house.

When I opened the door I saw a lanky, narrow-shouldered young man in a gray suit and tie, with horn-rimmed glasses on a face that looked too small for his height, and with a hesitant expression in his eyes. He apologized half-heartedly for being late, saying that he had booked a room by phone from Jerusalem, and was promised a room with a sea view. But when he arrived, it turned out he had been given a back room, so he decided to move to another hotel...

Laughing, he added that the first person he met coming out of the hotel was a drag queen, who tried to pick him up...

We sat down and he placed the parcel he brought from his father on the table—he had white, delicate hands with long fingers—muttering: "I have no idea what's inside." I opened the parcel and found two books in French, *Les Juifs* by Roger Peyrefitte, and *The Truth about the Protocols of the Elders of Zion* by an author named Francois Ducat. On each title page was written a warm inscription, 'with love,' mentioning our 'unforgettable' meetings in Israel. I pointed my finger at the drawing of a bird above Foiglman's signature and said how nice that a poet has a sort of 'coat of arms,' like pedigreed English families. And he replied, with a pursed smile, "Yes, he sees himself as a bird of passage." I asked how his father was, and Irving answered in his nasal voice, "I suppose he is all right. I don't see much of him. On my way here I stopped in Paris for only one day. He looks well. He really does."

I asked him about the conference he attended in Jerusalem. He shrugged and said, "Not important. Completely insignificant." And a moment later he added, a crooked grin on his lips, "There was one professor there from Jerusalem...Ehrlichman? Lehman?...who spoke about ontology and time, but who hadn't read Heidegger's *Sein und Zeit*... Ridiculous..."

I offered him coffee, tea, a drink. He said he did not drink alcohol, but would take coffee, no cream, no sugar.

I served the coffee and asked if he had already been to see his uncle in Ramlah. No, he hadn't had the time, and didn't think he would be able to now, but he had spoken to him on the phone. They

could hardly communicate, since his uncle could not speak English
and he himself could barely speak Yiddish. I expressed surprise that
the son of a Yiddish poet and a Yiddish actress was not fluent in Yiddish. When he was a child, he said, he could speak it, of course, but
since leaving home… His father's books stood on a bookshelf in his
room at Oxford, but he had not read them. Yes, a few poems here
and there. He did not think his father was a good poet.

I said I was not a great expert on poetry, but some of the poems
moved me deeply. He gave me a quizzical look, as if doubting my sin-
cerity. He sat there, his long legs crossed, his arms folded, his shoulders
hunched. He said there were a few Israeli students at Oxford—he
saw them at the library, pubs, the bookstores—and could always tell
they were Israelis by their behavior. They had one characteristic no
other foreign students had, neither Indians or Pakistani nor German
or Norwegian: absolutely no inhibitions. That always amazed him;
they would address a salesman, a librarian, a clerk at the bank or at
the travel agent's without manners or courtesy, without hesitation,
directly, freely, as if they were playmates. The Englishman behind the
counter would be taken aback, embarrassed, often revolted by such an
attitude; he would never comment on it, of course, but would resent
such disrespectful and socially unacceptable conduct. How did the
Israelis come to possess such a trait—Irving wanted to know—was
it Jewish atavism? But no; true, Jews are noisy, boisterous, but they
approach strangers warily, perhaps even fearfully… Is this, then, an
idiosyncrasy of the new race being brought up here in this land?

I said something about this being "the first generation to be
redeemed," celebrating its freedom, its deliverance from the prison of
Diaspora existence, which was why it flaunted all social conventions;
I also said a few things about a society in the process of forming itself,
still lacking in amenities and procedures. But I could tell, from the
way his eyes stared at me, unblinking, that he was not convinced. I
asked if this was his first visit here, and if he had managed to see
anything in those few days. He said, yes, this was his first visit here,
and he did walk about a little in Jerusalem, especially in the Old City.
Those merchants there are very clever, he chuckled. However, no
sooner had he reached the square by the Western Wall, he hastened

to leave. The commotion, the noise, the swarming crowds heading in all directions. He found himself surrounded by a bunch of swarthy kids, all wearing skullcaps who, for some reason, were pointing at him and giggling. A bearded fellow in a colorful skullcap, probably their teacher or guide, had come over to him and said something in Hebrew. But, he continued, the city as a whole was pretty. It had the splendor of 'an ancient kingdom,' and its inhabitants are a motley crowd of strange and diverse characters. On the way from the Holy Sepulcher to the Jaffa Gate, a handsome Arab boy followed him and talked to him, though he could not understand what he wanted, until he came out of the gate. "A beautiful and disturbing city," he grinned. He could not sleep at night and had to take a sleeping pill. On his last day there he went to spend a few hours in Ramallah.

Ramallah? I wondered. He explained that when he first arrived in Jerusalem he phoned an old friend who had studied with him at Oxford and was now teaching at Bir-Zeit University. A man of 'Victorian manners.' He had come to his hotel and taken him in his car to his spacious home, surrounded by a huge orchard, which reminded him of the rose gardens in the poems of the Persian poet Hafiz. In the parlor, Irving said with a slightly romantic smile, were hanging wall-rugs embroidered with verses and maxims, in Arabic and other languages. He found there an English quotation of Tagore to the effect that we gain our freedom only after we've paid the full price for our right to live, and in French a quote from Beaumarché: "I force myself to laugh at everything, lest I cry." His friend's wife was Scottish, the daughter of a Glasgow minister. After having been served oriental delicacies she had baked, he and his friend drove to Bir-Zeit University. There he heard from the faculty how the occupying military forces harass the college, by detentions, arrests, closure injunctions. What does the Israeli academic community think about this, he demanded—lacing his long, thin fingers on his chest.

I explained that Bir-Zeit University was a hornets' nest of subversive activities, both overt and covert, a center for the most ardent supporters of terrorists' organizations. The army, or the military administration, trys to contain that activity, sometimes by moderate means, sometimes by harsher means. A certain situation, I said, dictates a certain behavior. A change does not depend on us alone.

Irving looked at me in silence. Then he said that when he was there he understood what Sartre meant when he said that during the German occupation the Nazi poison had seeped so deeply into people's hearts that any precise idea seemed like a triumph, an exact word—like a declaration of principles, any human gesture—like a commitment to fight oppression.

"Poison..." I repeated, and told him that at a biologists' convention in Jerusalem, which my wife, who is a biologist, attended, a professor of epidemiology from Bir-Zeit University took the floor and accused the Israeli military of contaminating the springs and rivers of the West Bank, of spreading toxic material and epidemic viruses among the Arab population. He even cited so-called 'scientific' evidence to prove his allegations. Exactly the kind of libels the Christians used to spread about the Jews in the Middle Ages, claiming that they were 'poisoning the wells,' I said.

Irving remained silent, his eyes fixed on me, unblinking.

After a long moment, a dim flicker seemed to light his eyes, like the radiance of a distant sunset, and he asked if I had ever seen the movie *Lawrence of Arabia.*

No, I had not seen it, I said. I had not been to a movie in years. I wondered why he was asking.

There is a certain innate nobility in Arabs, he said. He noticed it while walking around among the students at Bir Zeit and sitting down with the young faculty members. An inherent nobility that emanates from their faces and bodies.

Then he added, "My father tells me that you teach Jewish history."

He wanted to know the periods I was researching, the subjects, the method I was employing. He listened very attentively to my reply and nodded after every sentence, as if in agreement. When I finished, he wrapped his long arms around his shoulders, as if huddling from the cold, and said, "To tell you the truth, to me all this doesn't mean much. I can't really say that I feel like a Jew. Except by birth, of course, which is something beyond my control."

99

I was silent and he felt obliged to elaborate: attachment to a nation depends on a sense of fellowship, of solidarity. He himself feels a greater affinity—intellectually, even spiritually—with a Japanese professor who shares his philosophical ideas, than with a Jewish shopkeeper from the 'Pletzel' in Paris. Or, an even more extreme example: between himself and a young German doctoral candidate, whom he met in Oxford, a shy, introverted fellow with whom he meets frequently, there exists a much greater closeness of spirit than with his sister from Orlean, with whom he has nothing in common.

"And what about history?" I asked.

"If you're referring to the common past…let me ask you this: is there any reflection of the common past on the relationship between, say, a Jewish *Kapo* in a concentration camp and the Jew he is shoving into the gas furnace?" And after a short reflection he added, "Yes, history may be a certain factor, a very tiny one. To me, personally, it means very little."

As if sensing the grave impact his words had on me, his expression suddenly relaxed, he smiled at me and said, "But Jerusalem is certainly a beautiful city. Yes, it's very special."

He eyed me, as from a distance and dispassionately told me the following: "One night, in the hotel there, I dreamed that I was in some camp…rows upon rows of barracks, hundreds of barracks looking identical…perhaps it was a concentration camp… A huge black man, naked, looking like a gorilla, was chasing me. I ran between the rows of barracks and he's pursuing me… I had a terrible fright… but at the same time I knew—and this is the strange part—that I would soon wake up, and everything will return to normal. When I woke up I said to myself: if a dream knows that it is a dream, is it still a dream?… This is a very significant metaphysical question that has implications in many other areas. Interesting…"

When he got up to leave, I asked him to convey my regards to his father and thank him for the present. He promised to do so. On his return to Oxford, he said, he would call him.

At the door, with his hand on the handle, he asked if I could recommend a store that sells leather clothes. He had heard that leather jackets are much cheaper here than in England and thought he might buy himself one before leaving. I could not remember any such store, and he smiled and took his leave.

ॐ

It was one day after the *shiva* and the house emptied of those who had come to console me in my bereavement. Many had come, day after day, and sat for long hours. All her colleagues from the Biological Institute came in twos and threes, in the afternoon, at night. Among them was a young laboratory assistant, a beautiful woman with jet black hair and big round eyes; from time to time she would remove the handkerchief from her face, raise her red-lidded eyes to me and mutter that she couldn't grasp it, just couldn't grasp it. Nora always radiated happiness; she was so warm and affectionate to everybody... And another woman, about forty-five or fifty years old, with parted hair pulled tightly back and a heavy Russian accent, confirmed that impression, but added that, in the last few days, she had noticed Nora was absent-minded; she took a jar of spores from the lab to the autoclave, but returned a few minutes later angry with herself for having taken the wrong jar, which had already been sterilized... "She plunked it on the table with so much force that it almost broke. I was very surprised because that was very unusual for her." And she added, "She was always so neat. So neat and tidy."

Dr. M. came, too. He sat and said nothing, but just looked around as if to see if there were any changes in the apartment.

When the house was empty and only the two of us, Yoav and I, remained, he suddenly asked me... It was shocking! He was sitting on the sofa, hunched, his arms on his knees, without lifting his head, only his eyes glaring at me from under his brows, saying in a quiet voice:

"One thing I don't understand... Why, when you found her in the morning...you didn't send for a doctor right away, or call an ambulance?... Sometimes they can save a person..."

Good God!—an electric charge shot through my body—next thing he'll accuse me of murder!

"I have nothing to say to you, Yoav," I said trembling.

What could I say to him?

I was stunned. She had been cold. White as a sheet. I shouted at her, called her name, her body was as stiff as log. When I let go of her arm, it had knocked against the side of the bed. On the chest of drawers by the bed, under the yellow light of the night lamp, a faded light, paler than the dawn, stood the bottle of pills, empty. I was stunned, shocked, I trembled from head to toe. The first thing that occurred to me to do was to call you, Yoav!

In such moments darkness descends and covers everything! Reason ceases to function.

You were not there. Shula answered the phone.

It took quite a long time—twenty minutes or more—till she got here.

Downstairs there was the clangor of the garbage cans being hauled by the garbage men, and from time to time, the quiet rustle, as from another world, of a passing car, and then another, and I'm here with Nora's body, lifeless... When Shula came in and saw her, she gave out a shout, cried like a child, cried on and on.

She was as stunned as I was.

It didn't occur to her, either, to call anyone. Whom could we call? The worst thing of all had happened, it was dreadfully clear. It was only when we recovered from the shock—how long did it take? half an hour?—did we think what to do, and then I called the police. Then a policeman and a doctor came. The doctor confirmed her death. He said she had been dead for hours. They took her down to an ambulance.

A day after the funeral a police officer shows up at the house. He is courteous, apologetic, assures me that the interrogation is routine, as in all cases of suicide. He opens a file on the table, sits with knees spread apart, pulls out a pen, lights a cigarette, begins his every question with 'Professor.' What time did I come home that night? What had I been doing until eleven? Why didn't I come into her room when I noticed the light on? Since when had we been sleeping in separate rooms and why? Had we quarreled that day? He writes down the hours and the minutes meticulously.

"It's not as if I'm suspecting you, Professor, far from it," he tries to placate me when he sees my stunned face. "It's just a matter of procedure, you understand…"

Then he silently reads what he has written, and just like Yoav a few days later, asks me, "Why didn't you call the doctor right away, Professor? I mean the moment you found her unconscious? Usually one thinks instinctively that perhaps…"

When I explain, still shattered from the tragedy, he nods as if he understands, then writes down my answer.

He asks if I could say anything about the motive. I am not obliged, but perhaps I have an idea or a conjecture. It was better if it were included in the file. I spread my hands; I have nothing to say on that score.

"Yes," he closes the file, full of understanding and compassion. "Quite often, the person closest to the deceased hasn't a clue as to why…"

He gets up and shakes my hands in condolence.

Chapter twelve

My father had an obsession about archeological finds from the Israeli and Canaanite period. Prehistoric flint knives, Hellenistic tombs, Roman capitals, Byzantine mosaics—those held no interest for him. But in order to capture a figurine of Astarte, a piece of earthenware from Gideon's time, an ostracon with five faded words written in Hebrew script of Jeroboam's reign, a course of stones from a fort dating from Uziah's time—for these he would leap upon the mountains and skip upon the hills. He could sniff these out like a bloodhound. When I was twelve or fourteen years old, he used to take me in his ancient beat-up Ford, a veteran of bumpy, jerky dirt roads, to some destination in the Judean mountains or in the Galilee. On the way he would stop four or five times, turn his head from side to side, as if on the scent of prey, then cut the motor and call out, "Come on out!"

Cane in hand, on his head a colonial cork hat that had gone out of fashion dozens of years earlier, he would climb at a brisk pace up some bald *tel* where nothing could be seen, and I would follow him, panting, trying to catch up with him. From the top of the Tel he would look around, then tap on the stones with his cane, like a

Texan prospector with a divining rod, and declare, "There's something here!" If he chanced to see a Arab villager plowing a field at the bottom of the Tel, he would dash down, dragging me behind him, and question the man—he was fluent in Arabic—about the name of the place, its history and the legends surrounding it. Back in the car he would write all this in his notebook, in his fast, undisciplined handwriting that was totally illegible to me. We continued on our way, and he would lay out his plans for the next digging expedition: first approach the official head of the archeological department at Rockefeller Museum in order to obtain a permit, then go to Mount Scopus to discuss it with Professor Sukenik, to recruit five volunteers from the Boy Scouts...

I traveled with him the length and breadth of the land. He was fearless. He would drive in unbeaten tracks, climb mountains, walk through villages in areas inhabited only by Arabs. Once he wanted to take a shortcut from Beit El to Jericho and drove through a winding, impassable, dirt road and we almost skidded into an abyss when the car was swept down in an avalanche of rocks. Fortunately, he managed to swerve into a shallow wadi and we came to a stop at the bottom of the riverbed. We had two flat tires and the motor had died and would not start again. My father did not lose his head. His sharp eye had spotted a Bedouin tent a couple of kilometers away. He left me in the car—the year was 1940 or 1941 and he carried a licensed gun—and an hour later returned with the Bedouin and two camels. We hitched the car to the camels and they hauled it up. It took us five hours, until sundown, to get back onto the road. From there a truck towed us to a garage in Jericho. We spent the night at the house of the garage owner; he offered us food and drink and let us sleep on the floor. All evening long my father pumped our host for information about sites in the vicinity and listened to his stories. At noon the next day the car was ready. Suddenly my father changed his plans: he decided to go to Novomeysky, at the Dead Sea Potash plant, to check out the feasibility of an archeological survey of the caves of the Judean Desert...

On these hikes with my father I became acquainted with the

land and learned to love it, but I couldn't stand going with him on the actual excavations.

I remember a summer I went on a dig with him, near Gush-Halav in the Upper Galilee, when I finally yielded to his entreaties. I had just finished my junior year in high school, and those were the days of the Arab uprising of 1936–39; it was dangerous to travel, and every night Jewish settlements were attacked by Arab marauders. The ruins of a second century synagogue in a rocky area surrounded by olive groves had already been excavated—lintels, a stone candelabrum with seven branches, engravings of pomegranates and a *shofar*, a ritual ram's horn—but my father clung stubbornly to his hypothesis, based on certain verses from the book of Joshua, that underneath this layer ought to be found remnants from the First Temple era, and further down—from the Patriarch's era.

My father had a theory, which very few scholars of Israeli history subscribe to, that there existed a dense Hebrew population in the country even before the conquest of Canaan by Joshua, and that the name 'Israel' derives from 'Asherah-El' (Astarte-god), and that the Phoenicians and the Hebrews are one and the same. With monomaniacal zeal he would dig and explore the land in order to extract concrete evidence that would corroborate his theory. "In the Galilee of all places?" I protested when we went out on the dig, "Harosheth of the gentiles?"

"Zvi, Zvi," he would shake his head, "Honor thy Father. He wouldn't be running around from one end of the country to the other merely on a wild goose chase." And he launched into a lecture on the Phoenician empire whose southern border once extended all the way to Jaffa, and about the 'Hebrews' some of whom migrated from Mesopotamia to Egypt, while others had settled in the land of Canaan.

Together with four others, two young men in side locks from Safed and two members of the Labor Squad from Rosh Pina, I raked dust and ashes with a spade and a mattock, filled wicker baskets and emptied them behind the dike. The sun above our heads was scorching; the powdery dust penetrated our eyes, nostrils and mouths.

The first four days we found nothing except shards and splinters of basalt rock. On the fifth day, however, our spades hit a rocky surface and we started scraping off the dust. My father was elated. It looked as if his hypothesis was confirmed: a temple of Asherah or of Baal! At noon, in the shed, he read us chapters from the books of Joshua and Judges, and from recently discovered Ugaritic texts. But we did not unearth any figurine or ritualistic object. Every evening, my father would drive the two Safed boys back home, and the four of us would sleep beneath the skies, among the olive trees, taking turns to watch. From time to time we heard shooting in the distance that seemed to be aimed at the rocks. The *ghaffirs** driving by in their pick-up trucks would look in on us, concerned about our safety. At night I asked my father why he was convinced that it was the site of a temple even though no evidence of religious worship had been found. Inferring from dents and bulges in the stones, he explained, from a certain recess. One rectangular stone with 'horns' was, in his opinion, the altar. I did not find his explanations convincing in the least. The surface seemed to me the floor of a residential house, and the stone with the 'horns'—a chair, an anvil, or a stand for cookware. Even if our mattock could unearth a figurine buried in the sun-baked dust, and even if our brush could polish an engraved Biblical name in Hebrew script—as my father had hoped all along—what was so remarkable about that? Why was he seized with such excitement at the sight of a spout of an earthenware vessel or a splinter of Phoenician glass as they bounced on the sieve? What could all these finds prove? Or was he in fact looking for material evidence to confirm our claim to this country? On the eighth day, when my father realized how sick and tired I had become of that work, he decided to release me and send me home.

Yes, that summer is indelibly engraved in my mind. In those days there was no direct bus service from Safed to Tel Aviv, so you had to change buses at Tiberias. I arrived in Tiberias at ten, and waited for the Tel Aviv bus at the restaurant of the bus station, across

---

* *ghaffirs*—paramilitary Jewish policemen during the time of the British Mandate in Palestine

the street from Central Park. Suddenly there was a great commotion
and a great many people rushed into the restaurant, seeking shelter
and shouting: "An attack! The *shabab* is raiding the Jewish quarter!"
Some of us were pushing our way to the door to see what was going
on when we heard distant shots echoing from the mountain above us.
Storeowners hurried to pull down metal shutters, and street vendors
folded their stalls and vanished into the alleys. A few people were still
seen running, ducking, seeking shelter along the walls, and soon the
street emptied completely. A few moments later a barrage of stones
was hurled at the row of stores where we were. In the park and on
the mountain slopes behind it, groups of Arabs were seen picking
stones and darting them at us, shouting, *"Itbah el Yahud!"* ("Slaughter the Jews!"). While the people in the restaurant huddled together,
squeezing into the back, in the corners, a window was shattered and
an elderly man was hit in the forehead. A jet of dark red blood gushed
down his face. He did not utter a word, only stopped the wound with
his hand and went to the kitchen. A woman fainted and collapsed.
Somebody rushed to bring some water to sprinkle on her face. The
stones—large round basalt rocks and small sharp ones—kept flying
around us, shattering windows, hitting the door and walls, ricocheting
from table and chairs and scattering on the restaurant floor.

I stood among these frightened, pale, helpless people, clinging to each other, whispering: "Where's the police? Why is nobody
coming? Why don't we see them?" Tears choked my throat, tears
of shame and humiliation. It's just like a pogrom, I cried inwardly,
like a pogrom. And in my bitter desperation I asked: Where are the
members of the Hagganah, or Beitar, the proud and hot-tempered
Sephardi boys? Why is nobody hitting back, not even with stones?
It seemed to me quite despicable, that this should take place while
we were here in the Land of Israel, in this town where Jews formed
the majority of the population…

The nightmare lasted for about twenty minutes. Army vehicles
carrying British soldiers in white helmets were coming down the
street, a few bursts of shots shook the air, the *shabab* were seen fleeing
toward the houses on the mountain, armed policemen appeared at
the intersections, and when the firing had died down, people emerged

from out of their hiding places, the stores opened, the traffic resumed in the streets and everything went back to normal. But the memory of that shameful incident was never erased from my heart.

Chapter thirteen

Each of us is surrounded by a circle, the circle of our destiny out of which we cannot step—this is how de Toqueville described it—but inside the circle, man is free to do as he pleases. But I, like the proverbial partridge of folk tales, was irresistibly drawn to the snare and was caught. Three months after Irving's visit, I was invited to an international conference on Jewish Studies at the University of Strasbourg, to give a talk on the Shabbetaian controversy and its corollaries in Poland. I suggested to Nora she take off some time from work and join me, but she saw no point in going on such a short trip, a mere ten days. "Go by yourself, enjoy, have a good time, paint the city of lights red, as long as you don't contract some loathsome disease...," she teased.

The conference lasted five days. When it was over I went to Paris where I decided to spend the remaining three days in total idleness, walking around the town, visiting a few museums and rare bookstores, enjoying the city's splendor. Except for one appointment I had with a publisher who was interested in my work and considered publishing my paper on the Frankist movement, I had no other obligations. I stayed in a small hotel, near the Jardins du Luxembourg, whose owner knew me from previous visits to Paris. I had made up my mind not to see Foiglman—not even to call him—so as to have all my time to myself. Perhaps I did not want to spoil my pleasure with 'Jewish troubles.'

And yet, on my second day there, before noon—was it guilt feelings for not thanking him for the books he had sent with his son that guided my hand to the telephone?—I called him up.

"In a hotel?" he protested vehemently. He was angry, offended; had he not told me several times that I was a welcome guest at his house at all times, that he would be happy to accommodate me for as long as I wanted, so why was I doing him such an injustice—him and his wife, who at that moment was standing at his side, equally offended—and besides, why was I wasting my money on a miserable hotel room and restaurants... And he announced that he was coming to take me to their house and that I was going to have lunch at their table... No, he would never forgive me if I turned him down...

At that moment I felt a searing regret in my heart for my irrevocable act; here I was, ruining my brief stay in Paris with my own hands.

Less than half an hour later he called me from the lobby downstairs. I went down to meet him, and he opened his arms, hugged and kissed me and again chided me—loudly, in Yiddish, to the amazement of the guests lounging around—for the great injustice I was doing him. Should he call a cab? Or, since it was such a pleasant day, should we walk to his home? Yes, we'll walk, I said, consoling myself with the thought that at least I would enjoy a stroll in the streets in this gorgeous fall season.

In his town of residence Foiglman walked around like a landlord. He took my arm in his—his cheeks were flushed, a mischievous glint in his eyes, his step nimble and vigorous—and every historic building we passed elicited a story from him. He stopped at a stall of roasted chestnuts, bought a bag and handed it to me, "Take, eat, you don't have these in Israel," and he stuck the bag in my jacket pocket. When we passed by a rare book store he said, "Come, I'll show you something." We walked into the dimly lit store and he exchanged a few sentences with the owner, who apparently knew him, and the latter took an old leather-bound book down from a top shelf. "Letters to Jews in Portugal, Germany and Poland" by Voltaire, published in 1782. "I wanted to buy it for you, but the price he's asking is exorbitant, simply exorbitant." He gave the book back to the seller and laughed, "This anti-Semite, Voltaire, he read the Bible backward!"

When we crossed the Jardins du Luxembourg he said that every time he goes through that park or near it, he is reminded of Rosa Luxemburg, who was born in Zamosc, though the park is not named after her. He told me about her ancestry and about the branches of her family who stayed in town until they perished.

"Oh, Rosa, Rosa," he sighed. "She left the nest thinking she could thus escape the fate of her people, and what has become of her?...the Germans murdered her in the streets of Berlin and threw her body in the gutter, twenty years before they did the same to her brothers in Zamosc. She wrote 'Spartacus' on her banner, instead of Bar-Kochba, and what good did it do her?"

"And what about Liebknecht?" I said, "who was not Jewish?"

"Liebknecht was murdered because he was her friend! Woe to the Jew and woe to his friend!"

Later, when we were walking down Boulevard Saint Michel, he said he had been rejuvenated, and his eyes lit up. Rejuvenated, he repeated, saying the phrase in Hebrew, and he told me how he had written close to fifty poems. "You'll love them, Reb Hirsch!" he pressed my arm tightly.

We crossed the bridge over the Seine and, at his request, I told him about the Strasbourg conference. I reported about a talk given by a gentile professor from Upsala University in Sweden, who had written a very interesting paper on Jewish history in which he tried to disprove the concept of a 'Jewish race,' claiming that, since its inception and throughout its history, the foreign elements that intermingled in the Jewish people have constituted a decisive majority.

"So what?" Foiglman stopped in his tracks. "Suppose he's right, and we are all a mixed and motley crowd, what conclusion can we draw from it? What difference does it make? You know what Heine used to say? Judaism is a family tragedy...a family tragedy!" He gave a loud chuckle. "For me it really is a family tragedy. How about you?"

It was a lovely day. Very mild. Light, white clouds were drifting in the sky, and a soft, rarefied and ethereal light penetrated through the defoliating treetops. But the 'Jewish troubles' followed me from the Jardins du Luxembourg to the end of Boulevard Sebastopol, more than an hour's walk, and would not let go of me even by Notre Dame cathedral, or by Sainte-Chapelle, or by the Hotel de Ville, or by Pompidou Center, and not even when we got to Foiglman's house.

We walked up the narrow, spiral wooden staircase to the third story of an old house whose dark hallways smelled of gas. Foiglman rang the bell, and we were greeted by a tall, erect woman, with a prominent chest and shoulder-length thick, black hair. "Ah, Professor Arbel, finally!"

She offered me her hand and gave my palm a vigorous shake. She scrutinized me, her face was white as marble but full of vivacity, and said, "Just as I imagined you, except taller."

Unlike the hallway and the narrow staircase, the apartment itself was spacious and pleasant. The living room was filled with heavy furniture: a large table, sideboard, chairs and armchairs, and a grand piano that occupied about a third of the room. My hosts were obviously proud of the pictures on the walls: a painting of an old Jew with Torah scroll by Mane Katz; two autographed drawings of the painter Ben; a lithograph of Vitebsk by Chagall with a handwritten dedication on the bottom, "To my friend, the sad poet whose eyes have not ceased smiling." Foiglman explained that that was Chagall's way of thanking him for a book of poems he had sent him. Then there were two photographs of a group of writers including Foiglman himself. On the sideboard and on the piano stood cardboard framed pictures of Hinda, Henrietta Fogel, in roles she played at the theater: Mirale Efros, the Madwoman of Chaillot, Hedda Gabler and others. "My old loves," Hinda said smiling, and her eyes, under the long lashes, reflected deep Jewish grief, "It's been years since I left the theater, but I'm independent, and that's what counts!"

She gave me a resolute look. With her long, black hair, her well-fitting brown dress with the round décolletage and the white muslin collar that seemed to heighten her stature, she looked much younger than her husband. Her thin, pointed nose gave her face a 'classic' appearance.

From the living room they led me to the adjacent rooms: one was Foiglman's study and contained a large library; on the wall opposite his desk hung the pictures of his father and mother, and between them a painting of a black bird, a sort of raven, perched on the bough of a naked tree surrounded by snow. The second room was a bedroom. Foiglman opened a third door to a room containing merely a bed, a table and a chair and explained that it used to be the children's room, but was now empty. "I said you could always stay here without in the least inconveniencing us!" and he added in Hebrew, "The one enjoys, and the other wants naught."

We went back to the living room. Hinda had laid the table. She asked if I ate meat, and if I kept kosher. "May I call you Zvi?" she asked. "Call him Hirsch," Foiglman said, "he's one of us!"

"Yes? Hirsch?"

Hinda examined me as if to decide whether the name suited me, and then went off to the kitchen. Two minutes later she was back, wearing an apron and said, "If Zvi is Hirsch, what would Hinda be in Hebrew?"

"A gazelle," I smiled at her. "How wonderful!" she clapped her hands. "You were sent from heaven!"

"Oy, oy, what trouble have I brought on myself," Foiglman clapped his hands to his cheeks, "she's already flirting with him!"

When we were alone, I asked him if he had had any particular motive in sending me Peyrefitte's and Ducat's books. "Particular motive?" he wondered. "I only wanted to show you that many things come and go in the world, but anti-Semitism always stays. Not only does it stay, but it never changes—the same old libels repeat themselves, from Apion to Hitler, and even forty years after Hitler. I wouldn't be surprised if, in this Paris of ours, this bastion of liberty, a rumor will spread tomorrow that a Catholic child has been murdered and his blood used for baking matzot for Passover. Two million people will credit it!"

I told him he was exaggerating: not too many years ago a Jew was elected prime minister of France, and nowadays Paris has an archbishop of Jewish extraction, who announces publicly that although he is a Christian by faith, he has not ceased to be a Jew.

"Yes, yes," Foiglman nodded, "Yes, yes, yes…"

And he leaned forward as if to share a secret with me, "Me, I have made up my mind, I'm going to Israel. To settle there. I'm resolved; once and for all!" When I congratulated him he added, "Not right away. After my book has been published there, in Hebrew."

I said it was a very good idea; his book should be the vanguard leading the way for him.

"But who will translate me, for God's sake?" he stretched his arms, "I don't know any of the translators there."

I promised to inquire when I got back to Israel, and to let him know.

"You will inquire, Reb Hirsch?" his eyes beseeched me.

In the meantime lunch was ready and we were invited to come to the table. Hinda served simple Jewish fare: chopped liver, chicken soup with noodles, tender chicken with *tzimmes*, potato and plum stew, kugel… Foiglman opened a bottle of port and we toasted each other. When I sipped from the boiling soup with the floating golden rings of chicken fat, I felt I had been transported back to Poland, Lithuania, Ukraine, Rumania—fifty years earlier, far away from Paris.

During the meal Hinda asked me what had prompted me—a *sabra*, as her husband had told her—to explore the history of eastern European Jewry. I said many of my colleagues who are native Israelis study the history of Rome, the Crusaders, the Napoleonic wars, the American Revolution, and nobody wonders about it. What, then, is so amazing when a scholar studies the history of his own people?

"But our story, Zvi, is a tearful story. With us—*altz dreyt zikharom broyt un toyt!*—that is, everything centers around bread and death."

I said that in my childhood my grandmother, who had come from the region of Podolia, used to tell me very amusing stories about her hometown, and I got a picture of a life full of joy and laughter and even frolicking in the bosom of nature.

"But you yourself write about pogroms, Professor!"

Indeed, I conceded, but from my thesis about the gloomy Diaspora one could draw the antithesis about the light of *Eretz Yisrael*... Hinda looked at me, her fork in her hand suspended over her plate, then said excitedly, "For years I've dreamed of performing in Israel—but it never worked out! They're obstructing me! A wall stands between me and them, as between Pyramus and Thisbe!"

She smiled and told me how her agent had tried several times to arrange for her to perform in Tel Aviv, but could find no association, institute or manager willing to sponsor her. She could not figure this out; from Uruguay to New Zealand she is much sought after; she is received with open arms, and only in the Jewish state, where there is a large Yiddish-speaking audience, Yiddish lovers...

I was the only representative of the Jewish state at that table. I felt it incumbent on me to explain this 'obstruction,' to find excuses, to rise to the defense. I said the reason must be the plethora of artists and the paucity of theaters: the stiff competition... All the while, Foiglman was absorbed in his food, refraining from taking part in the conversation. From his silence I inferred that the matter had often been discussed between them. Hinda sat erect, like a grand matron, one hand held to her white marble neck, as if protecting it, and her attentive look proclaimed that she respected my effort but was not at all convinced by my arguments.

"Professor Arbel," she rested her hand on the table, "I would like you to hear me, at least once, recite Manger's *Golden Peacock*, or Leivick's *I wasn't at Treblinka*, or Bialik's *On the Slaughter*, in Yiddish, of course..."

"She also sings Bialik's songs in Yiddish!" Foiglman raised his head from his plate.

"*Neither by Day nor by Night, Between the Euphrates and the Tigris, I Have a Garden...*"

"You should see the audience when she sings these songs."

Hinda's eyes narrowed and her nostrils flared as if she were relishing some unusual sensory pleasure, and flinging both her arms in the air said, "You know how it feels, Professor, when you're standing on the stage and sense the waves of warmth, love and empathy flowing from the audience toward you..."

She got up and went to the kitchen to bring the compote. When she served it, she said, "But the audiences diminish from year to year. Just now I toured three cities, Montreal, Toronto and Chicago..."

In Toronto, she said, only fifteen years ago, you could find schools run by *Arbayter-ring* and *Po'alei Zion-Left** where kids sang and played in Yiddish; and today—a wasteland. In Chicago, with a Jewish population of about half a million, you hardly see them at all! Scattered around in green suburbs, living in posh houses with swimming pools and tennis courts... They put her up at the Hyatt fifteen miles from the center of town, not even a bus line... She felt as if she were in an ice palace at the North Pole... "Yiddish is a language of poor people, Hirsch!"

When she had cleared the dishes from the table, we moved to the armchairs and Foiglman poured us some cognac. We chatted about this and that. Foiglman and I had only one shot, but Hinda kept refilling her glass. She soon became jovial, a blush spread on her cheeks and on her neck, she got up, walked light-footedly around the room, offered us cookies and chocolates, showed me a silver statuette she had received from her fans... Suddenly she hurled at me, "Why didn't you bring your wife, Zvi? Shmuel describes her as a Norwegian princess!"

"Norwegian?" I laughed, and said I had come for a conference on Jewish Studies and she was not interested in the subject. Hinda grew serious, her eyes opened wide, and she cried, "Oh, how I understand her! I understand her with all my heart! Believe me, Zvi, if I could... If Yiddish weren't the source of my livelihood—I would chuck it out and run to the end of the world! Yiddishkeit and Yiddishkeit and Yiddishkeit, morning, noon, and evening—I'm sick of it! Sick and tired!" She crossed her hands over her heart and, closing her eyes, lifted her head.

"She always goes on like this after two glasses," Foiglman whispered to me.

---

* *Arbayter-ring* and *Po'alei Zion-Left*—Socialist parties which Jews belonged to prior to the Second World War

"Shmuel!" She scolded him loudly, "you don't understand me, and you never have! You think," tears filled her eyes, "that when I travel thirty thousand miles to Montevideo to appear before fifty old Jews who nod their heads at me after every sentence as if they had spasms, that I enjoy it? That it fills me with joy? Pride? It fills you with pride! Because you live under an illusion! You always have!"

Her clear voice filled the room. She was Antigone, Cleopatra, Lady Macbeth, Mirale Efros all in one. Foiglman sank back in his armchair and looked at her sardonically.

"This house, Zvi," she stretched her arms as if to encompass its entire space, "this house reeks of Yiddishkeit like a morgue! Wherever you look! You can't breathe in here for all these Jews and Judaism. I'm suffocating! For the Poet Shmuel Foiglman the world is divided into two: Jews and gentiles! And a chasm between the two! The Jews may not all be good, but the gentiles are all evil. Tell me, Professor," and she leaned toward me, her hand on her knees, "Are all the gentiles evil? No exception? If it weren't for them, I would be soap and ashes now! You know," she lowered her voice and her eyes glared, "On October 21 in the year 1941, when the Germans surrounded the eleventh arrondissement, not far from here, they captured all the Jews they found in the streets and in the houses, like dog catchers, and sent them to Drancy. Nobody came back, as you probably know. My father took me, I was ten years old then, through backyards, to the house of Marcel Picard, a journalist, a socialist, a *goy*, who was his friend from the Party, and he, at enormous danger to himself, smuggled me outside the city to a convent near Saint Denis. I stayed there until 1945 when my parents came back from the Pyrenees, from Spain. This is how I survived. Do I have the right to curse all gentiles? Aren't there decent human beings among them? Do you know gentiles at all?" She turned to her husband, "All your life you lived among Jews? Only among Jews!"

"Oh, Hindele, Hindele," Foiglman nodded, scrunched in his armchair, his face mournful, "I don't know any gentiles, no…"

Hinda froze for a moment, her face, when she looked at him, seemed to have turned into stone. Then she said in a harsh, dry voice, "Yes, you do know." She sank back in her chair and covered her eyes with her hands.

A heavy silence prevailed. I got up and said it was time for me to leave.

"Already?" Foiglman's eyes widened in alarm. "We hardly had time to talk! And tomorrow you're leaving!"

"You must forgive me, Hirsch," Hinda straightened and her white face, which looked very pale, now assumed a serene, languid and beautiful expression. "I don't know what came over me that I burst out like that. I'm so terribly impulsive, what can I do? I'm a victim of my own impulsiveness. I'm ashamed of the nonsense that comes out of my mouth."

I said it was by no means nonsense. Within each of us the prosecution and the defense struggle constantly, each trying to gain the upper hand. Foiglman implored me to stay, sounding offended and reproving. I said I wanted to visit the Pompidou Center, which I had missed on my previous visits to Paris.

"Closed!" they both cried triumphantly, "all the museums are closed at this hour today."

Hinda got up and with great animation suggested that we go to the theater.

I was their prisoner. I could not decline. A great bustle filled the room: Hinda was looking for the magazine *Ce soir a Paris,* Shmuel was looking for the daily paper, and when they found them, they quickly scanned the list of shows; and he started calling box offices one after the other only to discover that no tickets were available, whereupon Hinda took over, to try her luck. She started each call with, "This is Henrietta Fogel speaking," and asked to speak to a specific person. Finally tickets were found for the first show of Arrabal's *Hangmen,* at a small theater, the Huchette.

After a quick snack Hinda changed into a purple velvet gown and put a string of pearls around her heck, Foiglman exchanged his black bow tie for a red one and called a cab, and we were on our way to the theater. I offered to pay for the tickets but they would not hear of it.

I was finally in Paris. Amid the hubbub in the street, the odors of cooking from Algerian, Greek and Turkish restaurants mingled with the fragrance of roasted chestnuts and *Gauloise* cigarettes. I stood among the crowd waiting for the theater to open—youngsters chatting, laughing, sipping beer from cans, here and there someone leaning against a wall with an open book or absorbed in thought, couples embracing at street corners, pale-faced girls who seemed to have stepped out of Romain Rolland's *The Soul Enchanted*.

After the show Hinda announced that we were going to a restaurant to have a proper French meal, to make up to me for having suffered through a 'Jewish meal' at lunch. I declined; I said I had better go to my hotel as I had to get up early. "Nothing opens before ten in this town," Foiglman informed me. "And now the choice is yours, between the 'Meshuggene Ferd' and the 'Meshuggene Faygalakh,'" explaining that the former was the famous night club, 'Crazy Horse'—where you could see magnificent nude shows with 'a cast of a hundred kosher maidens.' The 'Meshuggene Faygalakh' were the Yiddish writers, who were all sorts of crazy birds, and some of whom he wanted me to meet. To please my host, who had been so generous in his hospitality, I chose the birds.

We hailed a taxi and drove to Café Select in Montparnasse where, according to Foiglman, three or four of his companions usually met nightly.

The waiter greeted my hosts as old friends, complimented Hinda on her regal look, made a deep bow when I was introduced, and led us to a table where a single man was sitting in front of a glass of tea, a yeast-cake and a book.

"Please meet Professor Arbel, the famous historian from Israel, whose book, *The Great Betrayal*, was published here in France and received excellent reviews. And this is my friend Mendel Weissbrod, a journalist and writer at *Unzer Vort*. I never miss his satirical columns because each one of them is a *chef d'oeuvre*."

Mendel Weissbrod shook my hand without getting up, and his gloomy face did not light up. He invited us to join him at the table. He had a big head mounted on broad shoulders, a thick nose, lizard-like—like heavy eyelids and deep furrowed cheeks.

All the while Foiglman was telling him about me, about our meeting, about the happiness I brought him with the wonderful things I had written about his poetry, Weissbrod was staring at me with a grim and scrutinizing look. Hinda ordered a carafe of wine, cheese and cold cuts. Weissbrod asked me about people in Israel— journalists, writers, public figures—people he had met here and there, many of whom I did not recognize. He knew about the departments of Yiddish that had opened in two or three universities in Israel, but did not attach much importance to it. He complained about the 'egocentricity' of Yiddish writers in Israel, who in their journals and publications hardly ever include works by their colleagues from other countries, and who assume no responsibility for the state of Yiddish in the Diaspora. The yearly prizes awarded there are given mostly to local residents. Once in a while they deign to give an award to some big shot writer from America in return for donations he helped solicit for some Yiddish institute. "I have written about this several times, but they don't even see fit to reply," he said. A bitter man of about seventy, with profound anguish lodged in his wrinkled cheeks.

In answer to my questions he said he was originally from Warsaw but spent the war years in Kazakhstan, then in Moscow, where he published articles and stories in *Eynikeyt* and *Haymland*. He later returned to Poland, stayed until 1956, published in *Yiddishe Shriftn* and *Folks-Stimme,* then realized there was no future for Jewish life there and came to Paris. "What has been—will never be," he summed up and fell silent.

"After such a dirge—it's mandatory to have a drink!" Hinda was trying to cheer us up, raising her glass. But Weissbrod did not touch his glass. Instead he turned to me and said, "I know Hebrew literature exists in Israel. I have read some of it. You have clubs, 'The Authors' House,' literary cafés where writers gather—but what existed in Warsaw before the war has never existed in Israel, and never will!" And he told us about Tolmackie 13, a house teeming with activity for more than twenty years, where writers and journalists used to meet at all hours of the day and long into the night, and even out-of-towners who could not find lodgings stayed there for the night. On Nalewki Street, a few blocks from there, were the offices of *Moment,* and on nearby Chlodna Street were the offices of *Haynt,* and on Lesnia Street, the actors' club. At any free moment, people would gravitate to Tolmackie 13, to argue, to exchange views, to read to each other from galley proofs right off the press. "It was hot there, steaming! The heartbeat of the Jewish people!"

"Downstairs, on the ground floor, was an inexpensive restaurant where you could always hear sounds of music and a tumult of voices, and where the two waitresses, Manya and Polya, were everyone's friends; they knew everyone's favorite dish and what did not agree with them; they fed the hungry—and many were hungry with not a penny to their name!—and gave credit, never insisting on payment. And the cloakroom attendant, Mrs. Geber, knew everything that went on in the lives of the regulars: who had got married, who divorced, whose work was rejected by an editor, who had been fired, who was nominated for an award, who was panned by the critics... She would pass on this information together with the coats as they were checked in and out... And the literary banquets! The receptions for visiting authors from abroad! The anniversaries! No other people had such a tempestuous literary and cultural life, so full of enthusiasm, exhilaration, and caring as we had in Warsaw!"

Foiglman confirmed all of Weissbrod's assertions. He said how he remembered Tolmackie 13 from his own childhood, since his father used to take him there. It had been one big family. Life didn't really take place in the homes—but there! With the women and the children, the loves and hates, the lovers and mistresses, the affairs and the fights...

"What's left of all that?" Weissbrod turned a bleak gaze at me. "A few troubadours wandering from land to land, singing to empty spaces with the echoes mocking them."

At that moment we were approached by a thin, lanky man with pepper-and-salt hair and a wavy crest cascading on his brow. He wore a red carnation in his lapel and a bright smile on his face. He greeted us all cheerily, shook everybody's hand, kissed Hinda on her cheek, pulled up a chair and asked us what happy occasion we were celebrating.

"A guest from Israel," Foiglman introduced me with all my titles, and him, too, Yossele Haft, who signed his poems with the pen name: Yossele Lav-Davka (not necessarily), "a lyric poet of enormous talent, who, considering his age, has a whole future in front of him."

"Your honor is from Israel?" the poet turned to me brightly and with his hand smoothed back the forelock from his brow, "Good, very good!" With smiling eyes he added, "I see a lot of Israelis here, almost every evening a few of them hang around here. They speak beautiful Hebrew, rolling, rollicking, but for some reason, they never come close to us; they glance at us from a distance, hear us talk in a beggars' tongue, and hasten to pass by as if afraid they'd have to give us alms. So tonight is really cause for celebration! Let's have a toast for our honored guest!" He raised his hand, snapped his fingers at the waiter and ordered cognac for everyone.

"An excellent poet!" Hinda whispered in my ear and added that his poems had been translated into five languages.

Yossele Haft proposed a toast in my honor, took a sip, wiped his mouth with the back of his hand and said, "I have never been to Israel: I'm simply afraid. I say to myself: I'm going to go to Tel Aviv, walk in the streets, and feel a total stranger! To feel oneself a stranger in London or Stockholm—that's fine, it's even an advantage. You say to yourself: All these people around you take everything here for granted, while you, Yossele, are able to see what they don't! I walk around like a swan among ducks. But in Israel? To be a stranger in Israel?!"

"You won't feel a stranger in Israel," Foiglman assured him, "Believe me, they're all circumcised there!"

"You think so, too? I won't feel a stranger?" he smiled at me.

I said that Israel was the only country in the world where if a Jew walks in the street and feels like a stranger, he knows it is not because of how others see him, but because of how he sees himself.

"Yes, yes," he nodded as if considering my words, "yes, yes."

And a moment later, "Very nice what you said. Very nice."

He had a youthful face, although he must have been at least forty-five, and a mischievous smile flickered in his narrow eyes.

"Unfortunately I can't read Hebrew," he said, "But I read some Hebrew poetry in French translation. There's also a small anthology... You have pretty good poetry there...pretty good... I was especially impressed by one poet...Shomron? Hermon?... No...it is a name of a mountain in Israel, but I have forgotten... He writes a little like

Apollinaire...very nice...explosive, tempestuous, with an undercurrent of biblical myth... I was very impressed... I can even remember the opening lines of one of the poems..." and he quoted in French two whole stanzas of the poem, evenly, fluently.

"Bravo! Bravo!" Hinda clapped her hands.

"I couldn't compete with you, Hindele," he flattered her, and to me he said, "Have you heard her reciting Manger?—It's like Yascha Heifetz playing Sarasate!"

"I know whole poems of yours by heart," Hinda said, and having closed her eyes for a moment, started to recite one of his poems in an impassioned voice. It was a love song entitled, *After a Day or Two*. Haft was looking at her affectionately, moving his lips silently with her recital.

"I know them by heart in French, too!" she declared after the three of us had applauded her, and immediately proceeded to recite another poem of his, in French, of many stanzas, each opening with the line, "I see you across the Seine." Soon people from adjacent tables turned to listen, and the waiter, too, came to our table. When she finished, they all showed their appreciation and applauded, and Yossele Haft got up and kissed her on both cheeks and hugged her.

It was about midnight when we left the café. Haft shook my hand and said, "Maybe I will go to Israel, after all. One mustn't be afraid! No, one mustn't!"

Foiglman hailed a cab and the three of us drove to my hotel. During the ride Hinda was wrapped in thought, her face to the window, and did not say a word. Only when they took their leave of me at the hotel entrance, with the cab waiting to take them home, did she kiss me warmly and sadly said that she hoped to see me again.

At eight in the morning, before I went downstairs, Hinda called to say goodbye again. She apologized for her behavior the night before, for her silence from the moment we left the café. She was depressed, she was not sure why. She admonished me, on my next visit to Paris, mine and my wife's, not to look for a hotel, but to be their guests.

Chapter fourteen

Your mother was not a simple woman, Yoav. Her moods were hard to predict. My flight back from Paris was delayed, and it was nine in the evening when I arrived.

Her face was pale, alarmed. "I was frightfully worried! I've been calling El Al since five o'clock. Finally, they said the plane would land at seven. That was two hours ago!"

I told her there had been a delay in the unloading of the luggage, and then I waited for a cab for half an hour.

"I was frightfully worried," she repeated, and the pallor did not fade from her face. "I thought...that perhaps the plane had been hijacked..." She looked at me is if she were feeling my face with her hands. "You must be terribly hungry."

I was not hungry. We had had a light meal on the plane before landing. We sat in the kitchen drinking tea, and I told her about the conference and about meeting Foiglman and his wife.

"Exciting time in Paris," she grinned.

She opened the refrigerator and took out a bowl of mousse with slivers of almonds sprinkled on its whipped-cream topping.

I was surprised. She had never remembered her making chocolate mousse before.

She said that the night before Dr. M. from the Institute had come for a visit. "You met him at the airport when you came to collect me, remember?" Yes, I remembered. She had nothing to offer him, so they had gone to the kitchen and made mousse together. He stayed for four hours. It was almost midnight when he left.

I asked what she had done for ten days. One night she visited with Yoav. One evening she spent with Raya Lubersky, her friend from Jerusalem, and the night before—Dr. M.

"Drank half of our cognac," she laughed.

"The bottle Foiglman gave us..."

"Yes, yes," she said, standing by the sink washing the glasses, and her voice sounded sad.

The ashtray in the living room was full of cigarette butts.

I took out the presents I brought her from Paris. A bottle of perfume, a silk scarf, three pairs of stockings with a pattern of leaves that I had never seen in Israel. "Why? Whatever for?" She laid them on her knees and seemed to study them. Didn't she have time to empty the ashtray? I wondered.

The next day, as soon as she returned from work, in a sudden spurt of energy, she announced that she had decided to make some 'drastic changes' in the apartment. Changes? I was amazed—and it was during my absence that she had come to that decision. She had the whole detailed plan worked out in her head, as if the spirit of Interior Design had possessed her: to knock down the wall between the living room and my study, so as to almost double the size of the living room, while I would move to Yoav's old room; to paint the whole apartment in lighter colors, the bedroom in peach; to change the lampshades... The plan was not at all to my liking. I said I saw no rhyme or reason to it.

She was not deterred by my reaction. With enthusiasm that was totally novel to me—a new, inexplicable spirit seemed to have imbued her in my absence—she enumerated the advantages of the proposed renovations. The living room will cease to be as cheerless and gloomy as it is now; it will be filled with light and air; I will be better insulated in Yoav's old room from noises inside the apartment and outside...

The longer she spoke—out of some strange inner compulsion, as if her life depended upon it—the more entrenched I became in my opposition to this fantastic plan. I told her I was not moving out of my study; I liked it there, I was comfortable there, I was used to it and it was used to me; I was not ready for any sudden upheaval. The remodeling she was suggesting could take months and would completely upset my work and, besides, I saw no reason for all of these changes.

"Tear down walls?" I tried to contain the fury that was rising inside me.

Quietly, but with a marked animosity in her look, she said, "You are a hopeless stick-in-the-mud. And stubborn as a mule to boot. The slightest change in life scares you stiff. Even your mind is atrophied!" And she left the room.

She grabbed a shopping bag and slammed the front door. For two days we did not speak to each other. On the second day, toward evening, she apologized. She said she had been wrong in imputing all those things to me. She could not understand what had possessed her. This whole business with the remodeling was not important. Irrelevant. She suggested we eat out that night, in a Chinese restaurant, if I had no objection. We drove to a restaurant in Jaffa where, she said, she had been with Raya Lubersky. The headwaiter greeted her like an old acquaintance. Toward the end of the meal, with only the wine glasses before us, she told me of a dream she had had when I was abroad. She had driven her car to a strange city full of ancient houses and winding lanes—"like an old German town," parked her car in an empty square, and went to look for the house where the two of us were living. She walked around in the empty town, going from street to street, but could not find the house because she had forgotten its number. Despairing of finding it, she decided to go back to the car, but, when she reached the square, the car had disappeared. How was it possible that both the house and the car had vanished?

she wondered. Then she realized that she was going out of her mind. At the thought that she was crazy, a terrible panic gripped her. She screamed and woke up in terror.

Later, still lying in bed, when she contemplated her dream, she remembered once hearing her father shout at her mother, "Your sister was crazy—and so are you!" There was some skeleton in the family closet, of which she heard only snatches of hints, about an aunt who one night left her home in Munich and drowned herself in the Isar River.

She told me that in her childhood she had lived in constant fear that her father might not come back home. In the evenings she would wait by the gate of their house in Rehovot, watching the street for his approaching car. When time passed and he was late in coming, the anxiety tore inside her and turned into despair. When darkness fell, she was still standing watch by the gate—her eyes popping out as the headlights of every passing car approached, then receded. She muttered to herself, "Father is dead, father is dead," or "Father has abandoned us." And then there were vows, incantations, whispered prayers. Sitting in her room, doing her homework, her ears were constantly strained to hear what was going on in the other rooms, lest her father's outburst at her mother break like a thunderbolt. When her two sisters left home, the pain was like an illness, and she was certain by then that the rift would never be healed.

"I have difficult relations with myself," she said with an anguished smile.

Then she added, "I'm afraid of the stillness within myself. It's an excellent breeding ground for viruses."

And a few moments later, "Sometimes I ask myself how I'm going to leave this life. Clean? Dirty? Completely destitute?"

Chapter fifteen

I hardly go out of the house. Mornings, I go to the grocery store nearby, buy a few provisions, prepare simple meals for myself. I refrain from going to restaurants. About once a fortnight I visit my mother who has been living in a home for the elderly in Gedera for the last five years. And I go to the university twice a week. It is amazing how this realm, which for so many years was a second home to me, is now so alien to me. I give the required amount of lectures, see students in my office, and answer their questions—absent-mindedly, completely absent-mindedly. I think about my life with Nora, I think about Yoav; it's as if I'm burning up inside.

The department secretary knows she should not bother me with unnecessary administrative matters. Once in a while, when I go to the office—to hand in some material for copying, to fill up forms, to sign documents—she asks me how I'm doing, as one inquires of someone sick who has become a burden to the family. My colleagues pass by with bowed heads and strained smiles, muttering greetings, eschewing conversation. There seems to be a general consensus that it is unseemly for people of my sort—whose lives center around intellectual activity—to wallow for so long in grief and dejection over the loss of a wife.

Students' papers pile up on my desk, and I am behind in handing in grades. I know that there are complaints behind my back. I pull out one of the papers, start reading it, turn over a few pages, and then my thoughts drift to other spheres. I feel bad for my students whose progress depends on my output. I am sorry for one student in particular, Gita Jacobovitz, who last year wrote an excellent paper on the *Yevsektsia** and its relations to Zionism in the first years after the revolution, and now... She is the only one of my students this year who does not regard me as merely an issuer of passes from semester to semester, but as a human being. She comes into my office, and before opening her notebook—with a list of questions relating to her present research, the *Bund* and Zionism—gives me an inquiring, hesitant, sympathetic look and says, "Am I disturbing you? If it's inconvenient, I could come another day..."

"Disturbing me? That's why I'm here!"

"I thought... Perhaps you're tired today..." and hesitantly she opens her notebook and reads one of the questions, then listens to my explanation, and when I'm finished, again gives me a quizzical, concerned look, "Shall I go on?"

She is twenty-three, or twenty-four, born in Romania. Her accent, with its rolling Rs, betrays her as a 'newcomer'—only seven years in the country. She has a clear, round face surrounded by an arch of black hair, exuding a kind of motherly benevolence. When she smiles, round dimples appear on her cheeks. She called me at home three or four times with an excuse having to do with the material she was collecting; but when she heard my answer she said, "Is there anything I can do to help you, Professor?"

"Help me?" I laugh.

"You devote so much time to me...I feel I ought to do something for you..."

"What could you possibly do for me?"

"Look up some material in the library for you, copy some-

---

* *Yevsektsia*—the Jewish section of the Communist Party in Soviet Russia

thing…I can type…" Her voice is soft, a little chirpy. I thank her. I am grateful to her.

I invited her over once. She brought me a bouquet of red carnations. She found a vase in the living room, filled it with water in the kitchen, and put in the flowers. She sat facing me in my study, listening to me lecture on the subject of Jewish parties within the Pale of Settlement in Russia. She listened with the tip of her pencil between her lips and her green eyes fixed on me in an expression of approval and affection. When I finished, she said, "You know, my parents were born in Kishinev*…" and she told me that, during the war, her parents were in the camps in Transnistria, and when the Soviet Union annexed the region, they moved to Romania. She herself was born in Bucharest.

As often happens when people recount their history or their parents' history during the war in Europe, a cloud descends on me for a brief moment and a dark and narrow corridor seems to open into those dismal, sinister days.

"You have such a terribly melancholy look." She smiled, and the two little dimples gleamed in her cheeks.

When she got up to leave, she bade me goodbye with a light tap, as if in encouragement, on my arm. Such an unusual gesture on the part of a young student to a much older teacher.

⁂

Leafing through some documents I had used in writing my paper 'Controversy and Resolution'—in particular, Jacob Sasportas's *Zizat Novel Zvi*, Jacob Emden's *Sefat Emet Ulshon Zehorit* and *Va-Avo Ha-yom el Ha-ayin*, attributed to Rabbi Jonathan Eybeschuetz, of which I have a facsimile—I was once more filled with amazement, astonishment and marvel at the breadth and depth of the 'universal' unity of Jewish life in the Diaspora in the seventeenth and eighteenth centuries.

The Shabbetaian movement and the controversy it had

* Kishinev—the city in Bessarabia in which the infamous pogrom of 1903 took place.

generated, which lasted a hundred and fifty years, embroiled the entire Diaspora and shook it like a powerful earthquake, from Izmir to London, from Jerusalem to Amsterdam, from Salonika to Hamburg, from Krakow to Fez, from Zhitomir to Prague. And it all happened in the days when communication between countries and cities was primitive, before trains, automobiles, telephones, and telegraphs; before the Jewish press had come into being, except for two irregular newsletters published in Amsterdam, one in Portuguese and one in Yiddish. Had there been a popular, widely circulated press in the second half of the eighteenth century, with news agencies and correspondents stationed all over Europe, Africa and Asia, one can assume that the Emden-Eybeschuetz controversy, which had all the ingredients of a major scandal, would have produced such sensationalist headlines as: "Secret Shabbetaian messages found in amulets distributed by Rabbi Eybeschuetz among childless women," or "Emden accuses Eybeschuetz of disseminating Shabbatean propaganda at the Pressburg Yeshivah," or "Eybeschuetz's youngest son revealed as a crypto-Christian," or "Eybeschuetz calls Emden's allegations "libel and signs the *herem* on the Shabbetaians," etc, etc. The amazing thing is that, despite the lack of mass media at a time when news and polemic literature were delivered from town to town, from country to country, by messengers riding in coaches and carriages, carrying with them epistles and books written in the lingua franca of Diaspora rabbis—a mixture of Hebrew, Aramaic and Yiddish—the entire Jewish nation was shaken to its foundation by a controversy between two rabbis of one community—Altona near Hamburg. Jewry then proved itself to be one unified body, whose every limb and sinew is interconnected, to such an extent that, when a nerve in one finger is injured, the entire body is alerted to immunize itself against the infection. We are witness here to a unique historical phenomenon—a sort of 'para-territorial state,' extending over three continents; for it was not only common religion, rituals, customs, and the fate of a persecuted minority that unified the disparate Jewish sections, but also a superstructure comprising an elaborate system of organized interconnected communities. Thus, even a small community such as Zamosc, numbering only several hundred families, was ripped apart by the controversy of the Altona rabbis and reverberated with its thunderous echoes. It produced one courageous and fanatic detractor of Eybeschuetz, Rabbi Abraham Cohen, who took his stand against the majority of Polish rabbis who supported Emden's adversary.

But, as I contended in *Controversy and Resolution,* the Shabbetaian controversy, both during Shabbetai Zvi's life and after his apostasy and death, was not merely a theological-intellectual struggle between rationalism and the delusions of mysticism, between the sovereignty of the *Halacha* and antinomian messianism, but more profoundly (and covertly) it was also a struggle for the very existence of the autonomous structure of the Diaspora. Had the Shabbetaian movement won—with its attempt to divert Jewry beyond the confines of the Diaspora—it would have dismantled the instruments of that autonomy and wiped it out completely. Hence, we have here the kind of warfare waged by a governing authority of a state against the subversive elements intent on undermining it. This is why the struggle was so ruthless and uncompromising, involving extreme measures such as ostracism and excommunication, expulsion, vilification, forgery and false accusations. They even went so far as to ask for outside intervention from the Christian world, appealing to Frederick the First, king of Denmark, heir to the Duchy of Holstein, to remove Rabbi Jonathan Eybeschuetz from his position as rabbi of Altona when the amulets, with alleged Shabbetaian formulas, were discovered. The king appointed a commission of inquiry, comprised of Christian theologians, proficient in Hebrew, among them the Protestant scholar Friedrich Megerlin to decide what was true and what false in the charges against the Jewish rabbi. It was a defensive war on the part of Diaspora Jewry to maintain its existence as a viable entity, with its sovereign authority, and to guarantee its right to exist as a permanent structure. And, at the same time, a recurrent phenomenon of Jewish history manifests itself again: wars between the powers and upheavals in governments give rise to persecutions, restrictive laws, and pogroms. When a war breaks out between Prussia, under Frederick the Great—in alliance with France—and with Austria under Maria Theresa, and the Austrians lose Prague, the Jews are accused of treason, and Rabbi Jonathan Eybeschuetz, the rabbi of

Metz at this time, is charged with having secretly conspired with the Prussian-French enemy. The rabble launches a massacre of the Jews of Moravia and Bohemia, Empress Maria Theresa issues expulsion orders to all the Jews of these two crown-states, the expulsion is carried out with extreme brutality, Jewish property is looted, exorbitant fines and taxes are imposed on the other communities, and so on.

More than any other inter-communal event, more than the verbal polemics between the warring camps among the Jews at that period, it is the controversial figure of Rabbi Jonathan Eybeschuetz— as I demonstrate in my work—that epitomizes the clash between two conflicting perceptions of the exile as either a temporary or perpetual state. Scholars in the last few generations are divided as to whether Eybeschuetz was, in fact, a crypto-Shabbetaian, as Emden and most of the rabbis of Germany claimed, or whether he was a faithful adherent of the enemies of Shabbetaianism, as is attested by his declarations and by the fact that he signed the proclamation of excommunication in Prague. Not holding with either interpretation, I maintain that the titanic moral conflict was raging inside his soul—and therein lies the greatness of this genius. On the one hand, his exegeses of the *Shulhan Aruch* and of the commentary of Maimonides reveal extreme conservatism and adherence to the letter of the sacred *Halacha,* (interestingly enough, it was his nemesis, Jacob Emden, who displayed more 'liberal' attitudes in rulings that deviated from the *Shulhan Aruch,* as well as in permitting the study of foreign languages and sciences—an attitude typical of a man free of moral conflicts that undermine self-confidence); and on the other hand, Eybeschuetz's theological-Kabbalistic book, *Shem Olam,* dealing with the godhead and its attributes, (which, unlike Graetz, Perlmutter and Scholem, I do not believe was written by him, despite its resemblance to the Shabbetaian *Va-Avo Ha-Yom El Ha-Ayin*) reflects a quasi-messianic conception which allows for the revelation of a tripartite divinity and its incarnation in a human redeemer (a conception close to Christian doctrine, which was indeed why Eybeschuetz was accused of having such tendencies). Such a conviction, by its very nature, negates the permanence of exilic existence.

At all events, this bitter, virulent dispute, which shook Diaspora Jewry to its very foundations even a hundred years after Shab-betai Zvi's death in 1676—despite all the divisions it brought in its wake—still bears far greater testimony to its 'universal' unity. The forgers of the *Protocols of the Elders of Zion* at the beginning of this century, who imputed to the Jews a conspiracy to take over the world did, after all, have a certain historical, factual element to base their false allegations upon.

Chapter sixteen

Nora never mentioned the 'drastic changes' in the apartment again. But one day, without consulting me, she changed the lampshades in the living room. I did not say anything.

I was now about to fulfill my promise to Foiglman concerning the translation of his poems into Hebrew. However, I had no experience in this area, so I talked to Professor L. and he recommended four translators. I called one of them, Shalom Hochman. He told me on the phone he had never heard of a poet by the name of Foiglman, but if I sent him the book, he would read it and see if the poems were to his liking. He refused to translate poems that had no merit in his eyes.

I sent him the book. Two weeks later, he called me back. "No, unfortunately the answer is no." A few of the poems "had something in them," but on the whole he found them, 'epigonic.' He would send the book back to me.

I felt bitterly disappointed at hearing them branded inferior imitations; it was as if the poems were my own. The second translator I approached was someone called Yehiel Brotzky. He, too, said: "I'll read them first before I decide."

Two weeks passed, then three; every day I would check my mailbox to see if he had written me or—worse—sent back the book. After a month I called him and asked about the poetry book I had sent him. At first he had no idea what I was talking about, then he said, "Oh, that French poet, yes, now I remember… I'll tell you the truth, I'm in the midst of translating a big book, a novel, and I can't tell you when I'll have the time…at any rate not for a year." He promised to return the book.

Another two weeks passed, and I still had not received the book. When I called him, he cried in amazement, "What? You haven't received it? I sent it a long time ago! The same day, I think." And he blamed the delay on the vagaries of Israeli mail service.

The next day he called me. He apologized and said he had erred and misled me. He had asked his wife to mail the book that very same day, but she had apparently neglected to do so. The trouble was, he could not find the book. He had looked in his library and did not find it. Somebody must have borrowed it. I was very annoyed and told him the book was valuable to me, it was dedicated to me by the poet, and I demanded it back. "It will be found, I'm sure…" he muttered. I warned him, I threatened him…Two days later the book was delivered to my house.

The third translator on the list was Menachem Zelniker.

A few days after receiving the book he called me up and said, "Okay, we can talk." We arranged to meet in a small café on Arlozoroff Street. Zelniker, who had arrived before me, was waiting there with Foiglman's book lying in front of him. He was a man of about fifty or sixty, with black hair, mottled with silver and parted in the middle into two waves, and bushy eyebrows overhanging his glasses. I ordered tea, and he put a caressing hand on the book and said, "Fine, fine." He wanted to know about the connection between the author and me. He opened the book, leafed through and scanned some of the poems. "A bit maudlin here and there…but no wonder. The man lived though Majdanek and Kungskirchen and Auschwitz… When I read such poetry, I dare not judge it with the usual criteria of literary criticism. They transcend it, they are beyond criticism." He lingered on one page, pointing a finger at the title of the poem *Grass* and said, "Very powerful, very powerful."

He closed the book, set it aside and planted both arms on the table in the manner of a man of business. "Well, let's turn from the sacred to the profane," he said. "As I told you on the phone, I am willing to undertake the translation." Then he wanted to know what the deadline was, who was going to pay, and how.

I had no experience in such matters. When my two books, *The Great Betrayal* and *Controversy and Resolution* were published in Hebrew, I had very little to do with it. I signed contracts without paying much attention to their clauses and then read the galleys. The translation of the first book into French was undertaken by the publisher and I had no part in it. Thus, I responded to Zelniker's first question by saying that there was no urgency, and that I assumed six months would be adequate time to complete the translation. As for the payment, I asked him how much money he would require and Zelniker mentioned a sum equal to two months of my salary, which I found reasonable, perhaps even too modest.

"As for the payment arrangements," Zelniker said, "it is customary to pay a third in advance, a third in the middle, and a third upon completion of the work. Is it the author himself who is paying? Is he sending the money from France?"

I wondered at myself for not having thought of all these matters beforehand. And since the whole translation business was merely a wish when Foiglman brought it up, I had not asked him for any practical details concerning such an undertaking. After deliberating for a moment I decided to pay the advance on the translation from my own pocket, as a loan I might make to a friend, so that the work might start.

"Fine," Zelniker said, "and now about the contract. We need a written contract. How do we go about it? Is the agreement between me and him? Me and you? Are you his representative? Do you have power of attorney?"

I laughed and said, "I haven't thought of it."

Zelniker laughed, too. He evidently regarded me as an 'effete intellectual' ignorant of practical matters. We eventually agreed to write a simple memorandum with three or four clauses that I would sign on behalf of the author. Zelniker was an easy-going fellow, with a soft voice and kind eyes. "You are a well-known man, a university professor, and I believe you," he said.

I took out two sheets of paper from my briefcase. We wrote the memorandum in duplicate, and we signed it. I took out my checkbook and wrote him a check for a third of his remuneration and we shook hands.

Joy filled my heart when I went out into the street. I felt as if I were the poet, I was Foiglman, and I was walking on air. It was as if the whole weight of my scholarship was lifted from me, the burden of sitting at my workbench, tied down in one place, my head buried in books. The poems themselves seemed to have taken over my whole being. Lighthearted, folksy Yiddish verses rang inside me. I was Daedalus, with the pair of wings glued to his body, escaping from the labyrinth he had built to imprison himself.

That same day I wrote him a little epistle apprising him of the good news that his dream was about to come true. I did not mention any financial matters. A week later I received a cable saying: "Thousand thanks. Warm kisses from Hinda and me."

Nora, who had seen the cable before I did—it had come in my absence—asked what the 'thousand thanks' were for. I told her how I tried to engage translators, and how I finally found one who was willing to undertake the job.

She was silent.

"Do you have any objection?" I asked.

She looked at me. "So you went from one to the other and begged them…you simply begged…"

Then she got up and said she was going to Yoav. She came back around midnight.

Chapter seventeen

Y ou, Yoav, if the truth be told, never had any respect for my occupation.

"Why do you always have to deal with those rabbis?" you would ask at dinner, between one spoonful of soup and the next; you, still in high school, sneaking a curious and amused look at me to see how I would react. But the truth is, my answer did not really interest you. You always hastened to finish dinner and go out.

'Rabbis'—because I was then studying the Shabbetaian movement, and you, when you walked into my study, always in a great hurry, looking for a fountain pen, paper clips, transparent tape, messing up my desk—the names of those 'rabbis' would leap at you out of my papers. When asked about your father's profession, you used to say, "He works in the Rabbinate." You always had a sense of humor.

I tried to arouse your curiosity about Jewish history, a subject you 'hated' at school, so you claimed, by introducing you to novels of suspense and action. I brought you the same books that used to excite me when I was your age—*The Witch of Castille*, *The Jew Suess* and *Under the Gallows*—but you would take one look at them, scan the first lines, look at me playfully as if to say, You must be kidding, and hand me back the book as if I had offered you tainted food.

From my study I would sometimes overhear your mother moralizing with you, "Why do you aggravate your daddy like that? Can't you see that your attitude depresses him?"

"I'm depressing him? His line of work depresses him! He found himself an occupation that can only make you cry!"

But, in fact, your mother saw eye to eye with you. She, too, had no affinity for the subjects of my study, although she held my work in great regard and was proud of my achievements, as a teacher as well as an author. I did not hold it against her. Nor was I very interested in her biological experiments. I used to drive her to the Institute, pull up by the gate, give her a kiss, and then return to Tel Aviv, to the university. Alternatively, she would drive me to the university, kiss me at the gate, and drive to the Institute; those hasty kisses being, as it were, the only points of contact between our two professions: history and biology.

In fact, there was so much hostility in you toward my field of study that you avoided my room as much as possible. When you needed a reference book, you would hastily grab it from the shelf and flee, as if you were afraid you might catch a disease. When I was awarded a prize for 'Controversy and Resolution,' you refused to accompany your mother to the ceremony. There was a broadcast of the basketball game between Maccabee Tel Aviv and an Italian team on television that evening. The European Cup, if I am not mistaken. To this day my heart is heavy when I think about it.

Yes, you did read *The Great Betrayal.* You said you found it fascinating. But by then you were an officer in the regular army, and you probably found it fascinating because of the din of 'military movements' that fills the book: descriptions of the marches of Chmielnicki's rebels in Volhynia, White Russia and Ukraine; the raids of bands of Hajdamaks and Zaporozhyes; treaties with kings, princes and bishops that were made and broken. The names of 'rabbis' were scattered sparsely among the names of Tartar leaders such as Morzhenko, Genia, Chodki, or the names of Polish kings and noblemen such as Potocki, Wisniowiecki, Kazimierz, Wladyslaw. Only in the last part of the book, which describes the details of that bloodbath in which six hundred thousand Jews were massacred and hundreds of communities were destroyed, do the names of the rabbis cluster and huddle together, driving out the foreign names.

But even then, you found your hostility—the fundamental, deep-seated, hostility from early childhood—hard to conceal. By now it had assumed the guise (or should I say the uniform?) of a respectable, intellectual opposition, a matter of principle, so to speak. A little exaggerated, too, (don't you think?) to my views as they were expounded in that book. "No alternative?" you protested angrily, anger that amazed me, because after all, you never showed much interest in those problems. "There was an alternative! Who betrayed whom? The Poles betrayed the Jews? The Jews betrayed themselves! That was the 'Great Betrayal!'"

You said this despite all my explanations of the conditions of the Jews at that period, that they had no choice, yes, I must stress this again. They had no alternative but to rely on the patronage of those in power, because they had no 'territorial basis' for any mode of independence, let alone for amassing arms or organizing for self defense. But you pooh-poohed all my explanations and launched on a 'system analysis' as if this were an officers' training course. Chmielnicki's rebel army was divided and split up from within—as you had gathered from my book—so armed Jewish organizations could have found allies among the Russians, Prussians and Swedes who were also fighting against the Cossacks...

The army slang you were using in discussing the pogroms sent shivers down my spine. It was as if a bareheaded ragamuffin had burst into the synagogue in the middle of Yom Kippur prayers. You walked to and fro in the room, in your officer's uniform, excited, emphasizing your arguments by gesticulating with your hands. When you realized—apparently from the flabbergasted expression on my face—that you had gone too far in your overzealous attack on me and my ideas, with a condescending smile, as if you were more mature and experienced than me, you said good humouredly, "Okay, Dad, stick to your guns. After all, you academics first develop a theory and then arrange the facts around it, in circles, to keep it from breaking away; and if the facts don't fit the theory precisely, then you bend them a little, here and there... Why should I waste my breath? I know you won't budge an inch from your position! It's a lost cause!" You chuckled and patted me on the back.

But you also had another period. A period of calm. When you got married and started a family. I remember, and tears fill my eyes. Is it a sign of old age? Of the solitude I live in? Your wedding party in Beer Tuvia. I remember that all your harshness toward me melted away, vanished completely. You took my arm and led me. There were red and green light bulbs threaded among the trees; on the lawn someone was playing the guitar, surrounded by a large group of village youth singing folk songs. The summer air was redolent with the scent of oleander mixed with the smell of manure from the cowshed—and you led me from person to person, introduced me to your friends from the army, your commanders. You were proud of me, praised me, even mentioned the books I published, the two awards I had received. "My dad is a great man!" you said, good humouredly and with deep affection, when you presented me, hugging my shoulder, to a certain colonel, bald and pudgy, who looked up at me with an inquisitive smile, "versed in all the military moves of the Thirty Years' War!" And you threaded your way through the dense crowd to the other end of the lawn in order to introduce me to a woman soldier who had told you that her sister was a student of mine and 'admired' me...

And I am reminded of the wonderful days after the wedding, when the four of us, your mother and I, Shula and you, ran all over the town and its suburbs, looking for an apartment for you—driving from address to address, climbing up stairs, looking at rooms, arguing with landlords, with realtors—and Shula, yes Shula, the girl from a *moshav,* proved more practical than the three of us: she knew how to bargain, how to expose defects, how to insist on details that we were not even aware of. And I remember how the two of us, you and I, used to sit up at night, shoulder to shoulder—after you had already bought the house in Ramat Efal—calculating property taxes, mortgage rates, interest, and to your great astonishment, you discovered that your father's head was not always hovering among the somber clouds of Jewish history, but that he knew a thing or two about the affairs of this world.

I remember the many evenings we spent in your house babysitting, when Sarit was born; sometimes your mother went by herself, sometimes I did, playing with the child until she fell asleep.

That was a wonderful period. Our disputes over, we again became a close-knit family. Saturday afternoon visits, a grandchild on my lap, tea and cookies, discussions about price hikes and politics and military affairs.

You did not neglect—or was it Shula who reminded you? Was it at her instigation?—to send me flowers on my birthdays with cordial wishes. And I found it really touching when, in the middle of the Lebanon war, you called me from Sidon—with the hubbub of the command room in the background—to wish me a happy birthday. But then suddenly, the way you changed the moment you sensed the rift between your mother and me. It's beyond my comprehension, to this day, what made you decide, without knowing the reason, that your mother was right, and what made you side with her. Then came your silences. You used to come to our house, with Shula and the child, to demonstrate your hostility to me. You avoided looking me in the eye, you hardly bothered to answer my questions, and you deliberately prolonged your exchanges with your mother by joking or getting excited over something trivial. Banishing the criminal. What was my crime, Yoav?

You met the Yiddish poet only once. He spoke to you from his heart. He looked up to you admiringly, and you kept quiet. You knew nothing about the nature of the relationship between us.

And you knew nothing about what happened during the ten days that I spent with him in our house when Nora was in Jerusalem. Your mother was not a simple woman, Yoav. I doubt that you understood her. Underneath, within her soul, strange things were taking place. In darkness. Did you know that sometimes, in the middle of the night, she would shout in German in her sleep?

What are you punishing me for, Yoav?

Chapter eighteen

The three translators I approached, or perhaps it was only Menachem Zelniker, must have told the Yiddish writers in town that Professor Zvi Arbel of the university had become a 'repentant,' a devotee of their cause, even considering himself a patron of poets writing in that abused language. Shortly after I signed the memorandum with Zelniker, I began receiving various Yiddish publications and periodicals in the mail and the occasional green slip, which meant a parcel was waiting for me at the post office. They turned out to be books inscribed to me by the authors. Nora laughed at the sight of this abundance showered on my head, "Those missionaries are taking you under their wing! Beware of their bear hug!"

As I had no time to read those publications, I would quickly skim over the journals and throw them in the trash. I put the books on a shelf with other useless publications. I did not even bother to thank the authors. But one day I found an invitation in my mailbox to a literary evening at the museum, in honor of the poet Herz Sharfstein's seventy-fifth birthday. Out of curiosity I decided to go. It was a revelation.

To my great astonishment, the hall was full to capacity. I even had trouble finding a seat in the back rows. I looked at the audience, several hundred men and women, most of them elderly, and could not find one familiar face among them. A festive hubbub pervaded the hall, and the Yiddish sentences bandied about from person to person, from seat to seat, excitedly, joyfully, invested the gathering with the atmosphere of a townspeople's reunion after a long separation. So numerous are the devotees of Yiddish poetry in this town—I marveled as I looked around at the audience—and I had no idea!

Up on the stage, behind a long table covered with a green tablecloth and a vase of gorgeous gladioli, sat a battery of nine dignitaries, flanking on both sides the guest of honor—a broad-shouldered, stern-faced man, with a knoblike protrudence on the left side of his bald head, and squinting eyes behind glittering glasses. He sat, as if in a straitjacket, in his blue suit, his head sunk between his shoulders, gazing indifferently at the audience. Next to him sat a long-faced man whose head shook incessantly. In the corner of the stage stood a grand piano.

Silence fell as the chairman approached the microphone—a tall, imposing man with a shock of white hair and a high forehead that made him look like a philosopher. He opened his speech with brief congratulations to the guest of honor, and concluded by reading one of his poems. When he sat down, a singer came on the stage and was greeted by applause. She wore a black evening gown adorned with a string of pearls. Her face was not young, but her jet-black hair, gathered behind, made her look years younger. The piano sounded the opening chord, and her voice rose gradually as she sang Sutzkever's song, *Unter Dayne Vayse Shtern*—Under Your White Stars. The tender, delicate notes—adagio, dolce-ascended yearning, then descended imploring, fluttered like broken-winged birds, cast their spell on the audience, which held its breath, completely enthralled. Many had tears in their eyes.

She sang three more songs. I recognized two of the tunes: *Oyfn Veg Shteyt a Boym* by Itzik Manger and *Reyzele* by Gebirtig; you could feel a tremor shooting through the entire audience at the sound of the music and lyrics, a tremor of longing, of shared memories, of the brotherhood of a large, bereaved family whose house lies in ruins. The mellifluous voice of the singer, plaintive, yearning, outpouring, languishing, containing its anguish—resuscitated for a moment a world that was forever gone. Gripped by a tremor sending shivers down my spine, I seemed to say to myself that that was the 'historical tremor of the Jewish people,' whose suffering knows no end.

A reader, who looked about sixty, with an emaciated, tormented face, approached the microphone and read two poems by Herz Sharfstein, *Beggar King* and *Even Now, in These Days* in an emotional, tremulous voice, but with excellent diction, as if he were etching each word with a chisel, stressing each metric foot precisely and succinctly. Then, one after the other, five speakers praised the guest of honor and extolled his achievements. They spoke about the 'broad diapason' of subjects and motifs in his poetry, which spanned more than fifty years and included intimate lyrical poems, narrative-epic poems, symbolic poems and quasi-polemic poems, poems of love and hope and poems of anguish and desperation. One of the speakers said that Sharfstein's poems consisted of *benchen un krekhtzen* blessings and sighs, whose vocabulary is simple, the language of simple folk, but at the same time charged with profound symbolism hewn from the quarry of his heart. Another speaker, (who spoke for so long that the chairman's face reflected his impatience, and he passed a note to the man on his right) discussed Sharfstein's tremendous contribution to Yiddish culture in general, and said that his poems, which spanned the whole spectrum from the epic and concrete to the abstract and symbolic, were enduring literary assets epitomizing Jewish existence both in the Diaspora and in Israel. He bitterly deplored the fact that so few of Sharfstein's poems had been translated into Hebrew. The audience listened attentively to the speakers, without fidgeting or coughing or clearing their throats. And I, who had never read any of the guest of honor's poems, wondered about all those hyperbolic praises that were heaped on his head, the like of which I had never heard in any ceremony honoring a Hebrew writer, scholar or scientist.

Sharfstein himself, however, received the compliments with complete indifference. Not once did he smile, nor did a flicker of joy or gratitude light up his face. Rather, he seemed to listen to it with hostility. When the speakers had finished and he was called upon to respond—he got up on his feet to applause from the audience—and approached the microphone with measured steps. He tried to adjust it to his height, turning it this way and that, but to no avail. The chairman hastened to offer his assistance, but he, too, was unsuccessful, and the mike slipped from his hand. An agile man, with a shock of black curls, jumped the front rows onto the stage and quickly fixed the mike.

In two or three sentences Sharfstein thanked the organizers and his well wishers, and added, eliciting laughter from the audience, that the praise had been "above his head" just like the microphone, "and you've just seen what a hard time I have with such heights." Then he launched into a speech that lasted about half an hour; but he did not discuss himself or his poetry, but rather the state of Yiddish in general, in Israel and in the world. First he delineated the 'geography' of this 'universal language,' and showed how, in the last few generations, its center shifted from city to city: from Odessa to Warsaw, from Warsaw to Vilna, from there to New York, and since the establishment of the State of Israel—to Tel Aviv. But at the same time, hectic activity is taking place in the 'provinces' that stretch from Melbourne to Buenos Aires. Then he mourned the destruction of European Jewry and said—his voice becoming hoarse, choking a little, but in a moment clearing up and gathering force—that when the six million were murdered, their thousand-year-old tongue was cut off, too, its treasures turned to ashes, and its heart stopped beating. But did it really stop?—he asked and replied. No! Like the concentration camp survivors, so the language slowly rallied and came to life; like them she tossed on rough seas until she reached the shores of countries where Jews were living, and the shores of *Eretz Yisrael*. And having mentioned the 'Fatherland' he reviewed the 'bitter and ugly battle' that Yiddish was forced to fight here, in Israel. With an expression of revulsion and defiance on his face, he related the story of the 'dispute of the languages' in the twenties and thirties, naming those who 'hit and battered her till she bled,' among them noted leaders, and on the other hand—those who took up the cudgels for her: Bialik, Agnon, Fichman, Uri Zvi Greenberg, to whom we owe a debt of gratitude…

At that point, in the middle of his talk, a minor incident occurred. Someone from the audience hurled at him, "We don't owe them any gratitude!" And from another corner of the hall someone else shouted, "Where are they all? Why don't we see them here?" Sharfstein was taken aback; he turned red as if struck by a stone, but quickly regained his composure, grabbed the microphone and turned to the unidentified heckler and said, "Are you asking me, dear comrade?" The man got up and shouted angrily, "I'm asking the esteemed gentlemen at the podium, the honorable chairman and the organizers of this evening, why hasn't even one member of the Hebrew Writers' Union come here tonight to congratulate such an important poet? Why no representative of the Ministry of Culture and Education? We're excommunicated in this country!" His words were greeted by applause from all directions. The chairman pounded several times with his gavel, then got up and quietly said, without the microphone, his voice barely audible, that all those mentioned had indeed been invited, and if they chose not to come, the organizers were not to blame. He requested that the audience show respect for the guest of honor by letting him continue his talk. One woman shouted from her seat, "Shame and disgrace! Not only on the stage, but here in the hall, too, you won't find one single Hebraist!" Hundreds of heads turned left, right and back, looking for the one 'Hebraist' as if his brow were branded by a mark. In the midst of the whispering and grumbling I thought for a moment that their eyes were directed at me. The chairman banged again with his gavel, and when silence fell, the speaker resumed his speech.

By way of responding to the hecklers and grumblers, he said that for a sick person, despair is the greatest enemy, and one should not ignore the silver lining. After all, in the last thirty years there has been a 'significant change' in the attitude toward Yiddish in Israel; Yiddish has acquired legitimacy, popularity even, among speakers of Hebrew—as can be attested to by the number of songs and musicals, and by the fact that Yiddish is taught in forty schools and in five universities; everywhere one can see signs of a comeback, of renaissance: one hundred and forty Yiddish writers, journalists and publicists live in Israel, there are twelve newspapers and important periodicals, and three publishers...

"I shall not die, but live!" he raised his voice dramatically, and concluded his talk with the verse, "The Lord hath chastened me sore: but He has not given me over unto death." The audience rose to its feet in a thunderous standing ovation.

The singer reappeared on the stage and a complete silence prevailed in the hall; in that silence the sounds of Gebirtig's "Our Town is Burning" quivered like an anguished cry, like a smothered shriek; and then, with the courage of desperate fighters, the notes of Glick's "Partisan's Song" throbbed in the air. Again a tremor went through the audience, an electrifying, unifying tremor, as if, en masse, it was on the verge of tears.

From the start of the evening, and increasingly as it progressed, I was filled with an emotion—unlike anything I had experienced at other gatherings—that this congregation, melded together by shared memories, language, suffering, hopes and bitter disappointments, united in one tremor, one heartbeat—was, in fact, the 'Jewish people' of which I read and write and which I have known so well for so many years. Nowhere else in Israel, when in a large crowd of people, had I found such homogeneity, a homogeneity of physiognomy, attire, manner of speech and gesture—the kind one finds among people of the same ethnic group, be they English, Swedish, Hungarian, Polish, etc. And though I myself was not of this congregation, after all, I had stumbled in accidentally, almost gate-crashing, sitting there like an outside observer, and although their tongue was not my tongue, my personal biography was different from theirs, and I had no friend or acquaintance among them—yet I had the distinct feeling of being at home with my own folk: the agitation that permeated me, the sorrow, the pain, the yearning, were flowing from the audience to me and from me back to them. And although I was well aware all the while that that crowd was only one part of our people—a people made up of other large and varied tribes, yet all sons of our motherland, builders of the national home where I live—in their midst I felt the warmth of familial intimacy the like of which I had never felt anywhere else. Moreover, it was coupled with a feeling of respect and admiration for the courage and persistence of this aging flock, clinging for dear life, like an isolated and besieged army unit guarding the last outpost of their language and culture, fully determined to defend them to their last breath.

The audience left the hall with a subdued commotion, obviously still enthralled by the magic of the melancholy, wistful and exhilarating songs that had just ended.

When I reached home I found Nora watching television. "How was it?" She got up and turned it off. I sank in my armchair—still agitated—and said nothing. "Did anything happen?" she looked at me, concerned.

When I told her what had transpired at the meeting and the emotions I experienced, she remained quiet. A few days later I bought a new album of Yiddish songs. When I played it in the living room, Nora stormed into the room from the kitchen, her hands on her ears, and shouted, "Stop this mawkishness! It's driving me crazy!" She rushed to the record player and took the needle off the record.

Chapter nineteen

Otto, Nora's father, died of a heart attack—nine years before these events—in a hotel in Cologne, where he had gone on a business trip. His body was shipped to Israel and he was buried in Rehovot.

For weeks after his death, Nora fell into a deep depression; at night, when I woke up, I would find her lying awake, her eyes open. When I pleaded with her to tell me what it was that was troubling her, she revealed her guilt feelings as a daughter. She said her father had suffered from a lack of love all his life. His wife and her sisters had deprived him of affection, they never supported him, never indulged or pampered him; he was 'surrounded by darkness.' When I remarked that he himself was a difficult, self-centered man, incapable of showing love, she said it was true, but that that caused him the most pain. "He locked himself up in a solitary cell. Do you know how agonizing that is? You could hear him banging the walls with his fists!" I said that no one should be blamed for that, not him, and certainly not his family. It had to do with his character. Yes, she said, it's the inescapable burden of one's own character that's the hardest to endure. "To think that a person can live his whole life in a darkness of his own making without seeing the light!"

Nora said she would remember little things from her childhood, from her youth, that were painful for him, and said that had she acted differently, everything would have changed. Had she asked him to take her to the beach on Saturday morning, they would have spent more time together swimming and playing in the sand; had she walked into his study only once—when she was fourteen or fifteen—to ask him about the buildings he was designing, to praise his work, to congratulate him on his success; had she and her sisters given him a surprise party for his birthday, which was never celebrated; had we taken him along on our trip to the Sea of Galilee and Safed after our wedding; had only she shown him some warmth, some warmth…

His heart had been ailing long before the stroke, she was certain, but he never told anybody. Whom could he tell? What for? Nobody would have shown him any sympathy or affection anyway. His heart got sick because it could no longer stand the accumulating pressure that mounted from year to year. He harbored it inside until his heart burst. "Father died alone, just as he had lived; alone, always in a foreign country."

The deterioration in her mother's condition began two years before his death. The exaggerated amount of make-up she put on aroused pity in those who knew her and derision in strangers. Blue and green were smeared so thickly on her eyelids and around her eyes that the eyes themselves looked sunken in darkness. She dressed in diaphanous black, brown and purple muslin gowns that had gone out of fashion dozens of years earlier. In the evenings she would spend long hours in a small café on a side street, the haunt of "unsavory characters." She would sit there by herself smoking, drinking coffee until closing time. Rumor had it that she participated in spiritualist séances, conjuring up the spirits of her relatives who had perished in Europe. Another rumor—which Nora refused to credit—had it that she had a long-time lover, the owner of a taxi fleet, a heavy-set and callous man.

Nora used to visit her mother quite often, after work at the Institute, short visits that left her shaken and perturbed when she came home. "She is destroying me. She is destroying herself—and she'll destroy me."

One Saturday we went together to visit her parents and found only Susie at home. I was shocked to see her emaciated face; the heavy rouge on the sunken cheeks only made her uglier. For the entire time we sat with her she talked about Yemenites. "Princes," she called them jokingly, "the illegitimate offspring of King Solomon and the Queen of Sheba." In their males, she claimed, you find the perfect fusion of strength and tenderness, of chivalry and sensitivity, of cunning and good nature, and what she loved about them most of all, "their sense of mystery."

"They possess secrets that we don't know," she raised a finger at us, narrowing her eyes in a mysterious expression, "ancient secrets that only they know the winding, narrow paths to. What we try to understand with our minds, they grasp with their senses. They flirt with Lilith," she chuckled.

When we came out Nora said, "She's gone completely off the rails." After Otto's death Susie took to drinking. All of Nora's efforts to dissuade her were in vain. Every time we came to see her she reeked of alcohol, and there would be a bottle of cognac or whisky standing on the sideboard. Before we even sat down, she would pour herself and us a drink. Nora tried to pry the bottle out of her hand and screamed that she was killing herself with drinking, but her mother, who had been soused before our arrival, looked at her with burning hatred and said, "Speak for yourself. Don't drink if you think it will kill you, but you have no right to deprive Zvi of a drink," and she handed me a glass—"he's a rational man, an historian, and he knows that a glass of cognac never killed anybody; on the contrary!"

I would put the glass down and tried to reason with her, but she immediately switched to another topic and did not respond. She would complain about the gardener who did not trim the bushes; about the next-door neighbors who torment her with their loud radio and television, which blasted away at full volume all day, and with whom she had already quarreled; about the bank which, since Otto's death, she said was 'cheating' her all the time. She went to a drawer and took out a large sheaf of bank statements, put them in front of me and furiously pointed to the figures printed on them.

"What's this five hundred here? And this hundred and eighty? Are these checks I gave out? I never wrote these checks! To whom? I have no note of it! Let them prove it! I told them to prove it, but they have no proof! They think I'm dumb and don't understand these accounts!"

The rage mounted in her throat. She was convinced, she said, that someone there, at the bank, embezzled her accounts, and she knew who it was. She had already spoken to a lawyer about it. Furiously, she gathered the papers and put them back in the drawer. She had been talking only to me, completely ignoring her daughter.

Quite often the two of them would struggle physically when Nora tried to get the bottle from her hand. Susie, who appeared to have been consumed and debilitated by her drinking, still had tremendous strength in her scrawny arms, and usually won in these struggles. Once, when the two were thus embroiled, their arms flailing and twisting, the bottle slipped to the floor and shattered. Susie, with scalding tears in her eyes, shouted,

"Get out of here, Kapo! I never want to see you again!" and then added quietly, in German, "You will be the death of me!"

But out of concern for her, we kept coming.

On one of our visits, she served us only coffee, but the glint in her eyes indicated she was in high spirits. She said, "I think now I can reveal the truth to you; Otto wasn't Jewish."

"Are you out of your mind?" Nora whispered.

"I know the truth!" she raised her voice. "You can't know! He wasn't circumcised! He was a gentile! His mother wasn't Jewish and his—his father converted to Christianity! And why did he come here to Palestine? Because he was kicked out of the firm of Schutz and Erckhardt, the architects. Zionism? He didn't even know what the word meant!"

"Why are you lying?" Nora asked quietly.

"I'm lying!" Susie chuckled maliciously. "All this happened after we got married, in a civil ceremony, of course. In Munich, all the Bavarians were Nazis even before Hitler's rise to power, and they did not like having an Abramson in their firm, although his papers said he was Christian. So they kicked him out: *Heraus!* I remember that day perfectly, when he came home, flung his briefcase on the couch, sank in an armchair, his face ashen, and said nothing. When I asked what was wrong, he said: 'My father was too proud to change his Jewish name, and I'm paying for it.'

"I said, 'Maybe you're paying for your wife. After all, I'm your *Rassenschande*.' He said nothing. It was my idea to go to Palestine. I had been a member of the *Blauweiss* youth movement until I was sixteen. So off we went to the East, with our three-year-old daughter. Here, of course, he was registered as a Jew. In those days they did not inquire who your mother was and did not pull off men's pants to check if they were circumcised." She burst into short laugh.

After a long silence, she said, "And why did he kill the dog before he left for Cologne? He poisoned him!"

"Don't you think that's enough, mother?" asked Nora, restraining herself, "You yourself told me the dog had been sick."

"Sick because Otto put poison in his food! And why? Because he didn't want me to have a friend in the house."

"The last friend," turbid tears gathered in her eyes.

When we came out, Nora said, "Even if it's true—so what? If it's true that he was not born Jewish—so what?! She thought she was dealing me a blow that I would never recover from. But nothing has changed in my eyes. I have long stopped reacting to what she says."

⁂

A month before Susie's death, one of her neighbors stopped by the house and said, "Forgive me for interfering, but you've got to do something about your mother, maybe check her into a detoxification center, or at least arrange for someone to be with her."

She told us that twice she had found her lying unconscious by the gate, late at night. The front door was open and her purse and all its contents were scattered beside her on the ground. The neighbor and her husband carried her inside and brought her around. "Lucky no burglars broke in; they could have picked the house clean."

161

She added that Susie wandered around in the night and some-times was heard singing loudly in German. Nora thanked her and said, "I've tried everything. I even hired a woman to live there and take care of her, but she won't accept anything, and I can't force her." The neighbor gave us an incredulous look and walked away.

One night the phone woke us up. It was a call from Kaplan hospital requesting that we come immediately. We dressed and drove to the hospital. Susie was already dead. The cause of death, the doctor said, alcohol intoxication.

That same neighbor had found her again, lying on the grass, and called an ambulance. It was a year and a half after Otto's death.

In the hospital bed, Susie's face looked as if it had been hit and disfigured by lightning: the heavy makeup around the eyes was blue as a black eye, the mouth was twisted upward, the eyes in a frozen squint, the coppery hair looked ruffled and sticky. The entire drama of her restless life was imprinted on that face.

Few people came to her funeral. One of Nora's sisters—who had cut off all relations with the family years ago—came from Naharia. The other sister, who lives in New York, telephoned that she could not come. Throughout the funeral Nora stood erect, clasping her hands tightly, her eyes lowered to the grave, as if wrapped in thoughts. I said *Kaddish*.

Silently we walked with the coffin to the cemetery and silently we returned.

Chapter twenty

Writing down these events of the last three years completely distracts me from my work. This morning I went to the university to look for a book for my research. While searching in the library, I forgot the name of the author and the book. Irritated with myself, I went back home, sat down at my desk and tried to summarize—from my notes—the incident of the Zhitomir massacre of January, 1919, carried out by gangs of Hajdamaks who had accused the local Jews of supporting the Bolsheviks. I could not write down one single line, and instead found my thoughts continually drifting back to the ten fatal days in March two years ago.

Meanwhile, I'm growing increasingly doubtful about the purpose of writing this research, about the purpose of writing history in general. The historian E.H. Carr claimed that 'objective' historiography is attainable provided the historian is free of prejudices; he compared the study of history to the study of science, maintaining that both disciplines are based on facts and hypotheses and on the constant juxtaposition of the two. This is wrong. Any comparison between history and science is spurious and untenable, for the simple reason that in history every event is unique, inimitable, whereas in the realm of natural phenomena—which is the subject matter of physics, chemistry, biology—events consistently repeat themselves, and thus reveal their governing principles. Moreover, the study of history does not allow 'experiments'—even in the abstract sense—in the way that other sciences conduct them in a laboratory, since in history, unlike the sciences, there is no separation between the object—which is the study matter—and the subject, namely the researcher. The historian, who deals in people and their biographies, is himself part of history, a particle of the material he examines, and thus is incapable of studying it as an impartial, 'objective observer.'

What, then, is the writing of history if not an arbitrary selection of facts and their organization in a certain logical order, and in accordance with the writer's proclivities, in an attempt to discover the 'governing principles' which best suit his purposes?

Insisting that the historian free himself of 'prejudices' is like demanding that he renounce all attitudes—mental, emotional, moral—toward the events of the past. Is the writing of history possible without such attitudes?

In my opinion, it is precisely such attitudes that motivate historical writing. They are its *raison d'être*.

Thus, as a chronicler, I select from the chaotic conglomeration of past events that are known to us—events with no order except for the innumerable causes and effects, as we see them—those that appeal to me because they serve my purposes. This is what happened when I was writing *The Great Betrayal*, about the Chmielnicki massacres, which peaked in 1648, and this is what happened when I was writing my study of the Petliura riots, which I shall probably never finish.

Soviet historians, like the Ukrainians who preceded them, described Chmielnicki as a national hero, an indomitable warrior, champion of the oppressed peasants whom he tried to free from the Polish landowners and aristocrats. Those historians did not distort the facts, they merely selected, from the 'garbage dump of past events,' those facts that best suited their purposes and underplayed or completely ignored all the others. The murder of about six hundred thousand Jews during the twelve years of the uprising were, for those historians, a marginal fact, not worth stressing. It was the grass trampled under the hoofs of horses carrying freedom fighters on their triumphal march. On the other hand, Graetz—the Jewish historian who was a great believer in 'the Jewish moral mission in the world'—in the chapters describing the massacres, underlined to a great degree the exploitative nature of Jewish innkeepers, tax collectors and merchants who, out of loyalty to their Polish landlords, oppressed and humiliated the peasantry—so much so that his account reads like an apologia for the marauders' actions.

But I, too, select, underline, underplay and ignore. And changes in the proportions between various parts and details in the picture result in a change in the whole picture. In my study of the Petliura riots, for example, I could have stressed the individual acts of rescue carried out by gentiles in almost all the towns. In Zamosc, according to one document, there was a Polish barrel maker who, during the riots, at great risk to himself, entered a Jew's house and rescued four girls whom he hid in the smithy in his yard and later in a ditch he dug in his garden. In Dubovoy, Krivoye-Ozero, Ribnica, Banow, there were Christians who argued with the Cossacks in Petliura's army and tried to dissuade them from harming the Jews; some deceived them and misdirected them on their way to the Jewish neighborhoods; some protected Jews with their own bodies or gave them refuge in their home. One could argue, of course, that such acts were a drop in the ocean, the exception that proves the rule, and thus irrelevant for the historian seeking some 'governing principles' in the material. But here one faces a fundamental question, a question I often thought about in my own work, both as a teacher and as an historian: if history is studied and written—as Burckhardt maintained—not only to view the past in light of the present, but also to view the present in light of the past, or as the Latin expression has it, *historia vita magistra*, in other words, to see history as a teacher of life from which lessons should be drawn—why then should the historiographer be bound by the quantitative aspect of the facts? Perhaps the guiding principle should be one that says: "One small candle can drive out the darkness, but darkness cannot extinguish one little candle. Surely, then, it is the good deeds—few and far between though they may be—that need emphasizing, so that hope, like a little candle, will light up mankind's path."

Materialist historians, like Montesquieu and Hyppolyte Taine, positivists like Comte and Spencer, idealists like Kant and Hegel, theologians, Marxists, all believed, from differing viewpoints, in the existence of a historical 'set of principles' according to which mankind is gradually progressing toward a better world. Only a purely rationalistic approach can foster such 'principles,' or else faith in providence, i.e., that "God does everything for the best."

However, the historian who examines hundreds of documents from a particular period, scrutinizing not only the 'events' but also the lives of the people involved, who are the makers of history, realizes the extent to which irrational, and unpredictable, elements can influence events and change the course of a period, such as the thirst for power, destructiveness, revenge, ruthlessness, megalomania, paranoia, etc. The historian is bound to agree with Benedetto Croce that historical laws are either nonexistent or simply cannot be detected. Did any historian, from those who discerned 'a set of principles' in human history, foresee how Europe would be overrun by Nazi barbarism? Or the extermination of millions of people in gas ovens?

It was an historian who rejected the notion of 'historical principles'—the Englishman H.A.L. Fisher, the author of *History of Europe*, who claimed that a historian must recognize the fortuitous and the unexpected in human reality—who, years before the rise to power of the Nazis, wrote that progress is not a natural law and that human thought and desire might flow in a direction leading to barbarism.

When I examine the material I have collected for my research, which I now do with great absent-mindedness, knowing that in order to create a coherent picture of life in a certain period, I will have to arbitrarily select facts, there is a question gnawing in my mind: Isn't this kind of historical writing a form of fiction? In what way am I different from a novelist who, just like me, draws his material from reality, but out creates a fictional picture of it? And if this is the case, can this history ever really become the *vita magistra*?

※

Ten Days that Shook the World was the title John Reed gave to his book about the Russian Revolution.

The ten days that turned my life upside down.

Two weeks after that 'literary soiree' in honor of the poet Sharf-stein, at ten PM, as I was working at my desk, I got a phone call from Paris. It was Foiglman; he would be arriving in Israel in a week's time for a ten-day stay. Since the purpose of his visit was to work daily with his translator, to check what he was doing with his poems, he did not wish to stay with his brother in Ramlah, but rather in Tel Aviv. Could I book him a room for him in an inexpensive hotel?

I said, "You can stay with us. We have an extra room. It will be at your disposal."

At that moment I knew—my heart sank and my stomach seemed to melt—that I had committed a grievous mistake by not asking Nora first.

"No! What for? Why cause unnecessary trouble for such good friends? I can afford...an inexpensive hotel..."

"No, no, we'll be happy to accommodate you," I said faintly as, in my ears, echoed his and Hinda's warm exhortations to be guests in their house whenever I and my wife would be in Paris.

"Well, if you insist..."

I hung up in a mood of deep dejection. Even today, knowing the fatal outcome of that hasty sentence I blurted on the phone and which turned my whole life upside down, even today, when I ask myself if I could have acted differently... In the life of an individual, as in the lives of nations, the 'leeway of alternatives,' more often than not, is determined by circumstances beyond the control of one's consciousness.

I told Nora about it the next morning, just before leaving for work; her face turned pale, as if she had heard horrible news. She gave me a cold and hard look—full of restrained hostility—a look I had never before seen in her eyes, and announced, "I won't be here during those ten days."

I tried to defend myself, to explain, but she marched resolutely into the bedroom, picked up her purse and left, slamming the door, without saying goodbye.

Toward evening, when she returned, I again tried to talk to her, to explain, to apologize. My words followed her from room to room, unanswered. Suddenly, in the living room, she stopped in her tracks and, livid with rage, called out, "I live in this house! How dare you invite a stranger to hang out here for ten days and ten nights, run around the house, muck up the bathroom and the toilet, crawl all over the kitchen, the balcony, the sofas, the bed, deprive me of my air!" And, in a voice choking with fury, she added, "You let this into the house?!"

She said 'this,' not 'him.'

I was more alarmed by her face than by her shrieks; it was yellow and the skin looked taut, almost as if cracking.

"You're right," I said quietly, "I made a mistake. What do you advise me to do now?"

"I should advise you?" Her stare challenged me, and the tautness in her face did not relax. She said, "When a fool drops a diamond into a well, a hundred wise men cannot retrieve it."

"A diamond," she said, and I seemed to sense an evil premonition inside me.

A thought momentarily crossed my mind to invent some false excuse; I'll call Paris and tell him that Nora isn't feeling well, or that our granddaughter will be staying with us at that time. But I knew right away that I would do no such thing.

"I can't go back on my word," I said.

"You…" she crucified me with her look and then said, "I refuse to be the victim of your complexes. I have plenty of my own." And she left the room.

On the eve of Foiglman's arrival, Nora carried out her threat. Dryly—with no anger this time—she informed me that she was taking a leave from the Institute to go to Jerusalem. After she had packed her suitcase, I asked her where she was going to stay. "I'm not sure, maybe with Raya. Maybe in a hotel." She told me she was taking the car.

Raya Lubersky was an old friend who had studied with her at the university. She worked at the Foreign Office, was married to a water engineer, had two daughters and a son. Two or three times a year she would come to our house and the two of them would engage in long conversations in which I had no part.

"Have a good time with your beloved," she forced a smile to her lips, standing on the threshold.

She looked so beautiful in her proud, erect stature that I felt jealous. She had the appearance of a girl all spruced up for a party who, when her father admonishes her to be back on time, reacts with a secret smile that proclaims her freedom. She would not let me carry her suitcase. Afterward I told myself that perhaps it was better this way. Had she stayed, there would have been unbearable tension in the house.

Foiglman arrived the next day at nine PM, panting, perspiring, a huge suitcase in one hand and a bulging overnight bag in the other. He dropped his bags and flung his arms around me and kissed me. When he walked in, he turned his head left and right and asked, "And where is the lady of the house?" I apologized for her and said she had taken vacation from work, she needed rest badly, so she went to Jerusalem. "Maybe it was I who chased her away..." he said with an expression of sorrow and disappointment. "Sure! You're such a beast!" I patted his shoulder.

I showed him his room, Yoav's old room, and he cried, "Great! The Prince of Wales doesn't have such a room!" And he assured me he would not impose on me. "You go about your work as if I'm not here. I'll walk on tiptoes around here. At any rate, I'll be out most of the time."

When he saw folded sheets on the pillow, he pushed them aside and said he had brought his own sheets. He tapped lightly on the little desk that stood in the room, like a master craftsman checking its workmanship, and said, "Good, good!" He raised his eyes to me sadly and said, "I'm really sorry Nora isn't here! What a pity! Hinda sent something for her, and I wanted to give it to her personally."

He walked to his suitcase, opened it. But then he went over to the bulging overnight bag and zipped it open. "First we have to unburden the vain pleasures of this world..." and took out a bottle of cognac, Dubonnet, three bulky salamis, a big jar of cherry preserves, a jar of pickled mushrooms, three wheels of French cheese.

"You'd better put these in the refrigerator right away." He handed me the cheese. I protested, saying he had brought a hoard of provisions as if we were in a besieged bunker. "But we are under siege, Reb Hirsch! Don't you know it?" His eyes smiled at me, "Always!"

When I came back from the kitchen, he was opening a jewelry box that he had taken out of his suitcase and drawing out a long string of pinkish pearls, dangled them before me. "This is from Hinda, for your Botticellian Madonna!"

I was dumbfounded.

"It will become her, don't you think?" He beamed at me.

I stood before him ashamed and confounded.

"What does it say in the Song of Solomon? 'With rows of jewels, thy neck with chains…like the tower of David…' Your Shulamith has a neck that was made for pearls. And these are real 'Margaritana.'" He rolled the pearls between his fingers. "Feel them!"

I could not find the words to thank him.

"They were her mother's." He laid them on the table.

I asked how Hinda was. "Not so good. So-So." She had not given any performances recently; a couple of bookings were canceled. That's why they were a little hard up at the moment… "But it'll be all right! It is written, 'A pauper is deemed as good as dead,' but it follows that the living are deemed as rich—this is my nickel-and-dime philosophy!"

And he added jokingly, "That's when I have nickels and dimes in my pocket."

When we were seated in the living room, he asked how the translation of his poems was coming along. I said I was not really keeping tabs on it, but I trusted Professor L.'s judgment, as it was he who had recommended Zelniker. He was a well-known translator and had been highly praised.

Foiglman kept quiet. A cloud had settled on his face. He seemed to have stifled a sigh. Then he said, "Zvi, go back to your room! I don't want you to waste even one hour on my account!"

The following day, he got up before six, walked around 'on tip-toes,' as he had promised, so as not to wake me up, although I wasn't sleeping because my worries had kept me awake. He occupied the bathroom for a long time and, when I went in afterward, the room was full of steam and a sweet smell of soap, perfume and aftershave.

When I peered into his room, his bed was scrupulously made, two or three books and his briefcase were lying on the corner of the table, the suitcase and the bag had been put out of sight, probably under the bed, and the floor was spotless.

We had coffee together; I told him about the anniversary celebration in honor of Hertz Sharfstein and the praise that had been heaped upon him that evening. "Was he really such a great poet?" I asked. A disparaging smirk appeared on his face. "You want to hear my opinion?... No, one mustn't speak evil about a colleague!" And after some hesitation, "But he is a prolific poet! Very prolific! The number of poems he has produced is ten times the number of his years! You could certainly say he is an accomplished poet! He deserves the honors lavished on him." He smiled and added, "You have to remember, though, that the word 'honor' in Hebrew does not mean exactly the same as 'honor' in Yiddish."

And *a propos* of that, he told me about the group in Paris. They, too, celebrated an anniversary, honoring the poet Yacov Sommer on his sixtieth birthday. The audience did not number hundreds, only a few dozen. The main speaker had been Mendel Weissbrod, whom I had met at the café 'Selecte'...

"Just imagine, that same Mendel Weissbrod, who at every meeting in the café maligns and casts aspersions on Sommer, accuses him of being a shameless tear jerker, a pale imitator of Moshe-Leib Halpern—now at this party extols and eulogizes him as if he were Peretz or Leivick! And why? Because without the donations that that busybody Sommer solicits from some tradesmen, *Unzer Vort* would have long breathed its last. That was his just reward for his pains. You will have noticed, Reb Hirsch, that with us, when money talks, honesty walks!"

To avoid wasting my time chatting with my guest and seeing to his needs, I decided to work in my office at the university and spend most of the day there. I gave him Zelniker's phone number and a key to the house, and I told him I would be back in the evening and that he could use the apartment as his own.

When I came home I was surprised to find him in the kitchen, Nora's apron tied around his waist, frying and cooking by the range.

With the mischievous smile of a child who has surprised his parents with unusual resourcefulness, he said. "You see? I found everything by myself; pans, pots, spices...even the grocery store."

And he related how, in the afternoon, after his appointment with Zelniker, he went to the grocery and bought provisions for several days—some he put in the refrigerator, some in the pantry—and now he was preparing a meal for both of us. "I hope you haven't had supper yet..."

A big omelet was sizzling in the pan, with slices of salami and chopped onion. Kasha was cooking in a pot and a large bowl of salad stood on the table.

I laughed and said that I had planned to take him out. He said he detested restaurants. He always came away hungry. And the etiquette and all those ceremonies with the waiters... At home, too, he prepared his own meals, since Hinda was "like a satellite orbiting the earth, transmitting messages in Yiddish, and once every few months landing at Place de la Concorde." I had told him he could use the apartment as his own—so he did. And besides, why should I spend money on him?

"And kasha to boot!" I laughed, "why kasha?"

"For tomorrow. I don't eat much for lunch. Kasha with milk and some fruit—that's all."

He took out plates and silverware from the cupboard and laid the table. I was his guest.

After the meal, he insisted on washing the dishes. Then we sat down in the living room drinking cognac, and I asked him about his meeting with Zelniker.

"Ah, not good, not good," he sighed, "I mean, he is quite precise in rendering word for word, as far as my Hebrew goes, but the music! the music! I give him the music of Schubert and he plays Mahler!"

Then he said, "What can one do with this Hebrew of yours? Such a conceited, stuck-up language... Each word attired in a purple gown with a crown on its head... You can take a reverential bow before her, but not throw yourself on her neck... Sometimes I feel like grabbing a Hebrew word by its forelock, bending it a little and saying: 'A little humility, young lady, lower yourself to our height, to the size of simple folk… Don't walk about so haughtily, like a rich man's daughter parading in her Sabbath finery on Main Street… You know what we say in Yiddish: 'May God spare me gentile greed and Jewish arrogance.' For example, take a simple lullaby by Leizer Wolf that starts with the verse: *A mol is geven a mayse/ Di mayse is gor nit Fraylikh/ Di mays hoybt zikh on/ Mit a Yiddishen Melekh.* I saw a Hebrew translation of this poem at Zelniker's house: 'A tale I will relate—/ It is a gloomy thing—/ It opens thus: / There was an evil king.' Relate a tale, indeed! A *Mayse* is not just a tale. And the *Yiddishe Melekh* has become 'an evil king!' And further on in the poem it says, '*Lyolinke mayn faygelle/ Lyolinke mayn kind,*' which reads in translation, 'Hush my fledgling/ Hush my darling child.' Fledgling is much harsher! Or take, for instance, a wonderful poem by Sutzkever: '*Unter dayne Vayse shtern/ Shrek tzu mir dayn vayse hant.*' How was this translated? 'Under the whiteness of thine stars/ You proffered your white hand…' The whiteness of thine stars?' Doesn't Sutzkever say plainly, 'Your white stars.' Whiteness is an abstraction, something distant and alien. And note that the word '*Mayse*' (story) is actually the Hebrew word, '*ma'asseh,*' but paradoxically, it is this Hebrew word appropriated by Yiddish that is impossible to translate. But this is precisely my point, that Hebrew is so proud and haughty that when one of her prodigal offspring comes back home, she receives him coldly, like a stepson. What should one do, Zvi? No two languages are so far apart as Hebrew and Yiddish! As if spoken by two different peoples!"

I said, as far as I understood these matters, in every translation the words of the original text are disguised when they appeared on stage. Shakespeare in Hebrew is unlike Shakespeare in English, and Yehuda Halevi in Yiddish is unlike Yehuda Halevi in Hebrew. "*Traduttori—traditori,*" as the Italians say.

"Yeah, words, words," Foiglman nodded, "but in a poem, melody is what counts, and to translate the melody from Yiddish into Hebrew…"

The following morning, when I came out of my room, I saw him on the balcony, watering the plants with a jar he had found in the kitchen. I said, "What are you doing, Foiglman? I watered them two days ago." He gave me a bemused smile and said, "I'm an experienced gardener, Zvi, don't you know? I was the gardener at SS Commandant Spengler's, near Majdanek! Actually his wife's gardener…"

He put down the jar, came closer to me, and with his hand brushed aside a clump of long hair, exposing a scar behind his ear.

"Do you see this?" He told me that the officer's wife showed him kindness, but once her husband came unexpectedly and found him munching a carrot he had picked from the vegetable patch. He clobbered him so hard with his stick that the flesh tore.

In the afternoon, when I returned from the university—earlier than the previous day—I found a group of people on the balcony: Foiglman, his twin, two women and a little girl. Glasses of grapefruit juice stood on the table and on the sideboard in the living room. Foiglman came toward me saying, "We have taken over your castle. But don't get mad, it's only a tactical takeover. We're about to withdraw." He introduced his guests, "My brother's wife, Malka, their daughter Zehava, their grandchild, Yaffa… You have already met my brother… All decent people." Katriel apologized: a thousand pardons, they stopped by for only a few minutes to see his brother, they're already leaving… I asked them to sit down, but they declined. God forbid they should disturb me. Katriel said, "That was a very good deed you did, finding a translator for my brother. He's the kind of man with whom words always precede deeds. Now that his words are coming to Israel, he's bound to follow them."

His wife, a short woman with a wan face and swollen feet, said, "Shmuel is our pride and joy. We read every word he writes and that is written about him. All these years I've been telling him: twin brothers with a sea separating them?—a family has to live together! But he has this fear…"

Foiglman smiled, "'*A foygel on fligel un an ureman a gadlan, shtarben beyde far hunger*'—a wingless bird and a conceited beggar both starve."

"You won't starve here," his sister-in-law assured him, "we'll see to that." Their daughter, a pretty, dark-complexioned young woman, with a black braid hanging down her back, was chasing her two-year-old daughter toddling around the living room, slapping her hands whenever she grabbed things from the table.

When they had left, Foiglman requested that I spend some time with him discussing his affairs. He had a list of words and idioms whose translation seemed dubious to him. Could I go over them with him? We sat down, poring over his notebook, trying to decide what should be modified. Here, he wrote *'Mayn gesel un mayn teikhel'* whereas Zelniker translated, 'My street and my stream.' In the original, he claimed, these words carry a note of diminutiveness, of endearment! He had written, *'Kh'bin aroys fun mayn heym'* and Zelniker had translated, and 'I departed from my dwelling-place.'

Foiglman asked, "And why not 'I left home?'"

He'd written, *'Mayne Bagern kenen nisht fliyen.'* The translation read, 'My thought-laden yearnings.' He had only meant to say that his longing had no wings! And why did he translate *'Zayn tzar'*—his distress? Why not 'his sorrow?' And *'dayn Shtilkuyt'* was rendered, 'still small voice,' as if he, Foiglman, were a prophet hearing God's voice in the desert. Simple words like *Bet ikh mayn tefila,* Zelniker translates into a highfalutin expression; 'I shall pour out my supplication'!

I tried to explain some of the deviations by the exigencies of rhyme and rhythm, for others I suggested alternatives. But Foiglman remained disgruntled. He sat there despondent and disheartened.

"Oh, Zvi, Zvi! Sometimes, when I reflect on how Hebrew has supplanted Yiddish among those who left Europe, it seems to me that not only their speech was changed but their nature, too! Hebrew has deprived them of the warmth, the heartiness, the folksy simplicity! The transition from language to language is like those sex-change operations they perform these days..."

Dejected, he retired to his room.

I woke up twice that night, and both times I found Foiglman awake. At one AM the light was still on in his room and various sounds, the turning of pages, a creaking chair, shuffling shoes—reached my ears. At three thirty, when I gingerly crept out of bed, I saw him standing on the balcony in his pajamas, his hands on the railing, looking down at the street. I went back to bed, leaving him standing there. I heard his bare feet on the floor, going to his room and then back again to the balcony where they stopped.

The following nights, too, whenever I woke up—and my concern for Nora deprived me of sleep—the light was on in his room, and sometimes a sigh would escape him and reach me from there. Does he ever sleep? I wondered.

In the morning, his face gaunt, he asked anxiously what would happen when Zelniker had finished his job. "Do you think I should contact a publisher before returning to Paris?"

I replied that in my experience no publisher would even consider such a proposition before seeing the entire manuscript, edited and ready for publication, and even then publishers were not eager to publish poetry books by unknown poets, let alone in translation. When the translation was ready, I assured him, I would offer it to several publishing houses.

He still looked perturbed. "Do you think I should get to know some influential Hebrew authors?"

I had already figured out that his requests were phrased as questions about my opinion, "Do you think it's worth my while…?"

I told him that while I had no connection with authors—I knew only two who taught at the university—I would try to invite them over some evening. "Won't it be too much trouble for you? Perhaps in a café…?" I said it would be better to have them here; we could sit and talk quietly, perhaps even read some of the poems already translated. He was extremely grateful.

In the late afternoon, when I was alone in the house, Yoav came in. As usual, "stopping by just for a minute, to see what's doing." He asked where his mother was. I asked him to sit down and told him what had happened between us.

"Good for her!" he pronounced. "I would never put up with some stranger, a Jew from Chelm, invading my space for ten days and ten nights!"

I told him a little bit about Foiglman, what had befallen him in his life, about the generous invitation he extended to me and to his mother to stay at his house, about the gifts he had lavished on us. "Dad, you are guilt ridden. All your life you're burdened with guilt, that's your problem. You should go see a psychologist, you'll hear exactly the same things. Aren't you aware of it yourself? You seem to think that you have to atone for something. What is your sin? That you were not there?"

Foiglman walked in. When I introduced him to Yoav, he stood reverently before his officer's uniform, asked him where he was posted, how long he had been in the service, etc. Then he sat down and told us when he had first set eyes on a Hebrew soldier; when the Americans liberated Kungskirchen, he was "a mere skeleton walking on crutches," so they immediately transferred him to a military hospital located in a nearby camp that had previously served as the German army headquarters. One day when he was lying in bed, he heard Hebrew spoken outside. He could not believe his ears. He had not heard a word of Hebrew all through the war. He went to the window and saw an army truck parked in the square and a few soldiers surrounded by camp inmates. From a distance he spotted the Star of David on the shoulder of one of the soldiers who was speaking Hebrew to the crowd. Foiglman thought he was dreaming. The Star of David was the yellow patch designating those condemned to death, but here it is on the shoulder of a young soldier speaking Hebrew! Suddenly infused with strength, clad only in pajamas, he dashed out of the hospital, ran to the square, and mingled with the crowd gathering around the soldiers. Somebody told him, "They are the Jewish Brigade from Palestine!" The Jewish Brigade! "Can you imagine what those two words meant to me? It was as if a *shofar* had been blown proclaiming the arrival of the Messiah!"

He told us how he had pushed his way through the crowd and kissed the soldier's hand. "That was the first time I saw a Hebrew soldier!"

Yoav listened attentively to the story. When it was done, he remained silent for a long moment, then took out the car keys from his pocket and said, "Well, I have to go now. When Mom comes back, tell her we're expecting her. She hasn't been over in two weeks."

That night I telephoned the two authors, my acquaintances from the university: the poet M.L., who used to make me a gift of every book he published, and G., the essayist and literary critic. I invited them to my house the coming Sunday to meet my friend, a Yiddish poet from France. They wanted to know what he had written, whether his poems had merit, and if any of them had been translated into Hebrew. I answered their questions as best I could, and they promised to come.

The following evening Foiglman had a minor accident. A few minutes after my return home from the university, when I was in the bedroom, I heard a terrified cry from the kitchen, "Oh, blood!" I rushed there and found him standing in the middle of the room, girded by an apron—I could not dissuade him from preparing supper for both of us—blood dripping from his finger; he had opened a can and cut himself on the jagged lid. It was actually a small matter, but apparently not to him; his face was ashen, his eyes wide open in despair and supplication, he muttered, "What shall I do, Zvi…" I quickly fetched cotton wool, iodine and a Band Aid. He dropped into a chair, and while I tended to his cut, he kept muttering, "Why did it have to happen to me… now…here…" I calmed him down, saying there was no cause for alarm, these things happen every day. For long moments after I had bandaged his finger, he remained seated, pale, his eyes closed. When he opened them, he looked at me terrified, and whispered, "bad omen…"

And then, as if to cheer himself up, a wan smile hovering on his livid lips, he added, "Maybe this is my circumcision…the second one…."

On Saturday he went to visit with his brother in Ramlah.

On Sunday he prepared and primed himself for the meeting with the authors. He came home earlier than usual, showered, meticulously combed his 'poetic' hair, covering his temples and his nape, put on a suit and wore his red bow tie. He had brought home a sheaf of translations from Zelniker, all typed up and vocalized. We conferred to select four or five poems to be read aloud, and concluded that we would read both the original and the translation; he would read the Yiddish and I the Hebrew. He asked many questions about the two authors he was about to meet. I told him that M.L. was a gentle, lyrical poet, a 'poet's poet,' timid and insecure in human relations, but very confident when it comes to his poetry, exacting and demanding, careful in the choice of each word, and highly regarded by discerning critics. About G., I said he was one of the distinguished literary critics in the country, extremely well versed in Hebrew and general literature, an energetic man, with a brilliant style and great influence in the realm of letters. The glint in his eye told me he was pleased with my descriptions.

At nightfall he left the house without telling me where he was going. An hour later he was back, his arms full of bags. He had bought snacks, nuts, cookies. He put them in bowls on the table, with a bottle of wine in the middle.

The authors were invited for nine. At ten past nine the phone rang. It was M.L. excitedly muttering apologies for being unable to come. His mother had unexpectedly arrived from Haifa half an hour earlier and he could not leave her alone. He felt very bad about it, since he was eager to meet the Jewish poet from France. He begged me to convey his apologies. When I did so, Foiglman said, "I commend him! Honoring one's mother comes before honoring a guest!"

While we were waiting for G., he told me about his own mother. She had been an ardent *Bundist*, an adherent of 'Narodnaya Volya'. She had organized classes for Jewish laborers in the shops. On May Day, she would march in the parade carrying the red flag and singing 'The Oath.'

I told him about my own mother, born in Rehovot, whose father owned a citrus grove and a vineyard. As a young woman she rebelled and refused to go and study in France; instead she worked picking fruit, packaging and watching the vineyard at night. When it was ten PM, and G. had not shown up, I seethed with fury and indignation and started denigrating him. I called him an irresponsible person, always late for his classes, never turning in students' papers on time, never keeping his promises, an inveterate liar. Foiglman listened to my detractions with a sad smile on his face.

"Zvi!" he said, "you're a wicked man! How can you denounce a scholar? While we're sitting here chatting and whiling away the time with stories about mothers, he's probably reading *Ethics of the Fathers* or writing a profound scholarly work on Ibn Gavriol's *The Kingly Crown*, or Becket's *Waiting for Godot*. Why should he stop his sacred work on my account? One day, when I come in a coach-and-four, I'm sure he'll come to welcome me!"

I asked what he meant by that, and he poured us both wine and told me the Hassidic story about Rabbi Zusya of Anipoli and his brother, Elimelech, who traveled on foot from town to town; whenever they came to Ludomir, they lodged in the house of a very poor but pious man, since the rich man of the town despised them and would not put them up in his house. Once, however, they came into town by carriage, and then that same rich man came out to welcome them and invited them to his house most respectfully. Zusya said to him, "If in your eyes our honor consists of a carriage and horses, then we might as well stay with our poor host, as we have always done…"

"Down the hatch, Reb Hirsch!" He refilled both our glasses. "Look at this poor bottle, standing here so shamefaced, eager for us to empty its content into our bellies, don't you think?"

He took a big swig, put his glass down and gave me a sidelong look, "You're worried, I can see, that's bad! Sadness is a sin, happiness is a virtue; this is what I learned from my forefathers. So drink, drink! Alcohol wipes out the worries just as kerosene wipes out lice!"

I raised my glass to him. The creases on his forehead and by the corners of his mirthful eyes looked like ancient script on a parchment. He wiped his mouth and said, "You know, after the war I used to drink a lot. At least a bottle a day. But I developed problems in my bowels. Once, about five or six years after I had come to Paris, I became so sick I had to be hospitalized. When I came out, Hinda decreed complete abstinence. I wasn't able to endure it. I would nip surreptitiously, then eat onions to cover up my alcohol breath. All these years she has stood guard over me, making sure I don't drink more than one or two shots a day. But right now we're bachelors, Hirsch!" He puffed out his chest, "We needn't fear our wives' wrath!" He refilled my glass.

I don't normally drink, but there was the disappointment, the indignity, all that had happened that night, in addition to my anxiety about Nora, which kept gnawing at the back of my mind. "Women are a tough race," a bitter expression clouded his face, "a tough race. You can never figure them out. You can never anticipate what they are going to say or do. For three days they can be as placid as a limpid lake, and on the fourth, suddenly—like the river Sambatyon, raging, fuming, hurling stones at your head, and you don't have a clue. My own dear wife, as I was about to leave, my suitcase all packed… Well, never mind, forget it. Let's go out. It's a warm, pleasant night, and we are a couple of bachelors now. Let's paint the town red!"

My head felt dizzy. We went down to the street. It was quiet. A full moon hung in the sky. Foiglman put one hand on my shoulder and raised the other one, "Look at the sky! Even the moon is showing us a bright face!" And he started to sing:

Ikh vel a lvone dir koyfen
A levone fun zilber-papir
Ikh vel zi baynakht oyfhengen
Iber dayn kleyner tir—

(I will buy you a moon
A moon made of tin foil
At night I'll hang it
Over your little door—)

"You see? There it is, right over your door! Peeping into the rooms! Not just the rooms, peeping into the soul! It sees everything!"

We wandered through the alleys around my house, and Foiglman kept pulling me toward what he called the 'Boulevard Saint Germain': "Come on, let's go to your Saint Germain." He grabbed my arm forcefully, "We'll walk into your 'Deux Magots' and you'll introduce me to the entire literary gang sitting there. You'll tell them that I am the flaming torch of Jewish poetry! You'll tell them that if they don't drink with me—I'll set their house on fire!"

I told him that it had been years since 'Kassit' had ceased to be the writers' meeting place, and that right now the place was probably populated by shady characters.

"Very good!" He threaded his arm through mine and pulled

me along. "And what about me? Aren't I a shady character? You bet I am!"

On the corner of Dizengoff Street he stopped to marvel at the busy traffic at that late hour, of both pedestrians and vehicles, at the lights flooding the streets from cafés and store windows, and then he fell silent as if his spirit sank. Two or three minutes later, the spark of gaiety lit his eyes again, "You know what, maybe I ought to stand here on the corner, sing and hope people will throw me coins. Or better still—I'll sing and you go round with a hat and collect small change…except you don't have a hat, what a shame…."

And with his back to the wall, his moist eyes fixed on my eyes, he sang softly Abraham Lyesin's song about a shopkeeper who sits in his little shop, shivering from the cold, waiting for the customers who never come, and dreams about a Jewish State, a land full of geniuses and kings.

He stretched his hand to the street and laughed. "Look at the people around here! A genius every one! All kings! Come on, let's go in and have a glass of cognac, Reb Hirsch! You don't want to? No way? My treat! Okay, let's go home, then."

We turned back, and Foiglman, leaning on my shoulder, swaying a little, kept muttering, *"A Yiddishe melukhe…. A Yiddishe melukhe…. Es tut mir vey*…* it hurts me, the Jewish State, it hurts, Reb Hirsch…" he sobbed.

On the last day before his departure, I told him not to prepare supper, as I was taking him out. If it was thus decreed, he said, he would accept. A host's wish must be respected.

Again, he prepared himself meticulously before the occasion; he spent a long time in the bathroom and then put on festive clothes.

At eight o'clock, when I entered the living room to take him out, I found him slouching on the couch, leaning backward, his limbs slack. The palms of his hands lay limply at his sides, his face desiccated, as if swept by a wind. "Shall we go?" I asked. He stared

---

* *A Yiddishe melukhe…. A Yiddishe melukhe…. Es tut mir vey*….Yiddish: "A Jewish kingdom. A Jewish kingdom. It hurts me…."

at me blankly and said, as if pleading for his life, "Would you be terribly offended if I didn't come with you?"

"Has anything happened?"

"I can't... I simply can't..."

I sat down and asked what was wrong, was he ill?

"All of a sudden...all this...it's too much...just too much...." And a moment later, "Pardon me, Zvi, I know I'm causing you grief, but...I don't feel up to it right now.... When I come next time, I'll make it up..."

Then he straightened up, put his hands on his knees, and said that he had already commissioned his brother to find him a small apartment in Tel Aviv. His brother promised to give him half the sum required for its purchase, and the other half would come from the sale of their apartment in Paris. It was too large for them anyway. They would sell it and buy a smaller apartment instead. He would divide his time between the two cities. A few months a year there and a few months here. "I can't leave Europe altogether."

A shadow clouded the wide face that resembled a plowed, arid field. His eyebrows bristled, his thick lower lip quivered.

"You have to understand..." His eyes pleaded, "All this life I... What am I doing here anyway? I'm living a stolen life. I deceived the Angel of Death. You are probably saying to yourself: This man must come and settle here, must stop wandering from place to place. But to me the whole world is not altogether clear, you understand? I mean, not so real. I'm not absolutely sure that it exists. A sort of hallucination. Sometimes I think that my whole life up to now, that is, my second life—is only an allegory. An allegory for what, you may ask? What is the analogy? I'm an atheist, Zvi, you know, from way back, but when I ask myself why am I alive, why was I chosen when I was already on the other side—I have no answer except that some Providence, (God?) decided to make an example of me for all to see. A man walks about in the world and he is a conundrum—and the conundrum has no solution! This is probably what God wanted to tell us: a mystery with no explanation. Don't try to look for one..."

With a forced grin on his lips he added, "Go back to your

work, Zvi! Don't waste your time. Go write Jewish history!" And a moment later, "Perhaps it, too, is only an allegory."

⁂

During those ten days, my concern for Nora gnawed at me.

On the second day after her departure, late at night, when Foiglman had retired to his room, I called the Luberskys and asked if she was there. She had been there the previous night, Raya said, spent a few hours with them. "We had a very pleasant talk." They invited her to stay with them, but for some reason she preferred to stay in a hotel. "I almost fought with her." She said she would call but did not, so they did not know in which hotel she was staying. Was there a message in case she called? No, I said, she would probably call home anyway.

I felt extremely uneasy when I hung up. Why did she refuse to stay with her best friend? Why hadn't she called them or me? My apprehension hung inside my head like a spider's web. Every so often, while sitting in my office at the university, busy with my work, or at night, like the sting of a scorpion that jolts one from sleep, I would see the look she gave me when I told her I had invited Foiglman to stay in our house. A hostile look, as if convicting me of treason.

I remembered that only once before—once only—did I see such a look in her eyes.

We were in London. I attended a historians' meeting at the London School of Economics. We had been married ten years then. We decided to go to the theater that night. At three o'clock, I had gone to a party given for the participants at the old town hall in the City. Nora remained in the hotel. I told her I would be back by five. The party lasted longer than I expected. The drinks flowed and I became a little tipsy. It was seven-thirty when I returned. I found her sitting in an armchair, dressed to go out, her purse on her knees. And just like this time: the same implacable, censorious, condemnatory look. I had betrayed her. No explanation, no apology could mitigate the verdict. And after the punishing silence, her categorical pronouncement: Tomorrow morning I'm flying back home.

Then, too—even after the reconciliation at the end of the

184

night—I could not understand; from which dark hiding place did this hostility stem? It was as if I were threatening her life.

All the time I waited for the phone to ring. On Wednesday night, at nine o'clock, consumed by worry, I called the Luberskys once more. Raya answered the phone, "Yes, she called. She's staying at the Scottish Hospice…"

"The Scottish Hospice?" I blurted out loud. I am not sure why I did.

Raya, too, was surprised at my alarmed reaction. "It's a very nice place…quiet, inexpensive. Do you want the phone number?"

I called the Scottish Hospice. There was no answer. When I called the next morning, a woman asked me to wait while she went to see if Nora was in her room. When she came back she said Mrs. Arbel must have left. Any message? I said to say her husband called.

But Nora did not call. Not even once.

Like a dull, blunt ache, the worry kept turning in my head.

Two or three more times I was about to call the Hospice, I dialed the first digits, but then I held back. I said to myself: if she's not calling, it means that she's still angry with me. A stranger has invaded her house, and driven her out. And I—aren't I in collusion with that man? Better let things settle by themselves, I said. It never occurred to me that there could be another reason for her silence.

Chapter twenty-one

Yesterday, after a month's absence, I went to visit my mother at the sanatorium in Gedera. I found her in the same condition as on my last visit, nothing had changed; she was lying on her back, her head propped high on two pillows, her white hair gathered behind her head, her creased face shrunken while her thick glasses magnified her eyes to monstrous proportions. Her first question was, "Why doesn't Yoav come?"

I had to remind her again that Yoav and his family had been overseas, in South America, these many months.

"South America? What's he doing in South America?"

Like many old folks who suffer from sclerosis, she tends to forget things that happened a short while ago, yet remembers in great detail things that happened many years ago. Three months after I told her of Nora's death, she asked how she was doing. From time to time I bring her books to read, but she puts them aside, and rereads the ones she had brought along from home: Dvora Baron's *Episodes*, Moshe Smilansky's *Family of the Earth*, Tolstoy's *Resurrection*, Berl Katznelson's letters. Now I find Menachem Posnanski's *Accompanying Pictures* on her bedside table.

"You should read this," she said when she saw me open the book and leaf through the pages. It reminded her of Chekhov; it appealed to her more than Gnessin because of his 'humility.' She was surprised that his writings were not taught in the schools, and that few people recognized his name. "He makes such quiet music that one can barely hear it."

Tiny wrinkles appear around her mouth when she talks, and her lips purse tightly, almost involuntarily.

"And the letters he wrote to Brenner! 'My dear man,' he writes to him, 'my cherished friend'… But he doesn't mention his wife Haya… She suffered more than him… Why did she leave him and go to Europe with the child? Because she could no longer live with him. Everyone knew that! He banished her! Haya Broida was a nobody, while Brenner was a famous man, so no one took her side."

I asked if she wanted me to wheel her to the balcony. It was such a nice day. No, when she sits there she begins to cry, she said. And already her eyes were filling with tears that she tried to push back by contorting her face. From the balcony, she said, she was able to see the bluish Judean mountains in the distance, the orchards of the plain, the fallow fields strewn with poppies, chrysanthemums, thistles, thorns and hedges of prickly pear; the intoxicating fragrance of citrus blossoms waft to her face by the hot summer breeze, the redolence of mown wheat, of dill—all her childhood and adolescent memories assail her, thronging, pressing against her heart—and she begins to cry. She wants to lie only here, between the white walls. "The whiteness soothes me. When I see it around me, I'm resigned, yes, resigned." She purses her lips, and the look in her eyes becomes bitter, sullen.

Afterward, as on every visit, she starts talking about my father, who died nineteen years ago, of a brain hemorrhage while on an archeological dig near the town of Arad.

"At sixty-five he had to quit this world?" She reiterated things I had heard her say scores of times before. "I always said to him, Nahum, the sun will kill you. It beats down on your head and eventually it will destroy your brain cells! He returned from every dig with a headache. But he was stubborn, how stubborn! When we got married I told him: Why do you want to deal with things that are buried in the ground—stick with what's above the ground. My father is giving us five acres of citrus groves and an acre of vineyard, all fruit-bearing; so be an agriculturist, 'hereupon the face of the earth,' as the poetess Rachel has written. Archeology is the past, I said to him; agriculture is the future! He wouldn't listen. I could never understand what it was he was looking for in the bowels of the earth. If he had been searching for water, or oil, or copper ore—but he was looking for things of the past. As if it were relevant to our lives that three thousand years ago the Hittites or the Amorites or the Phoenicians inhabited this land. It's all written in the Bible anyway. He couldn't come up with anything new. And how excited he was when he found a crumbling figurine of Astarte! You're a heathen, I told him. Abraham smashed the idols, and you glue their shards back together and worship them! And he would say: What do you know about these matters? and then go off up and down the country, summer and winter, rain and shine, drought and hail, leaving me by myself for entire days and nights. Even when you were a baby, I had to do all the housework by myself. Later, when I worked in the day care center, and you were a year or two old, I had to take you with me to the center and slave and sweat—and why? Because he had unearthed the bones of Jerubaal's concubine near Shechem! I warned him. You will die before your time if you go on like this, just like those who opened the Pharaoh's tombs—they all died before their time! The heavens punish idol worshippers!… But he wouldn't listen to me."

About ten years after my father's death her health began to fail. At first it was rheumatism that caused her pains in the neck and shoulders. The rheumatism developed into arthritis. She had pains in her hands, knees, hips. Then she began to have trouble walking. Then her feet swelled up. Still, she continued to run the day care center and never complained. When we came for a visit and pleaded with her to close down the center and retire—by then she was over seventy years old, she always said, "That would be the end of me." One day, when she was alone in the house, she was struck by a severe pain in the spine; she fell to the floor and could not get up. A neighbor heard her cries and helped her to her bed. The medication prescribed by the doctors did not alleviate the pain. She had broken her hip. Even after undergoing an operation, she still could not walk because of the pain in her spine. Five years ago, when she could no longer stand on her feet, we sold the house in Rehovot and put her in the sanatorium in Gedera.

The softness that was once in her face has vanished. Suffering—and the thick clusters of wrinkles around the eyes and mouth, together with the enlarged pupils behind the thick lenses—all gave her face a mean expression. But she never talks about her pain. Suddenly she is reminded of neighbors, of old settlers, of bygone affairs. "Do you remember Altshuler? A dishonest man. I used to buy on credit at his store, but at the end of the month he would always swindle me. Three kilos of semolina, he would put down. I never bought three kilos of semolina from him," she emitted a broken, old woman's chuckle. And a few moments later, "To this day I don't understand why Menuha Libai sent her son to me with a caseful of avocados. Was she trying to bribe me? I would not take in her little girl even if she had given me a diamond necklace. Infested with lice. Those people never washed..."

She never inquires how and what I am doing.

When I came to her, three weeks after Nora's death and told her about it, she gaped at me for an interminably long time and then asked, "What of?"

"The heart," I said.

Again she was silent. "Did she have a heart disease?"

"No, it was sudden."

Then, after a long silence: "It will be hard for you now." That was all she said, although she had been fond of Nora. When we would come to visit on Saturdays, when she was still living at home, the two of them used to go for walks in the fields and come back with arms full of wild flowers. She was also interested in Nora's work at the Institute.

About three month after Nora's death she asked me how she was doing.

"Mother!" I stared at her. And then, without batting an eye, she said, "Yes, you told me."

And she never mentioned her since. Yesterday, before I left she said, "Tell Sarit I would like to see her."

I returned from Gedera with a splitting headache. I took two pills and within an hour the pain abated. I sat down to write, but the pen was not responsive to me.

I doubt that I shall be able to recount what I had been through from the time Nora returned from Jerusalem through the last morning of her life. Everything seems so trivial to me, and at the same time looms so large and portentous. It was evening, and the sea to the west of the city swallowed the silence. These rooms that used to teem with life, with the quiet sounds of conversation, with peals of laughter, with yearnings and agitation—are now silent, lifeless. Quite often I call out her name. I walked about the room, my eyes roaming over the hundreds of books lining the walls around me, as if they could help me. I asked myself what good was all the wisdom stored in them to me. In a few months I shall be sixty-two. Tiresias was blind, yet he saw better than anyone. But I—I was sighted.

When I raised my eyes, my gaze fell on the brown package on the top shelf that has been lying there since Foiglman's death. It is the package that his daughter, Rachel, gave me, and I hadn't opened it yet. I climbed up and took it down. I untied the string that was wrapped around it. There were five notebooks inside. I opened the first notebook. Notes of different lengths separated by asterisks. I became absorbed in reading them. I am copying a few paragraphs translated from Yiddish:

❦

When Katriel and I were traveling on a train from Warsaw to Lodz, after looking in vain for relatives in Zamosc, we heard a young Polish fellow saying: "They're just like cockroaches: you exterminate them with spray or with gas, you think you have wiped them out, then suddenly one pops out from under the stove, another from behind the cooking range, and a third comes crawling out of a crack in the wall... The Germans are said to be a very methodical people, but in this case they didn't do a very thorough job, I must say..."

It was at that moment, more than during all the war years, that

*the absolute conviction hit me, like a red-hot iron branding my flesh, that
we are the lepers of the world, from time immemorial to eternity.*

*In Majdanek it was Satan. And Satan is beyond humanity. Here,
in the train, were human beings, simple, ordinary people, sitting huddled
together in a train compartment, looking quite pitiful, having suffered
considerably during the war. Peasant women wrapped in shawls and
kerchiefs, between their feet, under their wide skirts, baskets full of rags or
cabbage heads or eggs in straw; laborers in dirty overalls, in rags stained
with machine oil or coal dust, their faces furrowed, somber. The young
fellow who had spoken, had a bottle of vodka at his feet, and he kept
pouring from it and passing the glass around. He was a 'nice' country boy:
flaxen locks falling to his brow, smiling blue eyes. What he said was not
spoken maliciously, but good-humoredly, and his listeners nodded their
heads in approval. One of the peasant women, added in agreement: "In
our village, one of them came out of the woods all naked, hairy as an
ape, covering his whatcha macallit with his hands, eyes like an owl. Our
blacksmith, who was fixing a cart in the field saw him and thought it
was a devil. So he fell on him with an axe and…" With a swift motion
of her hand she demonstrated how he chopped off his head.*

*The men threw us a glance from time to time, probably suspecting
that we, too, were 'them.' They were not sure, or perhaps they were and
deliberately said those things within our hearing.*

In Lodz, Katriel joined a local branch of the religious party, Ha-
poel Ha-mizrahi. *I said to him, "After all you've been through, you start
believing in God?" And he said, "What else is left for me to believe in?"
I said, "If there is a God, why did he abandon the world and let Satan
take over?" And he said, "To show the world what Hell is like."*

"On our flesh? Why on our flesh?"

*"Because he teaches the world everything through us, including this.
This must be the reason for our existence."*

This is his 'optimistic' philosophy, a sort of paradoxical optimism.

*The miracle that happened to me is not that I survived, but that I
did not go crazy. Every day I ask myself how it happened that I did not
go out of my mind, and how it is that even today I am almost sane.*

❧

The words I am using and am about to use, the words I have written and am about to write, do not contain even a fraction of the truth that I know. They are disingenuous, glib, hypocritical, mendacious. I write 'wall,' and it is not a wall; I write 'ditch' and it is not a ditch; I write 'bread' and it is not bread. Even when I write 'sun,' 'light,' or 'cornflower'—these words reflect nothing of what my eyes saw during and after the war. When I was riding in a cart from Lublin to Zamosc, after the liberation, on both sides of the road were green cornfields dotted with blue cornflowers. To me they looked as if they were growing on blood. Nothing 'afterward' was the same as 'before,' but the words stayed the same: the same letters, the same stresses. People who were not there cannot understand this.

At Majdanek, we were summoned one afternoon to the parade ground to witness a public punishment. In the middle of the square stood a Jew of about sixty, with a long face, high forehead and bald head. He belonged to our barrack. A doctor from Bratislava, a taciturn man who commanded great respect from us. Kommandant Kugel stood before him, his cudgel under his arm and bellowed: "Did you or didn't you steal?" The man answered in funereal voice, "No." The doctor had been accused of stealing a package of margarine from the camp kitchen. Kugel motioned to an SS man who was standing near the doctor with a whip in his hand, and he lashed him ten times on his back. Again Kugel barked, "Did you or did you not steal?" and the doctor, who could hardly stand on his feet, tried to straighten his back so as not to fall, shook his head: No. When he was beaten for the third time—twenty-five lashes—he was lying on the ground like a heap of rags, and still he would not confess. The Kommandant straightened up, thrust his chest forward and turned to us, "Do you see the nature of a dirty Jew? Not only does he steal, but he's also a coward and a liar!" And he ordered the SS to hang him. He and his aide hung a noose around the old doctor's neck and carried him, like an empty sack, to the gallows. But when they pulled the rope, the doctor suddenly raised his head, in defiance, or in pride, and opened his mouth as if to utter a curse to the world. But his voice was not heard.

We stood there, facing west, and the sun which had not yet set was behind the hanged man. Huge, red, indifferent.

For a moment it looked as if the head of the doctor from Bratislava was merged with the sphere of the sun and consumed in it. I shall not forget the sight of that sun to the day I die. But today when I use the word 'sun' in a poem it is as if it is nothing but the Greater Light from the fourth day of creation.

⁊⁊

We are the lepers of the world. From time immemorial to eternity.

Heraus—outside the human race. In every generation. Does this sound hysterical? Paranoid? Historical facts confirm it. And the myths too. Myths tell truths, no less than facts, but they are written in a different script; with the chisel of angels upon flying tablets. Pharaoh dictated: Every son that is born, ye shall cast into the river. The man of common sense asks: Why did he have to kill all the males? He could have used them for building cities like Pithom and Ramses. That man is looking for logic… He does not understand: Heraus!—outside the human race.

The man of common sense, during those years of colossal Hell, asked, Why did Hitler have to send the Jews to the gas chambers? He could have used them as manpower in his war effort?

That man is looking for logic… And we, the few who were spared and sent to work camps, asked every day, every minute, Why is he starving us, torturing us, harassing us, so that we can barely stand on our feet, move our hands or breathe—when he could have fed us but one loaf of bread a day and two bowls of pea soup and have derived some benefit from us. Logic, logic… Heraus!—outside the human race. Lepers, lepers.

⁊⁊

When Nora returned from Jerusalem her face had changed. There was no trace of anger or resentment in it. Only sadness and weariness. But it had undergone a change that amazed and troubled me. She came back at ten in the morning, the day after Foiglman's departure. She sank in the armchair in the living room, looked around her, as if to make sure there were no changes in the room, and asked wearily, almost apathetically, "How was it?"

"Quite all right," I said, and briefly told her about the ten days with my guest and his strange whims. When I described how he prepared his own meals, wrapped in her apron, she smiled," Really?" but it was obvious that her heart was somewhere else.

194

"How was it?" I asked in my turn. She looked at me for a minute, as if deliberating how to answer, then said, "Something's wrong with the car. When you brake, you hear a strange squeak. On the way back, I stopped at a gas station to have it checked. They told me to bring it into the garage tomorrow. It has to be repaired without delay."

We were silent for a moment, then she said, "It's quite a gloomy place, that Scottish Hospice. Like a lonely castle. But it's very quiet, and there's a lovely view of the Old City and the Valley of Hinnom from the window."

I asked why she had not called me all that time. "I thought you were angry with me. Also, I had nothing special to say."

"Did you have a good time?"

"Not bad. Jerusalem is fascinating, as usual."

Then she said that she spent one evening in Ein Karem at a café that is also a gallery, owned by a Dutch artist. There was a young American woman there who played the guitar and sang Negro spirituals. When she returned to the Hospice after midnight, she had to knock on the gate and wake the housekeeper, a devout and stern-faced Scot.

"On the whole, did you enjoy yourself?" Again, she looked at me, hesitant. "I'm not so young anymore, Zvi, I'm past fifty."

She smiled at me very wearily, like a person who has not slept through the night, then said, as if delivering an important message, "I met Professor Schlesinger in the Old City. He asked me to give you his regards."

I got up and went to the study. I took the string of pearls out of its case and brought it to her. "A present for you from Foiglman's wife."

I placed it on her lap. Nora took it in her hand and examined it, not knowing quite what to do with it. "I certainly don't deserve it."

I hung the necklace around her neck. "It's very becoming." She removed the necklace and put it on the table. She yawned, covered her face with the palms of her hands and bent her head to her knees.

"Tired?" I said. She sat in that position for a long moment, hunched to her knees, then straightened up. "Well, I have to unpack and freshen up."

At night, when I tried to make love to her she said, "Not now, Zvi, I'm awfully tired," and turned her back to me.

꙳

The next day, when she came back from work, everything seemed to have returned to normal. She busied herself, perhaps more than usual, with cleaning the house and preparing dinner. She called Yoav, talked to Shula and Sarit, and at dinner told me about a labor dispute that was raging at the Institute over salaries and seniority. She never mentioned Jerusalem, and I did not mention Foiglman.

But at night, when I tried again to make love to her, she said, "I can't, Zvi, forgive me."

It was uttered in distress. And it was then that my suspicions were first aroused... In all our thirty three years of marriage...

Nora was a woman to whom men were not indifferent. I was well aware of that. When she walked in the street, she attracted attention, and at parties—either at the homes of friends or at formal dinners—men would seek her company, talk with her in whispers, intimately, as it were, crack jokes, try to touch her arms, shoulders, hair. Wherever there was dancing—she was never left alone for a minute. If I never doubted her fidelity, it was mainly because she never concealed anything from me. Humorously she would tell me of the inane passes made at her by this or that man, of their attempts to pick her up. One Independence Day, in the backyard of a brigadier-general friend, I myself witnessed how a colleague of mine, an ambitious young associate professor, obviously tipsy, tried to hug and kiss her under cover of the dark trees, and she laughingly and gently pushed him away, exposing his foolishness. Another time, on the balcony in the house of a certain artist who was celebrating the opening of an exhibition, the house crammed with guests, I overheard that famous artist 'confessing' to her that, since he had first set eyes on her he had been dreaming of painting her in the nude, in the position of Goya's 'Naked Maja,' and he proceeded to extol the beauty of her limbs, one by one. "A man of your imagination does not need a model," she laughed in his face.

These blandishments flattered her, of course—flattered me,

too, to some extent—but I always remained confident that a deep-seated sense of self respect and pride, as well as the tacit agreement between us to tell each other the truth, guaranteed that she would not overstep the boundary.

"Has anything happened?" I asked.

"I'm dying to sleep, Zvi," and she wrapped herself up, away from me, at the corner of the bed.

But she did not fall asleep. For a long time afterward she tossed and turned and her irregular breathing often sounded like sighs. Two or three nights later she submitted to me. But it was done almost in pain, as if she were forced. She, who had always been the more eager one. We both lay awake, she was on her back, her arms under her head, her eyes open. Without my asking her she said, "Be patient with me; it will pass," and a moment later, "a little confusion, that's all. I'll get over it."

I waited for her to continue, but when she kept silent, I said, "Did anything happen in Jerusalem?"

"Never mind, it's not worth talking about."

"Tell me anyway."

She kept silent.

My suspicion was now divested of the doubt that had covered it and stood out naked and hideous. I asked no more questions. I was stunned. Everything was suddenly shattered. The trust, the deep friendship based on honesty and openness. Now I understood her reluctance: it was as if she felt contaminated.

I conjured up all the men both of us knew in Jerusalem, and those she had known from her university days. No, I could not imagine her making love to any of them. Her pride would not let her, her body would surely recoil. Then I remembered the remark she made the morning she came back from Jerusalem, which sounded irrelevant at the time, inappropriate as a response to my question if she had enjoyed her vacation. "I'm not so young anymore. I'm past fifty." But she was still a woman at the prime of her ripeness. Desirable. And she knew it. Did she say this in order to allay my suspicions? To cover her tracks?

Did she possess a trait that I had been unaware of throughout our married life—I thought to myself—cunning? Duplicity?

I could not sleep a wink. She fell asleep just before dawn.

For the next few days we did not mention the subject, not a word. We tried to pretend that nothing had happened. We seemed to have told ourselves: If we don't discuss it, it will go away. But I was tormented by the question: Was it an insignificant accident, a frivolous flirtation she succumbed to—with whom?—and why would she not tell me about him? Didn't she know that even if it hurt me, I would forgive her.

No, it was not an insignificant matter, I told myself. Because in the nights when I withdraw from her, she lies awake for long hours, tossing and turning, and emits a sigh when she finally falls asleep in the morning. And this fatal, mysterious event, that so troubled her soul, that is now turning our lives upside down, I thought ironically, happened while I, here, was wracking my brains, with Foiglman, how to translate from Yiddish into Hebrew words like *nebekh*, *tekhterlekh*, *arayngezugt*, or *prost* and *poshet*.

Chapter twenty-two

Last night, at eight o'clock, once again: Elyakim Sasson. As usual, without prior notice, a brief, cautious ringing at the door. I open, and he whispers softly, as if afraid to disturb someone's sleep, "You're busy with your sacred work, aren't you?"

I have no patience for guests—my mind is full of the bitter memory of what happened between Nora and me after her return from Jerusalem. But I cannot very well turn him out. He walks in, hunches himself and throws glances around stealthily, takes a couple of silent steps and again whispers confidentially, "Can you offer a bed to a weary wayfarer? For one night?" I invite him to spend the night here. He puts his hand on his heart by way of thanks, and whispers, "You—go back to your sanctum sanctorum. I'll take care of myself in the other room. God forbid a worthless and despicable man like me should disturb the High Priest at his work!"

But after many entreaties he consents to sit down with me in the living room. No, he won't drink anything tonight. He studies me, trying to gauge my mood, smoothes his thick mustache with a finger, "I see I have come at the wrong time. Woe is me, star-crossed friend that I am!" When he sees that I am not amused he says, "You look a little peaked. More than usual. Has anything happened?"

I grin, "Just tired, that's all." He stares at me with his black eyes, whose mischievous glint has not waned, and pretends to be angry with me, "I won't call you to account, Zvi, but you have deceived me three times. I'm telling you again, listen attentively. If you were to come to us, even for one week, not only would your back straighten up, but your whole world view would change!"

I apologize. I'm got so much work on my plate at the moment that I couldn't leave the city even for a day... He smiles at me as if to say, "And you really expect me to believe you?"

The silence is very uncomfortable for him. Uncomfortable for both of us. "Go to work!" he enjoins me, but sees that I do not move. I look at him and think about the abyss that opened between Nora and me in those ten days, to which I, in my blindness, was completely oblivious. I think of the two distant worlds, antipodal as the poles, which the two of us inhabited. While I sat with Foiglman in this room, as in a Vale of Tears, breathing Jewish sighs, enveloped in lugubrious words, she was breathing the Edenic air of illicit amorous delights, eating sweet, forbidden fruit...

His face assumes a somber expression, and he says, "And me? Do you think I don't have bad times? Terrible depression? Truly horrid! Times I wish I were dead!... How do I snap out of it, do you think? I look around me! To the world, to the Jewish people, to Israel! And I see that the state of the world is bad, very bad, and within the world, the state of the Jewish people is hopeless, and within the Jewish people, the state of Israel is dismal, and within Israel, the state of the kibbutz is desperate, and within the kibbutz, the horticultural section is shot, down the drain, and then I tell myself: Compared to all this, who am I and what am I—a 'fetid drop,' completely worthless—to bewail my own predicament? By what right? What impudence! And then I bend down and get into the hot house to trim the 'princess crown,' the grandiflora."

"And this is your consolation for all the ills of the world, of the Jewish people and all the rest?" I was intrigued, despite myself.

"I'll tell you where I find consolation: in knowing that we

have sunk so low that there's nowhere further to sink; so from now on there is only one way: up! 'Life on the razor's edge—wholesome and strong' as Nathan Alterman-the-Wise wrote, 'At the point of the knife—we'll never grow old!' No, we won't grow old!"

He shakes his finger at me and fixes me with his blazing eyes. Then he lectures me about the way of the world: "Hear, Zvi, the instruction of your friend and forsake not the teaching of your mate. We, simple folk—and you, too, even though you have reached fame and glory, and I take my hat off to you, are a little man, a speck of dust on the wheels of history—have only one weapon against all the evil in the world: laughter! Laugh, Zvi, because without a sense of humor, you're lost. I'm telling you this because you are my buddy and I have your welfare at heart. Laugh!"

Suddenly he bends his head toward me and whispers, "Tell me, did you publish some poetry book in Yiddish?"

"Me?"

"I heard a rumor. Is it true?"

I laughed and said I had never written a poem, let alone in Yiddish. He looks me straight in the eye, scrutinizes, studies me, then says, "Me, I know maybe ten words in Yiddish, vulgar ones in fact. But Yiddish is a good language, pliant, bendable. Hebrew, on the other hand, is not easily bent. I once heard a nice phrase from one of our members who is Polish: Hebrew is a language of time, Yiddish is a language of place. I didn't quite understand it, but it sounded good. There's something to it."

Having said this, he gets up and announces that he is going to rest his weary bones because he has to get up at five AM. "Arise, ye worker!" He pats me on the shoulder.

When I woke up in the morning I remembered a dream I had. I'm in a foreign city, perhaps Paris, where crowds fill the streets, since apparently it is a holiday. In the crowd I see Foiglman, a clown's hat on his head and his face the face of a bird, like the illustrations in the "Bird Haggadah." He is walking and dancing and making funny gestures with his hands, like a harlequin entertaining the crowd. I try to approach him, but I am pushed back by the crowd. I call his name from a distance, wave to him to draw his attention, and when he turns his head to me, I realize my mistake. It is not Foiglman, it is Elyakim Sasson. I am surprised: What is he doing in this city, which is Paris in all probability? He calls me and motions to me to come closer, but I am pushed further back and the distance between us widens and I know I will not reach him. I am seized by a terrible despair. I shout: Nora! and wake up.

❧

Nora could never hide things from me for long. Not so much out of a conscientious commitment to me but due to her inability to carry the burden of a secret. One night—it was in the third week after her return from Jerusalem—she left home and did not return until midnight. I was sitting at my desk reading and heard her walk in and go directly to the bedroom. When I went there half an hour later, she was already asleep, or perhaps pretending to be.

In the morning, over coffee, she put down her cup, and while still holding its handle, gave me a look that was both amused and painful and said, "Why don't you ask me about last night?"

I replied that there were many things I had not asked her since her return.

"I saw the man I met in Jerusalem," her smile darkened.

The blood rushed to my face. I asked who the man was. Her eyelids fluttered.

"Look, there's no sense keeping it from you…" Her hand rose to her neck protectively, "While I was there…" She stopped, as if weighing her words.

"You slept with him."

Her eyes were staring at me.

"Yes."

I could hear my heart sink inside, hitting bottom. For a moment my eyes grew dim as in a faint.

"Did you enjoy it?"

She did not answer, and her eyes, staring at me, were slowly filling with tears. "I understand that it is all over between us," my lips quivered.

After a moment she said, "If you send me away, you will be right. But it'd be the end for me."

She covered her face, then wiped her tears with her hands, got up, picked up her purse and left for work. I had a very difficult day. I could not imagine that, after more than thirty years of marriage, in which we lived in perfect harmony and were both happy, and Nora, who had a 'talent for happiness,' as I used to call it, confirmed it on many occasions, that something like this would befall me. When both of us were nudging sixty. I left home and walked all the way to the university. A long way. I locked myself in my study, tried to read, to grade papers. Not for one moment could I chase away the visions of lovemaking. With whom? Where? At the Hospice? In the Jerusalem Forest? At the Valley of the Cross? The Valley of Hinnom? At the copse near Yad Vashem?

I could not believe that all that time I had been sitting with Foiglman, selecting poems to read before the two Hebrew writers— who never showed up—he in Yiddish and I in Hebrew: "She plucks the slaughtered fowl/ And opposite, on a stool, sits the boy/ His flesh all trembling/ Seeing how ugly and unglamorous Death is…" How cynically Fate plays with marital relationships, I thought. What was the point of sitting and grading a student's paper on "Hassidism and its attitude toward the *Hibat-Zion* movement"? What is done cannot be undone. And even if we did not separate, I knew that nothing would ever be the same. At the same time I told myself that what she had done was the most banal, common occurrence in marriage, something that happens every day all over the place. But it could not even begin to allay the pain I felt.

When I came home in the evening, Nora was not home. I called the Biological Institute and a cleaning woman told me everybody had left hours before. Where could she be? With the 'Man from Jerusalem'?

I went downstairs and walked up and down the street, from end to end. Yes, I told myself, our life together has come to an end. Even if she breaks up with that man—who was he? A single man? Younger than me? How did he capture her heart?—you cannot set the clock back. What would be the point of such a life?

Darkness had fallen. When I passed by the house, I saw a car weaving into a parking place. Nora got out, and when she saw me, she was startled, "You…here?" I said I was out for a breath of fresh air. She hesitated for a moment (how could the warm, sensuous look turn so cold and alienated in the space of a few days! I shuddered) then said, "Would you like to go for a little walk?"

We strolled from street to street in silence, like two strangers. No son, daughter-in-law, grandchild between us. Her heels pounding the sidewalks, one two, one two. Only when we reached the Yarkon River, and started walking along the grove by the bank, did she begin to talk. She uttered a few sentences and broke off; again a few sentences, then silence. I did not pose any question. I did not say a word. It was eleven when we returned home. Here is what had happened. She spared me no detail.

৵

When Nora got to Jerusalem, she went to the Luberskys' house. There she met a young man, about thirty five, working for the Nature Conservation Authority, who told fascinating stories about tigers in the Judean desert, around Ein Gedi. He described how they stalk them and capture them in order to tie transmitters to their bodies to keep track of them and to protect their young from other animals. When she declined to stay with Raya—since she wished to be by herself—he suggested the Scottish Hospice and took her there. Early the next morning, he called her and asked if she would like to accompany him on a trip to the mountains near the Dead Sea. She accepted, since she did not have anything else to do. They drove in his jeep to Jericho, and from there to Ein Feshha, where they took a break, dipped their feet in the water, ate from the provisions he had packed, and continued to Mitzpe Shalem. From there they descended on foot, by a winding, spiral path, to the deep canyon of Wadi Hazaza. They entered a large cave, deep and dark, and watched the birds nesting there: owls, falcons, Nubian nightjars. (When she came to nature descriptions, Nora's speech became fluent, colorful, exuberant even, as if it had nothing to do with the excruciating matter at hand.) When they emerged from the cave, they happened to see an unusually large bustard, flying over the wadi. "A real nature man," she said, "who can name every plant and every bird. A great expert on birds." They climbed back to Mitzpe Shalem, ate there and drove on to Ein Gedi, where he had a few errands at the Nature center. Then they walked to Nahal Arugot and he was going to show her one of the tiger's dens, but she was too tired, so after a while they returned to the jeep. In the evening he brought her back to the Hospice. (Here Nora kept silent for a long moment. The headlights of passing cars flickered on her face, and for a while it was imbued with deep anguish and a ghostly pallor, as if old age had suddenly crept up on her.)

The next day, he phoned her again. He asked how she was, wanted to know if she had plans for the night. She had no plans, so she accepted his invitation to go to a café on the outskirts of Jerusalem, in Ein Karem, where someone who sang American folk songs performed. He lived in that neighborhood.

There, by the flickering candlelight, in an atmosphere of intimacy, over wine, he told her about himself; born in Nahalal, born in nature. He had always liked to go on long hikes by himself, to collect fossils, rare plants, watch birds. After finishing high school and his army service, he studied botany and zoology at the College of the Kibbutz Movement in Kiryat Tivon, near Haifa. Then he went back to Nahalal, married a girl from a *moshav*, was allotted a house and a piece of land at Tamrat and started building a farm.

(This is torture! I told myself, walking at her side. The shadows of the trees, illuminated by shafts of headlights, fell on her face and receded. This is torture the way she's recounting the details of that snakelike nature man's *curriculum vitae*! She was piling up mounds of hay to bury warheads underneath!)

He soon realized he was not cut out to settle down like that, so he left the farm and became supervisor of forestry in the Galilee. That way he was able to wander from place to place and live among the rich flora and fauna of the northern regions. This nomadic life did not appeal to his young wife, and after three years of marriage they were divorced. He was not a family man to begin with, he told her. When the Nature Conservation Authority was created, he applied and was accepted, and for the last six years he had been roaming between

Jerusalem and Sodom, between the Judean mountains and the Dead
Sea, familiar with every footpath and wadi throughout that big desert.
He met Raya's husband, Michael Lubersky, when a dispute broke out
between the Nature Conservation Authority and the Water Department over the use of spring water for irrigation. Since then he had
been a frequent visitor at the Luberskys.

When they left the café he invited her to come to his house.

(From now on everything was predictable, each detail fell into
its appropriate place in my gloomy fantasies. We were now walking
under the Yarkon bridge, and the wood across the street was enveloped
in darkness. It was predictable and inevitable now. What was I doing
that night? Going over my notes on the Petliura riots? Discussing the
two languages with Foiglman? Nora remained silent, and I pressed
my lips tightly to absorb the blow without emitting a cry of pain.)

His house is made of stone, and stands alone on a hill, east
of Ein Karem, surrounded by fig and olive trees, and inside there's
a decor that invites adulterous dalliance: Bedouin rugs, Damascene
copper work, a carved nut-wood table, inlaid with ivory, earthenware
jars with desert plants in them, mineral gems in turquoise, purple,
pink—a canopied bed?

"I wasn't telling the truth when I told you that I had returned
to the Hospice after midnight. I stayed the night."

(Those words, like needles, pricked my heart, inscribing there
the final, indelible truth. They brought an end to the thin, nebulous
illusion that her admission of a few days earlier might merely have
been a vengeful figment of the imagination.)

For the next few days she was alone. The 'nature man' went to
Eilat for a business meeting. When he came back, on Monday night,
he went straight to see her at the Hospice. He stayed the night. He
confessed that he had fallen in love with her.

"He's a boy. Just a big innocent boy."

(A long silence, all along the road from the edge of the wood
back to the bridge.)

On the last day they toured the Old City together. He showed
her sites she had not heard of before, even though she had lived in
Jerusalem for four years. In the Armenian quarter they ran into Pro-

fessor Schlesinger, who sent me regards. He thought that the young man was her son.

In the bazaar he bought her a necklace of amber beads.

"When you showed me the necklace that your poet had brought, I wanted to laugh. Maybe to cry. Now I have two necklaces, neither of which I'm going to wear."

At night they dined at the Khan, and then…

"It's terrible, I know. And you'll be justified in whatever you do. I have nothing to say in my defense."

Every day he calls her at the Institute. He came to Tel Aviv twice, and they met at a café in Jaffa.

"A sad joke, this whole business. He's almost twenty years younger than I am."

And then, "I'm in a kind of whirl. The foolish illusion of rejuvenation. It'll pass. I'll come to my senses."

When we neared our home, I thought: After all, she could have concealed the whole sordid affair! Not say a word to me! I wouldn't have asked! And I was not sure if I should feel grateful to her or… No, a man cannot be grateful to someone who deals him a blow to the heart. Her frank confession only served to disarm me.

At night, in bed—with Nora at the other end, sleeping like a weary traveler after an exhausting journey—with all the scenes swirling in my mind: tigers, vultures, sunless caves, deep canyons, springs, canopied beds, gentle embraces, ecstatic love making, raging carnal desires—I suddenly remembered once seeing a brochure of the Nature Conservation Authority with its emblem: a buck with one pointed horn on its head.

A devil snickered inside me. I had not asked Nora for the name of her young lover. For myself I dubbed him 'Unicorn.'

Chapter twenty-three

I n Foiglman's Notebook C, in which the chapters were separated not by asterisks but by tiny birds, like those above his signature, I found the following paragraphs as I was leafing through.

➤

As soon as I walked into the house I felt I was an unwelcome guest. Yes, he did greet me with great politeness, but there was no gladness in his eyes, and a mist seemed to cloud his glasses. When I saw that his wife was not there—and to my question he replied that she had gone on vacation—I realized that I was the cause of her leaving the house. How else can you explain the fact that precisely before my arrival she sank under the strain of work she had been doing all year and needed a vacation? For the entire ten days he never mentioned her, and if I'm not mistaken, they did not talk to each other on the phone. I understood they had quarreled, and about me, of course.

As a matter of fact, on my first visit to their house, I already felt her reservations toward me. A tall, good looking woman—her legs a little too long and her chin a little too rounded for my taste—with something gentile about her: the arrogance of a superior race. When I told them about my experiences during the war, she sat listening with her head tilted, her straight, ash blond hair falling over a third of her face, almost covering one eye. I was reminded of my meeting with the actress Antoinette Devreux a few years ago. Hinda, who knew her from her days in the theater, introduced me to her at the foyer of the Odeon. "Henrietta told me that you suffered a lot during the war," she said, tilting her head, her golden hair falling on her left cheek.

"Yes, a little," I said.

"You were in Auschwitz."

"Only for two weeks. Most of the time I was in Majdanek." She had not heard of Majdanek, and I had to explain that it was a concentration camp in Poland, near Lublin.

"Must have been awful," she said.

"A lot of lice," I said.

"Lice!" she slapped her right cheek with her hand. "Do you remember, Henrietta, when I discovered lice in my wig? Can you imagine? Lice in the wig I was wearing as Marianne in 'Tartuffe.' We ended up burning it."

Z.'s wife, too, was condescending to me; this poor Jew 'has suffered.' He deserves kindness, compassion, perhaps even help. But only up to a point. Let's not go overboard.

And Z. himself?...Z. is a decent, gentle fellow. But I haven't quite fathomed his attitude toward me. On the one hand, he shows a lot of sympathy for me. And for the rest of my life I shall be grateful for what he has done for me. If it were not for him, my poems would not have been translated, and if he fulfills his promise—the book will also be published thanks to him. No Yiddish writer in Israel, let alone a Hebrew writer, would have taken all this trouble for me. On the other hand, there is no warmth there. He keeps his distance. Politely he walks with me, shows me the bus stop, this and that store, various offices. And I want to grab him by the shoulders and shout, "Reb Hirsch! Don't be so polite with me! Be warm! Warm! We are brother Jews, aren't we?"

When he found me standing in the kitchen preparing a meal for us, I saw his panic. That was something he did not expect! How could I?—I had invaded the inner sanctum of the family. And I, who took him literally at his word—"make yourself at home here"—said, "You know the saying: 'A guest who brings food from the mart warms the cockles of his hostess's heart.' He looked at me and smiled, "Here, even my daughter-in-law keeps out of the kitchen…"

His is a gloomy smile, tinged with mockery, behind his glasses. Why the mockery? Perhaps for our very existence in this world.

Now I know I made a big mistake when I accepted his invitation. Already in Paris, when he spoke to me on the phone, I sensed from his voice that his invitation was not sincere. But it was convenient to delude myself.

And to be on his back for ten days!

*"The first day: a welcome guest. The second day: a millstone round the neck. The third day: starting to reek. The fourth day: take to your heels and scram!" **

➤

In my honor Zvi invited two Hebrew authors to his house. Neither of them came. One found some excuse and apologized. The other did not even bother to apologize. As far as I'm concerned, I've endured worse misfortunes. But I felt very sorry for him. He tried so hard. And what's his reward? Only grief. I thought to myself: What does he need all this business that only brings him trouble and humiliation? After all, what am I to him? Maybe I'm an 'historical document' for him…

➤

At the store where I buy groceries, the woman behind the counter is short, heavy-set and lame. The effort of dragging her lame foot has etched a painful expression on her face, like an unuttered shriek. Whenever she needs to get something down from the top shelf—a can, a jar of jelly she asks one of the customers to climb up for her. When I came in there for the second time and asked in Hebrew for herring and pickles, a crooked smile appeared on her face and she said in Yiddish, "Reb Yid, why break your teeth? To me you can speak mame loshen." Naturally, as fellow Jews from Poland, we asked each other, Where do you come from? It turned out that she was from Krasnostav. I said,

* This is a Yiddish proverb.

"Krasnostav? I was there many times! My uncle used to deliver flour to
Krasnostav!"

"What's his name?"

"Foiglman."

"Foiglman the miller?"

"Yes, Foiglman the miller." Well, she had been to Zamosc several
times. In her youth she was a member of the Bund youth movement, and
every May Day they participated in the parade in town. She remembered
the promenade, the lake with the island in the middle, the ancient
prison, the statue of Valerian Lukashinsky… "I remember crates full of
fish floating in the river, which the fish merchants put there to cool for
the Sabbath…"

Other customers came in, and I was about to leave. "If you're not
in a hurry, wait a minute," she said. I waited. When we were alone again,
she asked if I knew what had happened to Doctor Lerner. I replied that
as far as I knew he died in the typhoid epidemic that broke out in the
ghetto in 1941. "That's it." she nodded. "That's it." She told me that he
used to come to their village every other week to lecture on Marx, Adler
and Otto Bauer at their club. Those were difficult topics, yet people would
come and listen, fascinated by his talk, he was so eloquent and his manner so captivating. "In the epidemic then…" she nodded. I asked where
she herself had been at that time. "Better not ask," she tightened her lips
shut and darted a piercing and bitter look at me.

Here, in the grocery store, I felt at home. There, in his house, I
felt like a stranger.

➤

In the night my soul is restless, I get up, I lie down, get up again, walk
about the rooms, careful not to wake my host. The street is quiet, stars
twinkle above the treetops. The Land of Israel. I feel my body: alive and
aware.

I remember the night when I fell on the snow, the column marching past, and suddenly on my back, like fire lashing…

➤

Sholem Aleichem House is blind and mute. Nobody comes or goes. In *the house where Peretz lived there are many rooms, many books, but there are no people.*

I was told that there was a Bund *club in town. I went to see it. A side alley in the old quarter of Tel Aviv with only businesses and offices. I could hardly find the sign, in Yiddish and Hebrew, at the rear entrance of the house. I knocked on the door—no answer. The blinds are shut.*

Twice I looked in on Leivick House. Like a deserted synagogue. Yes, there is a secretary there, a pleasant, hardworking woman; she types, makes phone calls, takes notes, seals envelopes, files, sells tickets to performances of singers and actors that take place once a week in the hall there.

A man walks in, leaning on a walking stick, goes to the shelf, picks out a newspaper, sits at a table and reads. Fifteen minutes later, another man walks in, a handkerchief clutched to his nose; he sneezes, wipes his nose, walks over to the shelf, rummages through the papers and cannot find what he wants. Realizing that he has been preceded, he walks to the other man and intimates that he is waiting for him to finish reading. In the meantime he sits down at another table and stares out of the window, both hands resting on his stick.

I went up to the secretary and introduced myself. She did not recognize my name. I asked if she had heard of the actress and singer Henrietta Fogel, my wife. She hadn't. I told her briefly about her performances all over the world and asked if she could come and perform here one of these days. The secretary said that the audience was more or less constant, numbering about a hundred and fifty people. Twenty performing artists compete for this audience. Once in a while guest artists from abroad arrive—from the theater in Rumania, Warsaw, the United States or Argentina—but those artists are sponsored and supported by certain organizations. If I know of any landsmanshaft or public council or some government agency that would agree to sponsor her, then we could discuss the possibility of two or three performances...

Every Friday morning, the secretary said, about a dozen writers assemble here, sip tea around the long table, discuss organizational, literary and theatrical matters. If I come between eleven and one, I could consult them, too... But on Friday I have to go to Ramlah.

➤

Sometimes I walk about this Mediterranean city and forget what country I'm in.

I pass by robust young men, wearing brief shorts, their bare chests gleaming in the sun, a towel thrown over the shoulder, a transistor in hand—returning from the beach, apparently—salty languor in their eyes. I pass barefoot girls, in ragged dresses that trail on the sidewalk, or in see-through T-shirts that reveal their protruding nipples, English logos splashed across their chests: 'Love me,' 'I'm Available,' 'Only on Sundays' and the like—throwing listless glances about them. On the sidewalk, in broad daylight, I see a couple embracing, in sublime ecstasy, the man in narrow white pants, perched on the railing, his legs apart, between his thighs a bare-shouldered girl, her face bent to his face, her arms clutching his neck, her mouth clings to his mouth, they are oblivious to the world around.

At noon, in the cafés that sprawl onto the sidewalks, dozens of young men and women sit, swilling beer, sipping coffee, licking ice cream, chewing pizzas, indifferently staring at the parade of passersby, or lasciviously ogling the proud golden haired beauties…who strut haughtily in front of them, or the latest, glittering Mercedes models, driven by young men in Italian-made shirts, sending the blaring of their musical horns into the air.

At night, outside the movie theaters, groups of noisy, clucking urchins, cracking loud jokes, idly roaming about, and young girls with enormous manes and short skirts, mill around or cling to one another's shoulders, giggling and twittering. What did I really expect to find here? Seminaries and synagogues echoing with Torah learning? Or circles of pioneers dancing the Hora with Hassidic fervor?

But why is everything so promiscuous? So extroverted? Where does this empty-headed arrogance come from? Where has the seriousness, the legacy of generations of Jewish grief gone? The contemplation? The introspection? Only yesterday…

And tomorrow too.

Chapter twenty-four

Last night I dreamed about my late father. The two of us were walking side by side, between two rows of tall earthenware jars. Every jar I passed by cracked and crumbled and broke into shards. He scolded me. Zvi, can't you be careful? These jars are used for storing grain! I cried out in a choking voice: But I didn't even touch them! I don't touch them at all!

These days I find myself thinking a lot about him. Our home was like a hotel for him, a lodgings house—a port from which to sail away and to return to rest from the hardships of traveling. Most of his conversations with us consisted of stories he gleaned on those journeys: a cave in which he found a disintegrating parchment; a trickling spring which he chanced upon between Herodion and Nebi Mussa and which is not marked on any map; an encounter with a Greek monk in Wadi Kelt; a feast in the tented camp of the Azazma tribe; a banquet in the house of Mussa Alami in Jericho; his escape from a gang of Arab hoodlums who pelted his car with stones when he passed through Jenin; a heated argument he had with a British police officer in Tulkarem; a herd of mountain goats he spotted on the cliffs above Ein Avdat—but he never brought any archeological findings home. There was no jar, figurine, capital of a column or piece of mosaic to be found in our house or in our yard. Strangers walking into the house would never have guessed that an archeologist lived there, unless they examined the bookshelves in his study, filled with history, archeology and travel books—in Hebrew, English, German and Russian.

Our house in Rehovot was an old one-story house. Three rooms and a porch. Devoid of charm or elegance. The orange color of its exterior had long faded, worn by the rain and the sun. Many slates in the roof were dislodged and warped, covered with moss. The sink in the kitchen was speckled with black dots and had never been replaced. The window frames were cracked, but my father never noticed any of this, and my mother was too busy to undertake any repairs, renovations or modernizations. She would come back from work in the nursery at two o'clock and all afternoon was busy cleaning, cooking, laundering; taking care of my father's and my needs.

When my father had to stay home for a few days, between digs, or due to the weather, he would absorb himself in professional books. He was a self-taught man. His education consisted of high school and three years of the history of antiquity and ancient languages at the University of Riga. He did not have a Master's degree. And yet he dug and discovered and deciphered more than most of his colleagues. And they respected him and consulted him often. However, he was reluctant to write anything down—he considered it a waste of valuable time. The university people implored him—demanded of him—to sum up his findings in writing, to write surveys and publish them in periodicals, but he shrugged them off: "I'm illiterate; if you want a paper, send me a student who can write; I'll talk to him and he'll write it down." And so it was. In all his years of work he did not publish more than twelve papers under his own name, and those, too, were written by his assistants.

The running of the household and all financial matters were entrusted to my mother. He never interfered and never questioned. He handed her his salary and she alone decided how to dispense the money that they both earned. She paid the bills, and each month set aside a small sum for a nest egg. She had a small book in which she marked the sums deposited. She never wrote checks, paying for everything in cash. She always carried a little money in her purse; the rest she hid in the pantry. Very rarely did my parents quarrel, and when he did lose his temper with her it was for lecturing him that he was 'killing himself with idolatry.'

He died probably the way he would have liked to die: at a dig. Just like an actor wishing to breathe his last on the stage, or a knight on a battlefield. It was a sudden death. He collapsed and lost consciousness. When the ambulance arrived from Arad, it was too late to resuscitate him.

Many came to his funeral; they came from all over the country. Archeologists from three universities, students and youngsters who had worked with him, kibbutz members who became his friends when he dug near their settlements, officials at the Antiquities Department. Many people from our village, his friends and my mother's friends. They did not come just to fulfill an obligation, but because they really loved and admired him. "Ashes to ashes and dust to dust," his archeologist friend eulogized when the grave was covered. "You are gathered to your forefathers whose remains you dug out of your beloved soil."

During the *shiva* I went through his papers. Among the pages of notes he had scribbled to himself in a sprawling, unruly handwriting, I found dozens of crumpled little notes with place names, words in Aramaic, Sumerian, Phoenician, inscriptions in square characters, snatches of biblical verses, signs and marks that only he could understand. On one of them was written, "The word will be passed from generation to generation."

When my mother and I walked around the yard, she pointed to the pomegranate, plum, guava and lemon trees growing there and said, "It says in scripture, 'For man's life is like that of the tree of the field.' But it isn't so. We go deeper and deeper into the earth, while they rise out of it and reach up to the heavens."

※

All the time that Foiglman stayed here he never inquired about the payment for the translation. I wondered what he was thinking: Could he be so naive as to believe that the translation was a labor of love and the translator expected no fee? Or perhaps he had decided to settle the matter with me when the work was completed?

For several reasons I, too, did not bring up the matter in our conversations. First, one does not embarrass a guest by reminding him of an outstanding debt. Second, as soon as he had arrived, he had said something about their being in financial straits because his wife now had fewer performances. And third, how could I ask him to pay for the translation, I said to myself, when the string of pearls he brought for Nora alone was probably worth a lot more than the sum I spent for him?

About a month after his departure—a very long month, when each day was a lifetime, with me containing my pain inside, trying to suppress it by forcing myself to continue my daily routine, restraining myself from alluding to what had happened and eating my heart out—Zelniker called me and cheerfully announced that he had finished the work and was ready to 'deliver the goods.'

We met in the same café as before, and he presented me with a sheaf of pages, neatly arranged, numbered, vocalized, tidily typewritten, ready for publication. I leafed through, running my eyes over poems whose translation I had already seen, and perusing others newly translated. Zelniker watched me intently, as if waiting for praise and said, "The truth is, when you first brought me the book and I read it for the first time, I didn't think much of it, but when I got involved in the work, I realized there was much more in the poems than meets the eye. They sound too sentimental, too maudlin, but no! What you have here is a complete *Weltanschauung* of a man who confronts death every day, struggles with it and triumphs. There are recurrent metaphors that derive from his private nightmares… Take, for example, the poem *In the Desert*…

Thumbing dexterously through the pages, like a bank teller counting banknotes, he immediately found the poem in question and read it:

A reversed shadow falls
On my steps in the sand
And wheels of fire

Scorch the skies.
I lift my eyes:
Where are you, Elijah?
I clutch at the hem of your mantle
And you, you ascend in your chariot into heaven!
A broad-winged hawk hovers in the skies
Circling, circling, casting its shadow on the land.
Is it my carcass you seek, Hawk?
The closed eyeballs of my life?
I lower my eyes to the ground;
From the heat of the noontime sun
Behind me I see:
How shadow upon shadow falls.

"Layers of profundity!" he thumped the page with a shaking hand. "A poem by a man yearning for salvation, seeking God, who receives no reply. This image of the shadow recurs in many of the poems. The shadow of a memory, the shadow of terror, the shadow of death—it is the biblical 'Shadow of Death'—and the image becomes a symbol. If only I could write, I would write an article on 'The Shadow in Shmuel Foiglman's Poetry.'"

"Write it!" I said. "It will be the first review of the book after its publication."

"Me?" he chuckled, "I've never written an article in my life. Besides, as the translator I can't do it. I had a part in it... It wasn't easy, you know. This poem alone, *In the Desert*, took me three days. I had to make many changes, deviate from the original, to find equivalents for the Yiddish alliterations. Instead of the 'Sh' and 'T' that are prominent in the Yiddish text, in the Hebrew—I used the sounds of 'Tz' and 'Kh'... But on the whole, I enjoyed the work. I was so absorbed in it that I even forgot to call you when I was half way through, to ask you to pay me the second third..."

I asked him if he had mentioned anything about the translation fee to Foiglman.

"Foiglman? Why? The agreement was between you and me! You surely have an agreement with him to repay your loan!"

"Yes, of course," I said, and took out my checkbook and wrote him a check for the balance.

He examined the check, folded it and put it in his wallet. I asked him if he could recommend a publisher I might approach with the poems.

"I'm telling you what I told Foiglman: It's not going to be easy. The state-funded publishing houses serve only the celebrated sabra authors, the commercial publishers pander only to popular poetasters," he grinned, enjoying his *jeu de mots*. "What's left? Small private publishers, those that will publish anything provided the author pays the expenses…"

A moment later he added, "As a matter of fact, for a fee, almost all the publishers would be willing to print…"

"How much money are we talking about? For a book of this order?" I weighed the bundle of pages in my hands.

"A book of this order…a hundred and twenty pages…" Zelniker reckoned in his head, "I would say…about three times the translation fee."

I let out a whistle.

"Does Foiglman have money?" Zelniker whispered.

"I don't know. I will have to write to him."

"But after having invested in the translation…he can't just abandon the book," he looked worried. "And what about me? What have I toiled for? Just for my fee?"

I said perhaps he hoped that the poems spoke for themselves and would appeal to the editors…

Zelniker sighed, "Yes, that's the way it is here. A poet's reputation is what counts, not his poetry. God save us from publishers."

Then he gave me the names of three publishing houses whose editors he knew. "They have some liking for poetry—maybe they'll give you a reduction."

Then, as he took his leave of me at the café door, he wagged his index finger at me, "One day Foiglman will be famous! An excellent poet!"

❧

Just as a few months earlier I had begged translators, now I started courting publishers.

And again, there was disappointment upon disappointment. The first person I took the sheaf of translations to was an editor who, several years earlier, had been a lecturer in Social Sciences at the university. A week later he called me, and in a friendly tone, colleague to colleague, said: "It's never going to work. Even if I throw all my weight around on the editorial board, they won't accept it. We've had similar manuscripts before, by Holocaust survivors—they were all rejected."

Another editor, at a state-funded publishing house, who was recommended to me as an energetic person, eager to discover new poets, contacted me after reading the manuscript, saying that it was "a very interesting document," and "there is definitely something there." However, he added, that sort of book was not in their line. He suggested the names of two publishers who "specialize in the subject of the Holocaust." When I called a third editor, a professor of literature at one of the universities, to ask about the manuscript he had been sitting on for three weeks, he told me laconically and categorically: "Not for us." When I asked him to explain, he said, "I have nothing to explain. You're in history, I'm in literature. You won't understand my explanation anyway."

When I look back on those attempts to interest the publishers and ask myself what possessed me to thus devote myself to publishing somebody else's book, without even involving the author himself, to dedicate the better part of my time and my money, it becomes more and more apparent to me that I did not do it solely out of altruism, or out of love for the man and for his poetry. It was an attempt to distract myself from the wretched affair that hovered like an evil spirit around our house; to distract my spirit by engaging in an uncommon activity that would absorb my energy, my thoughts, my ambition, and drive away other, bitter, poisonous, considerations. At the same time—yes, I have to admit—it reflected my rather infantile wish to take revenge on Nora by some act of retaliation: she transgressed our common estate—so I, too, would transgress it, damage it, by squandering our common savings, by offering it to a stranger.

The fourth editor I approached was a noted poet and the director of a publishing house. A few days after receiving the manuscript he called and asked me to come to his office. The bundle of pages was lying on his desk.

"Is the poet your friend?"

"Yes, he's my friend." I explained that he lived in Paris and had asked me to help him have the book published.

"So you're his agent, so to speak." The poet, a bespectacled, round faced man, about ten years my junior, smiled at me.

"Something like that." He laid his hand on the bundle, examined it, as if deliberating with himself, then raised his eyes to me, "Look, our terms are as follows: the author kicks in two thirds of the investment. Half the sum is paid at the signing of the contract, the other half when the book is out. The first edition—in this case, 500 copies, I reckon—if it's sold out, covers our production, operating and distribution expenses, and we don't make any profit on it. Naturally, the author doesn't make any profit either. If we print a second edition, he will receive the usual royalty—ten percent of the retail price of the book."

When I stared at him for a long moment in silence he asked, "Is it acceptable to you?"

I said, "If this is the standard procedure..."

I asked how long it would be before the book appeared. "As far as we're concerned, we can start printing tomorrow. In about three months, if there are no hitches."

I expected him to comment on the poems themselves, but he said nothing. "Shall I draw up the contract, then?" he asked. I told him to make the agreement between the publisher and Shmuel Foiglman, and I would sign it as his representative. In a rider they should specify that I would be responsible for the payments.

A week later I signed the contract and paid the first installment, a sum equal to two months of my salary. I wrote Foiglman the good news and enclosed a copy of the contract. His reply was replete with thanks and terms of affection. The large envelope also contained a chrome page with the illustration for the cover of the book, drawn by his friend, the artist Yacov Kramer: a bent bough of a tree in the fall, with a tiny bird at its top, shivering in the cold.

At the bottom of the letter he wrote: "As for the payments—let me make clear: as soon as I come to Israel, before the book comes out, I shall repay you every penny. Regard it as a loan for three months for which, as for everything else, I am eternally grateful to you."

"Eternally grateful" Foiglman wrote, not knowing how grateful I had been to him when I signed the contract. Once more, as in the matter of the translation, I felt myself lifting off the ground. I remember the moment, as I was coming out of the editor's office—my eyes blinked at the intense sunlight—I felt years younger and light-footed. I had delivered myself from the depressing, suffocating atmosphere I found myself in at home—into the sphere where the Muses hover. I wanted to call out to people in the street: "Poems are being published! Soon they'll flutter in the air before your eyes!"

And I pictured Foiglman dancing, clowning around, like a jester at a Jewish wedding.

Chapter twenty-five

I find this excerpt in Foiglman's second notebook:

I sat in a hall at the Sorbonne and listened to eight lectures by learned scholars who had gathered here from all over the world for this conference on "The Study of the Holocaust." A professor from Belgium, an imposing man, tall, elegant, in an immaculate suit, spoke for an hour on the attitude of the Red Cross toward Jewish refugees and inmates of the death camps. Another participant, from Canada, a short, bespectacled man, with a high-pitched voice, read a résumé of a paper he had written—as if reading clauses in a contract—about the negotiations between the Horty regime in Hungary and the authorities of the German occupation in 1944, concerning 'solutions' to the Jewish problem. A third, a Jewish professor from Philadelphia, a smug-looking pot-bellied man, with cheeks that hung like sugar packets from his face, and short legs that made him waddle like a duck, lectured with great fluency and gusto on the conflicting versions of the number of people gassed at the crematoria in each of the concentration camps. A young German professor, aged around thirty-five, spoke very excitedly, his youthful face all flushed, about the influence of the Holocaust on the German language and its syntax. A small woman from Israel, about fifty-five or sixty, with a very stern look in her eyes and a sharp, forceful tone of voice, spoke in good French about the efforts of Yad Vashem to collect and store testimonies, both oral and written. An Austrian professor, tall and reedy, with a rimless pince-nez and a square moustache, demonstrated with numerous citations that the Wehrmacht in the countries occupied by the Germans knew about the exterminations and even took part in them.

All the speakers read their papers and quoted extensively from each other's books and papers, and lavished praise on their colleagues who lectured before them or were scheduled to lecture after them.

I sat in the hall listening to the learned and lengthy talks, with the aid of earphones, and kept asking myself what they were talking about. Whom were they referring to? Were they talking about me, too? Citing testimonies, documents, books, studies, adducing statistics, statistics...

'And man isn't there,' as Chekhov says.

That is to say: Life. Death.

In the middle of a talk by a professor from Helsinki University on the extermination of the gypsies, I suddenly pricked up my ears at the mention of "Kungskirchen."

I almost let out a cry toward the podium: "I was there!"

But five other names immediately followed, the names of other camps, and without stopping at any of them, the lecturer continued to rattle off statistics and citations from documents. At one of the intermissions I happened to sit at the same table in the cafeteria with two of the speakers. I asked a naive question: If all the lectures are read from papers, what's the point of the conference? You could publish them, bind them together in a booklet, and send it to the four corners of the world. One of them, a young professor from the University of Lyon replied, "There is a difference! When you meet, you exchange ideas and information, argue, make contacts..." The other one, a thick yellow beard surrounding a puffy face from which peered narrow, mirthful eyes, a broad chest dressed in a T-shirt displaying a large UCLA logo, chuckled:

"Don't you believe him. For us Americans, it's simply an opportunity to spend a few days in Paris. Next year we're inviting them to Los Angeles, in two years, it's Helsinki, in three, Budapest...the same lectures only in reverse order... Am I right?"

He patted his colleague on the shoulder and roared with laughter. Then he turned to me, "And where are you from?"

I said, "I'm from here, from Paris."

"The Sorbonne?"—

"No," I looked him in the eye. "From another university, one you probably haven't heard of."

He fixed me with his mirthful, penetrating eyes, as if to say, "You can't fool me," and muttered, "Are you from Poland?"

"You have the perspicacity of a scholar."

I paid him a compliment in the same language. "You know what we're like," he bent his face to my face, our noses almost touching, "we sniff each other's asses, like dogs!"...and again he roared with a gust of laughter that made his belly quiver.

Apparently, a huge industry of scholarship is now processing the ashes of the victims. A thriving industry on an enormous production scale. At the conference I heard that in America alone there are already twenty-two faculties of 'Holocaust Studies' with fifty professors. Hundreds of books and papers have been published, and doctoral theses are turned out in the thousands. There is no shortage of subjects: The Attitude of the Doberman Pinschers Toward the Inmates of the Labor Camps; Rats as Carriers of Typhus in Buchenwald; The Manufacture of Brushes in Germany and Jewish Women's hair; The Effect of Maggots on Inmates' Intestines at Majdanek...

In one of the lectures, somebody said that history is the "collective memory of humanity." I have only my private memory; that's why I'm a total ignoramus in history.

Chapter twenty-six

Since Nora's confession, a worm had lodged itself inside my body—jealousy. Creeping inwardly, gnawing, burrowing, incessantly consuming. There was no way to eliminate it. The green-eyed monster and her evil, conniving offspring that trails her everywhere—suspicion. We never mentioned the affair again. Not a word. It was a forbidden subject between us. But the air was charged with it.

And the stranger was present at home, day and night, witness to the silences and the exchanges between us. He followed me in my comings and goings, assuming all manner of guises. Sometimes, despite the fact that Nora had told me he was around forty, twenty years younger than herself, I would picture him as a slender, tall youth, keen-eyed and sun tanned, with auburn curls falling on his brow, like a biblical shepherd boy; at other times, I imagined him as a robust man, broad shouldered and thick voiced, a member of the legendary military reconnaissance units; at times, a mischievous wag, a charlatan, who by regaling women with tall tales and pleasantries lures them to his den. Somehow, he was always dressed in shorts, exposing hairy thighs.

From time to time, Nora would come home late from work.

At six or seven, sometimes later. I resolved not to ask any questions. But my imagination, rankling with leprous jealousy and suspicion, would roam the alleys of Jaffa, along the beach, in the thickets of woods, creep into hotel rooms like a thief through the windows.

We kept up the pretense. We continued to be a couple of respectable intellectuals. Jealousy is a despicable, shameful vice that one conceals or never admits to. We were careful to continue our routines. As usual, I would go to work at the university and come home—as late as possible, so as not to precede her, not to have to face an absence that would unleash the Dogs of Suspicion. In the evenings I would lock myself in my study and pore over papers and books; the testimonies of the Petliura's massacres waging hopeless battle against the phantom of the stranger, that 'nature man' who rose before my eyes. As usual, Nora would do her household chores, with even greater application. She walked about the rooms quietly, gingerly, as if careful to let sleeping dogs lie. She served dinner quietly, soundlessly. "Do you want your coffee now?"

When I raised my eyes to her, I would see her high, handsome forehead under the straight line of her hair—the blond hair tinged with gray—imbued with gloomy, other-worldly pallor, as if touched by Cupid's hand.

Sometimes, in the evenings, when I stole out of my room and glanced in the living room, I would see her seated in an armchair, an open book on her lap, a hand stopping her mouth and her eyes staring ahead, as if totally absorbed in some inner trouble, and the sight lacerated my heart. It's him she's seeing in front of her. She's tormented, like Tantalus whose mouth could not reach the forbidden fruit

I could hear her, beyond the wall, turning on the television for some British program like Armchair Theater, and then a few moments later, getting up, turning it off, and with slow, despondent steps, going to the bedroom.

Every sentence we uttered was like a stone that dropped into a pond.

One night, when we were at a Philharmonic concert (they were playing Berlioz's 'Symphonie fantastique'), I noticed from the corner of my eye how, during the adagio—when the flutes' serene strains evoked scenes of pastoral tranquility, rustling of leaves in the wind, amorous musings—her eyes filled with translucent tears and her throat tightened in an attempt to swallow them.

I still drove her to the Institute in the morning, or else she drove me to the university. Only the light farewell kisses stopped. However, when Yoav, Shula and Sarit came for a visit, the dammed up spring of familial warmth would well up in her, and she was once again lively and laughing, engaging in pleasant conversation, hugging the child, kissing her, chatting with her, singing to her.

In the nights—we did not withdraw from each other. With a lust we had not experienced for many years we now clasped each other's arms. But it was mere lasciviousness, not an act of love but of fury: we would pour into each other's body the fury we harbored in our bones all day, the silences, the resentment of each other and of ourselves. Two accomplices, partners in debauchery.

And after release would come the long wakeful hours, she on her side, I on mine, without exchanging a word.

The stranger between us, the invisible man, snickered behind the lattice The Unicorn

The air was charged; it seemed that all that was needed was a spark, and it would burst into flame. And burst it did. And as often happens in families, the fight was over money matters.

One evening, Nora stormed into the house, pale, agitated, her eyes open wide, said she had gone to the bank to withdraw some money, and the teller informed her that we were a huge amount in the red. She was stunned, then claimed there must be an error. But he produced a statement showing black on white the withdrawal of the sum that I had paid to Zelniker on April 13. "What happened?" she asked flabbergasted, "did you buy something behind my back?"

I asked her to sit down. I sat facing her and said quietly, "I lent this sum to Foiglman. To have his book published."

She let out a shriek. "What?!" Her flaming eyes bore into me. "You took out that much money from our joint account without even asking me?"

I replied—containing within me another, bitter, rage that had been seething for weeks—that Foiglman was a trusted friend, and that

I had a right to do as I pleased with my money. This only incensed her more, and she lashed at me—anger choking her throat, almost exploding—that it was not my money alone, both of our salaries went into it; I had deceived her, I had tricked her, I had acted in an underhanded, cowardly way. From that moment on, our house shook with quarrels, like a raging heat wave that withers all spots of greenery in its wake.

We abandoned all the outward trappings of good manners and civility, the attributes that lend respectability to a professional couple that is concerned with culture and science. In rude, vulgar language, we would provoke each other.

The following day, returning from work, she entered my room, disdainfully slapped a sheaf of bank statements in front of me and, with a finger, pointed to three large sums, circled in red, that I had withdrawn from the account—the sums paid out to the translator and the publisher. Her eyes flashing, she turned on me, "So that wasn't the first time you cheated me! It's been going on for months! And all to ingratiate yourself with your beloved Yiddish poet; you surrendered yourself to him, body and soul; you even dipped into our savings! At a great loss, too! You were so confident I wouldn't find out!"

I retorted that if I had really intended to keep it a secret from her, I would have found another way to lend my friend the money— and I here emphasized the word 'my friend'—not through a regular checking account where every transaction is registered.

The mounting resentment, the contentiousness, the consuming urge to win the verbal swordplay, drove us both mad. Our tongues became sharp, dripping venom, at times as crass as fishmongers, at others as acrimonious as contending attorneys; we became completely irrational. Nora declared she would press charges against me for embezzlement; I laughed and said that the law was on my side, since each party to a joint account is entitled to unilaterally withdraw, deposit, transact, sign and cancel. She immediately demanded that we separate the accounts and that I reimburse her. I told her if that were indeed her wish, we would have to divide the property, too. I closed the windows so that our shouting would not be heard.

When I think back on how low we sank in our exchanges—

arguing about our share in the joint property, our salaries, our parents'
inheritance, monies we had each used for personal expenses—she on
dresses and jewelry, I on books, travels etc.—I feel so utterly ashamed.
I remember that even then, in the midst of our fights, I would tell
myself: These must be our doubles, not us, squabbling like this. This
isn't my voice emerging from me, and it isn't her voice. We are a
couple of impostors, putting on an act not of our choosing. After all,
Nora had never been interested in money matters, never checked the
accounts. Nothing could be further from her heart. Sometimes, in
the middle of a fight, I felt like stopping short, as if a verse from an
ancient prayer was echoing inside of me. "Remember the covenant,
contain your evil Inclination," and saying softly, "Nora, why are we
making such fools of ourselves? We both know that you're not yourself and I'm not myself now," then take her in my arms, cry on each
other's shoulders.

But the stranger always loomed before me, standing like Satan
between us, rekindling my bitter resentment, preventing me from
forgiving. During one of these fights, when our voices rose in the
evening, I took my bedding from our conjugal bed and moved them
to the couch in my study.

For a few days, silence reigned in the house, a hostile, tight-
lipped silence. I, ensconced in my corner, she in hers. In the morning
she went into the kitchen, deliberately avoiding me, drank her coffee
hurriedly, then left for work. In the evening she came back—where
had she been all these hours?—and when I locked myself in my study,
she locked herself in the bedroom, or shut the living room door
behind her. She left me hastily written notes on the kitchen table or
on my desk or by the phone, "I'm taking the car, you'll have to do
without;" "the insurance agent called, call him back;" "the plumber's
coming at three, make sure someone's home;" "the Brombergs have
invited us for Saturday; you can go by yourself;" "order gas;" "some
student called; I didn't get her name;" "please do not involve Yoav
and Shula in this disgraceful business!!!"

I would stare at those words, scan them for a sign of reconciliation, searching in the familiar handwriting for the tenderness and
gentleness that were now no more. But it was like a forest fire, which

burns unextinguished for days on end, the fire on occasion abates, subsides, smolders, but then, suddenly, the wind blows and fans the fire, the flames rise, crackle, and pounce on the boughs and consume everything in sight.

Then, suddenly, with no warning at all, after two or three days of silence between us, at ten or eleven at night, when I was sitting and grading papers in my study, Nora opened the door. From the threshold, she hurled at me, like a judge pronouncing a verdict, "You were ready to destroy our lives for the sake of that Yid!" She slammed the door without waiting for a reply. Another time, before leaving for work, she stopped at the door and declared, "You are a selfish man, completely impervious to other people's feelings. You're capable of watching someone writhe at your feet, howling in agony, and you won't even offer him a glass of water!" and stormed out. On another occasion, when I was standing on a ladder, looking for a book on the top shelf, she said, her voice choking with restrained emotion, "You've been living with me for more than thirty years. Have you ever, even once, asked yourself who I am? What's going on inside of me? What's eating me up? You can see things that happened two hundred years ago, thousands of miles away, but what happens under your own roof here, next to you..."

I hardened my heart and did not reply. And one night when I was sitting in the living room watching the news, she walked in vigorously and turned off the television. She demanded to know what was going to happen with the money I had given to that miserable poet, and when was he going to return it.

Taken by surprise by this sudden attack, it was only after a moment that I was able to reply calmly, "He'll return it when he comes to Israel."

"When is he coming?"

"When the book is published. Soon."

"Why can't he send it from there now?"

"He doesn't have it now."

"How do you know he'll have it then?" Her voice contained suppressed rage about to erupt.

"He gave me his word. I believe him."

"With no guarantees? For such an amount?"

I was silent for a moment, then replied that a man like him, who had shown such generosity to me, to her, deserved a little kindness on my part.

"What generosity has he shown me?" Her face was livid with rage; the taut skin made it look like a death mask.

I said the string of pearls he had given her was worth more than the loan I advanced him.

She threw me a sharp look and walked out. A moment later she reappeared, holding the string of pearls, shouting, "Give it back to him!" She hurled it at my feet and left. The string broke and the pearls scattered and rolled on the floor. I knelt and started gathering them, one by one. After that, like a lull after a tempest, there was silence in the house for many days.

Chapter twenty-seven

We spent my first sabbatical year in Boston. In May, Nora was in her fourth month of pregnancy, and what I remember most vividly from the spring and summer of that year, more than thirty years ago, are the many trips we took. On Saturdays and Sundays, we would get into the little car we had bought when we first arrived in Boston and drive off, first to the parks on the outskirts of the city, then to the neighboring towns of Concord, Amherst, Salem, Lexington, and Cape Cod. We would wander for hours in the expanse of Franklin Park to the south of town, walking along paths in thick woods, by little rivulets, among ponds and lakes teeming with ducks and swans with gorgeous water lilies floating on top. Nora had learned the names of North American flora, so foreign to our landscape, and from time to time, she would stop, her face radiant with happiness, to identify them: elm, hickory, maple, linden, fir, nut tree. "It's funny," she said on one of our walks, "I should be getting heavier and heavier but, in fact, I feel lighter and lighter, I'm pulled upward!" And indeed she looked as if she were hovering in that lush green temple, with the light streaming through the meshed boughs and foliage, scintillating on her face. She was attentive to the life growing inside and to the plants growing outside, as if the two processes intermingled.

In the first months of our stay there, in winter, she went every day to the biological labs at MIT; she had become friends with one of the senior researchers there, a woman of Polish extraction. But later, in spring, she succumbed to a lazy, languorous weariness, and stopped going to the lab. When I went to the libraries at Harvard, she would go for walks in the old town, in Beacon Hill, along the Charles, visit museums and galleries, and in the evening, curl up with a book.

She became an avid reader of nineteenth century American literature after we had visited the towns where those authors' memories were preserved and commemorated. After a visit to Emily Dickinson's house in Amherst, she hastened to the library to borrow her poetry, her letters and biography, and for weeks on end, was completely wrapped up in the poet's life, sharing her solitude, her illness, her loves and her beliefs. After we had spent two days in Salem, Nora immersed herself in Hawthorne's *The Scarlet Letter* and *The House of the Seven Gables*. She was so absorbed in the plots of those books that, between chapters, she would involve me in the fanciful vicissitudes of the characters' fates. Then she read Melville, Louisa May Alcott, Edgar Allen Poe, Longfellow. Sometimes, in the mornings, after reading until midnight—she would walk about the house daydreaming, her motions slow; she was elsewhere, at the Customs House in Salem, in the Indians' tepees in *Hiawatha*, on Billy Budd's boat. Again and again she would ask to visit those historical sites in the small towns around Massachusetts where the first settlers' wooden houses were still standing with their old rustic furniture, household tools, and agricultural implements of earlier centuries. But, more than anything else, she was fascinated by Henry Thoreau's philosophy. I became friends with Professor MacGregor, one of the greatest living scholars of seventeenth and eighteenth century European history, who lived in Concord. He invited us several times to lunch at his house, which stood on a verdant hill overlooking magnificent woods and meadows. Together with him and his wife, we walked the streets of the town—the 'Cradle of the American Revolution'—many of whose houses had not changed their appearance for two hundred years. We walked along the banks of the river that traverses the town at one of whose bridges the British expeditionary force suffered their first defeat at the hands of the rebels in 1775, and reached Walden Pond. After visiting Emerson's and Thoreau's houses, and after hearing MacGregor talk about the transcendental philosophy of their occupants, Nora decided to read their books.

Thoreau's book, *Walden, or Life in the Wood*, was like a religious revelation for her. While reading it—she was in the seventh month then—her face flushed with excitement; she would stop every once in a while and declare, "This is my ideal," or, "This is how I would like to live," namely, in the bosom of nature, in solitude, according to Thoreau's philosophical precepts which bespeak perfect harmony between man and nature, between the Laws of Morality and the Laws of Nature, a life of introspection and integration through nature. "If only we could find a secluded spot in the Jerusalem hills, above Sha'ar Hagai, or on that wooded hill where we spent our first night together..."

Only once during that period—when Nora was imbued with almost heavenly serenity, so attuned to the new life forming inside of her, raptly observing the blossoming of nature around her—did she explode with a violent rage that was totally incomprehensible to me, and so out of proportion to its immediate cause. About a month before our return to Israel, she received a letter from her friend Raya Lubersky, with whom she had been corresponding regularly throughout our stay in Boston, telling her about the divorce of mutual friends after two years of marriage, because of the woman's infidelity; she had been carrying on a long, secret affair with a young doctor, also an acquaintance of theirs.

"How could she do such a thing! Cheating! Living a lie! Carrying on behind his back ... leading a double life ... defiling herself like that...."

She lashed out in shrill tones, in a voice she had not used all those months, her face—with yellow spots high on her cheeks and temples from the pregnancy—flushed a bright crimson that spread to her neck and chest; she was at a loss for words to express her outrage. She could never understand, never—here she lifted her heavy, broad body, her hands outstretched—how a woman who had entered the covenant of matrimony with the friend of her youth, a covenant of love—we had all been witnesses!—and Tzachi trusted her completely, adored her ... how could she ... her voice choked with emotion. For a long time she could not calm down.

I gazed at her, amazed and concerned. I could not understand her violent reaction; after all, the affair had nothing to do with her life, with our lives... Later, when she sat down, she told me that when she had read the *Scarlet Letter* she could find no justification for Hester's adultery with the priest she had seduced, and when she ripped off the scarlet letter and thrust it at his feet when he refused to join her, she saw Hester as the epitome of evil.

A few days later, when we were walking in the park, she said, "I don't know what possessed me when I got that letter. I have been so careful all these months not to lose my temper..."

Like many women in their first pregnancy, she, too, believed that tranquility and exposure to nature's beauty affect the fetus.

Chapter twenty-eight

Bonds of affection and pain entwined my fate with that of Foiglman. Ten days before the publication of *The Crooked Bough*, Foiglman arrived in Israel. He called me and broke the good news—taking me completely by surprise—that he was calling from his own apartment in Tel Aviv. Realizing that I could not very well invite him to our house, I hastened to offer to come over and see him that very night.

Foiglman's brother, Katriel, opened the door for me, his face radiant with satisfaction, as if he had just successfully accomplished a complicated mission. Foiglman, after embracing me warmly, immediately produced a bottle of cognac and three glasses, and we toasted the apartment and the upcoming book. The two of them led me around the tiny apartment, comprising only one and a half rooms—the books were still scattered on chairs and on the floor, cardboard boxes stood in the corners—showing me the kitchen, the bathroom, the balcony; Katriel was proud of having bought the apartment for much less than the market price, since the sellers had to leave the country in a hurry, and for having equipped it with all the necessary appliances for his brother's convenience.

"I even bought him a pressure cooker," he boasted, opening the kitchen cabinet, "so now he won't have to spend too much time cooking!"

"How is your Woman of Valor?" Foiglman asked me in Hebrew. I said she had not been feeling well lately.

"Yeah," he looked at me with concern, "you know what we say in Yiddish, *A froy is a zeyger*—delicate as a watch and requiring as many repairs."

Later, when we were sitting in the living room, he told me that since his arrival, he had already been to the printer, checked that there were no errata, and that the cover, in three colors, was perfectly executed. "The barrel is fine. How the wine will be judged—that remains to be seen...."

It was only on the way back home that it occurred to me that when he had inquired about my 'Woman of Valor,' there was an ironic twist to his question—perhaps subconsciously—since the second part of the verse is, "For her price is far above pearls," and Nora had not even thanked him for the pearls.

The day the book appeared, he called me again and, with great excitement, announced that he had a baby born unto him and that the first copy would, of course, go to me. Again I had to say I would come to him to receive the book. I hastened to leave the house, bought a big bouquet of roses at a nearby florist and went to his house.

He welcomed me with a vigorous embrace and, after he had put the flowers in a vase and stood them on a table in the middle of the room, he brought out his book and, with a regal gesture, handed it to me. I turned the book from side to side, opened it, riffled through, read the rhymed dedication, replete with compliments and thanks, and expressed my admiration.

Foiglman was all agog, tears stood in his eyes. He said it was the greatest day of his life, the day his book was published in Hebrew, in the Land of Israel, and he was bringing it to his own house...

"Excuse me," he took a handkerchief from his pocket and wiped his tears. "One shouldn't be so sentimental, but, how is it expressed in the Psalms, 'Yea, the sparrow hath found an house...'"

He took me by the arm and led me to the table, then he sat

facing me, brought his face to mine and whispered, "How much do I owe you?"

I said there was no rush, he must have had many expenses lately, what with buying the apartment. I could wait a few more weeks.

"No, no, I am a rich man! Today I am a very rich man!"

And he added that he had already opened an account in the nearby bank, like a proper citizen, and that he had some money left from the sale of the apartment in Paris and, besides, his brother had helped him considerably. That said, he took pencil and paper, plunked both arms on the table, in the manner of a tradesman and commanded: "Let's hear the account!" I stated the sum I had paid as an advance on the book. The balance owed to the publisher he should pay directly. I did not mention the translator's fee. I reminded myself again that the string of pearls—for which Nora had not even thanked him—was worth more. And even if that was not the case, let that be my contribution to a Jewish poet who had come to live in Israel.

"Is that all?" he looked at me wide eyed.

"That's all."

"Cheap." He took out his brand new checkbook and, when he handed me the check said, "I think it's less than what Abraham paid Ephron the Hittite for a burial place…"

I asked about his wife Hinda.

His face clouded. "Don't ask! I left home after a big fight."

Hinda, he said, had from the outset been fiercely opposed to the entire 'project' of exchanging the Paris apartment and buying an apartment in Tel Aviv. They had argued bitterly. She claimed that his move to Israel would bring him neither honor nor profit, "neither Parnassus nor prosperity," as she put it, only disappointment. He countered by saying that since their Paris apartment was not a home anyway, and she flew all year round from continent to continent, he was entitled to maintain his own nest—for a few months a year—in the Jewish state. In the end she relented. But when they moved to the new apartment there, she plunged into a depression and almost stopped talking to him. She did not even see him to the airport. "Troubles. Troubles. A woman has ninety-nine souls, we used to say."

When I came home, I told Nora that Foiglman, despite her doubts and suspicions, had repaid his debt. She said nothing.

All those days she had been wrapping herself in silence. Eight days after the publication of the book, on Saturday morning, Foiglman threw a party in his apartment. "A double celebration, the birth—actually the circumcision of the book—"was how he announced it to the guests, "along with a house-warming party."

The tiny apartment soon filled with guests. All of his brother's family were there, the three daughters, their husbands and their children; the translator, Menachem Zelniker and his wife; Professor L. from the university; the editor and the manager of the publishing house, two printers and a proofreader; four or five Yiddish authors, some of whom brought their wives. I came alone. Foiglman no longer asked about Nora. He must have understood—in fact, he must have understood everything.

The table was laden with refreshment: bottles of wine, cognac and juice, cakes and pies, cold cuts and gefilte fish, tiny sandwiches and snacks, olives and pickles. The guests heaped their paper plates with as much food as they could, went out on the porch or else stood against the walls holding conversations. Foiglman pulled his sister-in-law toward me, hugged her shoulders and said, "All this is her doing! She baked the cakes and the pies, she made the sandwiches, she even brought the dishes from their house!" And having planted a glass of cognac in my hand, he exhorted me, "Reb Hirsch, it now behooves you to make the blessing on the wine!" I was embarrassed and sought to avoid it, but while I was hemming and hawing, he was already tapping with his fork on a glass, crying: "Kiddush! Kiddush!"

I am not used to making toasts. I raised my glass and said a few words about a Jewish poet returning to his homeland, I wished him smooth and easy absorption, and that his 'crooked bough' would soon straighten up, blossom and bear fruit. Foiglman—I could see it in his eyes—was disappointed. He had expected much more. Something warm and personal.

I walked over to Professor L., who was standing by a wall examining the book of poems and whispered to him to say a few words about the book. "How can I?" he looked at me smiling, "I haven't read it yet!"

I went next to Menachem Zelniker and repeated my request to him. "If only I could speak!" he, too, smiled, "I would say great things! There is no Yiddish poet like him in the country!"

A few moments later, while the guests were busy eating, drinking and chatting, Foiglman again tapped his fork on a glass, stood at the head of the table and delivered a speech in Yiddish. He opened with thanks—to the translator, who "took the tattered, ragged clothes off his poems and dressed them in the fineries of the Book of Psalms," to the publisher, to the proofreader, to the printers, and last but not least, "to me, for were it not for me, who toiled and labored with such dedication…" I looked around at the faces of the people standing on the porch, paper plates in their hands, food in their mouths, refraining from chewing audibly and disturbing the speaker, raising and lowering their eyes from him to their plates; I stared at the table with the abundance of meat and fish and pastries, and at the bottles twinkling in the sun—and felt like a captive. I am out of place here, I said to myself, an interloper, a stranger at this Sabbath meal, among this extended family, a stranger to these people—and suddenly I felt a sharp pang in my heart at the thought of Nora. I saw her wandering from room to room like a shadow, haunted, restless; some anguish—kept secret from me—tormenting her relentlessly. I was seized by great panic. I felt anxious to leave the place and rush to her side.

"It is said that a poet's homeland is his language." I heard Foiglman say, "this has never been truer than in the case of Yiddish writers… Since Yiddish is not attached to the ground, it is above the ground…it wanders from land to land…like The Holy One, Blessed Be He, one of whose attributes is omnipresence, Yiddish, too, is all over the world… And here I am, in the country that is our homeland… All my life I have been a common swallow, but now the Hebrew translator has transformed me into a hoopoe, with a feathery crest, as in the legend of King Solomon…"

A shattering sound and a child's shrieks interrupted his speech. We were all startled and turned to find out what had happened. It was

Katriel's two-year-old granddaughter: she had knocked over a bottle of wine from a stool, fallen down and hurt herself from the splinters. Foiglman rushed to her and picked her up. Her mother quickly came, took her in her arms and tried to mollify her. "Does it hurt? Is it bad?" Foiglman held her hand, panic in his eyes when he saw the blood dripping from her knee. "It's nothing, Shmuel, nothing," the mother wiped the blood with her handkerchief and carried the child, whose sobs echoed through the house, into the bathroom.

Katriel and his two other daughters picked up the broken glass from the floor and wiped up the wine, but Foiglman, pale and shaken, recoiled and leaned against the wall, and wiping his perspiring brow muttered, "Imagine such a thing…such a thing…"

"Nothing terrible has happened, Shmuel," his sister-in-law returned, soothing him, "it's only a little bruise. Aren't you feeling well?"

"Imagine such a thing…" he kept muttering.

The guests started to disperse, taking leave of the host, thanking and congratulating him.

I was the last to leave. "A premature celebration! One mustn't! One mustn't!" Foiglman smiled at me sadly as I was about to take my leave. I hugged his shoulders and kissed him. I choked back the tears in my throat.

Chapter twenty-nine

On October 16, 1973, at five in the afternoon, when Yoav's armor battalion was stationed at Refidim in the Sinai, they received orders to proceed toward the place that was known, in Israeli army slang, as the Chinese Ranch, in response to distress signals sent by paratroopers trapped there. The paratroopers, exposed to heavy shelling from the Second Egyptian Field Army, had already suffered heavy losses. Yoav was driving one of the tanks that set out westward to carry out the mission. But the narrow 'Spider Axis' was jammed with a long line of vehicles of all shapes and sorts, including the huge raft-carriers for the crossing of the Canal. Not until midnight did they reach the battlefield, and a ghastly sight awaited them under the light of a full moon; the sandy plain was strewn with dead bodies, and the shrieks of wounded men—crawling on the ground or carried on their comrades' shoulders—pierced the air from all directions in the brief intervals between artillery volleys. As soon as Yoav's company's tanks entered the fire zone, three of them were hit. The one closest to him, caught fire, and a soldier, his clothes on fire, his face bloodied, escaped and fell to the sand. Yoav stopped his tank and, under fire, with Sager missiles flying all around him illuminating the area and exploding, rushed to rescue him. He threw him over his shoulder—he had been wounded in the face and his arm was lacerated—and carried him to the tank. As soon as he resumed his seat and began driving, a missile hit the turret and blew it together with the gunner. The signaler called for help, but there was no response. Later they found out that the command tank had been hit, too, and that its entire crew killed. Yoav continued to drive, attempting to retreat, but when the shelling intensified the engine, which had been damaged in the attack, died and they had to abandon the tank. He and the surviving crew member put the wounded man on a stretcher and ran to look for cover. They were shelled from every direction, since an Israeli artillery unit, oblivious to their presence there, was also shelling that sector. They ducked, they fell down, they got up, they called out as loud as they could that they were Jews, Israelis, IDF soldiers, brothers, but their voices were drowned by the din of volleys and explosions. Finally, they reached a shallow ditch that offered some cover. The wounded man groaned in pain. Yoav tore off his shirt and staunched the bleeding with the rags. Shrapnel landed in the ditch not far from them and its fragments hit his comrade, wounding him. Under fire that continued to rage around them, Yoav had to bandage him, too. Dawn came. Air force bombers coming from the East bombed the enemy lines and silenced them. Dozens of corpses lay on the sand.

We sat at Yoav's side and listened tremblingly to his account. Nora did not stop hugging him, stroking his arms, chest, face, as if she had given birth to him anew.

Chapter thirty

Yesterday afternoon Gita Jacobovitz came. As usual, she did not come empty handed. This time she brought a big wooden box of Havana cigars. I laughed, "I don't smoke! Why on earth would you bring me such a present?"

"Well then, you can offer them to your guests."

"You don't have to bring me anything when you come here."

"I had no use for them." It turned out that her parents had bought them at the airport in Amsterdam on their way back from a trip.

She had run into some problems in her research on the *Bund* and its relationship to Zionism, she said, sitting facing me in my study, a fresh redness covering her cheeks, as if from the winter chill. The material in Hebrew sources is scarce. It is scattered here and there over hundreds of articles, mostly chance references in speeches delivered by the leaders of the Zionist workers' parties. Even when she had gleaned all those bits and pieces, the resulting picture was very one-sided, reflecting only the opponents' views. Most of the material, comprising charters, protocols and resolutions of the *Bund*, had been written in Yiddish. She does not know Yiddish; her parents spoke Rumanian at home. What could she do?

"Learn Yiddish!" I said.

"*In di gassn, tzu di massn,*"* she ludicrously pronounced the *Bund* slogan and laughed, "It'll take me at least two years to learn Yiddish!"

"Then get yourself an assistant! Find someone who knows the language and can translate for you or give you the gist of the material."

"I don't have such friends."

I said one could infer the affirmative from the negative. The polemical chapters in the writings of Borochov and Syrkin, for example, provide us with insight into the controversies that caused such a bitter rift among the Jewish working masses. I suggested she read Tartakover's major work on the history of the Jewish labor movement.

"Yes, but I would like to discover new things, not just recapitulate!" she said.

I commended her on having such aspirations, and added that an historian discovers new things when he takes up a certain, definite position toward the material. When a researcher develops a unique, original attitude, he is bound to come up with new findings.

She gave me a limpid, wistful look and said, "You know what surprised me most when I studied this material? The realization that between the two world wars, the *Bund*, especially in Poland, was much more powerful than the Zionist parties! I had always assumed it was the other way round."

"More powerful than the Workers' Zionist parties," I corrected her, "especially in the big centers of Jewish workers, such as Warsaw, Lodz or Vilna…"

I explained the reasons for that development and got a little carried away describing the life of the Jewish proletariat in the large cities; how the *Bund*—as a corollary of its perception of the Exile as a permanent state rather than a transitory one—tried to instill pride

---

* *In di gassn, tzu di massn*—Yiddish: "In the streets, to the masses!"

and class consciousness in the proletariat by fighting for its rights and endowing it with education and culture through its extensive network of schools, clubs, popular colleges, theaters, publishing houses and newspapers.

She listened to me enthralled, her eyes wide open, as if conjuring up scenes in her mind, her hands lying on her knees.

"What I would truly like to do," she put both hands on her chest, as in prayer, "is not to write a dry, boring paper, but rather… something like a historical novel, depicting life itself! Not the bare facts, but life!"

I said that that required not just information but also some imagination.

"That I happen to have," she smiled, dimples appearing in her cheeks.

"And knowledge of human nature!" I added. "You can't write a historical novel without life-like characters."

"Vladimir Medem!" her eyes glinted with enthusiasm, "A novel about Vladimir Medem."

She explained that from the little she had read about him, he seemed like a fascinating character! Absolutely fascinating! She excitedly outlined a whole 'novel.' She envisioned Medem as a child baptized into the Orthodox Church in his wealthy parents' house in Minsk; his father, a medical officer in the Czarist army, his cherished mother secretly hankering after her Jewish origins and speaking Yiddish with her mother… Medem the devout Christian youth, ardently worshipping in the Greek Orthodox church and aspiring to be a priest… Medem, the bright high school student, the prize pupil of his religious instructors, then as a law student at Kiev University… Medem as he is attracted to Judaism and revolutionary ideas, influenced by his Jewish-Socialist friends and the warm atmosphere at the 'Jewish restaurant'… His expulsion from the university for leading the students' strike against the Czarist authorities…

I felt laughter rippling within me as I listened to her description. It smacked of the innocence of 'scholarly idealism'—something so rare among the student population I am familiar with—those exuberant evocations of an historical figure so distant from us in time, place, and worldview. I felt a great affection for her.

"How does this relate to the topic of your paper, Gita?"

"It does! When, later in the 'novel,' I recount Medem's flight to Switzerland after his prison term and how he became one of the leaders of the exiled *Bundists* there, I could describe his meetings with Chaim Weizmann, who had come to Berne from Geneva, and with Doctor Hisin, who was then about to go to Palestine, and the arguments they had concerning Zionism, territorialism, and cultural autonomy. Later I could report his impressions of the sixth and seventh Zionist congresses in Basel that he attended as an observer in the gallery, witnessing the historic dispute about Uganda…"

"I can see you're very familiar with the material…" I said, and if I hadn't been ashamed, both for myself and for her, I would have taken her rounded face, with the smooth, black hair surrounding it, looking so ardent and thirsty for knowledge, in both my hands and kissed her for her enthusiastic diligence.

"No, I just piece together what I have read here and there… He had such an eventful life! Only twenty-two or three and he is already a noted leader, a popular speaker, traveling all over Europe, serving one prison term after another, hiding, crossing borders illegally…and by the way, I noticed something interesting: Herzl and Medem, leaders on opposite sides of the two greatest Jewish movements of the time, both came from assimilated families, completely alienated from Judaism!"

I smiled, and for a moment our smiles locked, teacher and student, in an understanding that requires no words.

Later I mentioned the nineteenth-century historian Thomas Macaulays's view on historiography; the truly great historian uses and transforms the same material as the novelist. When he epitomizes the spirit of an age and the character of its protagonists, his work, not unlike the novelist's, enriches the mind and entertains and uplifts the spirit.

"Yes…" she mused and regarded me unaffectedly, amicably. "And you, didn't you ever want to write an historical novel?"

"No," I replied. "Novels contain an element of fiction, of invention, of both events and characters, and I can't invent imaginary things."

"With me it's the other way around," she grinned. "When I read historical facts, I'm forever filling up the spaces with my own imagining."

"Then write a novel," I said.

Chapter thirty-one

The quarrels between Nora and me stopped, but her silence worried me constantly. A mute dejection had descended over her; she was restless and distracted.

It seemed as though she did not know what to do with her free time. Upon coming back from work, she would busy herself a little with housework, even when there was no need for it. Suddenly she would grab a rag and start dusting the furniture in all four rooms. I would say to her, "Why are you dusting again? You did that two days ago."

"No," she would insist, "the pollution penetrates from outside and covers everything."

Or she would spend hours with the potted plants on the sills, watering, trimming, loosening the earth. Once I caught her standing by the closet, its door open, staring at it for long moments, as if trying to decide what to wear, though she was not going out, then closing it, sitting on the edge of the bed wrapped in thought.

Once she caught sight of an ad in the paper about collecting clothes for the needy. She muttered, "I hope they come here too. I have plenty of clothes I don't need." She said it apathetically. On

Saturdays—so unlike her behavior in past years—she now remained lying in bed until almost noon. Then she would get up, perturbed, throw on a gown, wash quickly and hasten to prepare a light meal for the two of us. After lunch, she would walk around the room, looking for something to do, then go back to bed. And she stopped reading books, something she had always enjoyed. When watching television in the evening, she seemed not to see what was in front of her. After a few moments, she would get up, turn it off, and go to the kitchen to make a cup of tea, or to the bedroom to lock herself in.

One morning, when we were sitting at the table, I was astonished to see her put three heaping spoons full of instant coffee in her cup. I said, "Three? Isn't that a bit much?"

"I like it strong," she grinned, then when she got up from the table she smiled at me, "You're a well-meaning sort of person" and left for work.

One night, as we were both watching the news on television, she turned to me, and with a light smirk, asked, "Are you still seeing that librarian?"

The old suspicion, from five years ago.

"Nora," I smiled at her, but she had already turned her head to the screen, as if she did not really expect an answer.

One morning, three weeks after the party at Foiglman's house, we were both sitting at the table, I reading the paper. Nora suddenly asked, "How is that poet from France doing?" I looked at her surprised. "He's doing all right," I replied, "his book is out. It's in print."

"Yes, I saw."

"Have you read it?"

She did not answer. She looked at me for a long moment, then said, "How did he survive?"

I shuddered. "You were there when he told his story."

"I've forgotten."

After some hesitation, wondering what was going on in her mind, I said he had been in a forced labor camp and had managed to hold out until the liberation. Her brow furrowed, as if she were thinking hard, then smoothed; her face turned white, and she said with a faded smile, "Does he believe in the resurrection of the dead?"

A shiver shot through my body. I stared at her speechless.

Twice I picked up the phone and heard a strange male voice. The first time was at five in the afternoon, a few minutes after Nora's return from work. "May I speak to Nurit?"

"Wrong number," I said, "there's no Nurit here."

"Is this the Arbel residence?" All of a sudden I realized who the caller was, and a wave of rage, indignation and bitterness such as I had never felt before came over me. 'Nurit' that, then, was the intimate name she had given herself during their amorous trysts, the nickname he whispered as they bedded. It was the name my mother had given her! I put down the receiver, walked to Nora's room and said, "Someone is asking for Nurit!" She turned red, then white and for a long time said nothing. "Tell him I'm not here," she said almost inaudibly.

"He's waiting." I was standing at the door, my face glowing, burning inside, "I told him I was going to get you." She covered her face with her hands, then removed them and repeated, "Tell him I'm not here." I went back to the phone and hung up.

I dropped into a chair, feeling my heart contract as if it would burst. How far gone they must be, I thought, and an ugly, black malice raged inside of me, to have appropriated her childhood name? A secret name shared only by them! Separating her from me! I could forgive her everything, I said to myself, but not this!

I could not look her in the face. The sight of her filled me with loathing. For several days we did not exchange a word. I avoided her around the house, in the living room, in the kitchen, when she came and went. I thought I would never be able to call her name again.

The second time was at ten at night. I recognized the voice. A typical Sabra voice, a little hoarse, as if scorched by smoke and desert winds, self-assured. "May I speak with Mrs. Arbel?" he asked this time. Such insolence!—my blood was boiling—without shame, scruples or fear of retribution, to thus address the deceived husband, whose wife he had actually defiled, and ask him to summon her! Was he assuming that she'd concealed the affair from me? Perhaps he thought I was one of those men who don't care? "The man who calls you Nurit wishes to speak to you," I blurted at Nora, who was sitting in the living room in front of the television. She looked at me for a minute, got up, walked to the phone, and said resolutely, "She's not at home," then hung up and went back to the living room.

The following day, just before leaving, she stood at the threshold, her hand on the doorknob. I was on my way from the kitchen to my room when she blurted out, "I apologize, for everything," and left. A few days passed and, seeing her dwindling before my eyes—she walked around the house like an invalid, listless, mute—my anger and my humiliation evaporated. I felt sorry for her.

One Saturday, in the late afternoon, I saw her standing by the window, looking down on the street. When a long time had elapsed without her budging, I was overcome by great pity for her. I came to her, put my arm around her shoulder, and said, "Can I help you, Nora?" She turned her head to me, looked deeply in my eyes—I had never seen such profound sorrow in her eyes before—then raised her hand and stroked my cheek slowly, slowly. My eyes filled with tears.

One day, when I was home alone, Shula came in, sat on the couch, and said she wanted to have a word with me. She was worried about Nora. When she came to their house and Sarit hugged her and asked to play with her, Nora looked at her as if she did not see her at all. She stroked her hair with a listless expression on her face and did not even get up. She spoke very little with her and Yoav. When offered tea and cakes, she took a few sips, then broke off, hid her face in her hands, then apologized, "I'm awfully tired." When Shula saw her to the car and asked if she wasn't feeling well, Nora did not answer; she only said, "Yoav should quit the army. He has given enough. He comes back late in the evening, not even every day, and you and the child suffer. I can see you suffer." And she kissed her.

We were silent. Later—her hands on her skirt, her bespectacled eyes scrutinizing me—she said, "You must speak to her, Zvi. You don't talk to her enough."

After a concert, as we were coming out of the Mann Auditorium, Nora said, "Let's have something to drink." We drove to a café on the beach and ordered coffee and cake. After a long silence, Nora said, "Do you want to divorce me?"

I grinned and put my hand soothingly on hers. "You feel sorry for me." I said there had not been a single day, throughout our married life, that I did not love her. Even when we were fighting fiercely.

"You should divorce me."

"Is that what you want?"

"I must be punished," she said, with an inscrutable expression on her face.

I said, "You do not punish people for the way they feel. I can only regret what has happened, not punish."

She gave me a hard look, almost resentful. "Why don't you hit me?! At least once! Hard! Hurt me! Draw blood!" I pressed her hand in mine. Her look did not relent. "No point living with a wreck, Zvi. Let's go!" She pulled her hand out from my clasp and got up.

Chapter thirty-two

I think about my conversation with Gita Jacobovitz who dreams about writing a novel instead of a thesis. I think back to the novels I used to read before I became completely absorbed in research, and it seems to me that their authors were better than the historians at predicting coming events; they saw the future clearly and anticipated it. Orwell in *1984*, Huxley in *Brave New World*, Karl Kraus in *The Last Days of Mankind*, seventeenth-century Grimmelshousen in *Simplicissimus*. But not only these works, which are essentially allegories, but in any great novel that depicts the present, with all its complexities, on a broad canvas, there are intimations of things to come. Take Kleist's *Michael Kolhaas*, Dostoyevsky's *The Brothers Karamazov*, Kafka's *The Trial* or Camus' *The Plague*, Golding's *Lord of the Flies* and other masterpieces.

One would think that it should be the other way around; we, the historians, who delve into the past, who, supposedly, can figure out the mechanism of historical development from a combination of factors and causes—social, economic, political—that move the wheel of history—we should have been the ones capable of predicting: by inference, deduction, syllogism, what will happen tomorrow and the day after. But, as I said before, it is the great writers, the novelists, who see deeper and further than us. And the reason is that they, unlike us, focus not on events but on people; they plumb the deeper recesses of the soul. And the future, mankind's future, after all, depends on the vicissitudes of the human soul. And I, who have spent my entire life examining the minute details of events, did I hear the anguished cry of Nora's soul?

A month passed since the publication of Foiglman's book, five weeks passed, then six, and yet not one line about the *Crooked Bough* appeared in the press. From the third week on, I bought three or four newspapers every Friday, opened the literary section, scanned their columns, then put them aside in bitter disappointment. I felt as if it was not only my own failure, but my fault.

Foiglman pretended to ignore it all. When I came to see him, he greeted me cheerfully, produced a bottle of cognac, raised a glass and toasted either me, Tel Aviv, or Israel. He did not talk about the book at all. He spoke mainly about his impressions of people he had come into contact with, street scenes he chanced upon; occasionally he'd mention politics. He told me about his Moroccan greengrocer, whom he addressed in Hebrew and who tried to answer him in Yiddish; about the Arab who repaired his blinds, with whom he had a long discussion on Arab-Jewish relations and from whom he had learned much about life in an Arab village; about a wonderful coincidence, when he discovered that the man standing behind him in line at the post office was a native of Zamosc, and it turned out that they knew each other's family.

Once, while we were talking about the Israeli press, I made a *faux pas* and blurted out that I was surprised that nothing had yet been written about his book. "They'll write eventually! They'll write!" he heartened me, as if it were my own book. "The same thing happens in Paris. A critic is given ten poetry books to review; he writes first about the authors he knows, or the ones who are his friends; the others—can wait...I have patience!"

When two months had passed and, aside from five laconic lines in the Brief Reviews section of one paper, nothing had been written about the book, I called the manager of the publishing house and asked for an explanation. Had he neglected to send copies to the papers? No, he had sent them all copies, he assured me. Moreover, he had called the editors of the literary supplements and asked them to give special attention to the book, whose author was an important poet from France, who had recently settled in Israel. He was told that the book had been given to reviewers, but it was against their policy to rush them. "You have to wait," he concluded. I called Zelniker and he, too, voiced concern at the lack of public reaction. He had already spoken to a couple of writers, and they promised to read the book and write a review, but there was a long way between making a promise and delivering…

I went to Leivick House to meet with two members of the Yiddish Writers' Association. I said to them, "Look, one of your own has come to live here. Surely you would want to honor and laud him. This is his first book published in Israel—why don't you have a reception in his honor, a literary banquet, and give his book a little publicity?"

They said Menachem Zelniker had already been to see them about it, and then another emissary came to speak on Foiglman's behalf, and they could only repeat what they had said to the other two: if it were a Yiddish book, they would be happy to throw a banquet in its honor, but since it was a Hebrew book translated from Yiddish, it was really outside their province. They suggested I talk to the Hebrew Writers' Association.

I swallowed my pride and went to Professor's L.'s office to try to persuade him to write a review of the book. After hearing me out, he said, "Look, as a teacher and a lecturer I have to maintain a neutral position with regard to Yiddish literature in Israel. For reasons you can surmise, there is a lot of jealousy and competition among these writers, a lot of unsettled accounts. If I write about Foiglman, I'll be immediately inundated with requests, petitions and pleas to write about this and that author. And if I refuse, there will be such resentment that I won't be able to talk to any of those people any more. However much I'd like to help…you as a colleague must understand."

When I next went to see Foiglman, he looked haggard. Still, he produced a bottle of cognac and poured two glasses, but he sipped his as if it were a poisoned cup. His eyes looked dim, as from a sleepless night, and when we sat down he said, "What is this country of ours coming to, Zvi?"

I looked at him quizzically and, after a long moment of staring into the glass in his hand and twisting it with his fingers on the table, he raised his eyes to me and said, *"M'harget yidn!** Here too!"

He waited for my reaction, but when I remained silent he raised his voice and said, "They're murdering Jews! In the Galilee, Jerusalem, Hebron! No safety, none!"

I said a few things about Arab terrorism and the ways to combat it. With a lusterless look, the wrinkles in his face deepening and his voice broken, he said, "Before the War, in Zamosc, there were streets in the old quarter that were out of bounds for us. We knew it was dangerous to walk there, especially on Sundays and on their holidays, when they came out of the churches, or when they were drunk. Some hooligans would always attack us, with blows, bludgeons, knives. We were lucky to come out alive. Every few months, someone was killed there. And now here—it's the same thing…you can't walk around freely…a soldier waiting for a ride is kidnapped and murdered in some lonely place in the mountains, a child is kidnapped and brutally mutilated, a bomb is thrown in the marketplace…every day I watch funerals on television, 'Justice shall go before Him,' 'God full of mercy'… My heart bleeds…my heart bleeds…"

"Israel—and Zamosc?" I said.

He looked at me with piercing eyes. His lips trembled, as if he were looking in vain for words.

"Ikh tziter…" he murmured, and then with fear in his eyes, "I shudder at what might happen here!"

I tried to cheer him up, inform him a little about our strength. The pained expression did not leave his face. Dim tears gathered in his eyes as he listened to my assurances.

Later, when I was about to leave, he said, "You wrote somewhere that Jews had no alternative. But there is an alternative!"

---

* *M'harget yidn!*—Yiddish: "They kill Jews!"

He said it in an encouraging tone, as if emerging from his sorrow. I asked what the alternative was.

"We'll talk about it some day. But there is one!"

❧

Three weeks went by, then four, and not one word about *The Crooked Bough*. Out of shame and guilt, since it was I who had encouraged him to publish the book, who had deluded him with false hopes, thus sharing responsibility for the debacle, I stopped visiting him altogether. When I recalled his enthusiasm and warm optimism on his two previous visits in Israel, at our meeting in Paris, in our conversations, in his letters, and soon after the publication of his book—I could not find the heart to confront his anguish. And he, too, stopped calling me.

I tried to push him out of my mind, him and his book. Whenever his name popped up in my thoughts—while reading or writing, coming across a line in Yiddish, running into one of his friends—I would banish his memory from my heart.

One night (I now shudder when I recall it) as I was standing by the window, I saw a man pacing up and down on the sidewalk in front of my house, his head bent, his hands behind his back. When he reached the street lamp, I saw that it was Foiglman. I was alarmed. I thought to myself: He'll come up and ring the doorbell any moment now. Nora was at home at the time. But he continued to pace up and down, taking broad strides as if measuring the sidewalk with his steps. He reached the bottom of the street, turned around, and again passed by the house without stopping. His hair was disheveled; his shoulders hunched forward, his back arched slightly, like a hump. When he walked by the house again, I almost called out his name; I felt like rushing down, grabbing him by the arms, shaking him and asking what was wrong. I wanted to hug him like a brother. But something froze inside me and would not let me budge. He paced the street three or four more times, never stopping, never raising his head, then quickened his steps and vanished around the corner.

For several days I could not rid myself of that scene. It was as if he were crying for help, pleading for his life, but did not have the courage to ask for it.

Did he come to Nora's funeral? Was he among the large crowd that gathered at the funeral home, and then drove to Rehovot, walked with the coffin, then stood at her open grave? I do not know.

On the second day of the *shiva*, when Yoav, Shula and four or five of my friends were sitting with me, he came in, shook my hand silently and sat down. His reddened eyes glowed—was it fury or fright?—an unholy fire flickering in them. He sat thus for a long time. People were talking about one thing and another, to distract me from my bereavement, but he never said a word. He raised his eyes from one to the other, but did not utter a word. Finally, when he got up to leave, I got up, too, and saw him to the door. Again, he shook my hand and did not say a word.

About four months later, Katriel called me and said that his brother was sick and had been checked into Ichilov Hospital. I asked what was wrong with him, and he said something in his bowels. He had already been in the hospital for two weeks, and Katriel thought— he said that in his usual hesitant manner, reluctant to impose—that his brother would be happy if I came to visit him. "Of course!" I said, "Of course!" I put it off from day to day, until the news of his death reached me.

ॐ

Only now, when I read the last of the notebooks Foiglman left behind—and I am not sure that he left them to me because he trusted me, or rather as a grim reminder, a rebuke, an ironic lesson—do I find out what thoughts smoldered in his mind during those months when I avoided him, and how those thoughts engendered that absurd idea of his, which almost borders on lunacy.

In the opening pages of the notebook I find these passages, separated by drawings of emaciated, featherless birds.

Shaya, Alter Rabinovitz, Avremale Krook—don't you recognize me any more? When you first arrived in Paris, didn't you come straight to me? How you flattered me! Your lips dripped honey! And I fed you, put you up in my house, introduced you to all our people, even exchanged money for you! And you, Avremale, when you stopped in Paris on your way to New York to receive some literary award from some big shot—I threw a party for you! I gave a talk in your honor! I said things I didn't believe—just so you'd be happier with yourself! Now you don't know me any more! You hardly greet me when we meet.

➤

In the middle of the night I wake up screaming. A terrible nightmare. Yankale Perlmutter, who shared a bunk with me at Kungskirchen—we deloused each other's hair, we kept each other's bones warm—meets me on Allenby Street in Tel Aviv, a tattered jacket on his back and his eyes glowering at me. I say to him, "Yankale, what's wrong? Are you angry at me?" "I'll never forgive you!" he says, his eyes flaming, "You stole my last piece of bread, hidden under the mattress!" "Yankale, how can you suspect me of such a thing? Me of all people?" I cry, choking. But he vanished suddenly, as if the earth had swallowed him. I screamed and woke up. With a deep sigh I remember that Yankale Perlmutter is no longer alive. On the way to the mine, he collapsed from exhaustion and never got up again.

➤

There are two tall straight cypress trees on each side of the gate in my yard. I stand on the balcony, looking at them and thinking to myself: They are my guard of honor, standing like sentinels at the entrance to my palace. At the top of one of them a bird whose name I don't know has built a nest. In the morning I see it fly off, then come back with a twig in its beak. It rests there for a while, turning its head from side to side, twitters, pecks around then flies away again. Sometimes it turns its head to me and seems to recognize me. I smile at the bird and it peers at me. A sight for sore eyes.

But at night, when I come back home and pass between the two cypresses, I say to myself, Alas, you beggar king! These are the two cypress trees planted on both sides of your tombstone at the cemetery!

❦

In the middle of the notebook I find a long passage and I cannot tell whether it is a copy of a letter he has sent or just something he wrote for himself.

>

My dearest Hindele, my beloved! When I came from Poland to Paris, broken in spirit and penniless, I yearned for one thing only: a loving home! Since I was thirteen I had no home. For five years I passed through the Seven Regions of Hell, and for two years after I came out of there, I moved from apartment to apartment, from bed to bed; my bones could find no respite. For the first time since the war, I found a home: in your parents' house. I shall never forget the steaming chicken soup your mother served me the first time I ate at your table; it tasted like heaven; and the pure white sheets on the bed in the little room you provided me—the same bed that three months later became the love bed, and seven months later—our nuptial bed.

For seventeen years, from the time we moved to our apartment on the Avenue Sebastopol until the children grew up, we had a home. You worked in the theater and were a devoted mother and a loving wife. And I, who had been like a leaf swept by the wind, clung to you, to your strength, your security, to the family and to my desk. I started growing fine roots, like a shoot that has been torn off the tree and then replanted. But then ... then, gradually that home, too, fell apart. Reuben, gone his own way, far away from us, has become Irving. Rochelle embarked on her own Via Dolorosa, and you started flying around the world, like our language, the homeless language. 'The birds of the tree were all scattered by the wind,' as Ritzy Manger wrote. One month you're here, two weeks you're there north-south-east-west, and in my mind I follow you to the end of the world. I see you on stage, I pray for you, I bless you....

But all this time I was yearning for a home, Hindele, a home! And then, sitting alone in a home that was no home, shrouded in darkness, because your face was not there to light it up, I thought to myself: I do have a large family, teeming with life, activity and joy! I have many brothers under the sun, in the east, in the warm country! And I asked myself: Why am I so estranged from them? And if you are not here, what is keeping me here?

Then I told myself: I can split myself in two, I can divide my time. I shall have two homes! One with you, the other with my larger family! You said, "You're like a child whose mother has left the house, leaving him alone. He's afraid to stay by himself, so he goes to his aunt. What makes you think the aunt wants you to stay with her? Two homes, you say. Two homes are no home."

Yes, Hindele, the aunt does not want me. My habits, my manners, my face, are not to her liking. And her cold eyes keep asking me all the time, when am I going to get out of her house.

Where can I go now, Hindele? My soul is torn to shreds and I see them fly to the four winds of heaven, just like then, when I emerged from the gates of Hell.

⁂

The second part of the notebook, however, reverberated with 'Jewish anxiety.' Foiglman seemed to have been gripped by a holy frenzy. It started in a rather balanced, dignified, almost academic tone, as if he were about to compose a serious polemic refuting the Zionist premise that the existence of a Jewish state will do away with anti-Semitism in the world. But half way through the second page the sentences became truncated and frantic, gushing out helter-skelter, some words crossed out, others furiously underlined, almost tearing the paper, words huddled together, driving each other out. "Those fools who attended the congresses, in tuxedos and top hats … Herzl, Weizmann, Jabotinsky…. Sheer idiocy! None of them could read history correctly! They could not decipher its code! A minority? Is that why we were murdered—because we were a minority? It was Balaam who foresaw future events correctly when he said, 'The people shall dwell alone, and shall not be reckoned among the nations…' They're looking for rationality? There is no rationality! There are only devils, demons, raging, stirring up the winds of wrath… In every generation, yea, in every generation… And when finally there is a state?! The world hates that state when it is up and when it is down!

269

They even begrudge it the victory over its enemies! The whip lashes on and on… *Huliyet, huliyet, beyze vintn…**" An apocalyptic vision strikes terror in his heart.

The Islamic states, stretching over two continents, whose populations number hundreds of millions, possessing unlimited wealth, growing stronger and stronger—nothing can stop their growth—mobilize their armies on Israel's borders; if not five years from now, then in ten, fifteen, they attack from all directions, by land, sea and air. And Israel's putative allies, when they see her thus overpowered, all odds against her, abandon her, stand aloof, just as they stood by when the Germans exterminated Europe's Jews. The invaders launch a horrendous massacre of the Jews of Israel, leaving no survivors. "And God watches from above, and keeps silent, just as He kept silent then."

From the heart of this darkness, in the final pages of the notebook, Foiglman's crazy idea of redemption shimmered like a will o' the wisp.

Against all the forces of evil in the world—what are we to do? How can we hold out? We have one resource at our disposal: the force of the Jewish brain! In The Protocols of the Elders of Zion, *the gentiles have falsely accused us of a plot to take over the world. Let us turn this false charge into a fact! We will create a worldwide secret alliance of the Jewish brain! The Jewish brain that is scattered among a hundred nations; the brain that has given rise to all the great inventions—in medicine, technology, armament, the intricacies of economy and politics—must now be united and harnessed to rescue the Jewish people!*

And after listing the names of several dozen Jewish scientists, recipients of Nobel prizes in physics, chemistry, biology, medicine, and so forth—(names he must have gleaned from some encyclopedia), he mentions the fact that about a fifth of all Nobel prize winners throughout the years were Jewish. But in fact, had the donors not been afraid of being labeled blatant philosemites, the percentage would probably have been sixty or seventy. Then, in the middle of the page, he writes in large letters a slogan in the style of the banners unfurled at Jewish parties in Poland:

* *Huliyet, huliyet, beyze vintn…*—Yiddish: "Rage, furious winds…"

Long live the Internationale of the Jewish Brain!

And underneath this line he lists the objectives and the agenda of the Internationale. After the inception of the secret alliance, when its headquarters have established its authority over all its members anywhere in the world—subject to the strictest discipline—it will be capable of stopping or foiling the development and production of armaments threatening Israel's existence, of imposing sanctions on hostile countries by immobilizing their scientific institutions. And on the other hand, the Internationale will be able to design and develop secret combat means that will serve Israel in its defense—and the secret weapon that will defeat any other weapon in the world is the Lethal Beam. Not an atomic bomb—for those are already in the hands of the East and the West and soon will be in the hands of the Arab countries, and just one of those is enough to destroy Israel and wipe out its population—but a 'lethal beam' that is capable of destroying huge armies within a few seconds. Thus, if the enemy masses its troops along the borders and declares war, they will be annihilated by the 'lethal beam' and Israel and its population saved.

That, then, was the 'alternative' Foiglman hinted at when I took my leave of him, never to see him again. In the last two pages of the notebook he outlines his own plan of action for the implementation of his idea: he will drop everything else he is doing and dedicate himself to this alone. Poetry is a luxury, and to indulge in luxury when a sword is pointed at one's throat is a crime! He will fly around the world, to France, England, the United States, Canada; he will find the means to get his message across the Iron Curtain, meet with some of the greatest Jewish scientists, convince them that Israel is facing total annihilation, and that if it falls, it will be the "end of the Jewish people." It is absolutely vital to set up the International Alliance now...

No more shall I be a song bird. I shall be a black raven, flying around the world shouting: "Confound Satan! Confound Satan!" as we say in the Yom Kippur prayer!

But before he could take off, he himself was hit by the 'lethal beam.'

I should not have absorbed myself in writing these notes. So many months. Foiglman's spirit haunts me. It gives me no peace. When I walk in the street, he follows me like a shadow. Even when I tread on it, his shadow keeps walking with me. In the heat of the day, when the sun is in my eyes, I see him hovering in front of me, like a huge bird, flapping his arms like wings. Lines from his poem *Unlike Icarus* flutter inside me, repeating themselves again and again, while I am reading, lecturing, talking with a student or with a colleague:

> *My wings are tired of flying*
> *But unlike Icarus,*
> *Unlike Icarus I shall not melt in the sun.*
> *I shall drop down*
> *And a fire from the ground shall burn me.*

But like the Phoenix, he rises from his ashes and lives. He is not consumed: he walks around my house, sits on the couch, stands in the kitchen. I hear his thick, warm voice, mocking my despondency, smiling at me with his clever eyes—talking laughingly about Hell. He refuses to come out of me. As in the prayer, 'when I lie down and when I rise up on my way.'

In the nights I dream about him. Sometimes I see him appear at my door, over the threshold, in a tattered coat, perplexed, his face white as a sheet, his arms stretched out as if asking why. I ask him in, but he only calls out my name in protestation. At other times he is wearing a clown's hat, disguised, hopping to the left of me and to the right of me, skipping, dancing, chortling gratingly, mockingly.

I sit at my desk in the evening, silence in the house; from somewhere afar drift the sounds of piano and cello playing Liszt's 'Lugubre Gondole' sent shivers down my spine. I see him sitting in Charon's boat, his large head sunken between his broad shoulders, his eyelids heavy. He's floating in the river, drifting away, vanishing behind a steep bank. Dogs bark in the city.

Chapter thirty-three

A month after Nora's death I went to the Institute where she used to work. For many years I had driven her there, said goodbye to her by the gate, and returned to town. Never did I go in with her to see the laboratory where she spent so many hours every day—half her life, you might say—investing so much thought, imagination, creativity. Her colleague, Leah P.—a young, stern-looking woman wearing a white lab coat and short boots—led me from the gate to the lab building. There were long narrow tables with test tubes, bottles, beakers and jars filled with colored solutions. Tiny flat vials with transparent lids containing some corpuscles, either fibers or sprouts. Two microscopes, a scale, narrow tubings, syringes and tweezers. On the shelves above the tables were bags with labels, 'Wheat from Ruhama,' 'Cotton from Revadim,' and so on.

Leah P., with big, black eyes, somewhat alarmed, explained the function and use of each of the implements, then told me what the small lab staff under Nora's supervision had been doing in the last year: looking for species of fungi that can be used for pest control. She explained: Certain strains of fungi 'latch on' to insects—flies, aphids, beetles—that attack crops. The fungi's spores then contaminate parts

273

of the insect's body, sprout and spread inside, killing them. The fungi are cultivated in the lab and grafted onto an insect, which serves as their 'host.' Their progress and proliferation are observed to determine how harmful they are to the insect; if, indeed, they destroy the insect, then a large quantity of spores is cultivated in containers of sterilized solutions and sold to commercial pesticide-producing plants for agricultural use.

I asked where they found the fungi for the experiments.

"In groves and fields," she said. "Those of us who work in this area have an eye for discerning them. You see an insect lying on a leaf of an infected tree, or on a blade of grass, in an unusual position, or discolored, and you know it must have been attacked by a fungus. You take it to the lab, remove the fungus, diagnose it, put a sample of the tissue in a petri and then…"

Nora, she said, had loved going on those nature trips. "She was a little girl playing hooky, running to the field to catch butterflies. She was nature's child…" And she added, "But we did not go out that often. Most of the time, hours upon hours, we spent here, in the lab, in this and other rooms, with sterilizing tanks, microscopes, computers… Do you want to see the other rooms?"

I said I wanted to spend a little more time in the room where Nora had spent most hours of the day. I asked what pesticidal fungi they had succeeded in finding.

"There are over a hundred and fifty such species," she replied. "For several months we did a follow-up on a fungus that demolishes grain rust—itself a fungus. Nora used to joke and call it the 'Grim Reaper'."

"Grim Reaper. It was as if a thorn pierced my heart, and all of Nora's silences in the last days of her life came crashing down on me. I raised my eyes to the wall. Enlarged photos of plant or fungus tissue were hanging there: galaxies of circular globules, nebulous intricate webs…

"Grim Reaper?" I asked.

"Well, the experiment failed. That is, we succeeded 'in vitro,' in the sterile environment of the lab, but we failed 'in vivo.' It turned out that cultivating and breeding those fungi requires so much work that chemical pesticides are cheaper and more effective."

It was warm and stuffy in the room, as in a tropical greenhouse, and a smell of acids and decay stood in the air. In the last few months Leah P. said— and her serious face assumed an apprehensive expression, as if she were frightened of me—there were attempts to eradicate the Mediterranean fruit fly. She picked up a petri dish with a tiny fiber that looked like a capillary on a leaf, and told me those were the spore of the fungus in question. She opened a drawer and took out a glass slide with a colored stain, explaining that that was a specimen of the fungus attacking the fly. She asked if I wanted to see it under the microscope.

I sat on the chair that Nora used to sit on every day for so many years and put my eyes to the microscope eyepiece. On the slide I could distinctly see the tissue of a diaphanous, golden wing of a fly, and in it—as if trapped in a net—two or three tiny, bluish twigs.

"You see those azure substances that look like tadpoles? Those are the spores of the fungus that destroys the fly."

I could not remove my eye from the lens for a long time. "A silent world." That silent world in which, Nora once told me, fierce battles rage. A web of threads—and an azure, wooly, innocent-looking microcosm slowly, quietly destroying it. I straightened myself and asked if they had been successful in eradicating the Mediterranean fruit fly with that fungus.

"It's still in the experimental stage," she replied and, sitting down on an adjacent chair, she told me how excited Nora would get whenever she discovered a new species of fungus, and how infectious her enthusiasm was for the entire staff. "She would hug us, and her wonderful warm laugh created such a cheerful atmosphere," she said, and a smile lit her pale face.

Then she told me that once in a while Nora would get into a prankish mood and play practical jokes on one of the doctoral students: she would put a slide with a crumb of food or a fiber from a soiled rag under the microscope and ask him to identify the fungus. The student would strain his eyes and brain for a long time, offering various conjectures, while the people around him could barely contain their laughter. I asked if there had been something unusual in her behavior on the last day.

"No, nothing unusual. She was quiet, very quiet, but she went through her usual routine. At two o'clock she said she had to leave and gave us instructions for the afternoon."

"At two!" I blurted out, stifling the panic that engulfed me.

"Yes. As she was leaving I asked her if I should distill water for tomorrow. She looked at me for a moment and said, 'Yes, go ahead.' She stood there for a moment, glanced at the equipment on the table and said, smiling, 'Everything should be thoroughly clean, of course.' Those were her last words."

On that last day, I did not see Nora. In the morning, before leaving for work, I saw her watering the potted flowers. I said, "It rained only yesterday," but she went on watering and did not answer. Later, she turned to me, asking softly, her eyes imploring, "Shall I give you a lift?" I said there was no need; I would take the bus to the university. "Well, goodbye, then," she said with a faint smile of infinite sorrow, which is etched in my mind like the fading glory of a sinking moon. I thanked Leah P. and left.

"Everything should be thoroughly clean, of course." Her words echoed whisperingly in my heart.

I drove to the cemetery. I made a wide detour and passed by my parents' old house. The house had disappeared. The yard, with its trees and bushes, was gone, too. Instead, there was a big four-story apartment building, with rows of shuttered balconies. The entire street had been transformed beyond recognition. High rises, a greengrocer's, hair dresser's salon, an electric shop, and a small square denuded of any greenery serving as a parking lot.

I passed along rows of crowded tombstones; many of the names inscribed were familiar to me. I stopped by my father's grave. Next to it was the empty plot that my mother bought after his death, to be buried next to him. I had not visited his grave for many years and now, as I stood in front of the tombstone bearing his name, he seemed to be reproaching me, typically, with charm and good humor. "Where have you been hiding from me, Zvi? You look so crestfallen..."

It was a spring day, and the air was filled with the scent of orange blossoms. Bees swarmed among the wild flowers. Many rows further down stood the two tombstones of Otto and Susie Abramson. "To be buried next to my father and mother"—said the note Nora left. But there was no empty plot next to theirs; so five tombstones now separated their grave from hers, which was indicated by a mound of soil and a wooden marker. Many wreaths from the funeral were still lying on the mound, their flowers now wilted.

Thirty-five years together, since that night in the Judean mountains. Her overflowing exuberance, the 'talent for happiness,' the myriad emotions that stirred her, that unnerved her, her consuming integrity. All she left behind was a fungus that exterminates the Mediterranean fruit fly, and her memory in my heart.

Her body, in this dust, decomposing, decomposing—I thought—thus is history transformed into nature.

About the Author

Aharon Megged

Aharon Megged was born in Poland and came to Palestine at the age of six. He was a member of Kibbutz Sdot Yam between 1938–50, and later, a literary editor and journalist. He has been a pivotal figure in Israeli letters since the 1950s. His many novels, short stories and plays reflect the complexities of Israeli society over the past 50 years.

His work has been translated into a number of languages, including English. His novel *Foiglman* won the WZO France Literary Prize. Megged was the president of the Israel PEN CENTER (1980–87), the cultural attaché at the Israel Embassy in London (1968–71), and is a member of the Hebrew Academy. He has won many literary awards, among them the Bialik Award, the Brenner Award, the Agnon Award, and the much coveted Israel Prize for Literature, 2003.

He has two sons—Eyal, who is also a writer, and Amos, who teaches history at the University of Haifa—and is married to the writer Eda Zoritte.

The fonts used in this book are from the Garamond family